SUPERVOLCANO
THINGS FALL APART

ALSO BY HARRY TURTLEDOVE

"The Daimon" in *Worlds That Weren't*

Ruled Britannia

In the Presence of Mine Enemies

Days of Infamy

End of the Beginning

Opening Atlantis

The United States of Atlantis

Liberating Atlantis

Atlantis and Other Places

Supervolcano: Eruption

Supervolcano: All Fall Down

BY HARRY TURTLEDOVE
WRITING AS DAN CHERNENKO

The Chernagor Pirates

The Bastard King

The Scepter's Return

SUPERVOLCANO
THINGS
FALL APART

HARRY TURTLEDOVE

A ROC BOOK

ROC
Published by the Penguin Group
Penguin Group (USA) LLC, 375 Hudson Street,
New York, New York 10014

USA | Canada | UK | Ireland | Australia | New Zealand | India | South Africa | China
A Penguin Random House Company

First published by Roc, an imprint of New American Library,
a division of Penguin Group (USA) LLC

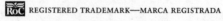 REGISTERED TRADEMARK—MARCA REGISTRADA

ISBN 978-0-451-46568-9

Printed in the United States of America

Set in Sabon LT
Designed by Elke Sigal

THINGS FALL APART

I

The windup alarm clock on Colin Ferguson's nightstand ticked like a bomb. A silent digital clock sat there with it, but too often was silent when it needed to make noise. Power in San Atanasio—power in the whole L.A. basin—had got too erratic to trust since the supervolcano eruption going on five years ago now. And Colin had always been a suspenders-and-belt man: a good way for a cop to be.

When the windup clock clattered, he jerked as if it really were a bomb. He groped at it till it shut up. Wan predawn light leaked between the slats of the venetian blinds.

"Did I—" Colin didn't finish asking his wife whether he'd bothered her too much to let her go back to sleep. Kelly wasn't in bed with him. He chuckled under his breath. *Her* alarm clock had gone off, and he hadn't even noticed. When Deborah woke up hungry, she wanted her mother's breast. Colin could do all kinds of things, but he wasn't built to nurse.

He got out of bed, opened the blinds, and went downstairs. He held on to the iron rail and stepped carefully. Even with the blinds open, not all that much light was getting in.

Kelly sat in a rocking chair in the front room. The baby was asleep on her lap, so she'd been there a while. She fluttered her fingers at him. "You didn't move when she started crying," she said. "I'm impressed."

He shrugged. "Yeah, well . . ." he said vaguely, and then, "I'm gonna make coffee. Want some?"

"Oh, God, yes!" Kelly said. He felt the same way himself.

They still had natural gas. Since the power was out, the fancy electronic ignition on the stove wasn't worth squat. When Colin turned a valve and lit a match at the burner, though, he got blue flames. He and Kelly both liked cream and sugar. He spooned in Coffee-mate instead. The refrigerator was an icebox more often than not. Sometimes the power stayed out so long, it wasn't even much of an icebox. They steered clear of milk products most of the time.

"Thanks," Kelly said when he brought her the cup. "Don't know what I'd do without this stuff."

"Tell me about it." Colin sipped hot caffeine. He looked out through the French doors at the back yard and made a small, unhappy noise. "Starting to rain."

His wife clucked in sympathy. "Just what you need."

"Yeah, right," Colin said. "I'd sooner stay in bed today anyhow. Heck, I'd sooner visit your old man than go in this morning." Kelly's father, Dr. Stan Birnbaum, bragged that he was the best dentist in the South Bay. He might well have been, too. That didn't make calling on him any more fun.

"Maybe the press conference won't be too horrible." By the way Kelly said it, she didn't believe it.

Neither did Colin. "And maybe—" He clamped down hard on that. Someone who tried not to swear in front of women shouldn't come out with *And maybe monkeys'll fly out of my ass* when talking with his beloved. But that was what he'd been thinking, all right.

By Kelly's soft snort, she knew it, too. She was almost fifteen years younger than he was, and took cussing for granted whether he did or not. She cautiously rose from the rocker, holding Deborah in the crook of her left arm and levering herself up with her right. The baby didn't stir or fuss. Kelly headed for the stairs. "I'll get her down. Then I'll figure out whether to go back to bed myself or just stay up."

"Okay." Colin finished his coffee, then cut a bagel in half and slathered Nutella on it. Nutella was great stuff when you could get it. Anything that tasted good and didn't need refrigeration counted as great stuff these days.

He went back upstairs after he ate. Shaving with cold water wasn't his idea of fun, either, but he methodically took care of it. A cold shower . . . He shook his head. Nobody bathed as often as people had before the eruption, not when hot water was one more thing that was hard to come by. A soapy washcloth here and there would have to do for now.

Somber blue suit. Blue shirt. Somber maroon tie. "Okay?" he asked Kelly. Yes, he would much rather have faced Stan Birnbaum's drill than the gentlemen and ladies of the Fourth Estate. Stan at least gave you novocaine before he got to work. There wouldn't be any painkillers this morning.

"Okay." Kelly nodded. For good measure, she came over and kissed him. She felt nice in his arms. He wished he could stay. Wishing did as much good as it always did.

"Off to throw the wolves raw meat," he said. Kelly laughed, for all the world as if he were joking.

He put on a rain slicker with a hood and slipped galoshes over his shoes. His bike sat in the foyer along with Kelly's and Marshall's. Deborah's squawks hadn't rousted his grown son from his first marriage. But then, from everything Colin had seen, Marshall was better than even money to sleep through the crack of doom.

One more sigh. Then out the door, up onto the bike, on with the helmet, and away. *Hi-yo, Silver!* Colin thought sourly. His bifocals sat in an inside jacket pocket. Hood or no hood, riding in the rain with them on was a losing proposition. He pedaled south to 154th, dutifully stopped at the stop sign, stuck his left arm straight out to signal a left turn, and went east on 154th to Hesperus.

Another stop sign there. A right turn this time: left arm out with forearm and hand pointing up. Hesperus was one of San Atanasio's major north–south streets. There'd probably be a few cars on it, even if gas was hard to come by and over fifteen bucks a gallon when you could get any.

Mostly bikes, though, bikes and skateboards and the occasional grownup–sized tricycle. Quite a few people rode with iPod earbuds to shut out the world. Colin didn't; he wanted to know what might be gaining on him. Traffic lights were out along with the rest of the power. If something came barreling down Reynoso Drive toward Hesperus, for instance, maybe he'd hear it and be able to take evasive action.

But nothing did—nothing more dangerous than other bicycles, anyhow. (Not that bike-on-bike crashes couldn't get messy. You could rack yourself up but good. You could even kill yourself, especially if you didn't bother with a helmet—at least as dumb as riding in a car without a seat belt.) He pedaled on. This was an old part of San Atanasio, with shops and offices dating back to not long after the war, some to before it.

The police station was near the corner of Hesperus and San Atanasio Boulevard, in the government center with the jail, the city hall, and the county library. They'd all gone up in the 1960s, when the town was flush. That was a while ago now. When San Atanasio got in the news these days, the people who didn't call it *gritty* invariably did call it *working-class*.

San Atanasio would be in the news today. Colin wished like hell that weren't so. One more wish he wouldn't get.

He chained his bike to the steel rack that had gone into place by the station's front door after the eruption. A lot of black-and-whites sat in the parking lot. They were in working order, but so expensive to put on the street that most of them sat most of the time.

Several news vans sat in the lot, too. Colin's mouth tightened when he saw one from CNN along with the local stations' machines. The only thing he wanted less than going on L.A. TV was going on national—to say nothing of international—TV. Well, a lot of what life was all about was the difference between what you wanted and what you got.

He walked into the cop shop. "Hello, Lieutenant," said the sergeant at the desk.

"Morning, Neil," Colin answered. A phone call from Neil Schneider at twenty-five past three in the bloody morning had got this nightmare rolling—or, if you looked at things a different way, the nightmare had been rolling for years and crashed to a stop with that call.

"Uh, Lieutenant, the mayor wants to talk to you before the press conference," Schneider said. "He's waiting in"—he looked very unhappy for a few seconds—"in the chief's office."

"Is he?" Colin said tonelessly. "Okay, I guess I'd better find out what's on his mind."

Colin tramped down the hall: a broad-shouldered, blunt-featured man in his mid-fifties. His hair was more salt than pepper, but he had all of it. Riding the bike and walking where he usually would have driven before the eruption had slimmed him some, but he'd never be svelte. He wasn't built for the role.

Mike Pitcavage, the plaque on the door said. Chief. No one had pried it off yet. Maybe no one had had the heart. More likely, Colin judged, it had fallen through the cracks. It wasn't as if nothing else was going on. He went inside.

Eugene Cervus was sitting behind the chief's big desk. The

mayor of San Atanasio stood up and held out his hand. "Thanks for stopping in, Lieutenant," he said. He had a pol's practiced grip. And why not? Along with managing a successful career running up apartment buildings, his father had sat in the mayor's chair before him. His younger brother was on the city council. All in the family. Uh-huh.

"What can I do for you, Mr. Mayor?" Colin asked.

Cervus studied him. The mayor was about ten years younger. He had an elegant haircut and wore a grayish brown suit of Italian cut. Mike Pitcavage had liked Italian suits, too. Probably not all the time, though. Not when he was out at night.

"Try not to make us look . . . too bad, anyway, all right?" Cervus said.

"It doesn't have much to do with the city, sir," Colin answered. "More with the police department." *And with all the other departments in the South Bay*, he thought. But the pigeons had come home to roost here. Oh, hadn't they just?

"I wouldn't say that." Eugene Cervus rolled his eyes. "What will you say when they ask you, 'How did it happen that San Atanasio not only had the South Bay Strangler on the police force but promoted him to chief?'"

Colin had never been long on diplomacy. That, no doubt, was why Mayor Cervus called him in here. But he actually chuckled. "That's simple. I'll tell 'em, 'Hey, they could've done worse. They could have promoted me instead.'"

He was kidding on the square. He'd applied for the job when Pitcavage got it. He'd been embittered for a long time at losing out, too. After a while, though, he'd realized the chief had to be almost as much a politician as the mayor. He wouldn't have been right behind this desk.

Of course, he wouldn't have raped and strangled a couple of dozen little old ladies, either, the way Mike Pitcavage had. No matter how good Pitcavage had been in this office, that wasn't part of the job description.

The mayor sighed. Then he said, "We'll have to fill the slot again, you know. If the man who ran down the Strangler were to apply, I'd think we'd have a hard time choosing anyone else. Wouldn't you?"

"I don't know," Colin said slowly. "Hadn't worried about it, to tell you the truth. Don't forget, I'm also the guy who couldn't catch him for all those years. And when I did, I didn't even know I'd done it."

"Mm," Cervus said. "I've heard—unofficially, of course—it was a friend of your son's who first reported that Darren Pitcavage was dealing drugs."

"Let's hope that stays unofficial," Colin said. Marshall's friend Tim hadn't exactly reported it. He'd just thought it was funny as hell, and figured his buds would, too. Things went on, and downhill, from there.

"Well, we'll see what the reporters know," the mayor said.

"See if they know anything." No, Colin wasn't diplomatic. He *was* distracted. He didn't want to be chief any more. But if Cervus told him the post was his for the asking . . . *Maybe I could try it for a little while—caretaker, like,* he thought, and then, immediately afterwards, *Kelly'd kill me.* Another thought followed hard on the heels of that one—*More likely, I'd want to kill myself first.* No, he didn't want it.

"One thing we'll show them is that California's policy of collecting DNA after felony arrests really pays dividends," Mayor Cervus said.

"Yeah." It wasn't that Colin disagreed with the mayor; he didn't. Mike Pitcavage had freaked at the idea of their taking a DNA sample from his son. He knew too well that it would point back to him. And so, instead of shooting himself the way so many cops did, he'd swallowed pills and put a plastic bag over his head to make sure things were final. Colin said, "Lucy'll be there, too, won't she? She's the one who really knows that stuff."

"She'll be there, yes," Cervus answered in a frozen voice. He explained why he sounded that way: "She did not want to consult with me."

In spite of everything, Colin had to hide a smile. Lucy Chen, the DNA tech who'd done the analysis that pointed to the late Chief Pitcavage, put him in mind of his own wife. She'd say what she'd say, what the facts told her to say, and the devil with anything else.

No wonder I get on with her, Colin thought. *No wonder I get on with Kelly, too.* He was talking with the mayor now, but they both knew it wouldn't do diddly to change what he told the news vultures.

Cervus checked his watch (a Rolex, of course). He sighed again. "Almost time. I suppose you'd better head for the press room."

"Happy day." Colin sounded like a man walking the last mile. He felt that way, too.

The press room was fuller than he ever remembered seeing it. As soon as he got inside, people started screaming questions. "Wait, please!" the San Atanasio PD public information officer said. She had a mike and the newsies didn't, but there were lots of them and only one of her. "Wait, please! Wait till Ms. Chen and Dr. Ishikawa come, too."

They didn't want to wait, even though Colin was a couple of minutes early. They always wanted answers immediately, if not sooner. They reminded him of spoiled three-year-olds. No matter how little diplomacy he owned, he knew better than to tell them so.

Lucy Chen and Dr. Maxwell Ishikawa came in together at nine on the dot. The DNA tech and the San Atanasio coroner both looked very scientific in their white coats. Dr. Ishikawa had plenty of practice meeting the press—much of it occasioned by the South Bay Strangler. Lucy Chen didn't. She seemed nervous. Well, it wasn't as if she hadn't earned the right.

Once they settled into their seats, the PIO said, "Shall we start?"

"Sure." Colin did his best not to show his lack of enthusiasm. The coroner and the DNA technician both nodded. The public information officer waved to the reporters. She wasn't really throwing wolves raw meat, as Colin'd said to Kelly before he left home. It only seemed that way.

"Why didn't you catch the Strangler sooner?" a newsie shouted. Colin would have bet that would be the first question. The reporter added, "How many years were you going to work with him every day?"

"Believe me, we've been beating ourselves up about that, too," Colin answered, which was nothing less than the truth. Lucy and Dr. Ishikawa nodded again. Colin went on, "But why didn't we? Because he was a smart crook, and a careful crook. We never got fingerprints or anything at the crime scenes. And I hate to tell you, but people like that don't wear I DID IT! signs on their backs. They look like anybody else. They act like anybody else, too, at least when they aren't killing little old ladies. Before the eruption, there was that guy in the Midwest who was a pillar of his church for years and years—except when he was murdering children. It can happen. I wish it couldn't. My life would be a lot easier. It can, though."

"But you had his DNA!" Two men and a woman bawled the same words at the same time.

Colin glanced over to Dr. Ishikawa. "We had the perpetrator's DNA, yes," the coroner said. "We did not know whose DNA that was, however. Unfortunately, samples do not come with name tags. We can say, *Yes, this matches that,* but when unknown matches unknown. . . ." He spread his hands.

"Then you arrested his son," the woman said.

It wasn't a question. She never would have got away with it on *Jeopardy!* Colin figured he needed to answer it anyhow. "That's right. We did, on felony drug-dealing charges," he said. "In California, anyone arrested on a felony charge has to give a DNA sample. So we took one from Darren Pitcavage."

"What was his father's reaction to that? The chief's reaction?" a reporter asked.

"Mike Pitcavage was upset. He wasn't just upset because his son had been arrested on a felony charge. He was upset because they were going to take a DNA sample. He told me so, more than once," Colin said.

"Did he put unusual stress on that?" the reporter asked.

"Looking back, I think he did. At the time, I have to say I didn't make that much of it. I just figured he'd come a little unhinged because of what Darren had done," Colin answered. "Then he killed himself that night. At first, we assumed it was because of his son's arrest and disgrace." Colin found himself making a small, unhappy noise down deep in his chest. Much the bigger part of the San Atanasio PD had blamed him for busting darling Darren. That was a very bad time. He made himself continue, "Then we found out he had other reasons."

"When you did Darren Pitcavage's DNA." Again, it wasn't a question. Again, it still needed answering.

Lucy Chen's turn. "That's right," she said. "You need to understand, I am very familiar with the South Bay Strangler's pattern. When I analyzed Darren Pitcavage's DNA, I saw at once how close to the Strangler's it was."

"Police departments in California have already solved several cases when the DNA from a criminal's relative led them to the actual perpetrator," Dr. Ishikawa added.

"But chief Pitcavage was already dead before you tested his son's DNA?" the reporter from CNN asked.

"Yes. He committed suicide the night after his son was arrested. He must have known Darren's DNA would point toward him," Colin said. "He didn't wait around to see what came of that."

"Hadn't Darren Pitcavage been arrested before?" the CNN guy asked.

"Yes, but never on a felony. We don't take DNA samples after misdemeanor arrests," Colin answered.

The reporter looked down at his notes. He'd probably carried an iPad before the eruption, but the Net was pretty threadbare these days. Scribbles on paper might not be cool or sexy, but they always worked. "Some of the things he was accused of seem pretty strong for misdemeanors. Did his father have anything to do with the light charges?"

Of course he did, Colin thought. That had pissed him off for years, though he'd chalked it up to nothing more than a prominent man protecting his only son. Mike Pitcavage had had other things on his mind, though—yeah, just a few. Aloud, Colin said, "I know the police recommended felony charges once or twice. The district attorney chose not to file them till this last time. You'd have to ask him about his reasons." He didn't usually pass the buck. Today, he did it without the slightest hesitation.

"He's not here." The CNN guy stated the obvious. Several reporters asked, "Where do we find him?"

"His office is in the city hall, around the corner from this building," Colin said helpfully. If the DA didn't like it, too damn bad.

"How do you *feel* about this, Lieutenant Ferguson?" one of the locals called.

Colin pursed his lips and blew out a long breath. He'd hoped they wouldn't ask him that. Talking about what happened wasn't easy, but he could do it. All he knew about feelings was that he didn't know much about them. If he hadn't known that, his ex-wife could have instructed him in great detail on his ignorance.

"You think you know somebody," he said slowly. "And you *do* know him. You know him as another cop, and you know him as a guy who puts on a nice barbecue in his back yard, a guy who it's pretty good to drink a beer with when you're off duty. But you never imagine the . . . the monster in the cave down underneath, the monster that only comes out at night."

Back in the day, he supposed, somebody could have got that kind of shock by suddenly discovering an old friend was gay. People now were harder to stun that way, which was bound to be a good thing. But there were still secrets, dark secrets. Colin was sure there always would be.

"May I speak to that?" Lucy said. Since nobody told her no, she went on, "When I recognized that Darren Pitcavage's DNA was close to the Strangler's, I didn't want to believe it. When I tested the chief's and saw that it matched the Strangler's, I felt like the world had come to an end."

"It felt that way to me, too, when Ms. Chen brought me the results," Dr. Ishikawa said. "I am a coroner. I work with many things most people do not want to think about. *I* did not want to think about this. But what choice did I have? What choice do any of us have?"

Colin hoped that would make the reporters shut up and go away. No such luck, of course. One of them asked, "Lieutenant Ferguson, what tipped you off to the fact that Darren Pitcavage was engaging in drug-dealing activities?"

Not drug dealing, mind you. Drug-dealing activities. Didn't anybody speak English any more? It seemed unlikely. Did the fellow with the sprayed hair know about Marshall? Colin took refuge in officialese of his own: "I'm afraid I can't comment on that right now. Darren Pitcavage hasn't gone to trial yet."

"Let me ask you a different question, then," the reporter said. "How difficult was it to implement the investigation when the person you were investigating was your police chief's son?"

"It was awkward," Colin answered truthfully.

"Chief Pitcavage wasn't aware of the investigation until his son was actually arrested?"

"That's correct," Colin said, and not another word.

The reporter kept prodding: "That was because you didn't trust him not to inform his son that he was being investigated?"

"Yes." Colin hoped he could get away with leaving it there, but the way the reporters all stirred showed him he couldn't. With a mental sigh, he went on, "You have to remember, at that time I had no idea Chief Pitcavage was the South Bay Strangler. I didn't know he would do anything he could to keep Darren from having to give a DNA sample on account of that. But I did know he was Darren's father, and fathers are liable to do anything to protect their sons."

"Suppose the chief hadn't been the Strangler. How much hot water would you be in now for busting his son behind his back, if you know what I mean?"

That was an honest-to-God shrewd question. With his jaundiced view of the press, Colin hadn't thought the man capable of such a thing. Fortunately, it was also a question he didn't have to answer. "I don't want to deal in hypotheticals," he said. "Haven't we got enough real troubles to worry about?"

To his relief, another man asked Lucy Chen, "You had access to Chief Pitcavage's DNA because of the autopsy after his suicide?"

"That's correct," she said. "I didn't know if Darren Pitcavage had other close male relatives, but I did know his DNA was highly similar to the South Bay Strangler's. I checked the sample I could get, and I found that it matched the Strangler's pattern."

"There's no possibility of a mistake?" the reporter asked.

That was a mistake. Lucy bristled. "I don't think so," she snapped. "And this is not just my judgment, not any more. Because the issue is so important, several other analyses have been made independent of mine. They all show exactly the same result. Without any doubt, Chief Pitcavage was the South Bay Strangler." *And you can go fuck yourself, pal.* She didn't say it, but her attitude did.

"That he killed himself as soon as he knew his son would have to give a DNA sample argues pretty strongly for a guilty conscience," Colin added.

"Thank you very much, ladies and gentlemen," the San Atanasio PIO said, which meant *Enough, already. Now get lost.*

They streamed away. Their trucks would send chunks of the press conference up to the satellites. People who had power would watch the chunks and decide they knew all about what had happened. Colin Ferguson knew only too well that *he* didn't. Only one man ever had, and Mike Pitcavage wasn't answering questions from any earthly authority.

"Boy, that was fun," Lucy Chen said.

"Not," Colin agreed.

"You all did a good job," the PIO said.

"Thank you," Dr. Ishikawa said.

"I hope I never have to do another job like that as long as I live," Colin said. The coroner's head bobbed up and down. So did Lucy's.

And so did the public information officer's. "I believe you," she said. "But you did it well anyhow. You made San Atanasio look . . ." She paused, perhaps wondering how to finish that.

Colin took a shot at it for her: "Just bad instead of really awful."

"That isn't what I was going to say." But the PIO didn't tell him what would have come out of her mouth. Colin didn't try to push her. Sometimes *not* explaining was better.

Colin stood up and stretched. Something in his back crunched. The city chair hadn't been what anyone would call comfortable. He hadn't been exactly loose while he was sitting in it, either.

"Back to work," he said. "If I don't have to mess with anything but punks and drunks and lunks for a while, I'll be the happiest man in the world, and you can take that to the bank."

For years, he'd walked to his desk in the big communal office in the cop shop without anybody paying attention to him unless someone needed to talk about the latest robbery or stabbing or whatever the hell. He'd taken that anonymity for granted. It was part of fitting in at your job.

Or it had been. He'd lost that immunity from notice when Mike Pitcavage killed himself. Most of the people in the San Atanasio PD had decided he'd driven Pitcavage to it by arresting Darren. The rest figured Darren had it coming, and that his father overreacted to the humiliation. Everybody on both sides stared at every move Colin made.

Now people knew the chief had had other reasons for committing suicide. They still stared at Colin. He wished like hell they'd cut it out. Chances were the world would warm up after the supervolcano eruption finally wore off before he got his wish—and the poor old world probably wouldn't warm up again till long after he was dead and gone.

He wasn't sorry to see Gabe Sanchez nod at him. "How'd it go, Colin?" Gabe asked. They'd worked together a long time.

"Well, it could have been worse," Colin allowed.

The detective scratched at the corner of his graying mustache. "Can't ask for too much more than that," he said. Like Colin, he had a limited sense of possibility—except for the ways things could go wrong. He stood up and headed for the door. "Gotta get my fix. They'd string me up by the short hairs if I lit one in here."

They would, too. Not many places had stricter rules against smoking indoors than San Atanasio's. Colin was glad he'd escaped one bad habit, anyway. His eyes followed Gabe to the exit. As far as he could tell, they were the only ones that did. He was jealous of his friend because of that.

He sat down at his desk. Yes, the eyes were on him. No, he couldn't do anything about it. All he could do was go on. People didn't stop robbing and fighting and shooting just because Mike Pitcavage grabbed some of the headlines for a little while.

He was checking to see if they'd found a match for the prints in a robbery at the Popeye's Chicken on Braxton Bragg Boulevard when the phone rang. He picked it up. "Ferguson."

"Hello, Colin." A woman's voice: familiar, familiar with him and familiar to him. For a split second, he thought it was Louise. But it wasn't his ex. He'd just realized as much when the voice—the woman—went on, "This is Caroline Pitcavage."

"Oh," he said, more an exhalation than a word. It was an exhalation of more than a little pain, as if someone had punched him in the stomach. After a moment, he managed, "I'm sorry, Caroline. I'm sorry for everything."

"Funny," Mike Pitcavage's widow said, though she didn't sound amused. "I was calling to tell you the same thing. After Darren got arrested, after Mike . . . did what he did, I thought some horrible things about you. I said some horrible things about you, too. I blamed you, is what I did. But now I know why Mike . . . swallowed the pills and put the bag over his head. I owe you an apology, a big one. I *am* sorry, Colin—God knows I am."

"It's okay," Colin said. "Before we knew, uh, what was up, I was kicking myself pretty hard, too." Before they knew what was up, he'd wondered whether Caroline would come after him with a shotgun. He'd also wondered whether a San Atanasio jury would convict her if she did. Not that he would have been in any position to appreciate the verdict either way.

"I believe you," she said. "*Now* I believe you, anyway. Now I just wish he would have done that years ago, the first time he got the urge to do . . . what he did. I lived with a monster all those years. I lived with a monster, and I had no idea. Not a clue. Not one single, solitary goddamn clue."

"I know you didn't, Caroline," Colin replied. As he'd said at the press conference, some people who did things like that were normal—at least on the outside—except when the compulsion grabbed them. It didn't happen often, thank heaven, but it happened.

Caroline Pitcavage went on as if he hadn't spoken: "Everything I had, everything we had together, it was all nothing. No, it was worse than nothing. It was a lie. How do you go on when most of your adult life all of a sudden turns out to be a lie?"

"It's not easy," Colin said slowly. He'd thought he'd had a fairly happy first marriage. And he had, at least from his point of view, till Louise decided she *wasn't* happy and decided to try her luck with her aerobics instructor instead. Colin had reacted to the ordinary tragedy the way an ordinary man would have. He'd drunk too damn much and he'd gone on vacation to Yellowstone National Park to run away from his troubles. And he'd met Kelly there, and his life had started to turn itself around.

But that was an ordinary tragedy. Ones just like it happened every day in towns from Nome to Key West. Caroline's was piled a lot higher and deeper. No sooner than that thought crossed his mind, she said, "You know what the real kick in the head is?"

"Tell me," Colin urged.

He was sorry immediately afterwards, because she answered, "If the son we raised hadn't turned out to be a stupid little shit, I'd still be glad I was married to a mass murderer. How about *that*?"

"Caroline . . ." Colin said helplessly.

"He didn't take all the pills. He knew just how many he needed. I'm sure I could find another plastic bag somewhere, too," Caroline said. Quickly, she added, "No, don't call 911. I don't mean it. That would be something he'd want me to do, damn him. I wonder how much Oprah or Ellen would pay me to turn myself inside out on national TV."

Probably quite a bit, Colin thought. Aloud, all he said was, "Maybe you don't want to do anything too real fast."

"Maybe I don't. But maybe I do, too. Gotta get on while Mike's still hot news, right?" Caroline sounded brittle, and who could blame her? She went on, "One more thing to talk to my lawyer about. He'll send his kids to Harvard thanks to me any which way, if it hasn't frozen solid by the time they get there. Take care, Colin. None of this was your fault, and I am sorry I thought it was." She hung up before he could respond.

"Jesus," he said as he set down his own phone's handset.

Gabe had come back from his cigarette break. "Who was that?" he asked from a couple of desks away.

"Caroline Pitcavage."

Gabe said "Jesus!" too.

"Tell me about it," Colin said. "Right this minute, drinking lunch looks like the best idea I've had in years. Wanna come along?" Gabe didn't tell him no. Colin hadn't thought he would.

II

Louise Ferguson looked nervously at the battery-powered clock on the wall in the condo's cramped little kitchen. She had to head for the bus stop if she was going to get to the Van Slyke Pharmacy on time. Where was Marshall, dammit? If she had to drag James Henry with her when she went in, nobody would be happy with her, not her preschool son, not her grown son, and not her boss, either.

The security gate at the front of the condominium complex stood open. When the electricity was out, as it was so much these days, the gate was useless. Arrivals couldn't buzz the people they were visiting. One of these days, the turbines on the Columbia that the dust and ash and silt from the supervolcano had killed would finally get replaced. One of these days, but who could guess which one? When the new turbines got to work at last, power up and down the West Coast would grow more reliable. So Washington claimed, anyhow.

Washington had claimed all kinds of things since the eruption. It delivered on about one in three, maybe one in four. Some disasters were too big for even the most powerful country in the history of the world. This one, for instance.

Feet on the stairs. The clank of a bicycle frame against the iron railing. A muttered "Shit!" outside the front window. A knock on the door. Marshall Ferguson, to the rescue! And just in the nick of time. The scriptwriters couldn't have done it better . . . if the bus didn't run late, anyhow.

She opened the door. In came Marshall, bike in one hand and typewriter case in the other. "You made it!" Louise said in relief.

"Yeah." Marshall grudged a nod. If she didn't pay him, he wouldn't be here. He set up his bicycle next to the dinette wall. "Just starting to rain."

"Oh, hell," Louise said. She had an umbrella in her purse— even in the L.A. basin, you could get rain any old time now that the supervolcano had done its number on the global climate— but she'd hoped she wouldn't need to use it today. Then she called, "James Henry! Come say bye-bye to Mommy!"

Out came her youngest son. That she should have a child not yet four still croggled her. James Henry Ferguson didn't look like his much older half-brother. Marshall looked like Colin, though he was rangier and had Louise's rather beaky nose. James Henry took after his father. He was much darker than any of Louise's children by Colin, and the shape of his cheekbones told the world Teo's ancestors came from Mexico.

He hugged Louise. "Bye-bye," he said dutifully, and then, "Hey, Marshall."

"Hey, kid," Marshall answered. James Henry yawned. He would sooner have slept in. Louise couldn't let him do it, though. She never knew for sure whether Marshall would show up on time—*he* would sooner have slept in, too. If he was late or didn't come at all, James Henry had to go to the pharmacy whether he or Louise liked it or not.

He didn't have to today, though. Louise damn well did. Out

the door she went, across the courtyard—the grass greener and shaggier than anyone before the eruption would have dreamt SoCal grass could get—and out through the security entrance that wasn't. She crossed the street. Nobody on a bicycle ran over her. The bus stop was half a block down.

She nodded to the regulars who waited there. Some of them nodded back. Others peered down the street. They cared more about the bus than they did about her. Everything was erratic these days. The bus was supposed to show up in about ten minutes. And maybe it would, and maybe it wouldn't.

It was late, but it wasn't *very* late. She fed three dollar bills into the slot, one after another. The reader didn't want to swallow one of the bills. She pulled out a different one. Everybody behind her was loving her to pieces for gumming up the works. The slot deigned to accept the substitute bill. She sat down. After the rest of the riders paid their fares, the bus pulled out into the street.

Three bucks each way. Five days a week. That sucked, was what it did. Not for the first time, Louise thought about buying herself a bike. It would save money in the long run. But getting what she needed for the upfront wouldn't be easy, not when she had to watch every penny as things were. And she hadn't ridden on two wheels for a hell of a long time. It was supposed to come back in a hurry. *With my luck, probably right after I fall down and break my wrist—or my neck*, she thought.

The bus went up to Hesperus, then swung left onto Reynoso Drive. It rumbled past what had been a drive-in movie once upon a time. For the past umpty-ump years, the big parking lot held a swap meet on weekends. Colin had always hated the place—he swore more than half of what got sold there was either hot or counterfeit.

Louise muttered to herself. She didn't want to think about Colin, no matter how long she'd been married to him. She was on her own. She'd wanted to be on her own, and she'd gone and got free. And, in spite of everything, she was happier without him than she had been with him. Not so secure, but happier.

By all the signs, he was happier, or at least as happy, without her, too. She hadn't figured on that—she'd assumed he'd flop around like a fish out of water. But she didn't want to think about that, either.

She stood up as the bus neared the corner of Reynoso Drive and Van Slyke. The bus stopped. The doors hissed open. She got out. The bus turned right onto Van Slyke and growled north.

Louise crossed Reynoso Drive. The pharmacy was in something half a step up from a strip mall on the northeast corner of the intersection. It shared the space with a liquor store, a Filipino market, and an optician's shop. None of the businesses except the liquor store was exactly thriving, but they all kept chugging along. She couldn't think of a disaster that would keep a liquor store from thriving.

When she walked in, Jared Watt was straightening the secondhand books on their shelves. "Good morning, Louise," the pharmacist said, eyes enormous behind thick spectacle lenses. He wore loud polyester shirts. His hair looked as if someone who wasn't very good with a lawnmower had mowed it. Along with the books and drugs (prescription and otherwise) and school supplies and the like, he also sold some of the ugliest tchotchkes God or the Devil ever made.

And Louise cared not a nickel for any of that. "Good morning, Jared," she said warmly. He'd given her a job when she needed one worse than a junkie needed smack. And, even if all his taste was in his mouth, he was a nice guy. Next to Mr. Nobashi, for whom she'd worked till the Japanese ramen company closed its American headquarters, Jared Watt was a saint on earth. A dweeby saint, no doubt, but a saint neverthenonetheless.

"Isn't that something about the chief of police?" he said now.

"Who could have thought such a thing? Terrible—just terrible. I met him a few times. I never had the faintest idea. Who would?"

"I knew him, too," she said tightly. She'd admired Mike Pitcavage. He had ambition, drive, call it whatever you want. He had style, too. Next to him, Colin was a lump of a man, somebody who'd stay a police lieutenant forever.

But, whatever you said about Colin, he'd never killed any old ladies. Praising with faint damn, maybe, but praising even so.

Jared must not have noticed the edge in her voice, because he went on, "And the fellow who arrested his son, who touched off the whole thing, he was smart and lucky both."

"That was my ex." Louise bit off the words one by one.

"Oh!" The pharmacist blinked. Louise could watch every eyelash move. Jared Watt continued, "His name *is* Ferguson, isn't it? I'm sorry—I didn't put two and two together."

"You didn't know. It's not exactly a rare name." Louise was trying to convince herself at least as much as her boss.

The landline rang. The interruption relieved them both. Louise answered it. Someone asked for a refill on a prescription. She took the prescription number, then checked a card file. The information was on a database, too, but with the power off a computer was just something to gather dust.

"It's Peter Aiso and his blood-pressure prescription," she told Jared. "He had three refills left on it—now he's down to two." She made a notation on the three-by-five. She'd do it on the computer, too, if and when the electricity came back on.

"He gets Aldovil 15/25 twice a day, right?" he said. It was a question, and then again it wasn't.

"That's right." Louise nodded. From everything she'd seen, Jared Watt barely needed the database or the card file. He almost always knew what his customers' meds were. Now he frowned. "We don't have any of that. I don't know when we'll get more, either. When some more comes into town. Whenever that is."

"What will you do, then?" Louise asked.

"I'll see what we do have. Then I'll call his doctor, and we'll work out something or other." He paused. "You ever see the Charles Addams cartoon with two witches over the cauldron? One of 'em's saying to the other, 'We're all out of dwarf's hair, dearie. Can we substitute?'"

Louise laughed. "No, I hadn't seen that one." She knew Charles Addams from the old TV show and the movies, not from the cartoons themselves.

"Well, that's where we are right now. That's where the whole country is these days, seems like," Jared Watt said. "We're all out of dwarf's hair, dearie, and we're doing our best to substitute."

"Only trouble is, our best mostly isn't good enough," Louise said.

"Welcome to the world," the pharmacist said. Louise looked at him in surprise. Colin might have come out with the same thing, and he would have used the same intonation if he had.

A little old Hispanic man walked in. He wore glasses almost as thick as Jared's. He peered through them at the shelves of old paperbacks. After due deliberation, he pulled out something called *Count Belisarius* and carried it to the counter. Louise looked at the price penciled on the first leaf inside the cover. "That'll be two dollars and fifty cents—two-seventy-five with the tax."

"Taxes," the man muttered, as if it were a swear word. "They've gone through the roof, too, since that stupid supervolcano blew up." He made it sound as if the eruption shot taxes into the stratosphere along with God only knew how many cubic miles of dust and sulfur dioxide and other climate-screwing crud. By the way he handed over a five, it was the last one he ever expected to see.

Louise gave him his change. "Even with the tax, the book's cheaper than bus fare," Jared Watt said. "That's a good one, too. You'll find out more about the sixth century than you thought anybody could know."

"It's fat," the Hispanic man said. "It'll kill time while the power don't work." He shuffled out of the pharmacy, tucking the book under his windbreaker. It was starting to rain for real, all right.

"How many of the books over there have you read?" Louise pointed to the shelves.

"Quite a few, anyway," Jared answered. "Reading kills time for me, too."

Colin read all the time. That prejudiced Louise against it. But she did some anyway. Batteries kept a Kindle going, even if you couldn't always download new stuff. And she read to James Henry. When the TV didn't run, stories entertained him.

We were so wired, so connected, she thought. *We were, and now we aren't any more. It's a different world.* A moment later, another thought occurred: *Christ, I wish we still were!*

Bryce Miller had known what post-supervolcano life in Nebraska was like before he took the assistant professor job at Wayne State. He'd known, that is, the way he'd known about girls before Brianna Davidson finally let him get lucky his senior year of high school. In the one as in the other, the difference between knowledge and experience was all the difference in the world.

People who'd grown up here had a tough time dealing with the new dispensation. They said average winter days now were as horrible as anything they'd ever known before the eruption. And the bad blizzards now, if you listened to them, had never been seen this side of the Great Slave Lake—or, if they were feeling charitable, this side of Saskatoon.

Bryce had little choice but to listen to them. He'd grown up in San Atanasio and lived his whole life till now in Southern California. His wife Susan was a SoCal girl, too. The depth of Midwest winter shocked and awed her as much as it did him.

So did the length of Midwest winter. Snow fell all the way

through Memorial Day. Right after the supervolcano went off, people had talked and talked about the Year Without a Summer, after Mt. Tambora erupted two centuries earlier. Now that they were looking down the barrel of a Decade Without a Summer, or maybe of a Century Without a Summer, Mt. Tambora suddenly seemed like mighty small potatoes.

Potatoes were a big deal at the local supermarket, though. Susan lugged a cloth tote full of oddly shaped, brightly colored tubers back to their apartment. "Gaah! Mutants!" Bryce exclaimed. "Do we eat them or exorcise them?" He made the sign of the cross with his forefingers.

"Fat lot of good that'll do when you're Jewish," Susan said with exaggerated patience.

"Maybe the spuds won't know. I don't look it," Bryce said. And he didn't. He was tall and skinny and very fair, with curly dark red hair and a lighter red beard that still wasn't so thick as he would have liked even though he'd slid to the tired side of thirty.

"You," Susan said, not for the first time, "are absurd."

"Thank you." He bowed.

"Anyway, these potatoes come from stock that's raised way the hell up high in the Andes, where potatoes started out from and where the growing season's always been about twenty minutes long," Susan told him. "The prices were pretty bad, but not terrible, and the produce guy says they'll be coming down because these'll grow in a lot of places where the kinds we used to plant just can't hack the weather any more."

"They'll still taste like potatoes, though," Bryce predicted gloomily.

"Hey, they're food." Except for being in the final throes of finishing a dissertation on Frederick II Hohenstaufen, Susan was a very practical person.

Since Bryce's thesis had been on the leading Hellenistic poets, and since his hobby was writing pastorals in the style of Theocritus, even Susan's field of interest seemed practical by comparison. Frederick was fifteen hundred years more recent and a hell of a lot more relevant to the modern world than Theocritus or Callimachus or any of the rest of the boys who'd done their damnedest to con lunch money out of one Ptolemy or another.

And food, in this long winter of the planet's discontent, was something you had to be practical about. Wayne, Nebraska, sat in the middle of what had been some of the finest farming country the world had ever known. *Had been*, unfortunately, was the operative phrase. Land that used to bring in bumper crops of wheat and corn now barely had enough of a growing season for the quickest-ripening strains of oats and rye.

"Potatoes," Bryce repeated, this time with resignation in his voice.

Potatoes they were, with a little pork sausage to perk them up. You could still get pork, and Bryce didn't let the religion he'd been born into keep him from eating it. Sometimes you could still find chicken without a bank loan. Beef? Lamb? The eruption had massacred the flocks and herds, and without corn and soybeans a lot of the animals it didn't directly kill starved. Milk and cheese and butter were hard to come by, too.

After a few bites, Bryce said "Potatoes" yet again, this time thoughtfully. "They don't taste *quite* like the regular kind, do they? I mean, they wouldn't even without the sausage."

Susan nodded. "I was thinking the same thing. Potatoes from before the eruption, ordinary potatoes, don't taste like anything much."

"Ain't that the truth? Born to be blaaand!" Bryce cheerfully goofed on a Steppenwolf song much older than he was.

His wife winced, whether at the lyric or the singing he didn't want to guess. Susan went on, "They've probably been bred not to taste like much for hundreds of years. These haven't. They're still—"

"Real roots," Bryce broke in.

"Something like that," Susan agreed. "If our regular potatoes are cows, these things are buffaloes."

"Cows," Bryce said wistfully. Then, more wistfully still, he said, "Buffaloes." Yellowstone National Park was the big reason the bison hadn't gone extinct at the end of the nineteenth century. No more wild bison there, not when the park literally fell off the map to form the supervolcano's latest and greatest caldera. As far as Bryce knew, no more wild bison anywhere. He supposed a few still lingered in zoos, but that wasn't the same.

A lot of things weren't the same, and never would be again—not for the rest of his life, anyhow, which was as much time as mattered to him.

"When you get a job," he said, "try really, really hard for something in Florida, or maybe Houston."

"Yeah, right." Susan rolled her eyes, the way one spouse will when the other comes out with something really, really dumb. "Nobody else wants jobs in places like those, of course, so getting one will be super easy."

His ears heated. He wouldn't have taken this slot in beautiful, romantic, subtropical Wayne, Nebraska, if he could have landed one in any warmer place. Given a choice between a slot in Wayne, Nebraska, and one in hell, he would have thought seriously at least one day in three—one day in two during Wayne's long, long winter—about taking Satan as his department chair.

When he said so, he got a snort out of Susan. Snort or no snort, though, she said, "If something does open up, it's likely to be somewhere like Winnipeg or Edmonton."

"Oh, joy," Bryce said. "We can wave hello to the glaciers when they roll down out of the north. Those are places that make Minneapolis look like it's got good weather."

Climatologists kept insisting at the top of their lungs that the supervolcano eruption wouldn't touch off the next Ice Age. They told anyone who would listen that this was only an episode. Even if they were wrong, the glaciers wouldn't start chasing musk oxen down toward Chicago and Philadelphia within a human lifetime.

Bryce hoped like hell they wouldn't, anyhow.

While he was ruminating, so to speak, on that, Susan said, "There's another problem with going north of the border, you know."

"Oh? What is it?" Bryce asked.

He thought she would talk about work visas or currency conversion or something like that. Instead, he got a pie in the face: "Neither one of us speaks Canadian," she said.

"Ouch!" He sent her a reproachful stare. "That's the kind of thing I usually come out with, not you."

"You're rubbing off on me. It must be love, or something," Susan said.

"Gotta be something," Bryce said. "I hope it's something you can take something for."

"I already did." She held up her left hand. The diamond in the ring on her fourth finger wasn't much bigger than a chip, but it sparkled all the same.

Bryce smiled. "I like the way you talk." His own wedding ring, a florentined gold band, had felt funny on his finger for a little while. Now he hardly noticed he had it on.

And he walked straight into another one. "Good," Susan said. "You wash dishes tonight, and I'll dry."

He made a face. But then he said, "Ha! Mwahaha, in fact. I'm the one who gets to put hot water on his hands."

"If there is hot water," Susan said. Wayne did have power and natural gas most of the time. That put it ahead of Los Angeles, but they were hideously expensive. The landlord at the apartment building reacted the way landlords have reacted to anything that costs them money since the beginning of time. He raised his tenants' rent and he set his water heaters so they didn't heat much water, and so what they did heat didn't get very hot.

Showers could be an adventure. So could dishes. Getting rid of grease with water that felt as if it came from some polar bear's pet iceberg at the North Pole wasn't Bryce's idea of fun. As a matter of fact, if he ever wrote a poem about modern labors for Hercules—an idea that had been bouncing around in his head for a while—there was one of them.

Tonight wasn't too bad, though. The water was still tepid when he got done. Susan put the dishes and glasses and pans and silverware in their places. Then she carefully shut all the cabinet doors. Dead-air spaces helped insulate the apartment. *Better to insu late than never*, Bryce thought vaguely. Colin would have appreciated that. He didn't have the gall to try it on Susan.

He spent the next little while reading his students' midterms. Any hope he might have had that the disaster could somehow make students write better had foundered during his gig at Junipero High. They were going to write things like *it's* for *its* and *effect* for *affect* (and the other way around) and even *you're* for *your*, and you couldn't do one goddamn thing about it. Half their alleged sentences looked as if they came from text messages.

Bryce was (almost) resigned to that. Languages *did* change. Thucydides would commit seppuku if he saw what Greek looked like these days. The tongue of Caesar and Cicero and Virgil had morphed into Spanish and French and Italian and Pig Latin. Buck the trend and you were shoveling shit against the tide.

But why did so many of the kids sound as if they'd never had a thought in their lives? They could give back the textbook, and sometimes even chunks of his lectures. Give them back, yes. Analyze them? Draw conclusions? Like the number five in *Monty Python and the Holy Grail*, those were right out.

He waved a bluebook—a C+ bluebook—at Susan. "I can't flunk them all, no matter how much they deserve it. People would talk," he said. They wouldn't just talk, either. They'd fire his nit-picking ass for disturbing the peace. "If this is what's up and coming, the country's in deep kimchi."

"You're right," she said. "You know what else, though?"

"What?"

"Everybody in college could turn into a cross between Shakespeare and Einstein tomorrow, and the country'd still be in deep kimchi."

He thought about that. He didn't need long. He nodded. "Well, you're right," he answered. He couldn't think of anything worse to say.

Marshall Ferguson clacked away on the manual typewriter his old man had found him. He didn't like it for beans, but it let him write when power outages left his Mac blind, deaf, and dumb.

He had all kinds of reasons for disliking the typewriter. If you'd learned at a computer keyboard, typing on a manual meant practically spraining your fingers every time you pressed down. That was bad enough. Worse was how user-friendly a typewriter wasn't.

If you made a typo on the Mac, a couple of keystrokes and it was gone. It you decided to rework a sentence, you selected it, deleted it, and rebuilt it to your heart's new desire. If you needed to put this paragraph above that one instead of below, Command-X and Command-V were all it took.

If you needed to do that stuff on a typewriter . . . He had a circular, gritty eraser with a green nylon brush sticking out of the metal holder for disposing of small mistakes. Correction fluid eradicated words, sometimes even sentences. For anything bigger than that, you needed to retype the whole stinking page, even if you were down near the bottom.

It sucked, was what it did. Bigtime.

Almost anything was better than retyping a page. He'd got to the point where, when he could see trouble coming ahead, he'd fiddle with things in longhand till he got them the way he wanted them. Then he'd transcribe his scribbles. The method wasn't elegant. It was butt-ugly, in fact. But it worked. He figured anything that let him turn out tolerably neat copy on a typewriter put him ahead of the game.

When the house had power, he would scan his typewritten pages to OCR. The copy that produced wasn't perfect—the scanner didn't care for the manual typewriter's imperfections. But it was, to borrow one of his father's favorite pungent phrases, close enough for government work. He could clean it up and then go ahead on the computer till the next time it went dark without warning. He learned to save very often. He never lost more than about a third of a page of text.

The next interesting question was whether the latest story was worth doing. It was about a guy whose friends kept looking at him out of the corner of their eye because he'd snitched when he found out somebody he knew was embezzling from the place where he worked.

Whether the story was worth doing in a dramatic sense mattered only so much. He knew damn well he'd finish this one. What he didn't know was whether it was more exorcism or expiation.

If Tim hadn't told him he'd bought dope from Darren Pitcavage, and if he hadn't told his dad . . . If that hadn't happened, Darren's father would still be alive. He'd still be chief of the San Atanasio Police Department. And, when the urge struck him, he'd still be raping and strangling little old ladies all over the South Bay.

Everybody was glad the South Bay Strangler was out of business. Everybody was especially glad the South Bay Strangler wasn't running the San Atanasio PD any more. In the ordinary run of things, passing on the information that made the South Bay Strangler shuffle off this mortal coil should have made Marshall a minor hero, or not such a minor one.

But he smoked dope. He'd ratted out a dealer. He'd never come right out and told his friends he'd done that, but they could add two and two even when they were baked. He knew what those sidelong glances he kept talking about in the story were like. He knew in the most intimate possible way—he'd been on the receiving end of too many of them.

His main character—a guy quite a bit like him—wondered if he'd have any friends left by the time things finally blew over. Marshall knew that feeling, too: knew it much too well. If he worked it out on the page and on the computer monitor, maybe he could work it through inside his head as well. Maybe.

He obviously couldn't talk about it with his buds. He couldn't talk about it with his father, either. Colin Ferguson just said, "You did the right thing." He was a hundred percent convinced of that. No doubt his certainty was meant to kill Marshall's doubts.

Only it didn't. It made them worse. Marshall was nowhere near a hundred percent convinced he'd done the right thing. Having somebody—especially somebody of the cop persuasion— tell him he'd absolutely done the right thing made him believe it less, not more.

His older brother might have understood him better. But Rob had been in Maine ever since the eruption. Maine was dimly, distantly connected to the rest of the USA a couple of months a year, when some of the roads sort of thawed. The rest of the time, it might as well have fallen off the map, or back into the nineteenth century.

And Rob went out and *did* things. He didn't worry about them as much as Marshall did. In a million years, Marshall wouldn't have had the nerve to try to pay his bills as a bass player in a band that would never make anyone forget Green Day or even Weezer any time soon. Marshall enjoyed hanging out with the guys in Squirt Frog and the Evolving Tadpoles. He enjoyed getting wasted with them. Hitting the road with them? That was another story.

So maybe Rob would have just told him to get over it and to get on with it. Good advice. Marshall knew as much. But he would have bet Rob couldn't tell him how to go about it.

He didn't ask his sister. Vanessa wouldn't even see there was a problem. She was about herself, first, last, and always (well, sometimes about whatever guy she was with, but she eventually decided each one in turn didn't measure up to what she figured she was entitled to). Besides, she had her nose out of joint at him right now because he kept writing and even selling stories every so often, where she talked a good game but never applied her behind to the seat of a chair long enough to produce anything.

Which left Kelly, pretty much by default. His dad's second wife wasn't the mother he should have had. She was too young for that, and too sensible. But she did seem like the older sister he might have had, all the more so when he compared her to the one biology had actually stuck him with.

And, like him, she was home most of the time. Taking care of a baby would do that for you—or rather, to you. She didn't mind listening to him. She said, "Hey, you could talk about the horses in next year's Kentucky Derby and I'd listen to you."

"You don't know anything about the Kentucky Derby," Marshall said. "Uh, do you?"

"Nope." Kelly shook her head—carefully, because she had Deborah on her shoulder. "But the other choice is talking about poopy diapers. I've got to change the goddamn things. I don't want to talk about 'em."

"I hear you." Marshall had changed some for his half-sister. Earlier, he'd changed some for his half-brother, his mother's child by the guy for whom she'd left Dad. Both kids were related to him. They weren't related to each other at all. How weird was that?

Kelly didn't try to tell him that of course he'd done the right thing when he squealed on Darren Pitcavage. She saw more shades of gray in the world than his father did. "I don't blame you for feeling funny," she said. "How can you help it? You didn't know all this was going to drop on your head. Nobody knew. Nobody had any idea. Darren's dad had been covering his tracks for a long time, and he was good at it."

"I guess," Marshall said. "It was even worse before we found out *why* he killed himself, you know? I thought getting Darren busted was what pushed him over the edge, like. That made me feel really great."

"Colin thought the same thing," Kelly answered. "Don't ever tell him I said this, but for a while I was worried about what he might do."

"Urk." Marshall hadn't thought about that. If there was a rock of stability in his life, it was his father. You didn't want to imagine that the rock could crack. Cops did kill themselves, even without reasons as good as Mike Pitcavage's. And somebody'd said that anything that could happen could happen to you. All the same . . .

Kelly nodded. "*Urk* is right. I couldn't say anything, I couldn't do anything. If he decided to, I couldn't even stop him. Too many chances away from me, too many ways for a cop to go, and to go quick. That was a *bad* time."

"Uh-huh." Marshall sent her an admiring glance. "You didn't let on that anything was bugging you."

"I was scared to," she said. "What would that do? Just make things worse. That was how it looked to me." Deborah made a small noise. One corner of Kelly's mouth turned down. "And it looks like this baby's never going to fall asleep."

"That's what babies are for, right? Driving grownups crazy, I mean." Marshall stopped in surprise, listening to himself. He'd just included himself among grownups, because Deborah sure could drive him crazy.

When he was a teenager, he'd desperately wanted to get older faster so he could be a grownup himself. Once he slid past twenty, though, he'd tried to put off the evil day as long as he could. He'd stretched his time at UC Santa Barbara as far as the university would let him, and then another twenty minutes besides. But they'd finally shoved the sheepskin into his sweaty hand no matter how little he wanted it.

And here he was, out in the world. Yes, he was living in his dad's house. No, he didn't have steady work. Even before the supervolcano blew, though, he'd shared that boat with plenty of others his age. He shared it with many more now. He figured he was a grownup anyhow—at least, if you compared him to a baby who didn't want to go to sleep.

III

Vanessa Ferguson was happy. Oh, not perfectly happy. That would have been too much to expect from anybody, and much too much to expect from her. Mr. Gorczany, the guy who ran the company she worked for, was a goose twit, and too big a goose twit to realize what a goose twit he was. The job was beneath her talents, and didn't pay her anywhere near what she thought she was worth.

But it did pay her enough to let her escape from the house where she'd grown up, the house she'd moved back to when she returned to SoCal. Escaping was nothing but a relief. She and her father's second wife hadn't hit it off, which was putting things mildly. And her kid brother seemed perfectly content to grow moss there. Marshall might still be living at home when he hit middle age. It would serve him right if he was, too.

Her own apartment wouldn't have been enough to bring her happiness, not by itself. It wasn't big. It wasn't new. It wasn't cheap. Too right it wasn't cheap! If Mr. Gorczany had paid her what she was worth to his miserable outfit, she wouldn't have worried about that so much. But he paid her what he paid her, and worry she did.

When she was in the ratty old expensive apartment with Bronislav, though, she didn't care about any of that stuff. She didn't even care that she thought Dad's second wife was a first-class bitch. All she cared about was Bronislav. He was what made her happy.

Oh, she'd felt that way the first few months with Bryce Miller, too, before she woke up to what a loser he really was. Back when she was still in high school, before she met Bryce, she'd been head over heels over a guy named Peter. She'd lost her cherry to Peter's peter, as a matter of fact. She'd been sure she would bear his children . . . till she lived with him for a little while. That cured her. She'd been glad—eager!—to jump to Bryce once Peter wore thin.

After Bryce, there was Hagop. Vanessa violently shook her head, the way she always did when she thought of Hagop. It wasn't just that the miserable rug merchant had been a year or two older than her own old man. She'd moved to Denver on account of him, dammit. That put her squarely in the line of fire when the supervolcano blew. All kinds of horrible things had happened to her on account of that.

Odds were Hagop was dead, of course. Almost all the people who'd lived in Denver were. Only a few had got out—the ones who'd fled first and fastest. She was one of them.

She didn't care about Hagop, not any more. Being dead was about what he deserved. Lousy schmuck. Lousy schmuck with his lousy schmuck . . .

Bronislav, now, Bronislav was different. Vanessa's sharp features softened as much as they ever did. Bronislav was the Real Thing. She was sure of it. (She'd also been sure of it with Peter, and with Bryce. And she'd done her best to be sure of it with Hagop as well, though even she'd suspected then she was trying to talk herself into it. She remembered none of her earlier certainties now.)

Bronislav Nedic was different all kinds of ways. Immigrant from what had been Yugoslavia. Looks somewhere between Nicolas Cage and an Orthodox icon. Big, dark, sad eyes. Beard thick as a pelt—the beard was the first thing she'd noticed about him, there in that New Mexico truck-stop coffee shop.

He had a musical Serbian accent. God help you, though, if you called it a Serbo-Croatian accent. To Bronislav, anything that had to do with Croats came from the dark side of the Force. He'd been a freedom fighter when Yugoslavia came unglued. He had some scary scars to prove it. He also had a tat on the back of his right hand—a cross with four C's, two forward and two backward, in the right angles. In Serbian's Cyrillic alphabet, those C's were S's, and they stood for *Only unity will save the Serbs*.

What had been Yugoslavia was now half a dozen little countries. Serbs dominated two and a third of them. So much for unity. And Bronislav, instead of plying his trade with Kalashnikov and RPG, was a long-haul trucker in America, going back and forth along I-10 to bring Los Angeles little pieces of the Everything it so desperately needed.

He was back in town now. He'd sent her a postcard and an e-mail and a text letting her know he was on the way. With the power grid so erratic, snailmail had advantages over its electronic rivals. It might not get there right away, but it *would* get there.

Vanessa kept telling herself she needed to buy a satellite phone. Then she wouldn't need to worry about whether the local plastic pseudotrees had power. But satellite phones dropped calls, too: the demand on the satellites was much worse than anyone had dreamt it could be before the eruption. And satellite plans didn't cost an arm and a leg. Like everything else these days, they cost an arm and both legs.

Bronislav usually brought stuff into San Pedro. That and Long Beach were the L.A. area's two main ports. Lots of warehouses and major distribution centers were there. And it worked out well for him another way—San Pedro had a sizable Serbian community.

It also had a sizable Croatian community. So far as Vanessa knew, they didn't go around firebombing each other or blowing up each other's churches. They limited their ancient feud to sneers and barroom brawls. Wasn't America a wonderful place?

Now that Bronislav had a lady friend in San Atanasio, getting in to San Pedro wasn't so convenient for him. He had to ride the bus up or Vanessa had to come down. He almost always came north. Her apartment might be cramped, but most of the hotels in San Pedro were only a short step up from flophouses (some of them *were* flophouses). They catered to sailors and truckers and hookers, not to producers or Silicon Valley gazillionaires.

Vanessa glanced at her watch. A quarter to seven, plus or minus a few minutes—he ought to be on his way now. The watch was a windup job she'd taken for herself while scavenging in Kansas for the Feds. It might not keep perfect time, but it didn't need a battery or a signal from the outside to work.

Like manual typewriters, windup watches were popular again. Unlike manual typewriters—Vanessa thought of Marshall's annoying monster—windup watches weren't annoying . . . except when you forgot to wind one and it lied to you about the time. That usually happened just when you most needed the truth, of course.

Footsteps on the stairs. Heavy footsteps. Bronislav was a big man. He could move quiet as a cat. He'd learned how in the fighting in Bosnia-Herzegovina. "Learn or die," he'd said. Most of the time, though, he didn't bother. This was America, where he didn't have to sneak.

That might not be him, of course. The apartment building had a secured entrance, sure. With the power out at least half the time, though, it just stood open. So did most buildings' security doors. Burglaries were way up.

A knock on the door. Four knocks on the door, in fact: one for each C/S in the Serbs' patriotic motto. Vanessa's heart leaped. Before she opened up, though, she peered through the little spy-eye in the door. Yes, that was Bronislav. He had a newspaper-wrapped package under one arm.

After a hug that stamped her against him, a fierce kiss, and murmured endearments in English and Serbian (he liked her learning bits and pieces of his language, even if the way she pronounced it could make him LOL), he set the package on her kitchen counter.

Blood leaked through the newspaper here and there. "What is it?" Vanessa asked eagerly. He was a good cook, a better cook than she was. And truckers got things and swapped things that didn't show up on their official cargo manifests. Americans didn't call the informal economy a black market, which didn't mean it wasn't one.

"Croat spareribs," he answered, deadpan. For a split second, she wondered if he meant it. Then he let out a harsh chuckle. "No, is not what you call long pig. Is only ordinary pig. I hear long pig and ordinary pig taste a lot alike. I hear, but I do not know of myself—*for* myself."

"Where did you hear that?" Vanessa did her best to make a joke of it.

But Bronislav wasn't joking. Or he didn't sound as if he were, anyhow. His voice was serious, even grim, as he answered, "In Yugoslavia, I knew people who could say because they did it. They said they did it, anyhow. Me, I believed them. People on the other side did it, too—oh, yes. Ethnic cleansing." He mimed picking his teeth.

"Gross!" Vanessa exclaimed. She hadn't thought she'd lived a sheltered life till she met him. She still wasn't sure how much to believe from his stories. If they were even a quarter true, though, a pretty good first draft of hell on earth had shown up in disintegrating Yugoslavia in the last decade of the last millennium.

"Too many things are," he said. The depth of sorrow in his dark eyes kept her from pushing him any more.

Instead, she asked, "What will you do with them?" She assumed he would fix them. She hoped he would, in fact. She appreciated what he did with food without worrying about matching it.

"You have prunes, yes?" he said. "And onions? And chilies?"

"Sure," she said. Onions she probably would have had anyway. The other ingredients she kept around because he liked them and used them. They wouldn't have been on the pantry's shelves if she'd been hanging out with someone who had different tastes.

"Good." His nod was all business. "I use pressure cooker, then. I get things done fast."

"Okay," Vanessa said as he fell to work. She also might not have had the olive oil in which he browned the ribs if she hadn't known him. She'd always thought it tasted medicinal. She didn't any more. That might have been love, or it might just have been better olive oil.

A wonderful smell filled the apartment. Bronislav grunted in satisfaction. "Now we are getting somewhere."

"When I had Pickles and I was making something that smelled good like this, he'd come in and try to scrounge." Vanessa sighed. "I miss Pickles."

"I am confused." Bronislav sure sounded confused.

"Oh." Vanessa explained: "Pickles was my cat. When I got to a shelter in Kansas right after the supervolcano, they made me turn him loose. He couldn't have lasted long, poor thing, not with all the ash and dust coming down."

"That is hard," Bronislav said. "Why do you not get another cat? I have seen some people in this building have them."

"I thought about it. I couldn't stand it," Vanessa answered. "What happens if—no, when—I have to do something horrible to this one, too?"

"You mourn. Then you go on. What else can you do? Sometimes life is hard. Always, in the end, life is hard. No one except our Lord ever got out of life alive. So do best you can while you are here."

Vanessa didn't believe Jesus had got out of life alive, either, not the way Bronislav did. She did believe avoiding pain was better than charging it head-on. Bronislav had a different opinion. They didn't argue about it. He rarely argued, which made him as different from Bryce as dim sum were from doorknobs. He knew what he knew (not all of what he knew was true, but he didn't give a rat's ass about that). And he didn't much care what you imagined you knew.

He put the lid on the pressure cooker and twisted it to seal it. Pretty soon, the steam-release valve in the lid started hissing away—chuff, chuff, chuff! Every chuff smelled great.

Pork ribs with prunes and chopped onions weren't something Vanessa would have come up with on her own. Bronislav waved her praise aside. "It is home cooking for me," he said. "My mother would have got angry because I do not have all my spices just right."

By *just right*, he no doubt meant exactly the way his mother and grandmother and great-grandmother and all his female ancestors for the past thousand years had fixed the dish. He was still a part of that ancient tradition, still involved in keeping it alive. Vanessa envied the rootedness that gave him. Nothing in her own life reached back further than the stuff her mother had told her when she was little.

She said so. Bronislav looked at her with those eyes out of a church mosaic. "You are American. That is how things are for you. I am Serb. This is how things are for me."

"But I don't want things to be like that!" she blurted.

"Life is not about how we want things to be. Life is about how things are." He sounded certain. He almost always did. After a moment, he went on, "I want things to be so I can open little restaurant, even if my spices in things are not just right every time. But I have not got money to do this. So I do not worry. Maybe one day I have money. Maybe I keep driving truck."

"Okay, sweetie." She put the dishes in the sink. Sooner or later, she'd do them. Odds were on later. She sent him a sidelong glance. "You aren't driving a truck right now."

The look he gave back said that, if she were a Serb, she would have been a slut. Since she was an American, he could make certain allowances. He got up and slipped a strong arm around her waist. They walked back to the bedroom together.

When everything worked right, Kelly Ferguson could sic one of the world's most potent computer networks on the climate changes and resulting ecological changes the supervolcano eruption was creating. She sometimes thought, though, that it preferred to remain a creature of mystery. One of its more obnoxious changes was playing merry hell with the North American power grid. Things didn't work right nearly so often as she wished they would.

When they didn't—and when she wasn't riding herd on Deborah, which also ate ridiculous amounts of time—she used what workarounds she could. She had a good scientific calculator. It ran on batteries. Its electronic brain was smarter and faster (and probably cuter, too) than a PC would have been a generation earlier. Next to the computer network she couldn't access at the moment, however, it might as well have been a retarded hamster.

Swearing, she ruthlessly simplified her assumptions and tried the regression analysis again. And the oh-so-clever scientific calculator choked on it again. Swearing louder, Kelly did some more simplifying. Not just regression for idiots this time. Regression for imbeciles. She hit the red button with the = sign on it. The calculator still choked.

"*Fuck* you!" she snarled, and drew in a deep, furious breath so she could really tell the stinking gadget where to go, how to get there, and what to do once it arrived.

Across the dining-room table from her, Colin was reading by the light of the same candles that shone on the uncooperative calculator's little screen. Before she could fire off all the ammo she'd stacked up, he shook his head. "Don't," he told her.

She glared at him. "What do you mean, don't?" He might be the man she loved. When he told her not to do something she damn well intended to do, though, he could take his chances like anybody else. And if he got in her way, she'd fire some of that ammo at him.

Or she thought so, till he answered, "I mean *don't*, that's what. If you cuss that thing the way you were fixing to cuss it, you'll wake the baby. Do you want to do that?"

Kelly opened her mouth. Then she closed it. After a few seconds, she said "Oh" in a small, sheepish voice. She sighed. "Well, you're right. How about if I throw the stupid thing against the wall, or maybe whack it a good one with a hammer?"

"Those'd make noise, too. Here. Wait." Colin got up. He picked up one of the candlesticks and lit his way over to the kitchen with it. Setting the light on the countertop, he rummaged deep in the bowels of the miscellaneous drawer. The drawer was extremely miscellaneous. Except for maybe the Lost Chord or the Holy Grail, Kelly wouldn't have been surprised at anything he hauled out of there. He'd recently produced a pair of polished-brass opera glasses whose existence she hadn't even suspected.

He let out a sudden, pleased grunt and pulled out something in a leather sheath. "What have you got there? A vorpal blade?" Kelly said. "If I can go snicker-snack on the calculator with it, bring it on."

Bring it on he did, or at least back to the table. He laid it next to the offending piece of electronica. "Not quite a vorpal blade. It was out of date by the time I went to high school, but hey, the high school I went to was out of date, too, so I ended up using it a lot."

Kelly opened the flap and drew out the enameled-aluminum body. "A vorpal slide rule!" she exclaimed. "Wow! This is retro like Marshall's typewriter."

"Uh-huh." Colin nodded. "The other way it's like Marshall's typewriter is, it still works and it doesn't need a plug, or even batteries."

"It still works if you know what to do with it." Kelly aimlessly moved the slide back and forth. "Hate to tell you, but this is the first time I ever tried." She was fifteen years younger than her husband. When she went to high school, slide rules might as well have been buggy whips. Well, buggy whips were probably staging a comeback these days, too.

"I can show you," Colin said. "Some, anyhow."

Multiplying and dividing seemed pretty simple . . . till Kelly said, "Wait a minute. How do I keep track of the decimal point?"

"Um, in your head," he answered.

"Tell me another one," Kelly said. "That's great for three times two equals six, but you start going batshit when it's 3.191×10^4 times 4.867×10^7."

He got a faraway look in his eyes. "That'd be about, uh, 1.5×10^{12}."

She punched the scientific calculator. She felt like punching it a different way altogether, but refrained. Sure as hell, it told her the answer was 1.5530597×10^{12}. "How'd you know that?" she yipped.

"Trick my uncle taught me. He's the guy who gave me the slide rule. This baby cost like thirty-five bucks, and that was a lot of jack back in the day. Me, I woulda bought an el-cheapo plastic job, but he wanted me to be an engineer like him, so I got this fancy one."

"The trick," Kelly said with the air of someone holding on to her patience, which she was.

"Oh, yeah. Your first number was about 3×10^4. Your second one was about 5×10^7. Multiply those two together and you get

$15X10^{11}$. That's the same as $1.5X10^{12}$. You do the same thing whenever you work something on the slide rule. It's the best way I know to keep the decimal point straight."

"I guess it would be," she said slowly, and looked at him as if she'd never seen him before. "If you knew stuff like that and you remember it all these years later, how come you *weren't* an engineer?"

" 'Cause I couldn't stand high school. I did okay, but I hated every minute of it. It was like being in jail, only I hadn't done anything to deserve to be there. Soon as I graduated, I joined the Navy—but you know that."

"Uh-huh." Kelly eyed him again, not the same way this time. "And the Navy wasn't like being in jail?"

Colin let out a small, very dry chuckle. "As a matter of fact, it was. More like jail than high school was, a whole lot more. I didn't know that going in, though. I was eighteen. I was dumb. But I repeat myself."

"Oh, boy, do you ever." Kelly thought back to some of the things she'd done when she was that age. And she didn't even have the excuse of testosterone poisoning.

"Yup." Her husband nodded. "I got used to it, though. After a while, I got to where I kinda liked it. Well, except for the living and sleeping arrangements. So when I took off one uniform, I put on another one. I'm what they call an institutional man, same as any other lifer."

"No, you put the bad guys in the institutions," Kelly said.

"Less difference than you'd think sometimes." Colin made a point of changing the subject: "Want to take a shot at square roots and cube roots and waddayacallems—trig functions?"

"Sure," Kelly said. If he didn't want to talk about it, he'd clam up bigtime if she pushed. He'd already come out with some things about his past she'd never heard before.

Square roots and cube roots seemed pretty straightforward.

So did trig functions. You slid the center piece. You moved the transparent piece with the hairline. You read the answer. It wouldn't be anything like 1.5530597×10^{12}, or even 4.867×10^7. You were kind of guesstimating the third significant figure, let alone any past that. In a way, that was cool. No one could accuse you of trying to be more precise than the data allowed.

But Kelly did wonder why no one had ever taught her the neat truck Colin used. Then she quit wondering. By the time she came along, nobody needed to keep track of decimal points in her head. The machines automatically took care of it. And if the machines screwed up, or—more likely—if some dumb human entered the wrong number somewhere, nobody would notice that the answer was also screwed up till something went horribly wrong. Every so often, something did. Maybe it wouldn't if people checked a little more.

If the scientific calculator was retarded next to the computers Kelly couldn't access, the slide rule was dumber yet. Trying to set up her problems so she could use it to work, Kelly feared she was simplifying so much that whatever answers she got wouldn't mean anything.

When she said so, Colin observed, "They built the first A-bomb off calculations from bunches of those babies." She grunted. She might have been playing with more variables than the Manhattan Project had. Then again, she might not have. She didn't know one way or the other.

After a while, she asked, "How do I raise, say, three to the 2.5th power?"

"That's what the log-log scales are for," Colin said.

"The who?" Kelly said blankly. He might as well have been speaking Cherokee.

"The LL scales. Here, I'll show you." And he did. It made sense once you saw how to do it. Well, damn near everything made sense once you saw how to do it. Kelly began to under-

stand how there'd been science in the ancient, primitive days before computers and even calculators.

She had more fun twiddling the slide rule than she would
have punching buttons on the HP. She knew she would have to
refine her results once she could get on the computer again, but
she would have had to do that with results from the scientific
calculator, too. Then Deborah woke up and started to cry. She'd
made a mess in her diaper. For the next little while, geology took
a back seat to motherhood.

Squirt Frog and the Evolving Tadpoles tuned their instruments
near the altar of Guilford, Maine's, Episcopalian church. Rob
Ferguson sighed. Even inside the crowded church, his breath
smoked. "One more acoustic set," he said quietly. "There are
times when I really miss cranking it up." He did some impassioned air guitar. You really couldn't impersonate an electric bass
without, well, another electric bass.

"I miss all kinds of things from the old days," Justin Nachman
said. Lead guitar was easier to do without a power cord than
bass was—not always easy, but easier. He was also responsible
for most of the band's vocals. Those didn't change a whole lot
even if he wasn't miked.

But lack of electricity wasn't all he was mourning. He patted
his hair. It was long and curly. It wasn't the aggressively permed
Brillo fright wig—Dylan with his finger in the electric socket—
he'd once worn to mark his status as a rock-'n'-roll not-quite-
legend. Perms were ridiculous luxuries everywhere these days. In
Maine north and west of the Interstate, which enjoyed very inter-
mittent power a couple of months a year, perms were flat-out
impossible.

Biff Thorvald, the rhythm guitarist, said, "Wish we had some
dope, is what I wish."

"Amen, Brother Ben!" That was Charlie Storer, whose drums

missed amplification less than anybody else's pet instrument. Just because Charlie said it first, though, that didn't mean Rob didn't agree with him. It didn't mean Justin and Biff didn't agree with him, either.

The only trouble was, Rob couldn't remember the last time he'd seen weed in Guilford, much less smoked any. It wasn't that he couldn't remember because he'd got too wasted to think straight. It had been a hell of a long time ago, if he'd ever seen any here at all.

Since the eruption, *Cannabis sativa* would not grow here. It wouldn't grow here even in greenhouses, which stretched the growing season from essentially nonexistent all the way up to ridiculously short. The only things that would—sometimes—grow in local greenhouses were the kinds of food plants that had been eaten in the Far North since time out of mind: turnips, parsnips, a few extra-hardy varieties of Andean spuds, cabbage, rutabaga, and the ever-unpopular mangel-wurzel. Rob had never heard of the mangel-wurzel before the supervolcano blew. Now he'd eaten it stewed, boiled, baked, steamed, fried. . . . If he never ate it again—that would mean he'd moved away from Maine.

Two or three months a year, enough snow melted to make road traffic possible if not easy. During what passed for summer up in these parts, the rest of the USA dimly remembered Maine north and west of the Interstate still existed. Food and machinery and some fuel came in. People who'd got sicker than the local quacks could fix or who couldn't stand living in these parts another second got the hell out.

The authorities reckoned that, next to food and machinery and fuel, dope was nonessential (to say nothing of illegal). Nobody seemed to see enough profit in this little tiny market to flout the authorities and bring some up here anyhow. Where were the Mexican drug cartels when you really needed them, dammit?

When the blizzards started rolling in again—say, about the

end of August—even the Interstate turned impassable. The rest of the country forgot about its northeastern extremity again. It had plenty to worry about where more people lived. The handful of cold-loving maniacs who stayed in the new Arctic were left to their own devices.

Which was why Squirt Frog and the Evolving Tadpoles were tuning up here in the church. They'd play after the town meeting. Before the eruption, Rob might have been caught dead in a church, but he wouldn't have been caught alive in one. Justin, Charlie, and Biff had piety every bit as notorious.

Before the eruption, odds were they all would have made loud, unhappy noises about the separation of church and state if they even heard about a secular town meeting in a building dedicated not merely to religion but to one particular religion. Now . . . Now Rob couldn't get his bowels in an uproar about it, even if he had no dope to keep him mellow. The church held more people than any other building in town. Okay, fine. The locals used it, and they worried not at all about the Supreme Court telling them they were committing a serious no-no.

Come to think of it, there were some serious advantages to being cut off from the rest of the world. You had the freedom to do what you wanted (within the limits imposed by frigid weather and nineteenth-century technology). Nobody called you at dinnertime to sell you on a candidate, to get you to take a survey, or to try to pry your credit-card number out of you. Since Rob's cell phone had been as dead as a doornail the past couple of years, no one called him at all. Nobody texted him, either. He found that he missed being hooked into everything 24/7 a lot less than he missed getting stoned.

Mayor McCann rapped loudly for order. The secretary—a real secretary, a gray-haired woman who actually knew shorthand—poised pen over paper to take the minutes. People paid close attention when the mayor read the typed transcript of last week's minutes. The church was packed. For people who couldn't amuse themselves with one electronic gadget or another, town meetings and screwing were your basic choices for fun. And hey, you could screw any old time.

No one moved to change the minutes, so they were approved as read. The arguments would come later. And they did, over hunting and over cutting wood. Without shooting lots of moose and deer, Guilford—like any other small Maine town north and west of the Interstate—would have starved. Rob had an ugly scar on his leg where an overeager hunter had shot him instead of a moose.

And, like any other small Maine town north and west of the Interstate, Guilford would have frozen if people hadn't chopped down acres and acres of the second-growth forest that had sprung up on great swaths of abandoned cropland. Rob didn't like denuding the countryside. He liked freezing even less, though. He'd swung an axe. He'd pulled on a two-man saw that came out of somebody's barn, too.

By now, though, not so many unshot moose were left. And there wasn't a whole lot of forest close to Guilford or any other town, either. The argument about what to cut now and what to leave for later was louder and more heated than the air inside the church.

"If we all turn into blocks of ice now, we won't have to worry about later, will we?" Dick Barber asked in loud, sardonic tones. Barber wasn't always loud, but sardonic seemed his default setting. Before the eruption, he and his family had run the Trebor Mansion Inn, a towered hostelry dating from the 1830s. These days, Maine got no summer, which meant it also got no summer people. Barber and his clan still lived at the Inn. The bank might have taken it away from him, but the bank also seemed to have forgotten about lands where electricity no longer reached. There were certain advantages to falling off the edge of civilization.

When Squirt Frog and the Evolving Tadpoles found themselves snowed in in Guilford, they'd lived at the Trebor Mansion
Inn, too. Charlie still did, in the tower room that had once been
Rob's. Like Rob, Biff and Justin had found companions of the
female persuasion with more spacious living quarters.

"If we cut down everything in sight now, what will we do
next winter?" someone else countered. Those were the two sides
of it, boiled down to a nub.

"If we aren't here next winter, what difference does it make?"
Barber said. "Jim Farrell's basic rule is, you do what you have to
do now, and you worry about later, later." Farrell's was a name to
conjure with. Barber had helped run the retired history prof's
Congressional campaign before the eruption. The winner, a blow-
dried lawyer type, hadn't been back in his district since the supervolcano blew. Farrell hadn't left. And he knew all kinds of useful
things—medieval things—that helped folks get by. He might not
be the law west of the Pecos, but he was the biggest cheese north
and west of the Interstate.

"He isn't God, you know. You don't quote him like you'd
quote the Bible," the other man said.

"As. *As* you'd quote the Bible," Barber said helpfully.

Bang! went the gavel. "You're out of order, Dick," the mayor
said.

"No, his grammar is," Barber replied.

The two sides wrangled a while longer. The meeting didn't
decide anything. As far as Rob could see, town meetings never
decided anything till they absolutely had to. Watching the fur fly
was at least half the fun.

Some of the rest came after formal adjournment. People
started clapping as the guys from the band ambled up to take
their places. They played "Losing My Tail" from their first CD:
an inevitable song for a band with their name and quirks. They
did "Came Along Too Late," which could be taken here as a trib-

ute to Jim Farrell, though it hadn't been conceived as one. They sang "Pleasures," the closest approach to straight-ahead rock in their eccentric orbit. They did "Impossible Things Before Breakfast," which was just bizarre. They did . . . a set.

They got a hell of a hand for it, too. That high was better than dope, even if it didn't last as long. As things wound down, a pretty brunette came over to Rob and squeezed his hands. "Good job!" she said.

"Thanks, gorgeous," he answered. "Can I take you home?"

"You'd better, since we're married," Lindsey said pointedly. And, in due course, he did.

IV

"N o," Colin Ferguson said.

Eugene Cervus sent him a look full of something between reproach and shock. The mayor of San Atanasio wasn't used to hearing that word from someone he reckoned an underling. He especially wasn't used to hearing it in tones that brooked no argument. He argued anyhow: "But you have to assume the chief's position, at least on a temporary basis. The political situation in the city cries out for it."

"No. I told you that before," Colin repeated. "Now I'll say it again. Hell no, as a matter of fact. I've spent a lot of time thinking about it since . . . well, since all this stuff happened. And I just don't want the job. I don't want it, and I wouldn't take it on a silver platter."

"Be reasonable, Lieutenant Ferguson," the mayor said, by which he meant *Do what I tell you, Lieutenant Ferguson. Take some heat off of San Atanasio, Lieutenant Ferguson.* "Why *don't* you want the position at this point in time? You applied for it. You competed for it when, ah, the previous holder was selected.

When we talked at the recent press conference, you didn't seem to find the idea hateful."

He was right about that much. And Colin didn't blame him for not wanting to speak Mike Pitcavage's name. Colin did blame him for saying things like *on a temporary basis* and *at this point in time* when he meant things like *for a little while* and *now.* You couldn't trust people who talked like that, because people who talked like that thought like that—which is to say, not too well.

He couldn't even explain that to Cervus, not so it made sense to him. People who didn't think too well didn't take kindly to having that pointed out. So Colin said what he could: "Back when I applied, I didn't know what all was involved. Mike was good at making nice. He made a fine chief, or he would have if he didn't get his jollies killing old ladies. Me, I'm not so good at it. I'd be a disaster in that chair. You'd want to throw me out inside a week. I'd want to tell you where to head in, and I bet I would. And all the cops would start hating me. Find somebody else."

Cervus studied him like a herpetologist examining a previously undescribed and very strange toad. "Doesn't the difference in remuneration between lieutenant and chief interest you?"

"It wouldn't make up for the headaches," Colin answered.

The mayor's gaze hardened. "If you feel that way, are you sure you should remain in the department under any capacity?" *Do what I tell you or I'll squeeze you out.* Yes, Colin understood Politico.

He went on being blunt himself: "The worst thing you can do is can me. If you do, I'll go home and play with my little girl. But I promise you one other thing—if you can me for the Pitcavage thing, you and the city won't have enough nickels to use a pay toilet by the time my lawyers get done working out on you. And nobody from here to Miami will be able to say *San Atanasio* without holding his nose when he does."

Cervus let out a pained hiss. "I assure you, Lieutenant, any such unfortunate course of events was the furthest thing from my mind."

"Glad to hear it," Colin said, in lieu of *My ass*. Even as a lieutenant who'd stopped caring about being anything more than a lieutenant, he needed a certain minimal amount of diplomacy. And the mayor was no dope, even if he was also no genius. He would hear the words behind Colin's words, the same way Colin heard the ones behind his.

His Honor tried again, asking, "Will you please take the position on an interim basis, until we can fill it permanently?"

"Thanks, but no." Colin shook his head. "Give it to, oh, Captain Miyoshi. He's back from his surgery now, and he's doing pretty well. It'll be a feather in his cap. If you promote me over his head, he won't like it. I sure wouldn't if I were in his shoes. And dropping back to lieutenant after I'd been running the department wouldn't be comfortable for me or anybody else."

"You are a difficult man," the mayor said with a sigh.

"Sorry about that," Colin answered: one of the bigger whoppers he'd told lately. "Can I go now, sir?"

"Yes, go on." By the expression on Cervus' face, he understood exactly why they'd passed over Colin when they chose the last chief. Well, so did Colin himself—now. He sure hadn't at the time, and losing out to Mike Pitcavage hurt worse than anything that had ever happened to him . . . till Louise walked out, anyway.

Both the city hall and the nearby police station were low-slung, blocky, modern stucco buildings—modern when they'd gone up, of course. Those had been good times for all the booming L.A. suburbs. Now the buildings were showing their age. So was San Atanasio. The city had no money to fix them up. Even if it had had the money, it probably wouldn't have had the will. People just didn't care.

By contrast, the grass and shrubbery between the two buildings were lush and green, even if they weren't well tended. San

Atanasio got so much more rain now than it had before the eruption that everything seemed green, green, green to people who remembered hills brown eight months a year and rationed water.

Well, almost everything. A couple of hibiscuses against the yellow-beige wall of the police station stood dead and leafless. The gardeners hadn't bothered to cut them down yet. God only knew when—or if—they would. Hard frosts had done in the hibiscuses. It snowed here every winter now. A lot of plants that had felt at home in warmer days couldn't take the revised weather.

A few, though, thrived where they hadn't before. Apples and pears had grown in and around Los Angeles before the supervolcano blew. They'd grown, yes, but they hadn't given fruit. They needed frost for that. They had it now, and they responded to it.

Colin remembered a story he'd seen in the *Times* a few days earlier. One of those newly fruiting apple trees had turned out to be a long-lost variety from New England. Horticulturalists were creaming their jeans over it, while local historians were trying to figure out how the tree had got here to begin with.

Also standing by the police-station wall was Gabe Sanchez. He couldn't smoke indoors. When he needed his nicotine fix, he had to come out here. At least it wasn't raining. Clouds scudded across the pale, bluish-green sky. While the sun wasn't hiding behind one of them, it shone wanly.

"Hey, Colin," Gabe said between puffs. "Can I kiss your ring now?"

"You can kiss my ass, is what you can kiss," Colin answered. "I told you I wouldn't take it."

The sergeant shrugged. "People tell me all kinds of shit," he said—he'd been a cop a long time. "Some of it, I believe. But I've heard too much bull. I wait and see most of the time."

"Can't hardly beef about that," Colin allowed. "I didn't take it, though. I'm not right for the job. I know that now, even if I didn't when I tried to grab the brass ring. And . . ." His voice trailed away. He looked around to see if anyone besides his friend was in earshot.

"And?" Gabe prompted.

Not spotting anybody who might overhear, Colin answered with what he'd been about to say: "And there are still a good many cops who're pissed at me on account of Pitcavage is dead. Yeah, there was stuff about him they didn't know, but that was stuff I didn't know, either. It's not why I took down darling Darren. They figure I had no business going after the chief's pride and joy. Running a department where half the people look at you sideways . . . That wouldn't have been a whole lot of joy."

"Not half the people," Sanchez said judiciously. "Maybe a quarter—a third at most."

"Okay, fine." Colin accepted the correction. "Still wouldn't have been much fun. And you know what else?"

"Tell me," Gabe urged.

"I don't get off on telling people what to do. Yeah, I know my kids'd laugh their asses off to hear me say that, but honest to God I don't. And you've got to do it, and you've got to like doing it, if you're gonna be chief."

Gabe Sanchez aimed a shrewd look at him. "You don't much get off on other people telling you what to do, either."

"I have no idea what you're talking about," Colin said, deadpan. They both laughed because they both knew what bullshit that was.

Gabe smoked the cigarette all the way down to the filter before he ground it out under his shoe. He pulled the pack from his pocket, contemplating another. With a sigh, he put it back again. "Christ, I'd be rich if I didn't get hooked on these fuckers. Especially with prices the way they are now—Jesus! Only thing that costs more than smokes is gasoline."

"You got that right," Colin said.

"So what is the mayor gonna do about the big office since you won't sit there?" Gabe might not want—or be able to afford—another cigarette right now, but he didn't feel like going inside and getting back to work, either.

"He can get somebody from outside or appoint a captain. I figure Miyoshi's the best bet. Or he can appoint a captain and then get somebody from outside. That's what I told him, anyhow. I didn't tell him he could go pound sand, but I wouldn't mind that, either."

"Heh," Sanchez said. "I got me a picture of Eugene Cervus pounding sand—and then turning over on his stomach and building a bunch of cruddy condos on top of it."

"He'd make money if he did." Colin had no doubts on that score. The mayor made money at everything he did. He had the knack. That didn't make Colin like him or admire him or trust him.

When they did walk into the cop shop, no one there asked Colin whether he was going to be chief. Everybody seemed to know already. Colin's cell was dead. He assumed other people's were, too. But landlines often worked even when other power was out. Only one call would have needed to get through.

The venetian blinds were open. That didn't make the big central office well lit, but it was lit. People *could* work here, at least from sunup to sundown. Some secretaries' desks sported typewriters as well as computer monitors and keyboards: portable typewriters, 1950s office jobs, even a few angular uprights from the 1920s. Getting them had been an adventure. Keeping them in ribbons was another one.

One of the secretaries typing away was Josefina Linares, who worked for Colin. She raised a questioning eyebrow as he walked past her desk on the way to his own. "You didn't, did you?" she said. It was as if she'd got the word but didn't want to believe it.

"Nope," he said.

She clucked in disapproval. "You should have. Whoever they end up getting instead of you is bound to be worse."

A dubious compliment, but Colin would take what he could get. He sighed. "Josie, I told my wife I wouldn't take it. I told you. I told Gabe. I even told the mayor. I told anybody who would listen. The mayor turned out to be one of the people who wouldn't listen. So I had to tell him all over again just now. I don't usually say stuff I don't mean."

"I know that. I ought to, after all these years." Josie still sounded mad at him. "But you should have anyway. Our Lord said, 'May this cup pass from me.' When it didn't, though, He went out and did what He had to do." She crossed herself.

"I'm not Him," Colin said, "and you can sing that in church."

"Well, who is? Nobody, not even Saint Francis." His secretary crossed herself again. "I still think the city needs you there."

She'd never been shy about telling him what she thought. She treated him as an equal and a friend. He always tried to treat her the same way; her friendship was worth having. "The city needs me there for its own PR," he said. "That's the only reason. C'mon—you know I'm a crappy administrator. And besides, putting me in Mike's office would just tear up the department worse than it is already."

"You'd manage. And I would make sure the administrative stuff didn't get too bad." She meant it. There was a pretty decent chance she could do it, too.

He wagged a finger at her. "You want me to be chief so you get to be the boss secretary."

"I'd like that." Josie nodded. "But I'd want you to be chief even if somebody else took care of the other things for you."

"Thanks." Colin meant it. "The only thing is, I really and truly don't want to do it. It'd drive me nuts."

She grinned crookedly. "And who'd know the difference?" He laughed. He wouldn't have kept laughing if she'd gone on with it. But she didn't. She'd said her piece. He'd said his. Now it was over . . . as much as something like this could ever be over. He sat down at his desk, started going through the latest robbery and homicide reports, and did his best to pretend he was nothing but an ordinary police lieutenant on an ordinary kind of day.

His best, he feared, wasn't close to good enough. He wondered if it ever would be.

The calendar swore it was spring. Rob Ferguson was more inclined to swear at the calendar, or else to burst into hysterical laughter. The only double-digit temperatures Guilford had seen since the beginning of the year were the ones in negative numbers. When your lows were below zero, that was one thing. When your highs couldn't jump the hurdle, you were talking about a whole 'nother ballgame.

He moved on snowshoes as easily as he would have in socks across a bare floor. He remembered how, when he first came to Guilford, the splay-legged, shuffling gait had left his thigh muscles sore, and how he'd had to think about every step before he took it. No more. As with Shakespeare's grave diggers, familiarity lent a quality of easiness.

He tramped through a barer, more open landscape than the one he'd known just after he got here. The pines and broadleaved trees that had grown this close to Guilford were long gone now—literally gone up in smoke. You could chop and burn or you could freeze. Not a pretty choice, but a real one.

He didn't expect to see a moose around these parts. To put it another way, he would have been astonished to see a moose around these parts. They'd been hunted out for a while now. But the Piscataquis River ran into Manhanock Pond east and a little south of Guilford. Most of the big pond was frozen hard enough for hockey. Hell, most of it was probably frozen hard enough for tank battles. But there'd be, or there might be, a little stretch of open water where the river came in.

Where there was open water, there'd be, or there might be, waterfowl. Mallards, maybe, or geese: Canada geese or the snow geese that grew more common in these parts as snow did, too. Rob's mouth filled with spit at the thought of roast goose. All dark meat—and all that lovely goose grease, too. If you were going to live in a climate like this, you needed fat. Vegans in Guilford—there were some—had a rough time because so little olive oil or even corn or soybean cooking oil came in. Corn and soybeans grew in the Midwest, or they had. Not much of anything grew there now.

Rob carried a shotgun in the crook of his left elbow. He wore an electric orange vest over his L.L. Bean heavy-duty anorak and backpack. His fur cap with earflaps had an electric orange nylon cover. He looked around and behind him every so often just the same. He'd used all the Day-Glo crap when he got shot, too. Just fool luck he hadn't lost a leg or got killed instead of only picking up that scar. If somebody was gaining on him now, he wanted to know about it as soon as he could.

Trust but verify. That had been a disarmament-negotiation mantra back about the time Rob was born. He wanted to verify, all right. Trust? After you'd got shot once, trusting wasn't so easy. He was glad when he didn't see anybody else.

He also peered ahead. Guilford wasn't the only small town that could send hunters to Manhanock Pond. Sangerville and Dover-Foxcroft might try it, too. Sangerville was so tiny, it had almost frozen up and blown away. Dover-Foxcroft lay farther off but, bigger even than Guilford, remained very much a going concern. It had a real hospital, for instance, not just an urgent-care clinic.

He didn't see anybody coming from the east, either. *Not even the Three Wise Guys,* he thought. Maybe over there they figured the whole pond would be frozen up. And maybe they were right, and he was just wasting his time hiking out here. As with any hunting, that was the chance you took.

His chuckle sent gusts of vapor spurting from his mouth and nose. *What would I be doing if I'd stayed back in Guilford?* The most likely answer was *Sitting around twiddling my thumbs.* He might be playing music with the other guys in the band, assuming they had nothing else shaking this morning. Or he might be over at the Mansion Inn, shooting the shit with Dick Barber.

But twiddling his thumbs was the best bet. He wouldn't be jumping on his wife's bones—he knew that only too well. Lindsey had a genuine, honest to God job: she taught chemistry at the high school east of the Inn. How useful that was in subarctic Maine might be a different question, but getting kids out of their folks' hair several hours a day several days a week had to prevent all kinds of child abuse.

There *was* some open water where the Piscataquis flowed into the lake. Rob clapped his mittened hands together. They made a Zennish almost-noise. (One of the mittens had a slit so he could stick out his index finger and fire the shotgun.) The only trouble was, no waterfowl swam in the water or waddled around by the edge of the lake.

Even more than trying to make a living in the music biz, hunting taught you patience. Either that or it drove you crazy, one. In his pack, Rob carried a little white pop-up tent. He took it out and popped it up now. *Voilà!* Instant nylon igloo. He turned it so one of the mesh squares that did duty for windows pointed toward the water. The mesh had been cut at the bottom and sides. He could push out the shotgun when he needed to. If he needed to.

He crawled inside. His six-one frame was crowded in there, but not terribly crowded. He settled down to wait. Maybe he would trudge back to Guilford empty-handed when evening came around. Or maybe he would be the primeval huntsman, bringing fat geese back to his mate. (The primeval huntsman probably wouldn't have toted his kill home in dark green Hefty trash bags, though.)

This whole business of killing your own food felt weird to a guy who'd spent most of his life grazing at roadside diners, and who'd always figured venturing into a supermarket and coming out with something raw was getting back to nature. Just as strange was having to think hard to remember the last time he'd actually spent money.

No, when you got right down to it, that was even stranger. He'd scuffled for cash ever since he went out on the road with Squirt Frog and the Evolving Tadpoles. Almost any band that toured all the time scuffled for cash. Yeah, there were exceptions, but SF and the ETs hadn't seemed likely to turn into one even before the supervolcano went kablooie.

Since then . . . With some wonder, Rob reminded himself that he hadn't filed a tax return since the eruption. The IRS and the FBI hadn't indicted him and dragged his evading ass to Leavenworth on account of it, either. Partly, that was because the Feds had written off this part of Maine as not being worth the bother. They kept trying to rehab the huge swath of the Midwest the blast had trashed: it would be worth something if they did. This piece of the country? Who cared? Washington sure didn't. Rob knew exactly nobody who *had* paid taxes the past few years.

Another reason for not paying was that precious little cash money had passed through his hands lately. He did spend some in the brief, chilly time alleged to be summer, when the roads thawed out and luxury goods from the south could come up. And he got a little sometimes when the band gigged in far-off places like Dover-Foxcroft and Greenville.

Mostly, though, the money economy in this cut-off part of the country had collapsed. Barter was the new king. You needed something done, you paid off in moose meat or paperback books or guitar lessons or whatever else you had that whoever was doing something for you wanted. A couple of women in Guilford had lost their reputations—or got new ones—by paying for things they needed in the oldest coin of all. So had one guy, a variation that might not have been seen so openly back in the old days.

Rob peered out through the mesh screen. Snow. Ice. Green water. No ducks. No geese. Not even any coots, though you had to be hungry even to think about shooting a coot. Rob had been hungry enough to do it a couple of times. He'd had coot roasted and boiled. Both took a long time and used up a lot of fuel. Neither was a success.

And coot soup made turkey soup smell good by comparison. Turkeys were such nice, tasty birds. Why their boiled carcasses smelled so nasty, Rob had no idea. But they did. Coot soup was worse yet. Boiled skunk might outdo it, but Rob wasn't even sure of that.

Time meandered by. "Patience," Rob muttered. "Yeah, right." That was also another game for solitaire. And it made a decent enough way to waste an hour or so. You found your fun where you could when TV and the Net and video games were only memories.

He pulled a beat-up British paperback about the Miracle at Mons out of his pocket. He'd got it from the Mansion Inn. Thanks to Dick Barber's book collection, he knew a hell of a lot more now about military history than he had when he got to Guilford. Like his own old man, Barber was an ex-Navy man who had a built-in excuse to be interested in such things. Rob didn't, but he'd discovered he was anyway.

Every so often, he looked up and looked out. When he saw nothing interesting, he went back to the British Regulars and their Lee-Enfields. Then noise outside told him he wouldn't see nothing if he looked out again, so he did. Half a dozen Canada geese were stumping around the edge of the water and cussing at one another the way geese did.

Rob slowly and carefully slid the shotgun's muzzle out through the window. He let fly with both barrels. The shotgun roared and slammed against his shoulder. The honking turned to frantic screeching. Two geese were down, one still, one thrashing. The others madly taxied on the open water to pick up enough speed for takeoff.

He hurried over to the thrashing goose. It still had plenty of fight left. A buffet or a peck from a goose was no laughing matter. Well, the shotgun had a butt end, too. He did what needed doing, then cleaned the butt in the snow. He never would have done anything like that if he were hunting for fun. He never would have *gone* hunting for fun: he didn't think it was. But hunting to eat was a different story.

He gutted the geese. The offal went into a trash bag, too. He'd take it over to Dick Barber, who'd feed it to the Maine Coons he semiprofessionally bred at the Inn. He owed Dick plenty. Cat food would pay back a bit of it. Money or not, you did need to take care of debts.

And he and Lindsey and maybe some friends would feast on goose. He'd trade the meat they didn't eat. He wasn't sure what he'd trade it for, but he was bound to come across something he wanted or needed. Money or not, that stayed true, too.

Dad and Kelly didn't get excited about the mail. Bills, ads, even the occasional letter . . . They didn't rush out to the mailbox as soon as the carrier had pedaled on by. Snailmail correspondence was alive again, like Frankenstein's monster, because e-mail here remained so unreliable. Even that wasn't enough to get Marshall Ferguson's father and stepmom off their duffs when the mail came.

It was more than enough for him. Some of the snailmail correspondence came from editors. Marshall was stubborn about putting stories in the mail and keeping them in the mail if they came back rejected. He needed to see what the ignorant editors had bounced today. He needed to do that every single today except Sundays, and he needed to do it as soon as he possibly could. Sure as hell, he had writer's disease, and he had it bad.

One of the reasons he had it so bad was that he didn't always get rejected. Every so often, he wouldn't find the folded manila SASE he'd stuck in whatever submission this was. Instead, one editor or another would use his or her own envelope and postage (usually keeping the stamps on the SASE) to let Marshall know he'd made a sale.

He was not going to get rich doing this. The odds that he'd never make a living doing this seemed much too good. Editors hadn't paid well when the supervolcano blew, which was just before he started selling. What they paid now hadn't come close to keeping up with inflation.

Of course, these days money needed a bicycle pump if it was going to stay even with inflation. Oil was through the roof. Food was even further through the roof. You paid up the wazoo every time you laid greenbacks on the counter for anything. And if you didn't grab it today, you'd pay even more tomorrow, and more still the day after.

Then again, as things went these days, Marshall didn't require a hell of a lot of money. He had a place to sleep and a place to work. If those were the room he'd grown up in, well, most of his friends were in the same boat. It beat sleeping in your car, especially when you couldn't afford the gas to move your car out of your folks' driveway. He had enough to eat. It wasn't always fancy, but it was what Dad and Kelly ate, too.

If he had to babysit for Deborah, he'd had to babysit for James Henry, too. By now, he was about as good at it as anyone who hadn't had his own kid could be. He did dishes, too, so Kelly wouldn't have to. That was part of paying his rent.

The other part was, thirty percent of what he grossed went to his father. It wasn't thirty percent of a lot. It wasn't nearly what a furnished room with board would have cost him. It was a reminder to him—and, no doubt, to Dad—that he wasn't a total freeloader.

"What happens if I write a bestseller and make, like, a zillion bucks?" he asked Dad after doing dishes following yet another dinner by candlelight because the power was shot to shit. "Am I gonna give you thirty percent of that?"

"It's a problem I'd like to have. I bet it's a problem you'd like to have, too," Colin Ferguson answered. He always took questions seriously. Maybe that went with his being a cop. Or maybe he was a cop because he'd always been the kind of person who took questions seriously. After a beat, he added, "So you know, of course you won't give me thirty percent of that. You'll bail out of here, buy yourself a big house, and pretend you never heard of me."

"Dad . . ." Marshall blew air out through his nose. It was something he did when he got pissed off. It was also something his old man did, but he didn't think about that. Then he made a different noise: a sheepish chuckle. "Y'know, if I'd hit it big when I was, like, twenty-one, I might've done that. But I'm not twenty-one any more."

"I noticed that," his father said. "I wasn't sure you had."

" 'Fraid so," Marshall said mournfully. "If I let my mustache grow, there'd be a couple-three white hairs in it."

Dad only laughed. "Welcome to the club." His hair was iron-gray, and the gray gained and the iron faded with every passing year.

"It's not one I want to join," Marshall said.

"Your only other choice is not lasting long enough to join it," Dad said. "Most people think that's worse, and most of the time they're right. Or that's how it looks to me."

"Me, too." Marshall nodded. "Um, if I do hit it big some kind of way, chances are I would move out."

"Makes sense. Moving out because you can afford to and because you need your own place is one thing. Moving out because you think this is worse than the city jail and you can't stand any of the other people who live here, that's a different story. It's one that gets told a lot, but it's not such a great one."

"You guys are okay." Marshall realized, too late, that he might have been warmer.

Even if he hadn't been, his father laughed. "Hey, compared to what you could've said, that's a five-star review on Yelp. So when *are* you gonna write that bestseller?"

"Um, it'd have to be a novel. Nobody makes eating money on short stories—you've seen that from the little bits of money I give you, right?" Marshall said.

"Right," Dad agreed. "Too right, as a matter of fact. Are you going to take a swing at it, then? It's your chance to make a living without working for anybody else. Nice work if you can get it."

"I guess," Marshall said reluctantly. Kelly had been after him to work on a novel, too. Doing something that somebody else had suggested wasn't his favorite plan in the whole wide world, though. He had some ideas. He had some notes. He didn't yet have any firm notion of how they all fit together, though, or even if they did.

And Dad, for a wonder, didn't keep pushing at him the way he would have when Marshall was younger. All he said was, "Well, either you'll figure it out or you won't. And if you don't, you'll just have to come up with something else instead."

"Uh-huh." To Marshall, *something else instead* translated into moving boxes from a truck to a warehouse, or maybe from a warehouse to a truck. Or he could stand near a cash register with a mindless smile pasted on his face and go *Hi! Are you finding everything you need?* to every third man, woman, or zebra that wandered by. If the power was on, a surveillance camera would tape him to make sure he didn't slack off on the important question. If he did, they'd dock him. If he did it too often, they'd can him.

Dad didn't try to talk him into following in his own flat-footed footsteps. To give him his due, he'd never tried to do that with any of his kids. Marshall laughed to himself. How many dope-smoking cops were there? Probably more than Dad wanted to admit, even to himself. But no. Dad had got himself a bass player, a graphic artist, and a wannabe writer. And whatever he thought about that, he never bitched where his offspring could hear.

Kelly came downstairs. "She's asleep," she said in tired triumph. Then she knocked on the first wood she saw. "With a little bit of luck, she may stay that way. So I get to be a human being for a while." She yawned. "A sleepy human being, but hey, you take what you can get."

"Hello, sleepy human being," Dad said. "We were just psyching out what to do with Marshall's millions after they make the Johnny Depp movie from his *New York Times* blockbuster."

"Hey!" Marshall said. "I wish!" What writer in his right mind—hell, what crazy writer—didn't wish for the exact same thing? "All we need is the movie. Oh, and the novel to make the movie from."

"Details, details." Dad waved them away. He could do that with the greatest of ease—he wasn't currently not writing a novel. "You should go upstairs and pound on the antique I found you."

"Dad . . ." Marshall was the easygoing kid. Rob and Vanessa would have opened fire on full auto. But staying easygoing wasn't always easy. He tried his best: "I am working on something right now."

"Get off his case, Colin," Kelly said, so she saw Dad was on it. She continued, "What did you do when your father gave you a hard time?"

"Me? Along with hating high school, my old man was the

other big reason I joined the Navy. Boy, did that show him! Showed me, too, by God," Dad answered. He held out his wrists to Kelly as if waiting to be cuffed. "Here y'are, Officer. I'll go quietly."

He would have barked at Mom if she'd told him to lighten up. But she would've been snarky when she did it, where Kelly wasn't. And maybe he'd learned not to bark all the damn time. They said you couldn't teach an old dog new tricks, but they were full of it as often as not. Marshall had gone through plenty of changes the past few years. Why shouldn't Dad have, too?

Marshall stopped thinking about his father. Some things in his vague scheme about what a novel might look like that hadn't fit together all of a sudden did. He jumped up, grabbed a scratch pad and a pencil off the bar, and brought them back to the candle's small circle of light so he could see what he was doing while he scrawled notes.

"You should—" Dad began. Kelly made a small noise, and he shut up. Kelly got the idea that sometimes someone who was writing needed to get something down without any interruptions. Dad didn't, not really, but he got that Kelly did, which was enough. Marshall barely noticed the byplay. He scribbled as fast as he could.

V

Vanessa wondered if getting back her old job at Nick Gorczany's wonderful widget works was the best idea she'd ever had. True, it let her get out of the house. She would have done almost anything this side of hustling tricks on street corners to achieve that. (Her mouth twitched, there at her window-side desk. She knew too well that the flesh could be made to pay, and that the biggest price was your own disgust every time you got near a mirror. *I did* that? you would wonder. But she had, and she knew it too well.) That she couldn't stand Kelly, and that it was mutual, hadn't helped, either.

Gorczany, the high honcho, did seem glad to have her back. He'd given her a fancy new title, senior technical editor, and a raise that at least made the wage living. Even a manufacturer of high-tech widgets sometimes needed somebody who could translate between techy and bureaucratese on the one hand and no-shit English on the other. Doing without somebody like that for a while must have rubbed his nose in the lack.

Whether she was glad to be back was a more complicated question all kinds of ways. Sure, a steady, nearly adequate paycheck was a Good Thing. Absolutely. No bout adoubt it. But did earning one require her to suffer fools gladly?

She'd never been the world's best team player. She knew that. She was proud of it. She knew when she was right, and she wasn't shy about saying so. Or about sticking to her guns when some subliterate tried to tell her she wasn't.

Being a team player at all came hard for her now. She'd spent way too much time on her own after the eruption. She'd escaped from Denver alone, one of the few who'd bailed soon enough to make it out. She'd been alone among tens of thousands of refugees in Camp Constitution, one of the many refugee centers that still blighted the fringes of the ashfall zone and probably would for years to come.

And she'd been alone, very much alone, on the team of scavengers that went into the devastated areas to get what could be got before it wasn't worth getting any more. She hadn't got along with anyone else on the team, and little by little she'd quit trying. She'd been glad to leave, and they'd been glad to have her gone.

She'd come back to L.A. on her own, too. Till she met Bronislav in that New Mexico truck stop, she'd figured she would stay alone pretty much permanently. That hadn't happened, and somebody to keep you warm at night was just as much a Good Thing as a paycheck.

Still, hanging out with somebody who kept you warm at night didn't take the same kind of talents as coping with the idiots who clogged your work day.

Speak of the devil, she thought sourly. Walker Ellis was an engineer who could do brilliant things with transistors and integrated circuits (odds were there hadn't been a segregated circuit since *Brown v. Board of Education* became the law of the land). But when he tried to write . . . Well, it was better when he didn't.

Which had to be why he was bearing down on her now, an edited progress report on his latest project clutched in his fist.

Vanessa edited in red. She could see her marks at long range, like zits on a clueless teenager's face.

He looked at her over the tops of his wire-rims, which meant he was really and truly pissed off. His mustache was a little lopsided. If he provoked her enough, she'd call him on it. For now she waited, wondering whether he'd provoke her that much.

"Was all this truly necessary, Ms. Ferguson?" he demanded, waving the offending—and offensive—pages in the air.

"I'm afraid so," she answered, and then waited some more. Often the worst thing you could do to them was make them come at you.

Ellis dragged a chair from across the desk around to one of the short sides so he could sit closer to her. He thumped the pages down on the wood-grain plastic desktop. "You're going to have to show me, and I'm not even from Missouri," he said.

Well, he'd asked for it. "Okay," she said. "Let's take the opening. 'It will be demonstrated that Gorczany Microsystems is in the process of becoming a bell weather for the industry.'" She quoted with savage relish.

He didn't notice. Away from his widgets, he was kind of dim. "What's wrong with any of that?" he said. "I see you've marked it up, but I don't see why."

"That's why Mr. Gorczany hired me," Vanessa said. "From the top, then. 'It will be demonstrated . . .' By whom? By what? God, maybe?"

"By the report," he said indignantly.

"'This report will show . . .' On to the next. How is 'in the process of becoming' different from 'becoming'?"

"Umm—" Ellis scratched the left, or shorter, wing of his mustache.

Since he didn't answer, Vanessa went on, "Now this 'bell weather'—"

"What's wrong with that? It's spelled okay. I did that part on the computer, and the spellchecker didn't hiccup. You can see for yourself."

Vanessa sighed, more in anger than in sorrow. "Just because the spellchecker passed it doesn't make it right. 'Bell' and 'weather' are both words, sure. But the word is 'bellwether'—w-e-t-h-e-r. It's got nothing to do with the rain outside. Do you know what a w-e-t-h-e-r is, Dr. Ellis?" He got pissy if you didn't use his title, so she loaded it with poisonous sweetness.

He blinked. "I never thought about it."

Why am I not surprised? But she didn't say that. She was being—relatively—good. "A wether is a castrated ram, the way an ox is a castrated bull. A bellwether was—still is, for all I know—a castrated ram with a bell around its neck. It leads the sheep where the shepherd wants them to go, and the bell tells him where they are if anything goes wrong. So that's why the word means getting out in front."

"Oh," he muttered. That he could grow the lopsided mustache proved he had balls of his own, but he didn't like hearing a woman talk about animals without theirs.

"Shall we go on?" Vanessa said. "I think you'll see I had good reason for the changes I made."

He considered. The next big flock of red marks perched two sentences farther down. There was another one in the next paragraph. "Never mind," he said, not looking at her. "I'll put the goddamn things in when I rewrite."

"Thank you, Dr. Ellis," she said demurely. *Fuck you, Dr. Ellis,* she thought as he retreated. And he wasn't the only one, and he wasn't the worst (though he was in the running).

She tried to think of herself as a plastic surgeon, making flabby prose look better with strategic nips and tucks. More often, she felt like a middle-school English teacher—only too many of them didn't know squat about grammar, either. She had to look at all the ugly stuff before it got improved, too, and came out not real gorgeous even after she'd done her best with it.

Once Walker Ellis decided he'd had enough, Vanessa went round and round with the company's HTML wizard. "A bunch of the apostrophes in the new post are upside down," she said. "You need to fix them."

"That's how Microsoft Word outputs them," he said with a shrug: a geek's version of *No tengo la culpa*. His name was Bruce McRaa, which he pronounced as if it were spelled *McRae*.

"That's how Word outputs them if you let it be stupid," she answered. *If you're stupid yourself* were the words behind the words. She'd gone round this barn with other alleged computer whizzes. She told him how to make Word behave. With a carnivorous smile, she added, "You don't even need a Mac to do it."

"Messing with special characters is a pain, though," he said. "Just typing is an awful lot easier and faster."

"Getting things wrong is a pain," Vanessa snapped. "Being lazy is a pain. Having people who look at the site think we don't care about what we put there is a big pain."

The HTML wizard—the evil enchanter, as far as she was concerned—threw his hands in the air. "Okay! Okay! When the power's up, I'll fix it." Behind McRaa's words lay a no-doubt heartfelt *Now fuck off!* Since she'd got her way, she left.

Standing in the rain waiting for the bus was a major pain. Watching Nick Gorczany head down to the Palos Verdes Peninsula in his BMW was a bigger one yet. No matter how obscenely expensive gas had got, he could still afford to drive whenever and wherever he pleased. The peons he deigned to employ? It was to laugh. *Come the revolution . . .* , she thought darkly.

Naturally, the bus showed up late. She stepped in a puddle walking to her apartment building and soaked her foot in spite of galoshes. The mail consisted of three bills and an ad. By the time she walked into her place, she was steaming.

Cooking odors greeted her. She got ready to scream and run, or to fight like hell. But Bronislav's voice greeted her from the kitchen: "They turn me around early, so I get into town and come up here."

"Oh. Uh, great!" Vanessa's rage evaporated. She'd given him a key, which was a mark of how much she cared for him. She threw down the crap from the mailbox and hurried into the kitchen for a kiss. Then she said, "What are you making? It smells . . . interesting."

"Even now, Americans think too much is not worth eating. In Serbia, we know better," he answered. "This is chopped beef liver with hard-boiled eggs, with onions and peppers and spices."

"Oh," Vanessa said again, on a different note this time. Bryce's mother had made her chopped liver—once. Once was twice too often. She'd tasted, then washed out her mouth with Manischewitz (which was also no thrill). Vile hepatic paste . . .

"You will like it," Bronislav said. "I make it properly, not like horrible stuff they do in delis."

She'd had to work to put up with Bryce's mom even when she'd still liked him (that they'd loved each other for a while was something she tried hard to forget). She loved Bronislav now. That got her to keep her mouth shut about what she was thinking. It got her to taste some of the stuff he'd worked hard to make.

Nothing on God's green earth, not even love, could make her like it or eat more than a forkful. "Sorry, dear," she said. "More for you, that's all." Too many aggressive flavors in her mouth all at once weren't her idea of a treat.

He looked wounded. With those sorrowful eyes, he did it better than anyone else she'd ever known. Then he brightened—a little. "If I serve it in restaurant, people who come there will know to expect food with strong Serbian soul."

"Sure they will," Vanessa greed. She started to tease him about Serbian chitlins and collard greens, but didn't. There probably were such things, or their close equivalents. Poor people, peasants, all over the world ate whatever the folks with more money didn't want to bother with. There was the root of Bronislav's crack about American tastes.

He'd also done something with potatoes and sharp cheese that she could say happy things about without making herself a liar. And he was here when she hadn't expected him to be. When you were in love, that even made up for things like chopped liver.

Once upon a time, going fifty or a hundred miles to see something was no big deal. Like anyone who'd grown up in Southern California, Bryce Miller had taken it for granted. He'd known plenty of people who'd commuted that far to college or to work every day. Oh, they'd bitched about how much driving they had to do and what a drag it was, but life wouldn't be life without something to bitch about.

Going fifty or a hundred miles through rural Nebraska, even after summer cleared snow from the roads and made a trip at least theoretically possible, was a whole different story. You not only had to go, you had to come back as well. That, of course, doubled the distance involved. It also doubled the expense for gas, even if his car happened to feel like running. Since he hardly ever used it in Wayne, he had some serious doubts about how trustworthy it would be on any kind of major journey.

Long-haul buses were few and far between, too. They weren't cheap, either. If you lived in or near a city, buses still ran. In this state, that meant Omaha and Lincoln. The rest of Nebraska was the terminal—or rather, terminalless—boonies, as far as the bus lines were concerned. Bryce was damn glad the state had found the money to keep the bus line out to the college going.

For longer jaunts through what had been rich farmland and

was now ash-dappled and heading toward tundra, choices ranged from bad to much worse. You could ride a horse—if you could find a horse to ride. Horses in the Midwest had suffered from ash-induced HDP as much as other livestock. They'd suffered much worse than people had, because they couldn't wear masks to filter out the crud. You could also ride a horse if you could ride a horse. Neither Bryce nor Susan knew how.

You could ride in a horse-drawn wagon. There were some. Again, as with so many things in these post-eruption days, there weren't enough to go around. They cost less than driving would have, but they were also much slower.

Speaking of slow, you could walk. That didn't cost anything to speak of, but you needed to be seriously motivated to walk fifty or a hundred miles to see something and then to walk back again. Bryce wanted to see Ashfall State Park, but he didn't want to see it bad enough to get shin splints in the process. Neither did his beloved, which was putting it mildly.

That pretty much left bicycles as the last surviving possibility. Bryce and Susan had both brought bikes from SoCal to the trackless wilds of northeastern Nebraska. Bryce hadn't ridden one a whole lot till after the eruption. As natural catastrophe and war in the Mideast teamed up to send gas prices past Mars and heading straight out toward Jupiter, though, he'd gone from four fat tires to two skinny ones like millions of other people.

Places like Denmark and Holland had taken bikes for granted since before the turn of the twentieth century. Two-wheelers had briefly swarmed in the States before the internal-combustion engine culled their herds. Without cheap gas, though, internal- turned into infernal-.

So bicycles were back, bigtime. Bryce rode his to campus whenever the weather let him—and, the longer he stayed in Wayne, the less fussy about the weather he got. "Hey," he said do Susan, "if we don't make the trip this summer, when will we do it?"

"Never?" she suggested hopefully. But when Bryce kept right on getting ready to try a bicycle tour, she got ready along with him. The martyred sighs she let out were only background noise. Bryce hoped like hell they were, anyhow.

The two of them pedaled north up State Route 15 for not quite twenty miles. They took the left fork when the road branched just south of Logan Creek. It was two lanes of bumpy, potholed asphalt; no one seemed to have done any work on it since the supervolcano erupted, or, for all Bryce knew, for quite a while before that.

When he said as much to Susan, she just looked at him. "That's not what I'm worried about," she said. "I'm worried about riding *north*. I keep expecting to see polar bears every time we come over the top of the next little rise."

"It's not that bad," Bryce said. "As long as it stays sunny, it's not." It was in the fifties. After you'd been going for a while, you could work up a sweat. Being warm felt good no matter how you did it.

No polar bears were in the neighborhood. A hawk circled in the air high above them. Jays and crows and little brown birds Bryce couldn't name perched on barbed-wire fences and occasional light and power poles. Robins hopped in the fields. So did rabbits, which probably accounted for the circling hawk. Bryce supposed it would have taken more than a supervolcano to clear the countryside of rabbits. The end of the world probably wouldn't have done it.

Just past the tiny town of Laurel—not deserted, because wood smoke curled up from a few chimneys—the state road ran into US 20. That was also a two-lane blacktop road, but a wider one. It had more traffic than State Route 15, which had felt eerily empty. Bicycles, wagons, people on horseback . . . The 405 at rush hour before the eruption it wasn't, but Bryce no longer feared he and Susan were the last two people left alive this side of Wayne.

They heard the approaching ambulance long before they saw it. Everyone did, and had plenty of time to get off the road and make way for the leftover from a different era. The ambulance screamed past them and turned down the little road they'd just left. It headed south, toward Wayne.

"Hospital," Susan said.

Bryce nodded. The hospital in Wayne wouldn't make anyone forget Cedars-Sinai or the UCLA Medical Center any time soon. But it was at least there, and boasted equipment a country doctor couldn't pull out of his ear. "I hope whoever's in there comes through okay," Bryce said, and then, "Boy, it sure was loud, wasn't it?"

Now Susan's head bobbed up and down. "I don't remember them being that loud in the old days." Her laugh sounded shaky. "Of course, we were usually in cars back then, with the windows closed and the radio or an iPod on and the AC going. And all the other cars and trucks and things made so much background noise, even a siren was just part of it. Not like that any more."

When the sun neared the horizon ahead of them, they camped by the side of the road. They fumbled putting up their little nylon tent, but managed. They ate MREs, which were uninspiring but did putty over any accidental empty space you had inside.

They pedaled through a succession of small towns strung out along US 20: Belden, Randolph, Osmond, Plainview, Brunswick, Royal. All of them looked to have been forgotten by everyone except the people who lived in them long before the eruption. They were even more forgotten now. The fall of ash had probably killed some of the locals and made others pull up stakes. Only the stubbornest still held their ground. In every little town, there were some.

Not far past Royal, a sign pointed Bryce and Susan north again, along a straight and narrow road towards Ashfall State Park. Susan said, "What do we do if they've decided to shut down the park because they don't have any money to keep it open?"

Bryce winced. California had done things like that even before the supervolcano hammered its tax base. But he answered, "We ride back, that's what, and we try and be happy for all the nice exercise we've got."

"Oh, boy!" Susan said in distinctly hollow tones.

"As of the day before we set out, the park's Web site said it was up and running," Bryce pointed out. Wayne did have power most of the time. You might wonder about polar bears there, too, but if they came at night you could at least turn on the light and spot them before they got you.

The park was open. Not a single car stood in the lot, but a few bicycles did rest in a steel rack that looked newish. Before the eruption, chances were that not a whole hell of a lot of people had biked out here to nowhereland.

A sign that also must have gone up after the eruption said LIFE IMITATES PARK! Bryce tried to decide whether that was funny or tasteless. He finally settled on *both at once.*

If the Web site mentioned that admission had gone up to fifty smackers a pop, Bryce didn't remember seeing it. Chances were it did somewhere, in pale lavender six-point type. Once you got way the hell out here, what were you gonna do? Turn around on your bike and go back to wherever you came from without seeing what you'd come for? Or pay the nice man? Bryce paid the man—he really did seem nice—and muttered under his breath. Inflation had kicked the whole country in the teeth since the eruption, not just Ashfall State Park.

Most of the park had been prairie. Here and there, ash still lay on the ground. More new signs said THIS HAPPENED 12,000,000 YEARS AGO, TOO. There was a visitors' center—how could you have a state park without a visitors' center? And then there was a trail down to what the people at the center called the rhinoceros barn: a structure with open sides and a corrugated-iron roof. It showed the fossils that had accumulated at a water-hole when the supervolcano blew all those millions of years ago.

"They moved some of these to the university's museum in Lincoln," Bryce said quietly. "I saw them there."

Susan nodded. "Yes, you've said so."

Bryce turned to a man in khakis, a work shirt, and a drill sergeant's hat: a park employee. "Will somebody twelve million years from now make a park around a waterhole all crowded with cattle and sheep?"

The man blinked. He smiled a slow smile that didn't quite reach his eyes. "Wouldn't surprise me one bit, sir," he said after a moment's thought. Yes, he was an employee, all right; otherwise, he never would have called anyone a good fifteen years younger than he was *sir*.

One of the skeletons of a female rhino had within it the tiny skeleton of an unborn baby. Looking at the splendidly preserved bones, Bryce wondered whether some far-future archaeologist would make a similarly amazing find. Then he wondered what the far-future archaeologist would look like. Not like a man, chances were.

He and Susan slowly walked the path in the barn. It was only sixty or seventy feet, but there were a lot of bones and plaques explaining what kinds of bones they were. At the end, Susan asked, "Now what?"

"Now we start back to Wayne," Bryce answered.

She sighed. "I was afraid you were going to say that." She sighed again. "Well, what else can we do?"

Colin Ferguson set his bike in the rack outside the San Atanasio station, then chained and locked it. This should have been, and was, one of the safer places in town to stash a bicycle. All the same, more than one here had walked with Jesus—or with Jesús, or with Eric, or with Terrell—in the past few months.

A reporter from the *South Bay Daily Breeze* waylaid him just inside the door. The desk sergeant sent a silent apology with his eyebrows. Colin raised one back, as if to reply *What can you do?* The reporter said, "Congratulations on your promotion, Captain Ferguson."

"Thanks—I guess," Colin answered. "If it wasn't for the honor of the thing, I'd rather walk."

The guy chuckled, so he knew what Colin was talking about, which surprised Colin a little. Then the man asked, "How do you feel now that they've finally appointed a new chief for the San Atanasio PD?"

"Glad. Relieved," Colin said sincerely. "It will be good to get back to normal, if we can."

The reporter made him regret the last three words, asking, "How likely do you think that is? With the cloud of Chief Pitcavage hanging over the department, and with all the lawsuits springing from it—"

"You have to ask the lawyers about that." Colin did his best to head the eager young man off at the pass. "Me, I'm just a cop. I want to do cop things. Today, paying a call on Chief Williams is number one on the list."

"Do you think you can ever be 'just a cop' again, Captain Ferguson? Won't people always think of you as 'the man who caught the South Bay Strangler'?"

That was a disconcertingly clever question. Colin didn't like reporters who asked such questions; they made it harder for him to think of the whole breed as twits. "I guess people will look at me that way," he answered. "But it's not how I look at myself, and it had better not be, or I'll have a tough time with my job. Now you've got to excuse me, 'cause I really do have to meet with Chief Williams in about five minutes, and he'll probably throw me off the force if I show up late."

The reporter's thumbs danced on his iPhone as he texted his story to the *Breeze*. It was a Web-only paper these days, and had been since not long after the eruption. With power so erratic in the L.A. area, a Web-only paper was a lot like one of Schrödinger's kitties: you couldn't tell whether it was alive or dead on any given day till you looked.

Colin escaped down the hallway. He nodded to a couple of cops and a clerk who walked past. They all nodded back, which he appreciated; he'd had a rugged time here after Chief Pitcavage killed himself and before Lucy Chen found that the late chief was the Strangler.

No spiderwebs hung from the door to the chief's office, but not many people had gone in there since the days right after Pitcavage swallowed his pills and fastened the bag over his head. Colin wondered whether the new chief had hired an exorcist before moving in. Well, that was Williams' worry, not his. He hadn't taken the job even when they tried to hand it to him on a silver platter. Along with getting Kelly to marry him, he figured that was one of the smarter things he'd done lately.

He knocked on the door. It was thick and soundproofed, but he heard the "Come in" from the other side all the same. He turned the knob.

"Chief Williams?" he said when he walked in. The door shut behind him with a click.

"That's me." Malik Williams stood up behind his desk and held out his hand to Colin. The chief was an African-American man of about fifty. His shaven head shone under the fluorescents in the ceiling. He wore a thin salt-and-pepper mustache. He was big, six-two or so, and in solid shape; when he was a kid, he might have played linebacker at a Division II school.

As Colin shook hands with him, he also noted the desk. It was a new one—or rather, an old one: an ordinary cop's desk, brought out of storage. It replaced the special oversized one Chief Pitcavage had used. Sitting behind that humongous flight deck, Pitcavage had had an easy time intimidating anybody who came in. Maybe Malik Williams didn't want to. That would be nice. Or maybe he hoped to be seen as not wanting to. That also wouldn't be so bad. From everything Colin had heard, the new chief was no dope.

"Have a seat." Williams waved to the chair on Colin's side of the desk. It was also an ordinary job. Well, so was the one in which the new chief sat down. It wasn't a leather-upholstered throne like the one in which Pitcavage had ensconced himself. More symbolism.

"I'm damn glad to have you here," Colin said. The chair creaked under him as he shifted his weight. So did the one on the other side of the desk. Chief Pitcavage's expensive model would never have dared to make such uncouth noises.

"I'm damn glad to hear you say that," Williams answered. His voice was a resonant baritone, with only a vanishing trace of accent to show his origins. He went on, "I don't think I could do this job if you didn't have my back."

"That's nice of you, but I don't believe it for a minute," Colin said. "Sitting in your seat, you've got the weight of the department behind you. Anybody dumb enough to bump up against you would find out how much weight that was, and in a hurry, too."

Chief Williams smiled. His teeth were white and perfect enough to belong to a TV anchorman; either he was very lucky or he'd had them fixed. "Anybody'd think you've been a cop for a while," he remarked.

"Guilty," Colin admitted. "Can I throw myself on the mercy of the court?"

"Maybe this once. After that, things go back to business as usual."

"Good," Colin said, which made one of the new chief's eyebrows rise toward the hairline he didn't have. Colin explained: "Like I was saying to the *Breeze* reporter out front a few minutes ago, nothing would make me happier than getting back to normal." *If I ever can.* He kept that to himself, not that Williams wouldn't get it whether he said it or not.

"If we look at the way things were before the supervolcano blew as normal, we're never going to get back there," Malik Williams said. "Not in your lifetime, not in mine, and probably not in our kids' lifetimes, either. And it's about time we started getting used to the idea."

"I'm going to *like* working for you, man," Colin blurted.

"Oh, yeah?" Williams looked and sounded dubious. "Most people I say that to, they look at me like I'm talking—what's that word from the Catholic Church? Like I'm talking heresy, and they don't want thing one to do with me."

"Chief, I'm married to a geologist who was studying Yellowstone before it blew. I met her in Yellowstone before it blew, matter of fact. Kelly was telling me then how bad an eruption would be. I didn't want to believe her, but she knew what she was talking about." Colin let out a small, wry chuckle. "She usually does."

The new chief grinned that ever-so-shiny grin at him again. "My Janice is the same way. Nice to know somebody else appreciates that in a woman." The grin faded. "How do we tie being different to police work, though?"

"I've been thinking about that. I've been thinking about it ever since the shortages started to bite," Colin said.

Williams' eyebrow climbed once more. "Somehow, that doesn't surprise me. What does surprise me is that you didn't want to sit on my side of this desk."

"I did, before Pitcavage got it," Colin answered. "But I don't put up with fools real well—not at all, if I can help it. Kissing up to the mayor and the city council and all would drive me to a coronary or a stroke. If you can do it and stay sane, more power to you."

"You don't beat around the bush, do you?" Williams said.

"Who, me?" Colin said, less innocently than he might have. After a beat, he added, "I try not to."

"Okay," Williams said. If Colin remembered straight, he'd

run a department in a little Sacramento suburb before winning this job. The new chief went on, "So what have you been thinking about the way things work now?"

"That most of the tricks we've picked up over the past hundred years have gone up in smoke—and dust, and ash," Colin replied. "We can't count on phones or electricity 24/7/365. We can't count on surveillance video or Internet databases. Sometimes we can manage all that stuff, but we can't count on it any more, and God only knows when we'll be able to. Back before the First World War, the cops with the big old walrus mustaches and the tall hats that made 'em look like London bobbies did without those things—hell, they'd never heard of most of them. Most of the time, they managed anyhow. We've got to be able to do that, too." He paused, embarrassed at himself. "Sorry. I made a speech."

"Yeah, you did," Williams agreed, "but it was a pretty good speech. Mostly. One of the ways the guys with the walrus mustaches managed was by pinning any cases they were having trouble with on the nearest guy my color."

"I bet they did," Colin said. "I don't want us to copy all their moves. But they had to solve cases and catch perps without the tools we still want to take for granted. We can learn from that. We'd better, or we're screwed."

"Tell you what. Work up a report for me, with ideas about how we can do a better job of what we need to do with some of the tricks the old-timers had. Not your top priority, but make sure you do it," the new chief said. "And before you finish it, talk to some of the oldest retired cops you can find. They won't go back to the days before phones and squad cars, but they'd type their reports with two fingers 'cause nobody ever taught 'em how to do it with ten. Those guys, the ones who half of 'em still don't have computers."

Now Colin looked at the man on the other side of the desk

with genuine admiration. "I've been doing that. Some of the fellows who were retiring when I came to the department are still around, even if they're old as the hills now. A couple of 'em started back in the Fifties."

"A long time ago," Malik Williams said. Colin nodded. The chief went on, "And I'm not surprised you came up with the same scheme that crossed my mind. Like they say, GMTA, right?"

"Oh, at least," Colin said, so dryly as to make Williams laugh out loud—or LOL, if you'd already started thinking with initials.

When Colin went back to his desk, the first thing Josefina Linares asked him was, "Well? What do you think?" Naturally, his secretary knew where he'd been. And if he didn't fancy Malik Williams, her fierce loyalty would make her ready—eager, even—to spit in the new chief's eye.

Quickly, Colin answered, "He'll do fine, Josie. I'm sure of it." He would have said the same thing had he thought Williams would prove a disaster—his loyalty was to the department, and to the chain of command. But he meant it. If the new man could get along with the people set over him, Colin figured he wouldn't have any trouble bossing the people he was supposed to lead.

Mike Pitcavage hadn't had any trouble bossing the department, either. No, Pitcavage's problems lay far deeper, somewhere in the twisted roots that made him do what he'd done. He'd been dead most of a year now, and Colin still brooded about him every day. He sighed. Even with the new broom of Malik Williams, this department wouldn't get swept clean any time soon.

All you could do was all you could do. Williams, Colin figured, would do that. He sighed again and started doing some of what he needed to do.

VI

As twilight deepened toward dark on Halloween, Guilford, Maine, reminded Rob Ferguson of a scene out of a Currier and Ives print. Snow dappled the few pines that hadn't been cut down for fuel. People on skis and snowshoes tramped the streets. Okay, they wore jeans and anoraks and watch caps, not nineteenth-century fancy dress, but you couldn't have everything.

A sleigh came by, drawn by two well-groomed black horses. In it rode Jim Farrell. His fancy dress—fedora and elegantly tailored wool topcoat over a suit with sharp lapels—was more Happy Days Are Here Again than Currier and Ives, but no denying he had style. Even 1930s finery made jeans and anoraks and watch caps mighty dowdy by comparison.

Not that Rob cared. Jeans and anoraks and watch caps weren't high style, but they were his style. The only reason for dressing up he'd ever found was trolling for pretty girls. Now that he'd actually landed one, he didn't need to worry about that nonsense any more. Lindsey wasn't of the let's-put-on-the-dog-to-impress-people school, either. If she were, Rob wasn't sure he would have wanted to marry her.

Plastic jack-o'-lanterns and black cats weren't quite from the nineteenth-century version of Halloween, either, but they did add splashes of color to the white landscape. The splashes were a little duller than they had been the year before, or the year before that—the plastic junk came from the days when the supervolcano hadn't erupted yet, and it was fading and cracking and otherwise showing its age.

Rob let out a mournful, fog-filled breath. Winter had Guilford firmly in its grip again. There'd been snow flurries every week or two all the way through the alleged summer. Even the quickest-growing strains of rye and oats had trouble ripening in this tiny growing season.

A few real jack-o'-lanterns went with the plastic ones. If you were both lucky and careful here, you could raise pumpkins and other northern squashes in a greenhouse. Some enterprising farmers and town gardeners had. People still enjoyed pumpkin pies—enjoyed them more than ever, because they were a surviving luxury where so many had perished. And the rinds (except for the ones grinning with candles inside them) and the vines would feed the local pigs. Less got wasted now than it had in the days when Guilford was connected to the outside world the year around.

Rob went back to the apartment he shared with Lindsey. A wood-fired stove vented to the outside had replaced the useless electric range long before he married her. Not only was it far more practical these days, it also helped heat the place. A delicious smell wafted out when he opened the door. Lindsey was using some hoarded nutmeg and cinnamon on a pumpkin pie. Rob didn't know what she'd swapped for the pumpkin flesh. None of the furniture seemed to be missing, so he wouldn't worry about it.

On an end table by the door stood a bowl of oat-flour cookies sweetened with maple syrup. Before the eruption, they would have been organic, gluten-free, super-expensive delights from

Whole Foods or Trader Joe's. Now they were just what Lindsey'd made to give to trick-or-treaters. The kids old enough to remember packaged chocolate bars would rather have had those. Rob fiercely missed chocolate himself. Well, you did what you could with what you had, that was all.

He filched a cookie. "Good stuff, hon," he called to his wife, who stayed in the kitchen to tend to the pot-bellied stove. It was a lot more fickle than the old electric, but it had the advantage of still working.

She made an exasperated noise, not at the stove but at him. "Try to leave a few, please," she said. "They'll start knocking on the door any minute now."

"You know me too well," Rob said.

"Much too well," Lindsey agreed cheerfully.

Before he could crank his dudgeon up to high, they did start knocking—pounding—on the door. In case he had any doubts, they also yelled "Trick or treat!" in a chorus of earsplitting trebles.

He opened up. The costumes were homemade, and warm. One kid was dressed as a polar bear, another as an Eskimo. Rob hadn't known there were any blue-eyed, freckled Eskimos, but who was he to criticize? He handed out cookies. "Thank you!" the boys piped. Gone—at least in these parts—were the days when mothers rejected any treats that weren't factory-wrapped.

Lindsey brought him a bowl of stew reheated from the day before and the day before that. By now, the pork was meltingly tender and all the chunks of root vegetables had kind of mooshed together. "Yum!" he said, and made everything in there disappear.

The libation that went with the stew was homemade whiskey turned out by a distiller in Dover-Foxcroft. It wouldn't knock single-malt scotch off the shelves any time soon. But it was here, while single-malts were only a memory. "Let's hear it for moonshine!" Rob said.

"I don't think he needs to worry about revenuers smashing

up his still," Lindsey answered. Since Rob didn't, either, he let that go. Lindsey continued, "Want some pie?"

"Wow! She's sexy *and* she cooks!" Rob exclaimed. She not only cooked, she gave him a dirty look—and some pumpkin pie, still warm and a little gloopy. He sounded as appreciative as he could with his mouth full. He must have done a good enough job, because after a while she went from glowering to giggling.

They expended almost all the oat-and-maple cookies by the time the trick-or-treaters stopped coming to the door. Then Rob got into his own costume: a tweed jacket, a shirt with a button-down collar, and a tie he'd got for an hour of guitar lessons. Since he never wore clothes like that of his own accord, they had to be a Halloween getup. Lindsey dressed in white from hat to shoes, and put white face paint on all her skin that showed: she was going as a snowdrift.

"Hottest snowdrift around," Rob said, which won him another dirty look. He grabbed his guitar. Lindsey carried a torch—an electric one with LEDs—to light their way to the Trebor Mansion Inn.

From somewhere, Dick Barber had got a big box of tiny Hershey bars. "Magic," he said smugly when Rob asked him how he'd pulled that off. For all Rob knew, he meant it. The taste of one brought tears to his eyes, so vividly did it evoke the bygone days before the eruption. You can't go home again. Someone had written a book by that name. Whoever he was, he'd known too well what he was talking about.

Lubricated by more moonshine and homebrew beer, Squirt Frog and the Evolving Tadpoles played for a while. They still gigged every now and then, here and there in this cut-off part of Maine. But the years when Rob and Justin and Charlie and Biff had lived in one another's pockets seemed almost as far from the here-and-now as the taste of a Hershey bar. And the music just didn't feel the same when it was all acoustic.

Again, you did what you could do. Or, if you decided you just had to have chocolate and electricity and the other marvels of what had been Western civilization, you got the hell out of Guilford and headed for a warmer clime. Rob had thought about it now and again, especially during summer snowstorms. But Lindsey didn't want to leave. And, by now, he had more roots here than he did anywhere else. He wondered how his folks and his brother and sister were doing, but he hadn't seen any of them since before the supervolcano blew, and he hadn't talked much with them since, either.

When he mentioned that to Jim Farrell, the retired history prof said, "If *things* matter to you, you'll do better somewhere else. If people matter to you, this is the place to stay. I could be watching TV in Florida, but I'm having more fun here."

"Hey, here you get to be *on* television, even if you don't get to watch it," Rob said. "That CNN crew that came in by dogsled last winter, to interview the Führer of Maine north and west of the Interstate . . ."

"No fair, Rob," Dick Barber said, wagging an indignant finger at him. The lord and master of the Trebor Mansion Inn went on, "That segment never aired. The CNN newsie was a lot cuter than Jim—"

"I resemble that remark," Farrell broke in.

"A lot cuter than Jim," Barber repeated, unfazed, "but she wasn't too dumb to see how dumb he was making her look. And in case she had been, her director and the camera guy saw it, too."

"It wasn't a beauty contest, or I would have been in over my imperfectly lovely head," Farrell said. He wasn't half bad—except for a certain glint in his eye, *distinguished* would have suited him as well as his outfit—but a broadcasting anchorwoman did have some unfair advantages. Chuckling, Farrell continued, "No, fool that she was, she wanted to talk with me. This sorry world has a great many things in it that I do poorly or not at all, but by God, gentlemen, I can run my mouth."

"It's why we love you so," Barber said. Farrell tipped his fedora: as much a trademark with him as it had been with Fiorello La Guardia a lifetime earlier. His silver hair shone, even in the relatively dim light of the fireplace and tallow candles.

Rob grinned. "Nobody talks this way down where things are still within shouting distance of what they used to be."

"Of course not. Nobody down there needs to," Farrell said. "Down there, they can still call a million songs and a thousand talk-show hosts—to say nothing of hot and cold running porn, which is all that should be said of it—out of the air whenever it strikes their fancy. They don't need to *talk*." His rich baritone freighted the word with scorn. "Here, now, this is a land where we have to make our own fun. And so we do."

"Speaking of fun, how about another song from you sociable Darwinists?" Barber said.

Thus provoked, Squirt Frog and the Evolving Tadpoles launched into "Justinian II," an underappreciated ditty about an equally unappreciated Byzantine Emperor:

> *"Justinian the Second lost his nose,*
> *Lost his nose, lost his nose.*
> *Justinian II lost his nose—*
> *The Emperor of Byzantium!*
>
> *They'd loved his father and his grandfather, too.*
> *His great-granddad would more than do.*
> *But he made them hate him strong and true*
> *As Emperor of Byzantium.*
>
> *So they overthrew him with effortless ease,*
> *Cut off his nose before he could sneeze,*
> *And exiled him to the Chersonese—*
> *Ex-Emperor of Byzantium!*

Folks say Jesus is coming, and is He pissed,
But Justinian, he was hardly missed
Until he decided to resist
The new Emperor of Byzantium.

A storm blew up on the high seas.
His friends, they got down on their knees
And said, 'Justinian, kindly, if you please
Forget about Byzantium!'

'If I forget, may God drown me now!'
And the storm just stopped—I don't know how.
And somehow on that wallowing scow
He made it to Byzantium.

He got his throne back with great vim,
Killed the guy who got rid of him
And the one who overthrew him
As Emperor of Byzantium.

Not all stories have happy ends.
He murdered so many, he lost all his friends.
So people turned on him again . . .
Friendless in Byzantium.

The moral's simple—keep an eye on your nose.
When you deal with people, watch how it goes
Or you'll end up like Justinian Number Dos:
A dead man in Byzantium."

When they finished, Lindsey turned to Rob and said, "You guys are weird, you know?"

"I had heard rumors," Rob admitted. Justin, by contrast,

took a bow. Rob went on, "You need to remember, though—you married me anyway."

"Oh, yeah." Lindsey spread her fingers and looked at her ring, as if to remind herself. She went on, "You probably drugged me. Rock-'n'-roll guys are notorious for that, right?"

"At least," Rob said, and then, "I wish! The last time I had any fun drugs here—well, except for booze—it was the Vicodin the clinic doc gave me when I got shot in the leg. Some things cost more than they're worth, if you know what I mean."

"What else could it have been, though?" Lindsey said. "Love?"

"Crazy idea, all right," Rob agreed. They grinned at each other.

Louise Ferguson often wondered how the hell the Van Slyke Pharmacy stayed in business. For one thing, it was a mom-and-pop up against the chains. Mom-and-pop hamburger stands went belly-up in short order when they butted heads with the Golden Arches and Burger King. They might make better burgers, but they took longer and cost more, and the people who didn't live in the neighborhood wouldn't know the burgers were better. Most of the time, being sure what you'd get trumped quality.

The Van Slyke Pharmacy certainly charged more than chains like Rite-Aid and Walgreens, both for prescriptions and for over-the-counter meds. The only people who came in for the stuffed animals and the gaudy ceramic horrors were obvious escapees from the local Home for the Terminally Taste-Impaired. Yes, the place also sold those secondhand books. But no one in the history of the world had ever got rich selling secondhand books. Even Utnapishtim had to declare bankruptcy after his Gently Used Cuneiform Tablets shop failed back in Sumerian days.

Then there was her boss. Jared Watt might be nicer than Mr. Nobashi, but he was also stranger. Considering how squirrely the salaryman from Hiroshima had been, that really took some doing. He not only managed, he passed with flying colors.

His wardrobe had some flying colors, too. He'd never met anything polyester or nylon he didn't love. The brighter, the better. If colors clashed, he either didn't notice or didn't care. His outfits were almost as horrendous as the china figurines clogging the shelves that weren't full of aspirins or decongestants.

Some people did that kind of thing as shtick. Louise could imagine either of her grown sons wearing some of Jared's clothes if they decided that was a hoot. But the pharmacist wasn't doing it to be cool. He did it because those were the clothes he wore.

And his hobbies . . . ! He was around Louise's age: in his early fifties. He wasn't gay, or she didn't think he was. But his music of choice was Broadway show tunes. He knew how many performances the most obscure musicals had run, and who'd replaced whom in the cast, and when, and often why. He knew songs that had got cut in tryouts, for crying out loud.

Louise had nothing against Broadway musicals, even if they didn't float her boat. When Jared started going on about European soccer clubs, though, that was when she started looking around for the closest handy blunt instrument.

Not that he cared. He went on and on about how Barcelona played the game the way it should be played, and how they were better than Real Madrid. He told her Barcelona wore blue and red stripes because the Swiss maniac who started the club there came from Basel, which already had a team in blue and red stripes. He talked about Bayer Leverkusen, and about the aspirin tablet on their coat of arms. He bored her with Juventus of Turin, and A.C. Milan, and Inter Milan. He blathered about Sir Alex Ferguson, Manchester United's longtime coach. He sang the praises of the Gunners of Arsenal, the Blues of Chelsea, and the Iron of Scunthorpe—though that last bunch seemed to be in whatever the Brits called the minor leagues.

His enthusiasm—his mania—didn't stop at the borders of Europe. He had kind words for the Black Stars of Ghana and the

Indomitable Lions of Cameroon and the Elephants of the Ivory Coast. He explained that there was a club called Corinthians in Brazil, a Liverpool in Uruguay, and another Arsenal in Argentina because of tours the original English sides had taken in the early years of the twentieth century. He even occasionally mentioned the L.A. Galaxy of the MLS, who were based in the South Bay (though he used Minor League Soccer as often as Major to spell out the league's acronym).

He was, in short, a piece of work. Louise cared nothing for any sport, a dislike she'd passed on to Vanessa. She particularly didn't care for American football. She'd never loathed soccer all that much before, mostly because it hadn't shown up on her radar screen. Now it did, and she discovered it was at least as annoying as its Yankee cousin.

And, short of using that blunt instrument, she was stuck listening to Jared go on and on about it whenever things got slow in the drugstore. Most of the time, in other words. Combining his obsessions, he even told her there'd been a musical about soccer.

"But only in London," he assured her. "They never brought it to the States—they didn't think it would draw." He sighed, mourning American ignorance. He soon brightened, though. "We did have *Good News* in the Twenties, about our kind of football. And *Damn Yankees*, of course." That last came out with a distinct sniff; he didn't care for baseball.

"Of course," Louise echoed. She'd at least heard of *Damn Yankees*, which was more than she'd done with all those stupid goddamn soccer clubs.

Jared paid her. She didn't exactly know how, considering that things at the pharmacy weren't what anyone would call swift, but he did. Except for talking too much about things that didn't interest her, he made a good boss. He never gave her trouble if she needed time off because James Henry was sick or had to go to the dentist or whatever the hell.

She knew she should count her blessings. She did, along with the dollars from her checks on the first and fifteenth of every month. She tried, as subtly as she knew how, to suggest to him that her interests ran in different directions. It didn't work. She didn't need long to decide that she could scream *Will you shut the fuck up?* without cutting the endless chatter about soccer and musicals, musicals and soccer.

She was there at the pharmacy the afternoon the blizzard hit Los Angeles. They'd had snow every winter since the supervolcano eruption, snow several times a winter most years since. But Louise, a Southern California native, had never seen anything like this swirling whiteness.

"Wow," she said, pointing out through the front window. "I mean, is this Chicago or what?"

Jared's eyes widened. The magnifying lenses of his glasses made them look owl-big. "That's amazing," he said. "When it gets this bad, a lot of the time they play with a yellow ball, or an orange one."

"Do they?" Louise said tonelessly. For all she knew, or cared, the ball they used when it wasn't snowing like the North Pole might have been pink with green polka dots. Before Jared could go *They sure do* and then tell her more she didn't want to hear, she added, "I'm just wondering how we'll get home in this."

He rubbed his chin. When he wasn't talking about soccer or Broadway, he sometimes said he wanted to grow a beard to see if it helped keep his face warm, but he hadn't done it yet. "I know they've got chains for the buses," he said. "They've used them before."

Louise nodded—they had. But if they had to summon the buses to some central garage to get the chains, the schedule would end up screwed, blued, and tattooed. And . . . "I'm glad the bus stop is right across the street. I'm not sure I could find it in this if I had to go much farther. I have to walk a little ways from where I get off to my condo. That should be fun."

"I've got a bit of a walk, too." He clicked his tongue between his teeth. "Something to look forward to. An adventure."

"I heard somewhere that an adventure was somebody else have a miserable time a long way away," Louise said. She startled a laugh out of Jared.

He let her leave early. It wasn't as if they were doing a lot of business, or any business at all. She was wearing Nikes. She wished she'd thought to stick galoshes in her purse, but she hadn't, so all she could do was wish. She also wished that, like a faithful Saint Bernard, she could carry a keg of brandy on a chain around her neck.

When she got outside and the wailing northwest wind smacked her in the face, she wished for the brandy even more. The traffic lights at the corner of Van Slyke and Reynoso Drive were working, but she could see them only by fits and starts, when the gale chanced to blow away most of the snow between her and them.

She crossed the street against the light. She didn't worry about getting hit by a car. Hardly anyone drove on the roads even when the weather was better than this. Anybody who'd get into a car now had to be crazier than Jared Watt, which was really saying something. The same went for bike riders—or she thought so till one pedaled past her.

She tripped over the snow-hidden curb on the far side of the street, but didn't quite fall. Brushing snow off the bus bench, she sat down. She hoped again the bus wouldn't be too late—it was bloody cold out here, and the wind didn't help. Duh! It was cold enough to be snowing. It never used to get that cold in SoCal. It wasn't just cold enough to snow now. It felt a lot colder than that. Cold enough to freeze to death in? Her coat was pretty good, but the side of her face the wind hit was starting to go numb.

Another guy on a bike zoomed by, head down, working hard.

That would keep you warmer than just sitting around. Louise wondered whether she ought to get up and start doing jumping jacks or something. It might be a good idea, but she didn't have the energy.

She also had no idea the bus was anywhere within miles till it loomed up out of the snow in front of her. The fare had just gone up to five dollars. She'd never been so glad to feed a fin into the slot. She would have paid a lot more to get out of that horrible wind. The bus' heater even worked after a fashion.

Getting off was a lot less enjoyable than getting on had been. It was growing dark—growing dark fast. The snow danced and swirled in the air, for all the world as if this were somewhere in Connecticut, or maybe in a movie from the 1940s. God only knew what things were really like in Connecticut these days. Movies had nothing to do with anything real.

By the time Louise made it home, she was wishing for both steaming coffee and earmuffs. *I want to get out of these clothes and into a dry martini.* Somebody'd said that, though she couldn't remember who. She didn't give a damn about a dry martini. If they'd made a *hot* martini, now . . .

"It's snowing, Mommy! It's snowing!" James Henry squealed when she walked through the door. It was a big deal to him. Hell, it was fun to him—he hadn't had to sit out in it or slog through it.

Louise had. "Really?" she said. "I never would have noticed."

Her younger son by Colin came to the door. "I'm outa here," Marshall said, "or I will be. . . ." He held out his hand. He didn't even pretend he was doing this for anything but mercenary reasons.

After she'd given him enough greenbacks to make him stick his hand in his pocket, Louise said, "Be careful when you're going back to the house. It's brutal out there—worse than I've ever seen it before."

"I'll cope," he said, but paused a moment right outside the door when the wind smacked him in the kisser. "Whoa! It is kinda rugged," he allowed.

"Ya think?" Louise closed the door on him—she didn't want the storm to chill down the inside of the condo. Marshall vanished from sight even before he got to the bottom of the stairs.

"Can we make a snowman, Mommy?" James Henry asked.

"Maybe right in the middle of the living room," Louise answered. James Henry clapped his hands. He didn't realize she was joking. Outside, the snow kept blowing and falling, falling and blowing. It wasn't freezing inside the condo, but it wasn't what anybody would have called warm, either. When Louise sighed, she could see her own breath. She might not have been joking so much after all.

Before she had Deborah, Kelly Ferguson had known babies were a lot of work—labor didn't stop once the kid popped out. She'd known, yes, in an intellectual way. In that same intellectual way, she'd had a fair notion of what would happen to the world after the Yellowstone supervolcano blew.

In both cases, intellectual knowledge was one thing. Actual experience was something else again. The difference between the two was at least as profound as the difference between a picture of a steak on the one hand and the real steak first on a plate and then in your stomach on the other.

With the supervolcano, the country's work afterwards boiled down to trying to pick up the pieces. Kelly did a lot of that with Deborah, too. But her work changed a lot faster than the country's did. Deborah was more than a year old now, toddling unsteadily on legs that were still figuring out how to hold her up and coming out with more and more words every day.

Mama and Dada and Asha—which did duty for *Marshall*—had arrived very early. Dada arrived well before Mama did, which annoyed Kelly and amused Colin. "Happened the same way with my other three, too," he told her. "That bugged the dickens out of Louise—oh, you bet it did." He chuckled. "Marshall said her new rugrat did the exact same thing, so my guess is she got bugged all over again."

"How about that?" Kelly remembered saying. From then on, she tried not to complain about how Deborah was learning to talk. Being thought of as like the first wife was nothing a sensible second wife wanted. And chances were that sooner or later, no matter how she learned them, Deborah *would* learn to say hard words like Constantinople and Timbuktu. From boxes, Colin had pulled out most of the Dr. Seuss titles that had also taught Kelly to read.

The biggest problem with kids was, they found ways to do dumbass things no matter how careful you were. Kelly was changing Deborah on a towel on the bed. She looked away for a split second to grab the baby powder. She looked back just in time to see Deborah, grinning from ear to ear, roll over . . . and off. Then she heard a thump, and then she heard a wail of surprise, pain, and fear.

She grabbed her daughter. She wondered if any of the cars would start so she could rush the baby to the ER. Then she realized Deborah wasn't badly damaged—wasn't, in fact, damaged at all. As soon as Mommy had her, everything was fine again.

"They'll do it to you, all right," Colin agreed when Kelly told the gruesome story over dinner. "Hey, I didn't have a single gray hair—not one—before I had kids." He ran a hand through his hair. His hairline hadn't retreated a millimeter, but the color up there kept fading toward silver. He scowled, interrogation-room style, at Marshall. "See what you did to me?"

Kelly guessed he intimidated suspects in the interrogation room more than he did his younger son. "Yeah, right," Marshall said. "Like, what are you blaming me for? I was third in line. By the time I came along, I bet you were already sneaking Just for Men into the bathroom."

"Why d'you think I'm blaming you?" Colin rumbled. "I can't get at Rob or Vanessa, but you're right across the table from me."

"That's how cops decide how to arrest people, too, right?" Marshall asked helpfully.

He didn't faze his father a bit. "A lot of the time, it is," Colin answered. "And you know what else? A lot of the time, we grab the perp when we do it. Not always, but a lot of the time."

From what Colin had told her of his older son, Kelly thought Rob would have yelled *Death to the pigs!* or some other endearment. Marshall just shrugged and shoveled another forkful of macaroni and cheese into his face.

Food was expensive, unexciting, and sometimes scarce. Kelly tended a backyard garden. So did most people who had back yards to garden in, in SoCal, throughout the USA, and in the rest of the developed world. Countries that had been hurting for food even before the eruption were worse off now. The messed-up weather disrupted their crops, and nobody was selling much grain across borders. Several small-scale wars simmered in Africa and Asia because too many countries had too many hungry citizens.

Deborah, of course, stuffed literally anything she could get her hands on into her mouth. What else were hands for but grabbing things and bringing them to your mouth? It might be food, after all.

Or it might not. Kelly discovered that the flesh of her flesh had swallowed a button when she found it as a souvenir Deborah left in her diaper. It obviously hadn't injured the baby. The button didn't seem hurt, either, but Kelly threw it out anyhow.

"I don't know where she got it," Kelly said that night, still jittery over what might have been. "I would have taken it away if I'd seen it, and I swear I kept an eye on her all the time."

Colin took it better than she did: an advantage, no doubt, of this being his fourth time around the track, as opposed to her first. "Babies do things like that, is all," he said. "Most of the time, everything turns out okay. They're tough critters. If they weren't, none of 'em'd ever live to grow up."

"I guess." Till she had one, Kelly'd thought of babies as hothouse flowers that would wilt if you looked at them the wrong way. What with her swan dive from the bed and the button sticking out of her poop, Deborah was changing her mother's preconceptions. All the same, Kelly said, "But what if the button'd got stuck inside her? We would've had to take her to the hospital, and they might have needed to operate to get it out."

"Purple fur," Marshall said.

"Huh?" Kelly wasn't sure she'd heard straight.

"Purple fur," Marshall repeated. "From Telly Monster on *Sesame Street*. He worried about everything, remember? So we'd say somebody who worried about things that weren't worth worrying about had purple fur—like you just now."

Kelly thought anything that had to do with Deborah worth worrying about. But now she knew what purple fur meant—and (again, in an intellectual way) she understood what Marshall was talking about.

Once Deborah reached the upright position, she could grab all kinds of things she hadn't been able to get at while she was rolling and crawling. Kelly and Colin kidproofed the house as well as they could. Anything Deborah could pick up and try to eat went on a shelf too high for her to reach. All the electrical outlets that didn't have cords sticking out of them got plastic plugs so the baby couldn't stick her wet fingers or anything else into them.

"This won't be perfect, you know," Colin said. "She'll figure out ways to land in trouble that we can't even imagine. They always do."

Kelly didn't like that. "We're supposed to be there for them, to protect them."

"Uh-huh." Her husband nodded. "But sometimes that means sweeping up whatever's broken and putting on the Band-Aids after it's too darn late to do anything else."

She didn't like that, either. She wanted to make her offspring perfectly safe, invulnerable to harm. The rational part of her brain insisted she couldn't do that, but didn't stop her from wanting to.

Little by little, Deborah got the idea that there were things she was supposed to do and things she wasn't. She was a good kid. Most of the time, she did what her parents wanted. Most of the time, but not always. Once in a while, she would throw things down on the ground to smash them and see how much noise they made. Or she'd try to bite the hand that kept her from doing something or going somewhere.

Kelly and Colin yelled at her to stop. The first time Colin swatted Deborah on her diapered fanny, Kelly was appalled. It created more noise than pain, but she was appalled anyhow. "She's a person! You shouldn't hit her!" she exclaimed. "It'll mess her up."

"I got walloped plenty when I was a little kid. I earned it, too," Colin answered. "I spanked my older kids. I never hit them with a belt or hit them in the face, the way I got it sometimes—I thought that was going over the line. But they aren't too warped, and I'm not, either. Little kids are a lot like puppies or kittens. Sometimes they need to know that doing the wrong thing means you get hurt."

"All the child-raising books are dead against it." Like most academics, Kelly valued expert opinions.

Colin only shrugged. "Mike Pitcavage never warmed Darren's behind, and look what a drug-dealing son of a . . . gun his spoiled brat turned out to be."

"Oh, boy," Kelly said. "If he'd scared his kid into being a law-abiding citizen, he'd still be going out there and murdering old ladies whenever he got the urge."

She did make Colin flinch; she had to admit that. But she didn't make him back down. "You know what I mean," he said.

"I may know, but I still think you're wrong," she answered. "A lot of the time, people hit kids to make themselves feel better. That's not a good enough reason, not in my book."

"Ha! You'll find out!" he said, and, much as she wished she could, she couldn't ignore the certainty in his voice. He had years' more experience in such things than she did. He went on, "I didn't say smack 'em all the time. I didn't even say to do it very often. You do it a lot, it stops meaning much. But every once in a while, you'll decide it's the only way you can make sure they get the point."

"Hmp," she said, a syllable that meant *I don't believe it for a minute*. They left it there; they didn't do much out-and-out quarreling. Time would tell which of them had it straight, or if either one did.

VII

Vanessa Ferguson swore in Serbo-Croatian—in Serbian, Bronislav would have said. She certainly imitated his accent, not the one a Croat would have used. As far as she could tell, the difference between the two was about as big as the difference between Brooklyn and Alabama.

She'd heard people say you couldn't get any satisfaction cussing in a language not your own. She wasn't so sure of that. Serbo-Croatian's gutturals and heavy rolled R's—she had a decent ear, and could do them pretty well—seemed made for telling other people where to go and how to get there.

Best of all, as long as she didn't scream out the foreign profanity, she could use it at Nick Gorczany's widget works. Even muttering *you stupid son of a motherfucking bitch* would get you talked about—possibly fired, if the stupid SOB in question was the boss, as it all too often was. But the Serbo-Croatian equivalent hardly got noticed.

She despised her job with the hopeless hatred of someone who knew how unlikely she was to find anything better. Fixing other people's dreadful prose all day was not the kind of work that inspired you towards admiration of your fellow man—or woman. Someone had once said that people were the missing link between apes and human beings. Whoever that was, Vanessa was convinced he'd been an optimist. As far as she was concerned, her coworkers still walked on their knuckles, picked fleas from their friends' armpits, and used sticks to hunt termites for a snack.

The widget works was trying to land a Federal contract that would make sure it stayed in business a few years longer. With fiendish gusto, Vanessa tore the first draft of the proposal to bloody bits. She did her best to translate it into something related to English. Her red marks didn't outnumber the black ones on the pages, but they came close. She tossed the bloodied document on Mr. Gorczany's desk.

Did he thank he for her diligence? Not a chance. He called her in on the carpet (the stuff in his office was softer and thicker than the industrial-strength junk the peons had to walk on). Patting the wounded proposal, he asked, "Did you have to be *quite* so thorough?"

"I'm sorry, Mr. Gorczany," she said, which would have been fine had she left it there. But then she added, "Which dumb parts do you wish I'd left in?"

He had a blunt, bulbous nose. If it had been a little bigger, it would have given him the look of a blond Elmer Fudd. Elmer Fudd couldn't flare his nostrils, though, and Nick Gorczany could. "The engineers and I worked hard on that," he said.

The *and I* told her she was in trouble. Nobody got off on having his own deathless words edited (Vanessa didn't herself, but chose not to remember that). More cautiously, she answered, "I do think I've made it better. I cut out a lot of repetition."

"Yeah, well, we'll need to put some of that back in," Gorczany said. "When you deal with the Feds, first you tell 'em what you're going to tell them, then you tell them, then you tell them what you've told them. Otherwise, they don't get it."

Vanessa's lips moved, not quite soundlessly: "*Jeben te u glavu bluntavu.*" The curse meant something like *Fuck you in your stupid head.* Bronislav thought it was funny that she wanted to learn obscenities in his language. A proper Serb woman, he made it plain, wouldn't come out with such things. Vanessa wasn't a Serb and wasn't proper, so she didn't care.

She wasn't soundless enough, either. "What did you say?" Nick Gorczany asked.

"Nothing," she replied sweetly. "I was just trying to figure out what to uncut, if you know what I mean."

"Huh," he said. He might be illiterate, he might bring out that stupid cliché about telling things three times as if he'd just made it up, but he knew an insubordinate employee when he saw one. But Vanessa hadn't been very loud, and she also hadn't spoken English. He suspected, but he couldn't prove, so he went on, "Never mind, then. Fix it up, uh-huh, but not like this."

"Repetitively repetitious," Vanessa said.

She was pushing things, but she got away with it. Her boss nodded. "That's right," he said. His sarcasm detector hadn't gone off. Maybe it needed a new battery or something.

She made the second revision of the proposal dumber than the first one. If she wanted to go on getting paid, she had to keep Gorczany . . . not too unhappy. The really scary thing was, he might have been right when he claimed the Feds needed everything spelled out more than once.

All the same, the rewrite was the dictionary illustration for the term *soul-deadening.* Vanessa was swearing in English when she walked out of the widget works. She swore some more as she popped open her umbrella and trudged toward the bus stop. Nick Gorczany's Beemer sat in lonely splendor in the company parking lot. He could still afford to drive in. Why not? He belonged to the one percent, not to the ninety-nine. Vanessa fought down the temptation to key the car. It would be just her luck to have a working surveillance camera catch her.

The supper she fixed herself was almost as crappy as an MRE. She couldn't imagine anything worse to say about it. That she was choking on her own bile sure didn't improve the flavor.

"There's got to be a better way to make a living," she said again and again as she washed several days' worth of accumulated dishes. "There's got to be."

Her dumb little brother sold his stupid stories. He didn't exactly make a living with them, but he did sell. Vanessa was sure she could outwrite Marshall in her sleep. She could . . . if only she found the time.

Here she was, all by herself in this crappy little apartment she could barely afford. If she couldn't find the time now, when she loathed what she did every day, when would she ever?

For the moment, her place had power. She plugged in the secondhand laptop she'd got after she came back to L.A. and waited impatiently for it to boot up. She ran the battery as little as she could, because sometimes she had to wait a long time to charge up again.

On came Microsoft Word, as familiar to her as the shape of her own hands. She frowned, nodded to herself, and started to type. *Beneath the bloated, leprous moon, Clotilda killed her lover.* Ignoring the squiggly red line that appeared under *Clotilda*—Word was a fussbudget—she plunged ahead.

She kept plunging for a little more than a page. That was as far as she got on inspiration alone. Then she had to stop and think and work out what ought to happen next, and why it ought to, and how it should look when it did. Fussing and cussing under her breath (in English now—this was serious), she fought her way forward for another page. She felt as if she were hacking and slashing through thick jungle with a rusty machete.

When she glanced at the time, she discovered in amazement that she'd been hacking and slashing for two and a half hours. The first page had flown from her fingers to the screen. On the second one, she'd kept going round and round, putting words in, taking them out, fiddling with commas and semicolons. Everything had to be perfect. Then, a minute later, she'd decide it wasn't perfect after all and change it some more.

"Later," she told herself. She saved the story to the hard disk and to a couple of flash drives. She was conscientious—hell, she was fanatical—about backing up.

She meant to get back to the piece when she came home the next day, but she was too damn tired. The same thing happened the day after that. Then the weekend arrived, and she had to run around and do all the shit she couldn't do during the week because she was stuck at the stinking widget works.

Monday, Mr. Gorczany was particularly fuckheaded. Vanessa swore in English. She swore in Serbo-Croatian. She swore in the half-remembered bits of Armenian she'd got from her rug-merchant ex-boyfriend. She would have sworn in Swahili had she known any. Her face must have been a sight—nobody on the bus wanted to sit next to her.

After she choked down another uninspired supper, she turned on the laptop again. "There's got to be a better way to make a living," she said once more, grimly. "I mean, there's fucking *got* to be." She was talking to herself, but that was all right. She was the one she needed to fire up.

She opened the story and read what she'd written before. She made a face. It was melodramatic. The prose felt purple. She'd have to clean it up before she went any further. An hour later, it didn't seem that different. She wanted to make some progress on the night, so she wrote a couple of new paragraphs. Then she stopped and tried to neaten them up.

"Hell with it," she said at last. She saved the document and went to bed.

Bronislav was in town the next weekend, so she couldn't very well write then. She could grumble about how the story was—or rather, wasn't—going, could and did. He listened with grave attention. That was one of the things she liked about him. When she finally ran down, he said, "Will you let me see this story, please?"

Vanessa hesitated. Some ways, that request was more personal, more intimate, than a lot of what they did in the bedroom. Yes, she wanted people to read what she'd written . . . after she got it just the way she wanted it. If she ever did. If she ever could. Till then, showing it off was like walking down the street not only naked but without any makeup. Who wanted to show off the zits on her ass?

If Vanessa had zits on her ass, Bronislav had seen them. She sighed. "Okay," she said—reluctantly, but she did. She started the computer and opened the filled she'd named *Story1.docx*. "Here."

While he read, his face showed nothing of what he thought. He would have made a dangerous poker player. He probably did, at truck stops along I-10. He scrolled through the piece, then said, "You should finish. Is good."

She would have put more faith in that if English were his first language. How many subtleties flew over his head? Still, she knew she would have been horrified—to say nothing of furious—if he'd told her it was lousy. That he could see the same thing, and that he could see which side his bread was buttered on, never crossed her mind. What surer sign she was in love?

"I don't know exactly where I'm going with it," she said. Up till now, she hadn't admitted that to herself, much less to anyone else. Love, indeed.

"You will find way to do it." When Bronislav said something

like that, he sounded as certain as a judge passing sentence. When he said it, he sounded certain enough to make Vanessa believe it, too. Whether she'd keep on believing it once he had to go back on the road . . . Well, she'd find out after he did.

When the computer worked, Marshall Ferguson lurked on several boards for writers and wannabes. Some of them were just sad—the blind leading the deaf, so to speak. Others, though, offered what seemed like good advice. One bit that struck him as sensible was to start at the top when you were trying to sell something, to aim for the highest-paying, most prestigious markets. If they said no, you could set your sights lower. But if you started with the bottom feeders, you'd never find out for sure how good you could be.

So Marshall first submitted his stories to either *The New Yorker* or *Playboy*, depending on what they were like. This latest one, called "Almost Sunset," went to *Playboy*, because it had a guy and a girl in it and they were fooling around while a spectacular post-eruption sunset painted the walls of the guy's place. Marshall wondered what had happened to Jenny, the girl at UCSB he'd fooled around with at a time like that. He couldn't remember her last name, which meant he couldn't find her on Facebook—and, if she'd got married since then, she might have a different last name anyhow . . . and might not want to be found by people like him.

He didn't think that much of *Playboy*. It might have been cool when his dad was his age . . . or it might already have jumped the shark by then. But he totally admired the kind of money the magazine paid. Some postage and a wait till the story came back were a reasonable investment. It was like buying a lottery ticket, only with somewhat better odds.

Since he'd moved back in with his father and Kelly and now Deborah, he was almost always the one who went to get the mail.

In *Animal Farm*, which he'd read for Western Civ, the "liberated" farm beasts had learned to bleat *Four legs good, two legs bad!* His bleat when he opened the mailbox was *Little envelopes good, manila envelopes bad!* A manila envelope was his story coming back rejected. A little envelope might be an acceptance letter or a contract or a check. It usually wasn't, but it might be.

He didn't think anything special was up when he grabbed the mail on a day that was trying to be springlike but didn't quite remember how. A couple of bills, a couple of catalogues, a Netflix DVD for Kelly to watch while she was up in the middle of the night with Deborah (if there happened to be power), and an envelope from Chicago he didn't even notice as he carried the stuff to the house.

Deborah pointed at him when he went inside. "Masha!" she announced. She came closer to his real name every day. Dad said little kids weren't human till they got potty-trained, but she was gaining on it.

He pointed back at her. "Vacuum cleaner," he said.

She shook her head. "No! Deb'ah!" She giggled. She knew who she was. She also knew part of her big half-brother's job was trying to mess up her mind.

"Oh, yeah," he said. "Pork rinds."

"No! Deb'ah!"

"You're bizarre, Marshall," Kelly said, more affectionately than not. "So what did the Post Awful inflict on us today?"

"You've got the latest *Hornblower* from your Netflix queue," he answered, which made her squee—she thought the actor who played him was majorly hot. Marshall went on, "Some people trying to sell us stuff, some people who want money, and . . . whatever this is. Oh, it's for me." He opened the envelope from Chicago.

He'd forgotten *Playboy*'s editorial offices lived there. The rabbit logo on the letterhead reminded him in a hurry. He read the letter. The farther he went, the more his jaw dropped.

"You okay?" Kelly sounded anxious. "You look kinda green around the gills."

"They're . . . They're . . ." Marshall had to try three times before he could get it out. "*Playboy*'s gonna buy 'Almost Sunset.' Holy crap! I mean, holy crap!"

"That's awesome! Freaking awesome!" Kelly hurried over and hugged him. "What are they giving you? *Playboy* pays good, doesn't it?"

"They're . . ." Again, Marshall had to try more than once before he could talk straight. "It says they're gonna pay me ten thousand bucks. That's their standard rate for a short story, they say."

This time, Kelly didn't squee. She let out a war whoop instead. Marshall felt grateful. She was acting out what he felt. He was too stunned to take care of it for himself. Even in these times of galloping inflation, ten grand was real money.

She hugged him one more time. Then she poked him in the ribs, which made him jump. "Who knows?" she said, mischief in her voice. "Maybe the centerfold for the issue your story runs in will be cute, too. Like a cherry on top of your sundae—only she probably lost her cherry a long time ago."

"Meow," Marshall said.

Kelly stuck out her tongue at him. Then she said, "Call your dad. You'll make the buttons pop off his shirt, and he could use some of that right now."

"Things at the cop shop are better than they used to be," Marshall said. "Half the force doesn't hate him for making Pitcavage snuff himself any more, and Pitcavage isn't sneaking around killing old ladies, either."

"I know, and I'm glad," Kelly answered. "But it's still a slog, and he's not as happy there as he was before things hit the fan. Trust me—he'll be glad to get good news from home."

"Okay." Marshall hadn't noticed Dad any glummer than usual, but he just lived with him—he wasn't married to him.

Noticing stuff like that was what wives were for. Husbands, too, Marshall supposed vaguely.

He took out his cell phone and smiled to discover he had bars. If he did, his father would, too, so he called Dad's cell. "What's going on, Marshall?" Colin Ferguson asked without preamble. Dad always hated beating around the bush.

Well, this time Marshall could be equally brusque: "I just sold a story to *Playboy*."

"Hey!" Dad did sound pleased, more pleased than Marshall had expected him to. Then, predictably, he asked how much they paid. When Marshall told him, he let out a low whistle. "Even with the dollar as messed up as it is, that comes pretty close to eating money, doesn't it?"

"Sure feels like it to me," Marshall agreed.

"And you know what else is cool about that?" Dad asked.

"What?" Marshall said, perhaps incautiously.

His father's chuckle wasn't quite a *mwahaha*, but it came close. "A good-sized chunk of that check'll be mine, to make up for the lean times."

"Oh," Marshall said, and then, "Right." He sounded as unenthusiastic as he was.

Dad laughed again, more wholesomely this time. "Believe me, the thing I hope for most is that you make enough to move out on your own and quit paying me rent. I've told you that before. I don't mind having you around—don't get me wrong. But if you do well enough to move out, you're really making it."

"Uh-huh." Marshall nodded, which his father couldn't see. Up until he opened that letter from Chicago, making enough to snag a place of his own had been no more than something he wished for when he got good and baked. Now . . . Now it suddenly felt possible, if not too likely.

"Way to go, son. I'm going to spend the rest of the day bragging on you," Dad said. "It's a lot more fun than grilling a wife-beater and an armed-robbery suspect—you'd better believe it is."

Marshall did believe it. He said his good-byes and powered down the phone. He didn't leave it on all the time, the way he had before the eruption. When you weren't sure when or if you could charge it again, you stretched the battery as far as it would go. You stretched everything as far as it would go, and then a little further besides.

One of these days, Marshall knew, he would make like an old fart—no, he'd be an old fart—and go on about the days before the supervolcano blew, and how there'd been so much of everything and it never snowed in L.A. And all the people under forty-five, the ones who'd grown up after the eruption—his half-sister and half-brother, for instance—would wish he'd shut the fuck up.

"Was he happy?" Kelly asked. Sure enough, she worried about Dad in ways that just never crossed Marshall's mind. Wifey ways, whatever those were.

"Y'know, I think he was," Marshall said. Had his own mother worried about his father in wifey ways? Much as he didn't want to—he was still furious at Mom for walking out—he supposed she had. She'd been ready to bite nails in half when Mike Pitcavage got named chief instead of Dad. *Yeah, and look how that turned out*, Marshall thought.

"Cool!" Kelly sounded happy herself, happy because Dad was happy. That was pretty cool in and of itself. Then she found another question, a sly one: "What will your buds think when they find out you sold *Playboy* something?"

"It's a ginormous check—I mean, it will be," Marshall said. "They'll like that. So will I." And if anybody paid quick, it was likely to be the rabbit magazine. A lot of publishers seemed to like—or to need—to play catch-me-if-you-can before they finally coughed up cash. He went on, "Otherwise . . . I dunno. I mean, I don't think any of 'em read it or anything. It's not, like, the latest thing."

"No, I guess not." Kelly's voice was dry. You could find much nastier babes in other magazines. And, when the power worked, online you could find anything anyone was weird or horny enough to imagine.

But hey, it was still a big market even if it wasn't the latest thing. The best writers from all over the world—well, the English-speaking world—busted their balls to get into it. They were all after those juicy checks. Writers could be as greedy as anybody else when they got the chance, and *Playboy* was one of the few places that gave it to them.

Now one of those checks had fallen into Marshall's lap. He shook his head. That wasn't right. *I earned that one*, he thought. *I wrote a story good enough so they pulled it out of the slush pile and bought it.*

"Wow!" he said as that slowly sank in. "Maybe I really am gonna be a writer after all."

"Maybe you are," Kelly said. "What would be so funny about that?"

"Only everything," Marshall answered. "I was just using creative writing for a major to keep from graduating as long as I could. I never would've submitted anything if Professor What's-his-name—Bolger, that's who he was—hadn't made everybody in his dumb class do it. You could've knocked me over with a feather the first time somebody bought something."

"Okay, you fell into it by accident," Kelly said. "But once you found out you were good at it, why shouldn't you take it as far as you can?"

"No reason . . . I guess. But if somebody'd told me Bolger would make us send our stuff out to an editor, I never would've signed up for his class." Marshall shook his head again, this time in wonder. A slow smile spread across his face. How totally green would Vanessa turn when she found out?

Colin Ferguson and Gabe Sanchez pedaled toward the scene of the crime. Gabe puffed away while he did it. Other riders and people on the sidewalk stared at a guy smoking a cigarette while he rode a bike, as if Gabe cared what other people did.

"You know what we need on these goddamn things?" Sanchez said, shifting the cigarette to the side of his mouth, tough-guy style, so he wouldn't have to lift a hand from the handlebars to take it out.

"Slaves to do the pedaling would be nice. I'm getting old." Colin was joking, and then again he wasn't. Gas shortages and astronomical prices had made pedicabs a popular way to get around for people who didn't feel like hauling themselves from where they were to where they needed to be.

He startled a laugh out of Gabe, who said, "Now that you mention it, so am I. But that's not what I was thinking of. Naw— what we need on these fuckers is a light bar and a siren so people will know we're cops."

"You don't figure maybe they suspect?" Colin said dryly, and Gabe laughed again. Many, many bicycles were on the streets. Except during commuters' hours, hardly any of them were ridden by middle-aged men in suits. If you looked closely at Gabe, you could see the bulge under his left shoulder. *If you look at me, you'll see the same goddamn thing*, Colin thought. Designers had talked about the invisible shoulder holster for more than a hundred years. The next guy who actually made one would be the first.

They both turned right from Hesperus onto Reynoso Drive. That was San Atanasio's most important street for businesses and shops. In the early days of the city, San Atanasio Boulevard, farther south, had filled that niche—which was why the city hall and the police station and the library were all either on or near San Atanasio Boulevard.

"If it wasn't for all the work I'm doing, though, I wouldn't mind this so much, you know?" Sanchez said. "You see the town better on a bike than you do from a car."

"You see it slower, that's for sure," Colin said. People on the sidewalk weren't just blurs. You noticed faces, clothes, attitudes. But you did take longer to get where you were going. With cell phones so unreliable, Colin and Gabe also carried little two-way radios in an inside jacket pocket. If they needed backup, they could call the station.

The bicycles were straight out of 1910. The radios were twenty-first-century gadgets. The mix, and using the one to make the other more effective, was a small part of the report Colin had done for Malik Williams. The new chief liked the report, or said he did. How much he'd use . . . Colin didn't worry about too much. Some of it struck him as plain, obvious common sense. Some was his own more left-handed thinking.

What Williams would make of that, Colin didn't worry about too much, either. The absolute worst thing the new chief could do was drive him into retirement. Colin didn't want that to happen, but it wouldn't be nearly so bad as if he'd had to quit because Mike Pitcavage killed himself. He'd go home, he'd enjoy his wife and his tiny daughter, and he'd cultivate his garden. You could do worse.

Meanwhile, he pedaled past the big B of A near Sword Beach. The gas stations at the corner of Sword Beach and Reynoso all flew the red flags that meant they had no fuel. Those flags were ragged and faded—they flew most of the time.

Past Sword Beach to the east was a shopping center a bit spiffier than a strip mall. The anchor store, such as it was, was a Vons supermarket that had been there since dirt. Colin and Louise and now Kelly all got their groceries there. The Vons was the place that had been knocked over. The armed robber had blown a plate-glass window to hell and gone; sparkling shards littered the concrete walk out front. A middle-aged woman who could only be the manager waited there for the cops to show up.

She gave her name as Rudabeh Barazani—Iranian, Colin guessed. One more ingredient in the SoCal ethnic stew. Her English had a ghost of an accent, no more. "Anybody get hurt?" Colin asked.

"No, thank heaven," she said.

"Okay, that's good," he said, both because it was true and to calm her down—although she didn't seem too flustered. "Tell me what happened, then."

"A man filled one of our hand-carry baskets with cans of hash and chicken and tuna. He filled it as full as he could. When he got to a checker, he did not take the items out. He tried to set the basket in front of her instead. When she asked him to take the cans out so she could see how many there were, he pulled a gun instead and told her to put all the money in the register into a bag. Since we have no bags any more, she just handed it to him. He left with the money and the canned goods, and fired a shot through the window to make sure no one would try to chase him."

"You have a description, ma'am?" Gabe Sanchez asked.

"A white man, or maybe Hispanic, in his fifties," Ms. Barazani said. "Medium-sized. Gray hair, getting thin here and here"—she sketched hair drawing back at the temples on her own forehead—"and a gray mustache and chin beard."

"Clothes?" Colin asked.

"Denim jacket. Khakis. Nikes."

Colin sighed to himself. You couldn't get more ordinary than that. He said, "I wouldn't want to lug a basket full of cans real far, not on foot I wouldn't. What kind of getaway vehicle did he use?"

"He had a tricycle with a wire basket big enough to hold our plastic one," the store manager replied. "A woman said she saw him turn from Reynoso north onto Sword Beach. I didn't see that. I was trying to take care of poor Carmela. She was the checker, and she was very upset."

"Somebody sticks a gun in your face, you usually are," Colin agreed. "We'll need to talk to her, though, and to the woman who saw which way the robber went. Gabe, radio the station and let 'em know what we have. I'll interview the witnesses."

"You got it." Sanchez drew the walkie-talkie out of his jacket pocket.

The checker had pulled herself together. Her story wasn't much different from the one Rudabeh Barazani had told. Colin discovered he couldn't talk to the gal who'd watched the getaway—she'd already gone home. But she was a regular at that Vons. The manager gave him her name and address. It wasn't far. He wondered whether he ought to go over there after he and Gabe finished up here.

Virtue triumphed over laziness. He was heading toward the witness' house, with Gabe puffing along beside him in more than one sense of the word, when his inside-pocket, not-quite-wrist radio squawked for attention. He took it out. "Ferguson," he said as he eased to a stop. "What's going on?"

"We just nabbed your armed-robbery suspect," answered the dispatcher back at the station.

"Oh, yeah? That's what I call service," Colin said. "How'd it happen?"

"A patrolman on a bicycle on Hesperus north of Braxton Bragg spotted an individual matching the description we sent out on a trike with canned goods in a basket in back. He made the arrest after a short pursuit."

"I bet it was short." Colin wouldn't have wanted to try to outspeed a bike on a trike, especially when the trike was weighted down with loot. "Any trouble with the suspect? I know he was armed."

"No, Captain, no trouble," the dispatcher replied. "Our man had the drop on the perp. The guy didn't try anything stupid."

"Roger that. Good," Colin said. "Okay, Gabe and I will come back to the station to question him. The witness I was going to talk to can wait. Out."

"We turn around?" Gabe said.

"We turn around." Colin nodded.

"Well, shit." Gabe ground out his cigarette under the sole of his shoe. "If we'd headed straight back from Vons, we'd be a lot closer than we are now."

"Piss and moan, piss and moan," Colin said. They grinned at each other. Then they rode back to the police station.

The suspect was already there. The dispatcher had sent out a black-and-white to bring him—and the canned goods, and the cash—in. His name was Victor Jennings. He was fifty-nine years old. He lived only a couple of blocks from where he'd been caught. Another five minutes, and he would have made a clean getaway. He had no previous criminal record.

In the interrogation room, he looked angry and embarrassed and hopeless, all at the same time. Colin had seen variations of those expressions on too many faces in that room. After Jennings waived his Miranda rights, Colin asked him, "Why'd you do it, Mr. Jennings?"

"Why d'you think?" Jennings sounded hopeless, too. "I was hungry. I was broke. Haven't hardly worked since that goddamn thing blew up. Had to get me food some kind of way. So I figured, what the hell, and I went and did it."

If he'd just stolen food, they might well have turned him loose. They might even have let him keep the canned meat. Even in cases like his, where the hungry thief pulled a gun to get what he wanted, juries often didn't care to convict. Too many jurors were either in the same boat themselves or had friends and relatives who were. But ... "Why did you have the checker empty out the register, too?"

Jennings shrugged. "Like I said before, what the hell? I was already a robber. After I ate what I took, I could buy some more food with the money." His mouth twisted. "You guys'll be feeding me now, won't you?"

Colin and Gabe looked at each other. The way things were these days, nobody at any level of government wanted more than the barest number of prisoners locked up. Feeding and guarding prisoners cost money, and money had been as hard to come by as work since the eruption. After a longish pause, Gabe answered, "That's not up to us. That's up to the DA."

Although Colin didn't blame him for passing the buck, he did add, "We'll have to hold you till the DA makes up his mind—a few days, anyhow."

Victor Jennings brightened. "A few days my belly won't be scraping my backbone, anyway. I know it won't be fancy food, but there oughta be enough of it." He went off to his cell a happy man.

"What does it say about us when somebody wants to get locked up so he can eat?" Colin asked when he was gone.

"Says we're fucked, man," Gabe told him, and he couldn't very well argue.

VIII

$\mathbb{N}$aked on the bed with Vanessa, Bronislav Nedic stretched luxuriantly. As the afterglow faded, she found herself chilly. He seemed plenty warm. Maybe that was because of the fur on his hair and belly: no surprise, what with how thick his beard grew. Vanessa didn't mind it; she found hairy guys more a turn-on than the reverse. Or maybe he seemed warm enough just *because* he was a guy. Something was wrong with half the human race's thermostats, though which half's had sparked arguments for thousands of years.

He rolled toward her. Did he feel like another round? She wasn't sure she did. But instead of reaching for her, he asked a question out of the blue: "Do you ever finish story you started during last winter?" His English was excellent, but he often left out articles.

"Huh?" Vanessa said brilliantly—no, she hadn't expected that.

Bronislav let his patience show. "Do you ever finish story?" he repeated, and went on, "I see—I saw—in *Playboy* story your brother wrote. Pretty good story. Not great story, but pretty good."

"Mrmm." Vanessa ground her teeth instead of answering. She thought it was a dumb story. She thought almost everything her kid brother wrote was dumb, so that came as no great surprise. She didn't mind that Bronislav had looked at the *Playboy*— and, no doubt, not just for the story. Men *were* going to look at women, and that was all there was to it. She did mind that Marshall had got a fat check from the magazine. It griped her belly as much as bad fish would have.

"You do not finish story." This time, Bronislav was telling, not asking.

"Well, what if I didn't?" Vanessa flared. "I didn't like the way it was going, so I put it away till I figured out how to fix it." She hadn't figured it out yet. She hadn't tried for a while. When she had time, she had no inspiration. When she wanted to do something with it, she was too busy.

"You should finish," Bronislav said. "If your brother can do, you also can do." Since Vanessa was convinced that was true, she found herself nodding. But then Bronislav asked, "Do you—will you—let me see what you do so far?"

She didn't want to. Then he'd see she hadn't done much more since the last time he looked at it. But if she told him no, she'd also have to tell him why not. Or, more likely, she wouldn't have to. You didn't need to belong to the FBI to work that one out for yourself. And so, with no great warmth, she said, "Um, okay."

Naked, he padded out to the dinette and brought the laptop back to bed. Since the power was on, he plugged it in. Then he said, "You find story for me. I have no GPS to find where you put things on your computer."

The way she organized her hard disk seemed perfectly logical to her. She quickly called up the story, not wanting Bronislav to see it lived in the same folder as one called "Strange Fish," which she also hadn't come close to finishing. Feckless lunges at fiction. Marshall could get things done, get them out, and get them sold, goddammit. Why couldn't she? She didn't know why. All she knew was that she didn't.

She felt nakeder while he was reading her prose than she had with him on top of her a few minutes earlier. Sex came naturally and, for guys, just about always had a payoff at the end. Writing, on the other hand, was almost the definition of an unnatural act.

He gave the screen his usual close attention. He didn't do anything halfway, which was one of the things that attracted her. She was like that herself, even if she'd never crawled under barbed wire clutching a Kalashnikov.

When he got done, he asked, "Why do you not go on more?"

"I couldn't find a way to end it that I liked," Vanessa said. That had the virtue of being at least partly true. The rest of the truth was that her enthusiasm for the story had dribbled away once she got past her opening burst. Sitting at the laptop till beads of blood came out on your forehead seemed much too much like work.

Bronislav made three suggestions. They were quick and neat and close together, like a burst from his assault rifle when he was fighting the Fascist Croats. Vanessa was sure one of them wouldn't work, but the other two easily could. The only thing wrong with them was that she hadn't thought of them herself.

"Maybe I'll try one of those," she said after a pause she hoped wasn't too awkward.

"Or do something you think of. Only *do*!" Bronislav said. "Your brother does, so why not you?"

Yeah, why not me? she wondered. Envy of Marshall was part of what had got her writing, or trying to write, in the first place. The other part was hating the crap she had to deal with at the widget works. She was still jealous of Marshall. She still hated the crap Nick Gorczany and the other linguistically challenged nerds at the widget works dropped on her desk.

But writing stories—all the way through, from beginning to

end—proved harder than it looked, at least for her. It wasn't a way out, a way to keep from having to go in to the widget works every day. That was what she wanted. That was what she needed, before dealing with idiots forty hours a week plus overtime drove her postal.

Could she explain that to Bronislav? She felt herself yawning. Not tonight, she couldn't. She was too damn sleepy. She went to the bathroom and brushed her teeth. Bronislav took the hint. He shut down the computer, made his own ablutions, and came to bed with her. She turned off the light.

When she woke earlier than she wanted to the next morning, Bronislav was sitting up beside her. His face, illuminated from below, looked scary—faces weren't meant to be lit that way. But the way he was lit wasn't what bothered Vanessa. "What are you looking at?" she asked sharply—she didn't want him or anybody else snooping on her computer.

"Oh, good morning. I am sorry if I bother you," he answered. "I am reading your story again. I managed to find it, you see." He turned the screen her way. Sure enough, there was the story, or as much of it as she'd done. "You need to write ending. It will be outstanding. It will be amazing." That was his all-purpose word of praise.

Vanessa's temper cooled almost as fast as it had kindled. That he liked the piece so much helped to relax her. Right this minute, she was sure he liked it better than she did.

"Since you are awake, I will make for us breakfast," Bronislav said.

"Okay!" Vanessa knew she sounded eager. With reason—she was. He could do outstanding things—amazing things—with the junk in her icebox. They might not be illegal or immoral, but they were sure as hell fattening. She didn't care even a little bit. They were also delicious.

This time, he got dressed before he went into the kitchen.

He'd be messing around with hot grease, after all. Spatters could get you in some of the most unkindest places if you let them.

Vanessa lay in bed for a few minutes, listening to the sounds of cookery. Listening to someone else cook was a lot more fun than doing it yourself. When savory smells started wafting back to the bedroom, she got up, put on a thick terrycloth robe, and went out to see what kind of magic Bronislav was working this morning.

It involved an egg or two, torn-up bread, a little bit (only a little bit, for flavor) of sausage, some leftover veggies, and spices in the pantry she'd forgotten she had. "What do they call this in Serbian?" she asked when she could stop inhaling it.

"I don't know." His powerful shoulders rose and fell in a shrug. "It is not Serb dish. Oh, maybe spices are Serb-style, but it is just what I do with what I find. I hope you do not get mad, but is poor-people food. It stretches what you have as far as it can."

"I'm not mad. It's great!" Vanessa tried to stretch what she had as far as she could, too. Food didn't turn out so tasty when she cooked, though. She got her attitude toward cooking from her mother, she supposed. And Louise Ferguson never aimed any higher than *Well, let's get it over with*. Vanessa went on, "You really ought to open up your restaurant. The place'd be packed, and they could roll the customers out after they got done, 'cause everybody'd be round as a bowling ball."

Bronislav's long face seemed mournful even when he was happy. Now he looked like a bearded Mask of Tragedy. "I want to try this. I am sick of driving truck back and forth, back and forth. But what can I do?" He spread his hands, both hard palms up. "I have not money to open restaurant. Not close, even."

That might have been a hint. Vanessa realized as much. If she'd had more money herself, she would have thought about helping to back him. But she was still trying to climb out of the hole the supervolcano had dug for her. Everything she'd owned before the eruption was buried in ash in Denver—except for her poor cat, who'd surely died in Garden City, Kansas. She had to regather the Stuff that made a life: an old end table here, the sec-ondhand laptop there, some used books somewhere else. She saved when she could—at a bank with a nationwide presence, not a crappy little local credit union like the Colorado one that had vanished and taken her funds with its dead computers—but she still lived from paycheck to paycheck a lot of the time. Bronislav's *poor-people food* rang a painful bell with her.

When she didn't say she'd fork over a few thousand smack-ers, he sighed. "Maybe one of these days. Maybe one of these years," he said. "I look for chance. I look for money. Could be I find it."

"I hope you do." Vanessa wouldn't have minded marrying him and helping make a go of a restaurant. She supposed it would involve moving down to San Pedro, which had the largest concentration of people from the ex-Yugoslavia. Well, that might not be so bad. It wasn't as if she were too close to her mother, or to her father and his obnoxious new wife and brat, or to the little brother who had the gall to sell things.

One sign she was serious about Bronislav was that she washed dishes after breakfast. She hated washing dishes. Sometimes they piled up in the sink till they started getting stinky and she had to do something about them. But Bronislav was grimly neat, in the way some veterans were (Dad had a bit of the same disease). The hurt look in his eyes when he saw a mess got her moving better than a top sergeant's chewing-out could have.

When the power was on, and when the gas was, the apart-ment building had hot water. Doing the dishes with it was easier than without it. And, after the dishes got done, she and Bronislav took long, lazy showers—Hollywood showers, her father would have called them. Once the showers were finished, they found something else to do with their morning together.

Another winter in Guilford. Every one seemed harder to get through than the one before it. As far as Rob Ferguson could tell, every one *was* harder to get through than the one before. They kept on getting colder, something he wouldn't have imagined possible after the first couple. And moose on the hoof and pines in the ground got scarcer and farther away every year.

Things would have been even more rugged if people hadn't kept giving up and moving south. Maine north and west of the Interstate probably couldn't still support the population that had lived here when the supervolcano went. But a lot of those people had gone, too. The new winters wore down even Mainers. And some people froze to death every winter, too.

"People shouldn't freeze here, dammit," Dick Barber said at a town meeting after such an unfortunate family had been found. "Back when there was a Red Army, they taught their men to get through a Russian winter night in the woods with only the greatcoat on their back—no fire or anything. If they could do it then, we should be able to do it now in our own houses."

Plenty of people in Guilford wore surplus greatcoats from the former Soviet Union and the countries of the late Warsaw Pact. They weren't new, but they were cheap and warm—a good combination. Barber had one, and often used it.

He was universally noticed in town, but not universally beloved. Like Rob's father, he had a habit of saying what was on his mind and letting other people pick up the pieces—or go after him with a two-by-four. One of his unadmirers called, "Do you know how to pull this stunt yourself, or are you just blowing hot air again?"

"Dave, if I could reliably blow hot air, I'd be the most popular man this side of the Interstate," Barber answered, which got enough of a laugh to make Mayor McCann rap for order from the pulpit of the Episcopal church. When order returned, the proprietor of the Trebor Mansion Inn went on, "Since I'm not, I probably don't. But I've read about how to do it, so I suppose I know."

Dave ran a junk shop, which made him both literally and metaphorically a man of parts in Guilford these days. He was lean and graying, with a blade of a nose. "Ayuh," he said, which meant he'd been born in these parts. "Then you won't mind doin' it for real, to show folks you mebbe for once know what you're goin' on—and on, and on—about."

Several expressions chased one another across Dick Barber's face. None of them seemed what you'd call happy. Rob could see why. If he said he didn't want to do it, who would take him seriously after that? If he tried and failed, the Trebor Mansion Inn would be under new management.

But his voice showed none of what he had to be thinking. All he said was, "You'll allow me a fur hat, too? The Ivans have them as part of their winter uniform—which probably means they wear them year-round these days." Guilford did a good impersonation of Siberia these days. What Siberia was like . . . *It's, like, cold, man*, Rob thought.

"You can wear a fur hat. You can wear your warm boots, too," Dave said. He seemed amazed Barber had taken his dare with so little fuss. "You sure you know what you're doin', Dick?"

"Of course I am," Barber answered easily. "And if I turn out to be wrong, I promise I'll do my best to haunt you." He laughed a spectral laugh better than any Rob would have guessed he had in him.

After the town meeting broke up, they agreed he would show off—that was the only way to put it—in the strip of forest that still ran along the southern bank of the Piscataquis. They hadn't cut that down because people hunted the birds and squirrels which used those trees. The test would take place in two nights' time.

"If a blizzard comes in then, you don't gotta do it." Dave didn't want blood, even frozen blood, on his hands.

"Thanks for your generosity," Barber said.

"*Do* you know what you're doing?" Rob asked him as he started back to the Inn.

"I will by night after next," Barber told him. "You can bet your life on that. Why not? I'm betting mine."

"You weren't . . . just making that stuff up about the Russian soldiers and their coats, were you?" Rob asked hesitantly. Maybe because Barber had experience in politics, every once in a while he would exaggerate. He didn't do it often, but Rob had seen it happen.

This time, though, he raised his right hand as if taking an oath. "Not guilty, your Honor," he intoned. "Not guilcup, even, if you remember your Pythons. I read it in a book by a defector. A Red Army man froze to death, and a general who'd been a front-line junior officer in the war against Hitler got pissed off when he found out about it. Weren't they teaching the troops anything any more? He went out in his greatcoat to show the rest of the brass it really could be done, and then they went back to teaching the draftees how to do it."

"Sweet," Rob said. "Does the book tell how to do it, then?"

All of a sudden, Dick Barber didn't sound so sure of himself. "Er—I'm going back to the Inn to find out. Been a while since I read it, and I don't remember."

"Sweet," Rob said once more, sardonically this time.

"Well, I'll find out one way or the other," Barber said. "If this were the good old days, I'd go online and Google it. Or if I lived somewhere like Florida, I could still—probably—go online and Google it. Of course, if I lived somewhere like Florida, I wouldn't need to worry about freezing to death in a snowstorm. I don't think I would, anyhow."

"Florida," Rob said in a wondering voice. When Maine's laughable excuse for a summer started, he could go there if he wanted to. But he couldn't imagine wanting to. Guilford was home now, and his horizons had contracted around it. Florida might as well have been another planet, not another state. Some memories lingered, though. Not quite apropos of nothing, he went on, "I dreamt about guacamole the other night."

"Guacamole." Barber sighed—the word sparked nostalgia in him, too. "There used to be a Mexican and Italian place down on Highway 7, between here and Newport. It wasn't *good* Mexican food, not with the ingredients they could get in the middle of Maine, but still. . . . They've gone under now."

"I remember driving past that place when we first came up here," Rob said. "Justin was driving. Right after we went by, a fox ran across the road. I'd never seen one before—I'd sure never almost turned one into roadkill before."

"Not something we need to worry about much any more," Barber said. "If by any chance my greatcoat doesn't do its job, I won't get squashed. You can use me for a fence post till I thaw out. The way things are, that should be quite a while from now."

"Heh." Rob's chuckle sounded uneasy even to him. Most of the time, Dick Barber knew what he was doing. Most of the time. When he didn't, the results could be interesting—as in the Chinese curse.

It wasn't a blizzard two nights later, but it was snowing again: dry, powdery stuff that stung and then numbed any skin it touched. The mercury read eleven below. It could have been worse. Rob had seen a mercury thermometer freeze, a new experience he could have done without.

On the appointed night, Barber looked like something out of *Red Dawn* if *Red Dawn* had been filmed in Nome rather than the Lower Forty-eight. He had a fur cap with earflaps, a wool Navy watch cap under it, a thick wool sweater with a denim jacket over it and his Red Army greatcoat over that, jeans (probably with long johns underneath, but Rob didn't know that for sure), two pairs of wool socks, and L.L. Bean winter boots.

Pointing down at his feet, he said, "They're what worries me. I don't think those boots are as warm as real Russian *valenki*."

Dave the junk-shop man surveyed him and said, "I expect you've made your point, Dick. You don't got to go through with it if you don't have a mind to."

"Damn right I'm going through with it," Barber answered. "I may as well. Pulling off all this shit would take me half the night anyway."

"Don't be a hero," Rob told him, wondering how many times his father had given testosterone-fueled young cops the same advice. "If you feel too cold—or if parts of you stop feeling anything at all—for Christ's sake come on back and warm up."

"Who appointed you my mommy?" Dick Barber inquired. No matter how cold it was, Rob's cheeks felt on fire. Barber thumped him and Dave on the back with a mittened right hand, then stumped across the bridge over the Piscataquis. He quickly vanished into snow and darkness.

Rob rounded on the junk-shop man. "You and your goddamn big mouth."

"I'm not the only fella around here who has one," Dave answered. "Still and all, I got to say I didn't reckon he'd take me up on it like this. I figured he was all talk, and I'd shut him up for a while." He kicked at the snow under his own booted feet. "Hope he comes back. Guilford'd be a boringer place without him—not that I'd say so to his face, mind."

"Right," Rob said wearily. He'd seen more than he ever wanted of small-town squabbles and feuds here. He reflected that

Dick Barber wouldn't have said anything good to Dave's face, either. Feuds and squabbles ran both ways.

Even after he went back to the apartment he shared with Lindsey, he didn't sleep much. The night seemed very long. In this season, at this latitude, the night *was* very long. It would be even longer in Russia. Those Red Army men had lived. Dick Barber . . . No, Rob didn't sleep much.

In his own warmest clothes, he hurried to the bridge at the first hint of twilight. More snow lay underfoot; as he slogged through it, he wondered if he should have put on snowshoes. He wasn't surprised to see Dave making his best speed toward the bridge, too.

"He didn't come in during the night, did he?" Rob called. The junk-shop man shook his head. Rob swore under his breath. Dick Barber was somewhere in the trees on the south bank of the Piscataquis, then. Where? No way to tell; snow and breeze would have swallowed his tracks. The bridge looked as if no one had walked across it for a thousand years.

Barber was somewhere in the trees, all right. But as man or fur-capped icicle? *Did* he know what he was doing? Rob hurried over the bridge, Dave at his heels. Several other people who'd been at the town meeting followed them. Some were getting down bets on how they'd find Dick Barber. The odds were against him.

Rob really wished for snowshoes on the far bank of the river. The going there was heavier, and the snow thicker. A jay screeched at him from the top of a pine. *Why don't its feet freeze?* Rob wondered. Somehow, the bird had got through the frigid night without a Red Army greatcoat to keep it warm.

"Dick!" Rob called. "You there, Dick?"

The others going through the narrow strip of trees with him also took up the call. "You there, Dick?" they chorused. If he hadn't known what he was doing, they might not find him till the snow melted, if it ever did.

No sooner had that thought crossed Rob's mind than he saw a boiling and heaving in the drift not ten feet ahead of him. Dick Barber stood up, so covered in white that he made a distinctly snowy abominable man.

"It's alive!" Rob shouted, as if a Hollywood Tesla coil had just activated a monster. Then, while the others rushed toward him, he asked Dick the obvious question: "How the hell are you?"

"Cold. Hungry," Barber answered. "I don't think I'm frostbitten anywhere, though. It wasn't much fun, and I hardly got any sleep. Hey, Dave!"

"Ayuh?" the junk-shop man said in an unwontedly small voice.

"Fuck you."

"And your granny," Dave replied, but his heart didn't seem in it.

"Now I'm going across to Caleb's Kitchen for some ham and eggs and hot tea," Barber said. The tea would be nasty; it was brewed from burnt grain and local leaves. But it would be hot. Anyone who'd just spent a night out in the snow was entitled to something hot, by God.

And, by God, Barber had proved his point. The luckless family that froze hadn't known what to do. No good deed would go unpunished, of course. Since Barber did know how to survive in horrible conditions, he'd have to show other people the tricks. Rob hoped they wouldn't test their new knowledge the same way he had.

The Great Plains ran a long way west from Wayne, Nebraska. They ran a long way north, too. Bryce Miller was convinced that, with nothing in the way to slow it down, the wind doing its goddamnedest to blow straight through him had got its running start right at Santa Claus' house.

It wasn't snowing just this minute, only blowing. He cast a curious eye heavenward, wondering whether he'd see any elves tumbling by up there. But no. Santa must have put rocks in their pockets or something. Nice to know good Saint Nick was up for emergencies.

Nice to know the wind is making your brain freeze up, Bryce thought. Along with half a dozen other shivering people, he waited for the bus to come and take them back to town from the Wayne State campus. The sun shone pale. Even though it shone, the sky was closer to gray than to blue. How many years would it be before real blue skies came back?

However many years that would be, Bryce sure hoped it wouldn't be too many more before the bus showed up. Otherwise, he would turn into a Brycicle. To his relief, the bus kept its schedule. His breath still smoked inside, but that wasn't too bad. Compared to what he'd just escaped, it felt like Havana in there.

As he walked from the closest bus stop in Wayne to his apartment building, he did some muttering he couldn't do once he got there. Susan wasn't happy, and he didn't see what to do about it. If she hadn't been happy with him, he might have figured out some way to make things better. But that wasn't the problem— not yet, anyhow.

The problem was, no college or university felt itself in dire need of an expert on Frederick II Hohenstaufen and the Holy Roman Empire in the twelfth and thirteenth centuries. Susan had taught a couple of adjunct courses at Wayne State. She'd taught a little online. She'd written three articles, expanding on chunks of her dissertation. Two had already come out, and the third was in the pipeline.

But she spent too much time staring at the computer monitor and the TV and the apartment walls. Wayne wasn't like Los Angeles; it didn't give you piles of things to do when you weren't productive or just needed to get away from the monitor and the TV and the walls for a little while.

Bryce had got a job. That was why they were here in Wayne. Susan had been so sure she could land one, too. She'd hoped she could land one someplace with a climate better than this one. There weren't a whole bunch of places with worse ones. There was Maine north of the Interstate, where Rob Ferguson had inexplicably washed up. And there was Minnesota. Shivering, Bryce tried not to think about Minnesota.

He clumped up the stairs to the apartment. If it looked as if he'd stay here a long time, he wanted to buy a house. They were ridiculously cheap by California standards. Well, more people lived, and wanted to live, in California than in Wayne, Nebraska. And the ashfall around here had been worse than in most of California, which didn't do real-estate prices any favors. Saving on an assistant professor's pay wasn't easy, but the only real vice he and Susan had was books. There were plenty of more expensive ones.

"Hey," Susan said when he walked in.

He went over and gave her a kiss. She squeezed him. No, nothing was wrong between them . . . yet. She slapped his hand away when he tried to reach under her sweatshirt, but she was smiling when she did it. "What's new?" he asked.

Too often, she said *Nothing* in a hopeless way that denied anything in Wayne, Nebraska, could possibly be new—and denied that anyone outside of Wayne, Nebraska, could possibly want a medievalist who'd specialized in the Holy Roman Empire. Today, though, she waved at the TV, which was on CNN. "They've finally passed the New Homestead Act," she said.

"Have they?" Bryce said. "Well, it's about time, don't you think?"

"Years past time," Susan replied. "But it's Congress and the President, so what can you do?"

"Nothing. Less than nothing." Politics had been dysfunctional at least as long as Bryce had been alive. It would have taken more than a supervolcano to change that. The President came from one party, but Congress belonged to the other. Whatever the President wanted, Congress hated. Whatever Congress wanted, the President was ready—eager—to veto.

When people proposed marching on Washington and impartially burning down the White House and the Capitol, they sounded less and less as if they were kidding. After a while, even That Yahoo in the White House and the Congresscritters took the hint. The New Homestead Act was some of the result.

That wasn't its real name, of course. The short version of its real name was "An Act to Facilitate the Resettlement of Lands Adversely Impacted by the Recent Supervolcano Eruption." The full version of its real name ran for a fat paragraph and had not a punctuation mark anywhere in sight. But the New Homestead Act pretty much described it. It let people gain title to property abandoned after the eruption by settling on it and improving it. That was the gist. The details had caused almost endless wrangling and produced a bill with the heft of a Tom Clancy novel.

"Do you really think it'll get people out of refugee camps?" Susan asked. Getting people out of camps was touted as the bill's main benefit. Millions—no one seemed sure just how many millions—of people had been stuck in camps since the supervolcano blew.

Before long, it became obvious that the refugee camps were doing for—or to—the United States what the gulags had done to Stalin's Soviet Union. They spread the pathologies of the prison system into the wider society. Maybe getting people out of them and onto the land would help turn back the clock. Maybe.

Bryce shrugged. "Mm . . . some people, I guess," he said judiciously. "But if you lived in a city or a town before the eruption, how much will you want forty acres and a mule?"

"It's supposed to help small towns, too," Susan said. "Those towns we biked through on the way to Ashfall State Park sure could use some help."

"Yeah. They could." Bryce couldn't very well quarrel with that. No one in his right mind could. But . . . "Those towns were dying on the vine before the eruption. Who knows whether anything will help them? And who knows whether people who've been in the camps for years will be good for anything once they get out and have to do stuff on their own again?"

Susan made a face at him. "You sound like Colin Ferguson, you know? We've got to try to put the country back together again."

"We've got to try, sure," Bryce said. "I think it's gonna be a while longer before the trying gets anywhere, though."

"You *do* talk like Colin Ferguson." Susan didn't sound as if she were paying him a compliment.

How much has *Vanessa's old man rubbed off on me?* Bryce wondered. It wasn't that they shared political opinions, because they didn't. But a cynical view of mankind and its follies . . . That, yes.

"Well, it doesn't make me a bad person," he said after a beat.

"Not too bad a person . . . I guess." There, Susan seemed to be giving him as much benefit of the doubt as she could.

The impeccably dressed, impeccably groomed talking head on CNN said, "It is hoped that the passage of the New Homestead Act will assist in the revitalization of eruption-ravaged states such as the Dakotas, Nebraska, Kansas, and Oklahoma."

He didn't say anything about Colorado or Idaho or Utah, and he *really* didn't say anything about Wyoming or Montana. The first three states were years away from being resettled. The western fringe of Montana remained more or less habitable. Nobody would be moving into the rest of it, or into any of Wyoming, for decades if not centuries to come. Big chunks of both those states, along with some of Idaho, had gone off the map in the most literal sense of the words.

"It would be nice to have people in those little towns and on some of the farms," Susan said.

"Yeah. It would." Bryce nodded. Things here were just bad. They weren't terrible—well, except for the weather. Of course, this was the eastern part of the ashfall zone, close to 750 miles from what had been Yellowstone. When you went farther west, things got worse and worse and worse again.

IX

D~r.~ Stan Birnbaum paused before plunging the novocaine-filled hypodermic into Colin Ferguson's gum. Kelly's father was in his mid-sixties, with gray hair, thick glasses, and a scraggly white mustache. He was heading for retirement, but he hadn't got there yet.

"Don't worry about a thing," he said reassuringly. "The building has a backup generator and a very smooth switching system. Even if the power in town goes out in the middle of things, the drill won't slow down even a little bit."

Colin cocked an eyebrow at his father-in-law. He very nearly cocked a snook at him, too. "Stan," he said, "I'd be happier if the drill weren't going at all. Then I wouldn't be getting this blinking root canal." He would have expressed himself in stronger terms, but Stan's assistant, a pretty young Asian woman, was in the room with them.

"Not going is good. Going fast is good—it doesn't hurt so much," the dentist told him. "Going not so fast . . . Going not so fast is why root canals used to have such a nasty reputation. Now open wide." With no great enthusiasm, Colin did. He clutched at the arms of the reclining chair as the hypodermic went home. Withdrawing it at last, Stan Birnbaum said, "That wasn't too bad, was it?"

"Depends which end of the needle you're on," Colin answered. His father-in-law chuckled. After a moment, Colin added, "I've had worse—I'll say that."

"Well, good. I'm a painless dentist—it didn't hurt me a bit," Stan said. Colin winced worse than he had when he got the shot. But he'd asked for it with his own crack. The dentist continued, "We'll give you a little while to get numb now. Come on, Ruby. Let's see how Mrs. Diaz is doing in room three."

"Okay, Dr. Stan," the assistant said. Out they went, leaving Colin alone with his thoughts and with a tongue that seemed more like a bolt of flannel with every passing second.

In due course, Stan Birnbaum reappeared. Dentistry resembled the Navy in its hurry-up-and-wait rhythms. Dr. Birnbaum poked Colin's gum with a sharp instrument. "Feel anything?" he asked.

"Only pressure—no pain," Colin answered—he knew the ropes. He'd been on antibiotics long enough that the sore tooth wasn't so bad, either.

"Let's get to work, then," the dentist said. In spite of all the modern technology, it wasn't what anyone this side of a dedicated masochist would have called fun. Still, Colin had been through plenty of bumpier rides in that chair. Stan Birnbaum knew his business, all right. Colin wouldn't have expected anything else from Kelly's father.

When the ordeal was over, Birnbaum gave him his marching orders: chew on the other side, and no strenuous exercise for a day. He also gave him a prescription for more Cleocin and one for Vicodin. "Drugging a cop, are you?" Colin said—thickly, because the left side of his tongue was still disconnected from his brain.

Dr. Birnbaum shrugged. "You don't have to take them. I've known macho guys and recovering addicts who got by on aspirin or ibuprofen. But these are better for pain, and they don't leave most people too blurry. The way things are nowadays, you're not likely to go driving while you're loaded, are you?"

"Nope," Colin said. Gas was around twenty-five bucks a gallon. The auto industry and all the ones related to it still hadn't started to recover from the eruption. Their collapse meant more hundreds of thousands out of work—and unable to afford even a motor scooter, never mind the tiny cars Detroit was still haplessly trying to sell. The only person Colin knew of who'd bought new wheels after the supervolcano blew was Vanessa's boss. The only reason he knew about Nick Gorczany was that Vanessa cussed him every chance she got. It sounded more like *After the revolution, we deal with swine like him* each time he heard it.

"All right, then. I'll call you tonight to see how you're doing." Stan didn't do that just because Colin had married Kelly. It was SOP for him. He was a damn good dentist, even if he did say so himself.

The building with the backup generator had a pharmacy on the ground floor. Colin filled both prescriptions there. He washed down one pill from each with a large apple juice. They told you to drink plenty of fluids (what else would you drink? rocks?) when you took Cleocin, and they meant it; the stuff would leave you nauseated for hours if it landed on an empty stomach.

That done, he walked to the bus stop to wait for the ride back to San Atanasio. Dr. Birnbaum's office was in Torrance, the biggest South Bay city. Kelly had grown up there. Torrance was . . . less strapped than San Atanasio, anyhow. It boasted the Del Amo mall, which it claimed was the second biggest in the country, after only the Mall of America. Since the Mall of America lay right outside subarctic Minneapolis, odds were pretty good the Del Amo mall was busier these days. *Busier* didn't mean *busy enough*, though.

He waited long enough that the Vicodin had kicked in before the northbound bus showed up. The bus ran late. Once he felt the pill, he cared less than he would have before. It distanced him from annoyance almost as much as it would distance him from pain once the novocaine wore off.

When the bus finally did show up, he climbed aboard and gave the driver six dollars—more thievery. He saw a Torrance police car and two civilian autos on the way back to San Atanasio. A few motor scooters, a Harley, bikes, trikes, pedicabs, skateboards, an honest-to-Pete horsedrawn buggy, Rollerblades . . . The streets were full of wheels, but they weren't full of engines. The pace of living had slowed down since the eruption. No one had wanted it to, but it had anyway.

He had to walk several blocks from the closest stop to the police station. Walk he did, hoping it wouldn't count as strenuous exercise. When he came in, Malik Williams was talking with the desk sergeant. The chief turned toward him and nodded, asking, "How'd it go?"

"I'll live. Like I told my father-in-law the dentist, I've had worse," Colin answered. Williams chuckled sympathetically. Colin went on, "Afraid I'll flunk a drug test for the next little while."

"Hey, I hear that," Williams said. "I had an implant done a couple of years ago—you know, where they stick a screw in your jaw and then mount a replacement tooth on top. The thing works great now, but you bet I was glad for the dope then."

"That's what the shit is for," the desk sergeant said. "The trouble is the people who get off on it."

"I'm a little buzzed right now," Colin said, "but I like scotch better."

"There you go," the sergeant agreed. "Something with some taste to it, not just a lousy pill."

"Uh-huh." Colin nodded, then glanced toward Malik Williams. "You need me for anything right now, boss?"

"No, no." The chief understood the question behind the question. "Go on to your desk, man. I bet you aren't real bouncy on your pins."

"Now that you mention it, no." Colin sketched a salute and headed towards a place where he could sit down. Between the root canal and the pain pill, the world felt less steady than it should have.

No sooner had he plopped his behind into his swivel chair than Gabe Sanchez came over to see how he was doing. Gabe smelled of cigarette smoke. Smokers always did, and hardly ever knew it. If you didn't light up, you knew they were around even before you saw them.

"So what's it like having your father-in-law drilling holes in your head?" Gabe asked.

"Just as much fun as it is with anybody else," Colin answered.

"You wouldn't want to go to him if you were giving Kelly grief," Gabe said.

"I didn't want to go to him today, but that stupid tooth wouldn't quit hurting," Colin said. "I'm just glad we've still got a decent dental plan. Otherwise, my bank account would've taken one in the teeth, too."

"Probably get wiped out the next time we have to talk contract with the city," Gabe said gloomily. He had too good a chance of being right. Every contract kept less than the one before. San Atanasio had been scuffling for money even in the good old days. Since the eruption, each year's budget turned into a dance with bankruptcy.

"Joys of being a civil servant," Colin said. "And if you believe that, I'll tell you another one."

"Save your breath," Gabe said. "I already know just how much fun this job is." He sighed. " 'Course, collecting unemployment's even more fun."

"You got that right." Colin shuffled through the papers on

his desk. After they found out who the South Bay Strangler was—and after that almost tore the department to pieces—everything else felt like an anticlimax.

Well, almost everything. He noticed a familiar name on a manila folder. Opening it, he read a carbon of a badly typed report a patrolman had submitted—one more place where old technology had more life to it than anyone would have dreamt before the eruption.

"How about that?" he said.

"How about what?" Gabe asked.

Colin tapped the folder with the nail of his right index finger. "Our old buddy, Victor Jennings, is back in business again."

"Oh, yeah?" Gabe sounded disgusted. The DA's office hadn't thought a jury would convict Jennings of armed robbery or assault with a deadly weapon, not when most of what he stole was food. So they'd told him *Go, and sin no more*. And go he did, but quit sinning he didn't.

"Yeah." Colin tapped the report again. "This time, he knocked over a check-cashing place on Hesperus. Probably would've made his getaway, too, if Jodie Boyer hadn't been coming by on her bike right then. She's the one who made the bust."

"Jodie's always had a pretty good bust," Gabe opined. Colin was inclined to agree with him . . . in a purely theoretical way, of course. He wouldn't have said so out loud, though. Gabe sailed closer to the breeze than he did. A crack like that could make Internal Affairs want to talk with you, and never mind whether you wanted to talk with them.

When he went out to lunch with Gabe, he ate soba noodles. Squishy was good right after you'd had a root canal. He hadn't been back to the office long when the root-canaled tooth loudly reminded him that, though the offending nerve was gone, it wasn't yet forgotten. His first Vicodin and the last of the novocaine chose the same time to wear off. He hurried to the water fountain to gulp another pain pill.

What would they do with Victor Jennings this time? Jennings had evidently decided that, if he couldn't work, he might as well steal. He'd have to get charged and tried and serve some kind of term this time . . . wouldn't he? Colin hoped so, but he wouldn't have bet anything that cost more than a McDonald's Happy Meal on it.

Nick Gorczany's chief accountant was a no-nonsense, short-haired woman named Mary Ann Flores. She was a dyke, and made no bones about it—the photos on her desk were all of her much more feminine partner. Vanessa Ferguson didn't care about that one way or the other. She did care that Mary Ann was the one who doled out the salary checks twice a month.

The head accountant set one on Vanessa's desk now. "Here you go," she said gruffly. It had nothing to do with her machismo. She gave Vanessa dubious looks because Vanessa wasn't corporate enough to suit her.

"Thanks." Vanessa let it go right there. Mary Ann was way too corporate to suit her. Mary Ann was also too gay to suit her, though she never would have admitted as much. She didn't care what people did in the bedroom. When they acted as if they wanted a medal for it, too . . . That got old fast.

No matter who brought it, the check was highly welcome. If not for the check, she wouldn't have had anything to do with this miserable, stupid place. Maybe that also showed enough to make Mary Ann Flores suspicious of her.

She waited eagerly for the (battery-powered) clock on the wall to announce that it was quitting time. Banks stayed open later than usual Friday nights, but she'd still have to hope the bus ran on schedule. If it was late, she'd have to go in on Saturday morning, which would be a pain.

She hustled out as soon as she could, or even a couple of minutes sooner. If Mr. Gorczany and Ms. Flores didn't like it, too damn bad. She was still standing at the bus stop waiting when Gorczany drove by. She ground her teeth. After his recent adventures at the dentist's, her father would have told her that was a bad plan. She did it anyway.

The bus came five minutes late. Normally, no biggie. When she was trying to get to the bank on time . . . "Nice of you to join us," she snarled as she fed money into the slot. The driver just looked at her. He didn't get it. When you insulted somebody and it flew right over his head, weren't you wasting your time?

She hustled into the B of A on Reynoso Drive just before the security guard would have kept her out. She filled out the deposit form and went to the end of the line. Before the eruption, she'd hardly ever set foot in the bank. She'd done as much as she could on the computer. But with both power and the banks' servers erratic these days, dealing with genuine human beings worked better.

Better, but slower. The line was long, and crawled forward. Somebody at one of the tellers' stations had trouble with something, which bogged things down even more. *I might as well be at the post office*, she thought sourly, going nowhere fast.

She finally reached the front of the line, made her deposit, stuck some cash in her purse, and got the hell out of there. Then she had to wait for the bus that would take her not quite close enough to her apartment building. It ran late, too. Of course it did. It ran later than the other one had, as a matter of fact. And rain started coming down while she was walking from the stop to her building. So she was not a happy camper when she turned the key in the lobby mailbox.

A linen catalogue, a coupon from a new pizza place that had opened a few blocks away, a bank statement, her cell-phone bill. If the world were beige and concrete-gray all over, her mail would have fit in perfectly.

Shaking her head, she went on to her apartment. At least she didn't need to hassle with cooking. She'd splurged on Thai take-out the night before, and she kept enough ice in the refrigerator to make sure the leftovers would stay good even if the power had been off all day.

It was on now, so she heated herself some dinner. After she put the dishes in the sink, she sent Bronislav a text. He was some-where out on I-10, either hauling something back from L.A. or bringing something this way. She hadn't heard from him in a few days. She'd been beat after she got home from work, and her cell hadn't been working anywhere close to all the time.

The cell proved it was working now by making the almost-hiccup with which it announced an error message. "The fuck?" Vanessa said. She hadn't miskeyed Bronislav's number. She couldn't have; she'd taken it out of the phone's list of saved num-bers, the way she always did.

But the screen said THAT NUMBER IS NOT CURRENTLY IN SER-VICE. NO REPLACEMENT NUMBER APPEARS IN THE DATABASE.

She tried it again. She got the same error announcement and the same message. "The fuck?" she repeated, louder this time. She wondered if he'd had an accident somewhere that she didn't know about.

Wondering, worrying, she called his cell this time. It rang, which encouraged her, but instead of him or his voicemail she got a computerized voice that said, "We are very sorry, but the num-ber you have dialed is not in service at the present time."

"What do you mean, we?" she growled, but insulting a com-puter was even more pointless than zinging someone who didn't notice he'd been zinged.

She watched TV and read a thriller till she got sleepy. Every so often, she tried Bronislav's number again. As far as her phone could tell, he might have dropped off the face of the earth.

Something was rotten in the state of Serbia or along the Interstate, but she had no idea what. All she knew was, she didn't like it.

She slept badly. She texted him in the middle of the night, but his phone hadn't magically come back to life. She tried yet again when she got up too early in the morning. Still no luck.

"Shit," she said. Breakfast was bread, which didn't need to stay cold, and jam, which could also do without much refrigeration. After breakfast, Vanessa knew, she'd have to bustle around taking care of the things she couldn't do while she was stuck at her nine-to-five. Shopping. Paying bills. All the exciting, time-swallowing stuff.

First things first. Vanessa wrote the cell phone company a check. Then she opened the bank statement. When she'd reconciled her checkbook the month before, she'd come out ten dollars lower than B of A thought she was. She figured the goof was likely hers, but maybe the bank had decided it was wrong. Stranger things had happened—they must have. *Name two*, she thought, hearing an echo of her dad's voice inside her head.

Because she was intent on the checking, she almost missed what was going on in her savings account. Almost, but not quite. "The fuck?" she said one more time, her voice far angrier than it had been when she was trying to figure out what was up with Bronislav. Two large withdrawals just before the statement mailed had almost drained the account.

The only problem was, she hadn't made them.

"Jesus H. Christ!" she said, loud enough to scare a cat if she'd had the heart to get another one after poor Pickles. Then she swore at the bank and all the swarms of idiots, morons, and perverts who'd ever worked for it. And then she hied herself off to the bus stop through the rain to give the idiots, morons, and perverts at the Reynoso Drive branch a jagged-edged piece of her mind—and, not at all incidentally, to get her money back.

Getting wet on the way to the bus and on the way from the other stop to the bank building did nothing to improve her mood. The line for the tellers was long, as usual. But she didn't need a teller today. She needed a supervisor. They had desks on the other side of the line from the tellers' stations. One of the people behind the desks had no one in front of her. Her name was Denise Yamaguchi, but she had blond hair, blue eyes, and freckles. She also had a wedding ring, which probably explained the surname.

"How can I help you?" she asked when Vanessa sat down at the other side of the desk.

Vanessa slammed the bank statement down on the Formica. "I've got close to ten grand that needs to go back in my account," she said. It wasn't worth anywhere near so much as it would have been before the eruption, but it wasn't chicken feed, either, not unless the chicken was the size of an ostrich.

Ms. Yamaguchi examined the statement. "Your problem is . . . ?"

"I didn't make this withdrawal, or this one, either." Vanessa stabbed at each item in the printout with her right forefinger. Water from her umbrella soaked into the rug. Steam from her ears should have scorched the ceiling.

"Let me see, please." The supervisor did things with her computer. She frowned as she studied the monitor. "I don't find anything wrong with the transactions. They were both done by computer. They used your password. It was given correctly at the first try both times. There was no reason not to release the funds."

"Then you've been hacked. You—" Vanessa broke off as a horrible fear filled her mind. She yanked her phone out of her purse and called Bronislav's number again. She got the automated announcement that it was no longer in service. "No. Jesus, no! I think I've been hacked. Oh, shit!"

He'd been looking at her laptop when she woke up that morning. He kept her story front and center to show her. Cover—

it had to be cover. Up till then, he'd been snooping. If he wasn't so dumb with computers as he claimed, he wouldn't have had much trouble finding her password list.

And then, when the time was right, maybe when he found a town where he could open a little restaurant, or buy into one, and needed some money for a down payment or whatever . . . She didn't know that was what had happened, not yet she didn't, but she sure would have bet that way.

"*Bog te jebo!*" she hissed.

"What does that mean?" Denise Yamaguchi sounded impressed in spite of herself.

"God fuck you," Vanessa answered absently. It sounded better, filthier, in Serbo-Croatian. Her mind raced in overdrive. "Listen—do you have the IP address of the computer or smartphone or whatever the thief used to get into my account? If you do, maybe you can find out who he was."

"Let me see what I can manage." For the next several minutes, Denise Yamaguchi fiddled with her computer. When she stopped, she looked as if she also wanted to say *God fuck you*, but she was too professional. She did say, "I can't access that from here, but I think our IT people will be able to run it down. Now . . . I'm afraid you're going to have to fill out about a ton of papers. They'll protect you, and they'll protect us. People work out schemes to defraud banks sometimes." She held up a hasty hand. "I'm *not* saying you're one of them, but they do. Am I right that you have an idea about who might have taken the money out of your account?"

"Oh, yeah. You're right. My boyfriend. My ex-boyfriend, I guess I should say." Vanessa had loved Bronislav. She'd thought he loved her back. If he didn't . . . She hadn't even started processing what that meant. All this was happening too fast. But you didn't rip off someone you loved. That, she was solid on. "Let me have those forms. As many dotted lines as you've got, I'll sign on them."

"Excuse me for a minute, please. I don't use these very often. I have to pull them from that file back there."

As the banker walked over to the file cabinet, Vanessa realized that, if Bronislav had been planning for a while to steal from her, he might have been lying when he said he liked her story. Somehow, absurdly, that seemed a worse betrayal than all the money he'd siphoned from the B of A.

A few minutes before the bus was supposed to pick up Louise Ferguson and take her to the stop across the street from the Van Slyke Pharmacy, three eighteen-wheelers came down the street. Because their motors were the only ones she could hear, they seemed ridiculously loud. She knew she and everybody else had taken them for granted before the supervolcano blew up, but she couldn't imagine how. Hadn't the growling, clanking, stinking monsters driven all the people within half a mile squirrely?

As each truck passed—slowly, to keep from mashing bike-riders and what have you—she peered into its cab. She didn't *think* Bronislav Nedic would come back to L.A. any time soon, but you never could tell. She wasn't all that sure she would recognize him in a truck, either, but, again, you never could tell. So she looked.

Vanessa had dumped a string of boyfriends in her time. She'd never been dumped by one till now. She'd never had her bank account cleaned out by one, either. She'd made more money than Bryce Miller had, but that wasn't the same thing.

Now she knows how it feels, Louise thought. She'd dumped Colin, but then Teo'd dumped her. Having it done to you left a different feeling from doing it yourself. When you did it, you did it because you were—or at least you hoped you were—heading for a better place. When you were on the receiving end, it felt more as if an earthquake knocked your life higgledy-piggledy.

Louise looked down the street. Where was the damn bus?

Her boss would understand if she got in late; Jared mostly rode a bus to the pharmacy himself. But Louise didn't like it. Living with Colin all those years had left her compulsively punctual. She hated running late, and she hated when anything in her life didn't run on time.

Which didn't mean she could do squat about it. Schedule or no schedule, the bus would come when it felt like coming, not when she wanted it to come or expected it to come. Fuel shortages, the breakdowns of an aging fleet, spare-parts shortages, the problems drivers had getting to work on time . . . Oh, the Retarded Transit District had all kinds of good reasons its buses didn't always show up when it claimed they would. Louise hated every one of those reasons. That didn't help, either, of course.

Half an hour late, the bus at last deigned to make an appearance. Instead of hissing open, the door wheezed and creaked. Motors and transmissions weren't the only parts showing the strain of too much use over too many years.

As she paid her fare, she asked the driver, "What will you guys do when the buses start dying and you can't fix them any more?"

The Hispanic man looked at her. "Maybe we get stagecoaches—you know, with horses. Or maybe we just pack it in on account of it's too expensive. Then everybody climbs on a bicycle, hey?"

He was only a driver. He didn't make transit policy. Louise had to remind herself of that as she sat down. The vinyl or whatever it was that covered the seats was wearing out, too. You could see bits of yellowish foam rubber sticking up through holes and cracks and tears.

The whole damn country was wearing out the same way, with things breaking down and falling apart faster than people could run around and fix them. There'd been worried talk about that even before the supervolcano erupted. Back then, though, the fixer-uppers had just about managed to stay even with the breakdowns. So it had seemed to her, anyway.

Now . . . The supervolcano had broken so many things and made so many others fall apart, the whole damn human race was scrambling to try to fix things up in its aftermath. And, for all its frantic scrambling, humankind seemed to lose ground every day.

Such cheery thoughts occupied her till the bus shuddered to a stop at the corner of Van Slyke and Reynoso Drive. The pharmacy was already open. Jared's bus must have shown up closer to the promised time than hers had.

Her boss greeted her with, "Morning, Louise. Have you heard the latest?"

"Nooo," she said slowly, wondering whether the latest revolved around soccer, Broadway, or some incestuous combination of the two.

It turned out to be none of the above. "The Russians have invaded Ukraine and Kazakhstan," he said.

"Good God!" Louise said. "Why?"

"Well, I was listening to Radio Moscow on the shortwave this morning"—yes, Jared was the kind of man who *would* listen to Radio Moscow on the shortwave—"and *they* said it was to consolidate the historic unity of the region. I'm quoting, you understand."

"Uh, right," Louise answered. "What does that really mean? Does it really mean anything at all?"

"I think it means the cold has hit Russia so hard, nothing's growing there at all," Jared said. "Ukraine and Kazakhstan are a little better off, so the Russians are grabbing with both hands."

"That will make everybody love them," Louise said. She'd grown up loving the Russians that way; like the pharmacist, she was old enough to remember the Cold War. To her grown children, it was as one with World War II and the Battle of Hastings and the Pyramids: something they had to learn about in school that didn't mean anything in their own lives. Thinking back to Cold War fears, Louise found a brand-new question: "Are they using nukes?"

"They haven't yet, or nobody's said they have," Jared answered. Louise nodded in relief. With several—no one seemed sure just how many—nuclear bombs tossed around in the Mideast, that genie was out of the bottle, dammit. Her boss went on, "But Ukraine and Kazakhstan are both screaming for NATO help."

NATO, Louise remembered from somewhere, stood for North Atlantic Treaty Organization. Kazakhstan was one hell of a long way from the North Atlantic. Well, so was Ukraine, but it did touch the Black Sea, which was connected to the Mediterranean, which was connected to the North Atlantic.

And the ankle bone's connected to the leg bone, and the leg bone's connected to the hip bone, and the hip bone's connected to the backbone . . . Louise wasn't even close to sure she had the old song straight. She also wasn't even close to sure she had all her marbles right now.

Then something else occurred to her, something that had to do with connections and that made her pretty sure she did. "When they're yelling for NATO help, that means they're yelling for American help. What are we doing about it?"

"Last I heard, the Secretary of State told the Russians that attacking independent countries was a big no-no," Jared answered, which surprised a laugh from Louise. He continued, "The Russians have told the Secretary of State that Washington needs to mind its own business."

Trying to picture a map in her mind, Louise said, "I wouldn't want to have to send soldiers to Kazakhstan."

"Neither would anyone else with all his brains," Jared said. Louise laughed again—he was on a roll. Then he added, "Some of the commentators are saying they don't want soldiers. They want us to tell the Russians we'll shoot missiles at them if they don't go home and play nice."

"Urk," Louise said. If the USA shot missiles at Russia, it wasn't like shooting at Iran or North Korea. The Russians could shoot back. Oh, could they ever! That was why the Cold War had stayed cold. Both sides could shoot back much too well to take suicidal chances.

"*Urk* is just about the size of it," Jared agreed. "You can get to Ukraine from the rest of Europe, anyhow. Or to Russia. You can assuming you want to, I mean. The last fellow who went into Russia from the rest of Europe was Hitler, and he didn't have such a great time afterwards."

"No," Louise said. "We don't *need* a war now. We're still picking up pieces from the supervolcano, and we will be for the next fifty years."

"You know that. I know that," Jared said. "I'll bet the Russians know that—they're picking up pieces, too. But does the President know that?"

As far as Louise could tell, the President was a twit. He meant well, but he was a twit regardless. And everybody except maybe him knew which road was paved with meaning well.

A little old Asian man with a fedora came in. It wasn't a hipster's stingy-brim. It was just a hat. He'd probably started wearing it when most men put them on every day, and somehow never stopped. He nodded to Jared. "Good morning. Is my Inderal prescription ready?"

"It sure is, Mr. Nakasone." The pharmacist went behind the counter and handed him a pill bottle. The Asian man handed back a credit card. Since the power was on, Jared could use the computerized system. After Mr. Nakasone signed the slip, he stuck the pills in a pocket of his windbreaker and tottered off. He wasn't going anywhere fast, but he was going.

He reminded Louise of the whole world these days.

She wondered what the world would do if Russia overran those two chunks of what had been the Russian Empire and then the Soviet Union. Then she wondered what Russia would do if it overran them. Just because you wanted something, you wouldn't necessarily be happy once you got it. (Hadn't somebody with Vulcan ears said that the first time?) Ukraine and Kazakhstan had been their own countries for a generation now. They'd got used to being their own countries. They wouldn't want Moscow ordering them around again. And they were big enough that trying to hold them down might not be a whole lot of fun for the Kremlin.

Well, that was the Kremlin's worry. It wasn't Louise's. She had plenty of worries of her own.

X

Cal State Dominguez Hills wasn't the most beautiful college campus running around loose. UC Santa Barbara had a much nicer natural setting. UCLA and Berkeley both jumped all over CSUDH when it came to architecture. Dominguez Hills looked more like a nicely landscaped office park than anything else Kelly Ferguson could think of. But Cal State Dominguez Hills had one enormous advantage over all those prettier places. Unlike them, it had given her a job.

She both was and wasn't glad to be back at the State University. She was because she liked research and teaching. She wasn't because going back to work took her away from Deborah.

She'd looked down her nose at women who let motherhood slow down their careers . . . till she had to start making those choices herself. Then, as people often do, she discovered things weren't so simple as they looked from the outside. She liked research and teaching. She loved her little girl, who changed faster and needed her more than the study of supervolcano eruptions did.

But if she stayed away too long, no one but her would care if she ever came back. So here she was, and there was Marshall, keeping an eye on Deborah back home. Kelly also felt conflicted about Marshall's progress as a writer. She wanted him to do well. But if he did very well, he could afford to say no instead of babysitting his half-sister.

A Frisbee flew through the air. A dog ran, jumped, caught it, and proudly carried it back to the kid who'd thrown it. Most of the students looked like kids to Kelly—one more sign she wasn't a kid herself any more.

She made her way to the room where she was privileged, if that was the word, to teach Introduction to Geology: geology for people who weren't geology majors. Some of them, by all appearances, had barely heard of rocks. There were good students in the Cal State University system, as there were in the University of California system. But there weren't nearly so many of them.

This lecture was about plate tectonics, and about how continents could slowly move across the surface of the Earth and, sometimes, run into one another. "India used to be a separate continent," she said. "Then it ran into the bigger Asian land mass. The collision pushed up the Himalayas, the tallest mountains in the world. It's still pushing them up to this day."

Some of the students in the room took notes. Some listened without writing anything down. Some, plainly, had their heads a million miles away.

"For a long time, people were sure continents couldn't move, even though the east coast of South America looks like it fits together with the west coast of Africa, and almost the same with North America and Europe. The first man who proposed the idea of continental drift, a German named Wegener"—Kelly wrote the name on the board—"got called a crackpot for his trouble. That was right after the First World War. It wasn't till the 1960s that enough evidence came to light to make people take another look at Wegener the weirdo."

She outlined what the evidence was. Then, smiling as she remembered her own undergraduate days, she went on, "The older profs I studied under were in college themselves when geologists started to realize continental drift and plate tectonics were true after all. One guy told me it hit geology as hard as the idea that the Earth goes around the sun and not the other way around hit astronomy in the days of Copernicus and Galileo."

After the lecture, a tall student named George Chun—Chinese? Korean?—came up to her. He was one of the bright ones. He would have been a bright one anywhere. Maybe he couldn't afford to go to a UC school. Kelly couldn't find any other reason why he'd be here and not at one of them. She hadn't learned all her students' names, but she knew his, all right.

"Talk about astronomy," he said. "I was in one of those courses last quarter. The instructor talked about the Ptolemaic theory. Then he talked about the Copernican theory. And one of the dudes walking out in front of me said to his bud, 'If that first one wasn't true, man, why'd he go and teach it to us?' "

Kelly laughed and groaned at the same time. "The really scary thing is, I believe you," she said.

"Some people are too stupid to live," Chun said with the heartlessness of nineteen.

"And of course you've never said anything or done anything dumb in your whole, entire life. And neither have I." Kelly waited to see how he'd take that. There were bright kids who really did think being anything less than bright was, or ought to be, a punishable offense.

But Chun laughed. "Well, when you put it like that . . . Take care." He turned away from the lectern.

"You, too, George," Kelly said. "And thanks for the story. That's a good one—or a bad one, depending on how you look at things."

The student shrugged. "Kinda weirded me out that there could be guys who need an astronomy class to tell 'em the sun doesn't revolve around the Earth. But hey, like you say, I bet there's stuff I don't know that a lot of people'd call intuitively obvious."

"We can all say that," Kelly answered. But her guess was that George Chun's failings, whatever they might be, weren't academic. If he was the kind of young man too shy to date much . . . either he'd get horny enough for his hard-on to push him in that direction or he'd stay social caterpillar and never turn into social butterfly.

She was walking to her office when groans announced that the CSUDH campus had lost power. She slowed down. The office was on the third floor and had no window. With the door open— more important, with the door to the office across the hall (which did have a window) open—it wasn't quite so dark as the inside of a politician's head, but it came close.

So, instead of climbing the stairs, she sat down on a concrete ledge near the doorway to the building. Anybody who needed to talk with her would likely spot her there. Anybody who needed to talk with her so much that he or she had sprinted on ahead would, she hoped, take a hint from the locked door and the gloomy hallway, come downstairs and back outside, and then spot her there. Chances were good that even students not rich enough or bright enough to win admission to one of the UC campuses could figure that out.

Sure as hell, another Asian kid buttonholed her. Rex wasn't doing nearly so well as George Chun. Kelly had a good idea why he wasn't, too: he was baked all the time. She recognized the signs from Marshall. But Marshall held the joint—he got loaded a lot, but he still functioned. Kelly thought the joint was holding Rex.

He had trouble remembering what he wanted to ask her, which couldn't be a good sign. Finally, a couple of his fried synapses clicked together and made a spark: "Oh, yeah! Plate, like, tec . . . waddayacallit."

"Tectonics," Kelly said patiently. Stoners *could* do it. They just couldn't do it very fast. "What do you need to know?"

Again, he had to grope for an answer. He reminded Kelly of that ancient Cosby routine where the dudes with the munchies went to Burger King and forgot why they were there before they could order. When one of them got asked what he wanted, he mumbled *Hey, lemme talk to the king.* Rex was too much like that.

At last, he managed, "Um, how's that work, you know?"

With a small sigh, Kelly explained how it worked. It was an abridged version of what she'd said during the lecture, but it was all new to Rex, even though he'd been there.

"Wow," he said, and she had to fight back giggles. She hadn't heard such a wasted noise, even from Marshall, for a long time. Rex went on, "That's pretty amazing. How'd they psych out it does that?"

Kelly fed him another slice of the lecture. Maybe it would stay down this time. She could hope so.

Another student, a Hispanic woman whose name Kelly couldn't find in her head, came up when she was halfway through her little talk on subduction and seafloor spreading. Kelly backed and filled so the newcomer wouldn't think she was speaking Urdu. The woman actually seemed to have some idea of what was going on. Kelly wouldn't have said the same thing about Rex.

She did feel virtuous that she'd stationed herself out here and drawn some students even though her office wasn't usable. When her office hours were done, she turned in a journal at the library, collected a handwritten receipt, and trudged off to the bus stop for the trip back to San Atanasio.

It would have been twenty minutes by car. The way things worked these days, it took one transfer and over an hour to get back to her stop on Braxton Bragg Boulevard. From there, she had to walk another ten or fifteen minutes before she was actually home.

As it did so often since the eruption, sunset looked like a pousse-café, with all sorts of gaudy, gorgeous colors piled one atop another and changing every time she looked at them. She didn't look at them as much as their beauty should have demanded. She'd seen too many sunsets not just like this one, maybe, but every bit as gorgeous.

When her key turned first the dead bolt and then the lock to the front door, she heard high, shrill squeals from inside. As soon as she walked through the front door, a small, friendly hurricane did its goddamnedest to kneecap her. "Mommymommymommy-*mommmy*!" the hurricane yelled, all one word.

Kelly let her backpack slide from her shoulders to the floor. She picked up Deborah and squeezed her and kissed her. "Hello, kiddo. I missed you," she said. "Have you been a good girl?"

"No," Deborah said proudly.

"Marshall?" Kelly asked, a certain apprehension in her voice.

"Not too bad," Marshall said. "She was gonna see if a coffee mug bounced like a rubber ball, but I got it away from her before she could make like Isaac Newton and experiment."

"Good for you," Kelly said, and then, to her daughter, "Don't throw cups, please."

"Why?" Deborah asked, which gave Kelly a sinking feeling.

Hoping against hope, Kelly answered, "Because they can break."

But she was doomed after all. "Why?" Deborah asked again.

"Because they're made of china."

"Why?" Deborah was ready to ask it all night long. And why not? Mommy was home, and the world was wonderful again.

With no great enthusiasm, Colin Ferguson dialed a number in Mobile, Alabama. His opinion of Mobile wasn't high. His destroyer had put in there for a few days while he was in the Navy. The weather'd been every bit as horrendously hot and sticky as

New Orleans'. Unlike New Orleans, though, Mobile seemed to have been settled by people who had no idea how to have fun.

Nowadays, Mobile's weather was probably better than it had been before the supervolcano eruption. It would be one of the few places in the world able to say that.

But he hadn't called Mobile to talk about the weather. In due course, a voice on the other end of the line said, "This is Lieutenant Randall Atkins, Theft and Fraud Unit." Lieutenant Atkins had a deep voice, and a drawl thick enough to slice.

"Morning, Lieutenant. I'm Captain Colin Ferguson, of the San Atanasio PD out in California."

"Ferguson . . . San Atanasio . . ." Colin could just about watch the pieces going round and round in the Mobile cop's mind like the wheels on a slot machine. Pretty soon, Atkins hit the jackpot. "Jesus! Aren't you the guy who—?"

"Yeah, I'm *the guy who*, all right," Colin agreed heavily. He knew too well he'd be getting that the rest of his career. "This hasn't got anything to do with that, though."

"Okay." Atkins seemed to pull himself together and act professional. "What does it have to do with, then, Captain?"

"There's a new restaurant in your town, a place called Unity," Colin said, remembering that Bronislav's tat with the cross and the two forward C's and the two backward ones stood for *Only unity will save the Serbs*. "One of the people behind it is a fellow named Bronislav Nedic."

"Named what? You want to spell that for me, Captain? Spell it nice and slow, if you'd be so kind." Colin did—the request was more than reasonable. When he finished, Randall Atkins said, "All right. I've got it. You don't mind my asking though, how come a cop way the devil out in California cares about a guy with a funny name in the restaurant racket here?"

"I don't mind," Colin answered. "We've got a warrant out on Nedic. Charge is grand theft. He hacked into his girlfriend's bank account, swiped almost ten grand, and used it to get a piece of this Unity place." The restaurant already had half a dozen online reviews, all of them good, a couple of them raves. After a brief pause, Colin went on, "I'd go after him any which way—believe me on that one, Lieutenant. But it just so happens that his girl-friend is my daughter."

"Ouch!" Atkins said. "Boy, what a dumb son of a bitch, rip-ping off a cop's kid."

"That did cross my mind," Colin said. "But he knew she had it, and he figured out how to get his hands on it, and he was talking about opening a place to eat for as long as he dated Vanessa—a couple-three years. Looks like he could resist every-thing but temptation."

"Heh," Lieutenant Atkins said. He paused for longer than Colin had before continuing, "Well, send us the particulars and we'll look into it." He didn't say they would bust Bronislav Nedic and send him back to California in leg irons. He didn't say any-thing of the sort—not even close.

Colin noted what he didn't say, and didn't like what he did say. "Look into it?" the San Atanasio cop echoed. If he sounded affronted, he sounded that way because he damn well was.

Randall Atkins just sighed. " 'Fraid so, Captain. You need to understand—things aren't real good around here right now. We've got swarms of folks in town who're just out of the camps, and it's like they're cons just out of prison. They don't give a shit—pardon my French—about anybody but them. Stealing's second nature to 'em. That and turning tricks are about the only way you can get stuff in those places. They'll lift anything that isn't nailed down, and they'll try and pry up the nails if it is. They'd sooner steal food than work for it, not that there's much work to get around here."

"I hear that," Colin said, remembering Victor Jennings and others like him.

"Yeah, I bet you do," Lieutenant Atkins said. "But anyway, that's where we're at. Somebody's actually opening up a business instead of closing one, we won't go after him real hard unless he grabs himself an AK-47 and starts shooting up the neighborhood."

"He's liable to," Colin remarked.

"Say what?"

"I said, he's liable to. Have you seen this dude, Lieutenant? He's very bad news. I always figured he'd be more likely to knock over a bank than to rip one off with a laptop. When Yugoslavia came to pieces in the Nineties, he did some nasty things over there. I don't know all the gory details and I don't want to, but he did. You can see it in his eyes."

"And he was going with your daughter?"

"It wasn't my idea. He's not any more—that's for damn sure." Colin sighed. "She's old enough to make her own mistakes, and it's not like she'd listen to me if I tried to show 'em to her. Not obvious she should, either, on account of I sure made my share of mistakes like that."

Randall Atkins chuckled mirthlessly. "I don't know what you're talking about, man—and if you believe that, I'll tell you another one. But seriously, as long as this, uh, Nedic keeps his nose clean around here, we aren't gonna go after him real hard. We've got enough day-to-day trouble. We don't sweat the other kind much."

"What would happen if I asked your switchboard to put me through to the chief there?" Colin asked.

"Go ahead," Atkins said. "Maybe he'll do you a cop-to-cop favor. But I've got a hundred bucks that says he'll tell you about what I just did."

A hundred bucks wasn't what it had been before the eruption, let alone what it had been when Colin was in the Navy— back in those days, a hundred bucks was serious money. But it still wasn't nothing. Instead of calling the chief in Mobile, Colin hung up. Atkins had convinced him the Alabama town really didn't worry about people like Bronislav as long as he stuck to his restaurant there.

"That sucks," Gabe Sanchez said when Colin told him the sad story over lunch. "Sucks big-time, matter of fact."

"Tell me about it," Colin answered. "But I don't know what I can do. Mobile's not like the LAPD—I don't get many chances to do them a bad turn if I owe 'em one."

"You could mail 'em a package bomb," Gabe said helpfully. "Make sure you put a long delay on the timer. The post office is as slow as Super Bowl losers in February."

"Ha!" Colin heard the uneasiness in his voice. He would never do anything like that. But he didn't plan to pass Gabe's joke on to Vanessa. He didn't *think* she would send Lieutenant Atkins something that went *boom!* when you opened it. He also didn't *think* she would try that kind of payback on Bronislav Nedic. He wasn't sure enough not to worry about giving her ideas. She was already righteously pissed off at the big, tough Serb.

Colin wished Vanessa were righteously pissed off at herself, too. She'd wasted years of her life on a man who saw her as . . . what? As a fuck toy and an ATM, that was what. But Vanessa had never blamed herself for anything that happened to her. No, it was always somebody else's fault, usually a man's, once in a while her mother's.

"If the city cops won't do anything, maybe you can get hold of the Alabama highway patrol or state troopers or whatever the hell they call 'em over there," Gabe said. "If Bron-whatever's doing anything bent outside of his fancy new restaurant, they could land on him for you."

"Huh." This time, Colin's grunt was thoughtful. "You know, you may not be as dumb as I look."

Gabe had opened his mouth to come back with a zinger of his own. He coped with self-mockery without shifting gears: "Jeez, I hope so!"

"Me, too," Colin said. "I honest to God may put a flea in somebody's ear about that place. Nedic never struck me as the kind of guy who stayed inside the rules all the time. Hey, he spent a while doing Christ knows what in a place where you made your own rules with an AK. He lived through that. What do you want to bet he thinks he can live through anything?"

"Sounds reasonable." Gabe nodded. Then he looked sly. "Suppose he did enough of that shit so you could get his ass in a sling on a war-crimes rap?"

"I doubt it. Far as I know, he was just a spear-carrier," Colin answered. "On the off chance, though, I'll poke around online." He didn't mention that he spoke not a word of Serbo-Croatian. Gabe already knew that. Colin couldn't even cuss in it, the way Vanessa could. And the Serbian half of the language was written in an alphabet he didn't read. Details, details . . .

"Have you told Vanessa the Mobile cops are sitting with their thumbs up their asses?" Sanchez could find the most intriguing questions.

"Not yet." Colin wasn't looking forward to that, any more than he would have looked forward to another not-social-enough call on Dr. Stan Birnbaum. Sighing, he went on, "Wish I could get out of it. Won't happen, though, not when she was the one who found Nedic when he surfaced."

"She was?" Gabe raised a shaggy eyebrow. "Either she takes after you or she's been reading too much Sherlock Holmes."

"Bet on the Holmes," Colin said dryly. There were ways Vanessa took after him. He didn't notice all of them. Neither did his daughter: one more way she resembled him.

"You know where this guy is at now, anyway." Gabe gave what consolation he could. "If he does go bad, the Alabama cops will bust his sorry ass. And if he starts banking profits, well, maybe you can find your own hacker to make 'em disappear." He grinned.

He *could* grin—it wasn't his problem. It wasn't really Colin's, either, but Vanessa was his daughter in spite of everything, so he wound up stuck with it. "Yeah," he said, "maybe I can." He only wished he believed that. If Bronislav Nedic wasn't the kind who stashed his cash in a coffee can or between his mattress and box spring, Colin had never seen anybody who was. You didn't need a hacker for that kind of job. You needed a strong-arm man. And any strong-arm man who bumped into the tattooed Serb might find out his arm wasn't so strong as he'd figured.

The apartment Rob Ferguson shared with Lindsey Kincaid— after a lot of hemming and hawing, she'd kept her own last name—enjoyed all the modern conveniences. It enjoyed the conveniences that were modern when the nineteenth century segued into the twentieth, anyhow. It had running water . . . when the pipes didn't freeze. Some of the time, it had hot running water. The icebox kept food fresh. The stove, which would burn wood or coal depending on how you adjusted the grate, not only cooked food but also did its share in heating the place.

There was even electricity. Sometimes. After a fashion. The Energizer Bunny's proud products were among the most import-ant goods that trickled into Maine north and west of the Interstate during the short summer season when most of the snow melted off most of the roads and the voice of the eighteen-wheeler was heard in the land.

Batteries powered flashlights and lamps. The most popular ones in these parts used LEDs and drew very little power. That stretched the batteries' effective lives. Batteries also powered music players. Rob was far from the only person who put miles and miles on a bicycle to nowhere to keep an iPod charged.

Listening to music from before the eruption reminded him the wider world was still out there. Listening to a shortwave radio did the same thing.

So did the occasional click from the Geiger counter Dick Barber had found wherever the hell Dick came up with such things. Sometimes, when the wind blew from the northwest, the clicks sounded less occasional. The Russians hadn't used atomic weapons in their war against Kazakhstan and Ukraine. But Kazakh special forces squadrons—Kazakh terrorists, Radio Moscow called them—had infiltrated into Russia and blown up two nuclear power plants. It wasn't a new Chernobyl (or if it was, the Russians wouldn't admit it). It did raise the background radiation level.

It also raised Barber's amusement level. "Of course the Kazakhs will know where the Russians have security problems," he said. "Their higher-ups went to the university with the Russians' higher-ups back in the days when the Kazakh Soviet Socialist Republic and the Russian Soviet Federated Socialist Republic were both parts of the same workers' paradise."

"Er—right," Rob said. People like Dick Barber and Rob's father could talk that way with a straight face. They remembered the Cold War from when they were young. And people like Jim Farrell, most of a generation older still, could talk that way and sound as if it were the most important thing in the world. For much of their lives, the Cold War, who would win it, whether anyone could win it, and the terrible fear it would turn hot, had been the most important thing in the world.

"Want some more cider, Dick?" Lindsey asked. She didn't fancy Barber's politics, but she did think he was interesting. And he was her husband's friend. That tipped the scales toward politeness for her.

"Much obliged," Barber said. Lindsey poured some for him and some for Rob. The cider was also an import from the south, from a land where the growing season stayed long enough for apples. Barley sometimes grew here, so local beer remained possible.

"You're not drinking any yourself, babe," Rob said.

"Don't feel like it," Lindsey answered. Rob let an eyebrow climb toward his hairline. Lindsey liked cider fine, thank you very much. But something in her voice warned him not to push it right then. It wasn't something Dick Barber would have noticed. Rob sure did, though. If you were going to make this husband-and-wife business work, you needed to pick up on stuff like that.

After more gloating about the Russians' embarrassment and distress, Barber went on his way. Rob turned to Lindsey and asked, "How come you didn't feel like cider?"

"It's not a good plan when you're going to have a baby," she told him.

He got up and hugged her. Even with the potbellied stove in the apartment, it wasn't warm. They both wore too many layers to make the hug as enjoyable as it might have been.

"That's wonderful," Rob said into her ear. He wasn't altogether caught by surprise. Any tolerably alert husband notices more about his wife than subtle shifts in her tone of voice. He knows how her calendar runs and when she's due. He also knows when she's late, even if he doesn't say anything about it till she brings it up herself.

This time, she squeezed him. "Now we have to decide where we're going to move after the kid comes out," she said.

His jaw dropped. "Oh, yeah? I like it here. If you don't, you sure did a good job on the coverup. Richard Nixon would be proud." Nixon was even more before his time than the end of the Cold War, but he prided himself on coming out with weird things every now and then.

To his annoyance, Lindsey barely noticed. "I like it here

fine—for us," she said. "But I want my son or daughter to have some possibilities in life. Possibilities that go further than moose hunter or fur trapper or beer brewer or scavenger."

"Ooh." Rob's mouth twisted. That hit close to home, all right—too close. Lives here, including his own, were catch-as-catch-can. He did whatever he could to help put food on the table. Whenever Squirt Frog and the Evolving Tadpoles had a gig, he played. He gave guitar lessons. He hunted. He fished. He'd never ice-fished till he came to Maine, but he sure had now. He chopped wood. He swapped this for that and that for the other thing, hoping he came out ahead more often than not.

As a teacher, Lindsey had more order in her life. What she didn't have was more money. Maine's state government ignored the great expanse north and west of the Interstate almost as thoroughly as the Feds did. It concentrated its attention on the part of the state that had some small chance of paying bills rather than just running them up.

With the collapse of cash in this stretch of the country, the local school district had given up trying to collect taxes. Families with kids in school helped keep teachers in food and fuel, and did other things they needed. If they couldn't or wouldn't, their kids stopped going, as they would have in the nineteenth century. Even Jim Farrell called the system ugly, but it worked most of the time. The locals had taken care of themselves and helped their neighbors before the eruption. They were more used to it than people in some other places would have been.

One of those other places was the Southern California where Rob Ferguson had grown up. He pointed that out to Lindsey, saying, "Are you sure you want to move? People who live here really belong. It's not like that in most of the country—I mean, totally not like that."

His wife stuck out her chin and looked stubborn. "Suppose the baby gets sick or gets hurt. Or you do, or I do. We're living on borrowed time here. People die every year because they run out of it."

She wasn't wrong. In the Guilford clinic, Dr. Bhattacharya did what he could with what he had. He didn't have much, and seemed to have less every year. The closest hospital was in Dover-Foxcroft, more than ten miles east along the Piscataquis. An ambulance did run during the brief summer. A snowmobile or two were kept alive for the rest of the year. But, for anything this side of the worst emergencies, the hospital was at least two hours away. And it hadn't been much of a hospital before the supervolcano. Like Dr. Bhattacharya here, its staff did what they could. They couldn't do enough.

"It's funny," Rob said. "For years before the band washed up here, I never had a home. Nothing close to a home except maybe our SUVs. We were on the road all the time. We'd play somewhere, overnight in some cheap motel, and then hop in the Explorers and play somewhere else—two states away, half the time. So I wondered if I'd go stir-crazy when we got stuck in Guilford." He broke into ersatz Dylan: "Oh, Lord, stuck in Guilford/With the SoCal blues again!"

"Oh, Lord!" Lindsey agreed. Rob winced. She went on, "If you didn't get stuck here, we wouldn't've met."

"I know. That's what I'm saying," Rob answered. "This is a good place even if it's the boonies—maybe especially because it's the boonies. Please, Mr. Custer, I don't wanna go."

"But we're on the ragged edge of civilization two or three months a year," Lindsey said. "The rest of the time, we've fallen over the edge."

"I know," Rob said. That he admitted it seemed to surprise her. He continued, "Is that a bug or a feature, though? As long as the rest of the world leaves us alone, aren't we better off?"

"You've spent too much time listening to Dick and Jim," Lindsey said, which wasn't a charge he could exactly deny. "And what happens when Junior"—she set a hand on her still-flat belly—"turns eighteen? Even assuming there's something like high school here then and he, she, whatever, graduates from it, what about college?"

The University of Hard Knocks trembled on the tip of Rob's tongue. He gave the serious effort he needed to keep it from falling off. Despite his love for smartass cracks, he came equipped with enough sense to see that that one would land him in deep, deep kimchi. It might be true, but that made it worse, not better.

Instead, he said, "Hey, the University of Maine at Orono is still a going concern, right? That's not super far away. It's—what? Sixty or eighty miles? Something like that. It'd be doable."

He did make Lindsey stop and think. But she shot back, "How will we pay for tuition? Moose meat?"

If there are any moose left when Junior hits college age, great. One more thing Rob didn't say. What he did say was, "We'll work something out. Not like we're the only ones up here worrying about this kind of stuff."

"Well . . . maybe." His wife still didn't sound convinced. But she also didn't sound like someone who wanted to pull up stakes and head for warmer country before dinner. To Rob, that felt like a victory, and not such a small one, either.

XI

Vanessa Ferguson had a way of walking around with a chip on her shoulder. To her, there was rarely any such thing as a slight. If something was big enough for her to notice, it was big enough to send her off to war, flags flying and bugles blaring.

Being as she was, she fired the first shot more often than not. And so she had even more trouble than most people might have in getting over the Pearl Harbor that Bronislav Nedic had dropped into her life.

She'd loved him. She'd trusted him. She'd opened the postern gate in the fortress of her self and let him inside. She hadn't just let him inside—she'd led him inside.

She'd let him inside her body, and she'd let him inside her heart. He'd screwed her and he'd screwed her, respectively. He'd taken what he wanted and he'd bailed out. Vanessa had disposed of a string of boyfriends. Now it was her turn.

It damaged her all kinds of ways. Her bank account, for instance. B of A admitted she hadn't made the withdrawals that drained her savings. But it said they were her fault; she'd given Bronislav access to her personal information. That she didn't know she'd done it till too late was no excuse. The bank's fug-headedness held just enough truth to infuriate her all the more.

And now there he was in Mobile, sitting pretty in the restaurant he'd always talked about. He'd cared more for the restaurant than for her. No doubt he figured he could always find another woman. With those Nicolas Cage-y looks and those big, sad eyes, no doubt he could, too. But a restaurant, now, a restaurant didn't come along every day.

A restaurant didn't go away every day, either. Not even her father the famous cop had been able to make the Mobile police get off their sorry, lazy asses and bust Bronislav. He was making money in their town. Such birds were so rare these days, they didn't want to pluck this one.

Her dad hadn't passed on Gabe Sanchez's crack about the package bomb. He hadn't needed to. Vanessa thought of it on her own. The only thing that held her back was a healthy fear of get-ting caught.

Messing up Bronislav's life with computer skullduggery, the way he'd messed up hers, also crossed her mind. But she didn't know any of his passwords. Even if she had, she lacked the com-puter *fu* to do anything with them.

Which didn't mean she didn't know people who had such arcane talents. Several of them infested Nick Gorczany's widget works, starting with the big boss himself. Vanessa disliked him too much even to think of approaching him about it.

Some of the other engineers and programmers, though . . . She spoke, in a hypothetical way, to Bruce McRaa. No, the HTML whiz couldn't navigate an English sentence with a gun, a camera, and a road atlas. But put him in front of a monitor and all of a sudden he knew what he was doing.

No matter how hypothetically Vanessa talked at lunch one day, he knew what she had in mind, too. Maybe he wasn't as naïve as he looked. Well, he couldn't be, not if he wanted to stay alive. "That's interesting," he said when she got done. "Illegal, of course, but interesting."

"That asshole didn't care about what was legal when he shafted me," Vanessa said savagely.

"That was his choice, not mine," Bruce replied. "He must have thought the reward was worth the risk. What kind of reward would we be talking about here?"

Vanessa remembered a bumper sticker she'd seen on a truck bumper—not Bronislav's. GAS, GRASS, OR ASS—NOBODY RIDES FOR FREE, that was what it said. She remembered *TANSTAAFL*, too: the annoying libertarian acronym and mantra. *There ain't no such thing as a free lunch*. She had no idea whether the enchanter Bruce was a libertarian, though a disturbing number of guys who did things with and to computers seemed to be. Whether he was or not, he understood *quid pro quo* just fine.

"How much do you want?" Vanessa asked. "If you think I'll pay you as much as he stole, forget about it. I don't just want revenge. I want to get back what's mine, if I can."

"Oh-kay." Bruce blew a speck—probably dandruff—off his glasses. "Well, there's money and then there are other things," he said at last.

She looked at him. That she thought about it, at least for a second, said she wasn't the person who'd moved to Denver not long before the supervolcano erupted. But she didn't think about it much longer than a second. She remembered too well how much she'd hated herself and the whole goddamn world every time she blew that stinking FEMA dweeb in exchange for services rendered. If she had a choice between stringing up Micah Husak and Bronislav, she would choose the FEMA dweeb every time. Bronislav stole her money, yeah. Micah had robbed her of her self-respect.

"Let's just forget about it, then," she told the enchanter Bruce.

He looked disappointed. What really pissed her off was, he looked surprised. "I thought you wanted this bad," he said.

"Badly." The correction came almost without conscious thought, as it would have were she editing him on paper. She went on, "Anything that went on between us, *that* would be bad."

"I don't think so." Lewd imaginings filled Bruce's voice.

Vanessa sighed. "Of course you don't. It's always good for guys. But letting somebody screw me to get even with somebody for screwing me . . . That still leaves me screwed, if you know what I mean."

If it could make a computer or a tablet or a smartphone jump through hoops, Bruce understood it the way Theocritus understood Doric dialect (that Theocritus had used the Doric dialect was one of the useless factoids she remembered from her time with Bryce). If it had to do with human beings and the way they worked, the HTML wizard was a clueless git.

One of the field marks of a clueless git was that he was clueless about being a git. The enchanter Bruce proved he belonged: "You might like me better after you get to know me that way."

"If you're the kind of guy who expects to get his dick wet in exchange for doing something for a woman, nobody in her right mind is gonna like you." Vanessa spelled it out as plainly as she could: plainly enough to make Bruce McRaa turn pink. Even Micah Husak hadn't been that dumb. In fact, the FEMA dweeb had got off on having her go down on him when she couldn't stand him.

"Well, excuse me for breathing," Bruce said, as snarkily as he could.

"Since we won't be doing anything for—or to—each other, I suppose I will," Vanessa answered. "If we were . . . If we were, you'd want to worry about whether you kept on doing it."

He started to laugh. Almost as soon as he did, he realized she wasn't kidding, not even a little bit. The laugh came out as a strangled snort and quickly cut off.

That left her with better feelings about herself than she'd had in Camp Constitution. But it also left her without payback on Bronislav Nedic. If men weren't such rotten horndogs... It wasn't as if she hadn't been plenty hot for Bronislav while they were together. The bastard knew what he was doing in bed, damn him. Which didn't mean he wasn't a bastard. It only defined what kind of bastard he was: a fucking bastard, of course.

Not too long after they got back to the widget works, Nick Gorczany called Vanessa into his office. He steepled his fingers and looked at her over them. "Did you ask Bruce to do something that might be illegal?" he inquired.

Bruce, Vanessa presumed, had been in there ahead of her, telling tales. "Who, me?" she said, doing her best to project innocence. "Of course not, Mr. Gorczany. Asking anyone to do something illegal would be, well, illegal."

"Right," Gorczany said tightly. Maybe her innocence projector had a burnt-out bulb. He went on, "Bruce went into some detail."

"Did he?" Vanessa said. Her boss nodded. She continued, "Was one of the details he went into that he said he'd do it if I put out for him?"

"Mm, no," Nick Gorczany answered. "You told him no dice?"

"You bet your sweet ass I told him no dice," Vanessa said. "Yeah, I want to get even with Bronislav. But I don't want to be even with Bronislav and then spend all my time figuring out how to get even with Bruce."

"Oh." Gorczany thought that over. After a few seconds, he nodded. "I think that's a good plan. I also think Bruce may not know how lucky he is not to get all the way on your bad side."

"Why, Mr. Gorczany, sir! You say the sweetest things!" Vanessa batted her eyelashes at him.

She made him laugh. "Okay. We'll leave it there, then," he said between chuckles. But he got serious again in a hurry. "Do me a favor, please. If you want to get even with this guy, that's your business. Can't say I blame you, either. If you use people who work here to help you get even, though, and especially if you get them to do things for you that are against the law . . . In that case, it turns into my business. So don't do that any more, all right?"

"All right," Vanessa said reluctantly. It wasn't, not so far as she was concerned, but she could see where Gorczany was coming from. If one of his employees got into trouble for doing something like that, the widget works could wind up in trouble, too.

She walked out of the boss man's office. A few minutes later, the enchanter Bruce walked back in. When he emerged once more, he seemed unhappy with the world. Catching Vanessa's eye, he sent her a dirty look. Her answering stony stare made him find a new direction for his gaze in a hurry.

That would have been funny had Vanessa been in any mood for jokes. She wasn't, and making Bruce flinch was no more reason for pride than scaring some other puppy. Damn his big, stupid mouth to hell and gone anyway! Because he'd tattled to Nick Gorczany, she couldn't recruit anyone else at the widget works to give Bronislav what he deserved (and a little more besides—anything worth doing was worth overdoing, wasn't it?).

Life wasn't fair sometimes. Life sucked, when you got right down to it. And so did all the alternatives.

One of the amazing things about kids, Kelly Ferguson was discovering, was how fast they changed. Deborah was rolling over. She was crawling. She started to talk, and to walk. All of a sudden, she was potty-trained. Kelly definitely approved of that. So did Colin. "Looks like she'll turn out to be a human being after all," he exulted.

Kelly looked at him. "And how long have people been saying the same thing about you?" she asked in her mildest tones.

Her husband didn't so much as blink. "Hey, babe, I'm a cop. Cops don't even come close to human beings. Ask anybody. Heck, even the stupid cat knows that."

The stupid cat in question lay asleep on the rug in front of him. The cat's name was Playboy, in celebration of Marshall's best sale. In spite of his name, he'd been fixed. One of the secretaries at the station had been sure her cat was fixed, too, regardless of the attention all the male felines in the neighborhood gave it. Four kittens later, she discovered she was wrong. Colin brought Playboy home with the idea that Deborah would like him.

Deborah did. She loved him, in fact. She squealed and chased him and rubbed his fur the wrong way when she petted him. Playboy was fine with grownups. Whenever Deborah showed up on his radar, he ran like hell.

He was a handsome beast, a gray tabby with an enormous plumy tail. Even the vet thought his tail was impressive, and the vet had seen and traumatized whole regiments of kitties. Unfortunately, while standing in the line for tail twice, Playboy had forgotten about the line for brains.

Colin leaned down to pet the cat. Playboy purred and stretched and rolled over so his belly fur stuck up in the air. He wasn't a lap cat, but he was friendly enough . . . on his own terms, and always provided you didn't shriek "Kitty!" in his ear when he wasn't expecting it.

"Remember when he met the mirror monster?" Colin said, chuckling.

Kelly snorted. "I'm not likely to forget it. Oh, my God!"

Playboy'd been a kitten then, and brand-new to the house. He'd staggered up the stairs and wandered into Colin's study. The study had begun life as a bedroom. It boasted sliding, mirrored closet doors, like the other upstairs bedrooms. Playboy, then, spotted another cat in the mirror.

The kitty in the mirror saw him, too. Playboy had thought he was the only cat in the house. He angrily arched his back. So did the kitty in the mirror. He stuck his majestic tail straight up in the air and bottlebrushed it. The kitty in the mirror did, too. Playboy hissed and showed off his pointy teeth. The kitty in the mirror did the same thing.

Provoked past standing it, Playboy charged. The kitty in the mirror charged, too. They slammed together at top speed. *Bang!* The kitty in the mirror turned out to have a much harder head than Playboy did. And Colin and Kelly, who'd watched the confrontation with wonder and amazement, rolled on the floor laughing their asses off and scared the cat.

"He only did that once," Kelly said: the best defense of Playboy's poor battered brain cells she could give.

"I should hope so!" Colin exclaimed. "If he'd done it twice, he would've killed himself."

Deborah came into the front room. Playboy rolled over onto his stomach again and got his feet under him, ready to light out for the tall timber if the small, noisy human launched a sneak attack. But Deborah didn't have killing cats on her mind right this minute. She was clutching a piece of paper, on which she'd been coloring in crayon.

"Look!" she said importantly, and displayed her artwork: a large blue blob.

"That's very nice," Kelly said, and then, "What is it?" With preschoolers, as with adult abstractionists, you were allowed, even encouraged, to ask such questions.

"It's a whale," Deborah answered.

"That *is* nice," Colin said. He'd picked up a whole series of children's nature guides on the cheap somewhere. Deborah loved them—she had some of them practically memorized. So if he felt chuffed just then, Kelly wouldn't have said he hadn't earned the right.

Deborah, though, hadn't finished. "It's a *sperm* whale," she explained. "But it's not done yet. I have to finish coloring in its sperm."

Kelly looked at Colin. Colin looked at her. They both fought the losing battle as long as they could—say, for a second and a half. Then they lost it even harder than they had when Playboy tried to assassinate the kitty lurking in the mirror. Playboy couldn't tell whether they were laughing at him this time. He decided not to take any chances and skulked away, his belly low to the rug.

Having lost it, Kelly and Colin couldn't get it back. They laughed and laughed and laughed some more. Deborah decided it must be funny whether she knew why or not, so she started laughing, too.

Marshall clumped down the stairs to find out what the devil the commotion was about. He scowled with a young man's stern severity at his ruined father and stepmother. "Some people!" he said. "You see what happens when you get into the dope with the weedkiller sprayed on it?"

"Is *that* what did it?" Kelly said when she could speak again—which took a while. "Oh, Jesus! I hurt myself."

"Me, too." Colin was holding his sides. Kelly'd never seen anyone actually do that before, but she also felt like trying it. He went on as if giving God a takeout order: "I want some new ribs, please. I went and ruined this set."

"They're silly!" Deborah informed her half-brother.

"Thanks for letting me know, kid. I never would've figured it out without you," he said. Warily, as the cat might have, he eyed his elders. "What *did* happen there? Whatever it is, it knocked my train of thought right off the rails."

Also warily, afraid of a new spasm, Kelly told him what. She and Colin got through the rerun with no more than a few extra giggles, but Marshall laughed almost as hard as they had. Playboy, who'd wondered if it might be safe to come back, turned tail and fled again.

"Wow! Oh, wow!" Marshall said when he got done cracking up. "Have to steal that some way. You couldn't make it up."

"That's why we keep cats and kids around," Colin said. "For their entertainment value." He eyed his younger son. "You were pretty darn funny once upon a time your own self. Shame it wore off."

"Did Grandpa think you were funny?" Marshall asked.

"He thought I was so funny, he walloped me with a belt," Colin replied. "I gave him a standing O after that, 'cause I sure couldn't sit down."

"Mm." Marshall sounded thoughtful now. "You never did that with us, did you?"

"Nope. Playing too rough, way it looks to me. A whack on the fanny is a different story. Sometimes you can't make a kid pay attention any other way," Colin said.

"Says you." Kelly still wasn't convinced, but she was less unconvinced than she had been before Deborah was born. Till she saw for herself, she'd had no idea how nutso little kids could drive you and how well they ignored anything resembling logic or common sense.

One of the reasons you swatted a little kid on the fanny, of course, was to make yourself feel better. Before she'd had her own, she would have dismissed that as a rotten reason. She still did, but less scornfully than she would have back in the days BC (Before Children, natch).

Playboy made another cautious approach. Since the grownups weren't making loud, alarming noises, and since Deborah didn't seem to want to ruffle his fur or yank his tail, he rolled himself back into a donut on the rug. Tail over his nose, he fell asleep. Kelly wished she could turn herself off so fast. Even tired from teaching and from riding herd on Deborah, she didn't have the knack.

The next Tuesday—a day she didn't have to teach at CSUDH—

she walked out to get the mail after the mailwoman pedaled past: a grownup trike had replaced the old delivery van. There was a water bill, what looked like a rejection for Marshall, a flyer announcing a hardware sale, and a postcard.

The postcard was black and white. It showed a mill on a river, with New Englandy–looking houses and pines in the background. When she turned it over, the printed legend read *View of Guilford, Maine*. The note (which, by the postmark, had taken upwards of three weeks to cross the country) was in Rob's spiky handwriting.

Hi Dad and other sordid family, he wrote. Maybe he meant *assorted*. Then again, from what Kelly had heard about him, maybe he didn't. *This will let you know that Lindsey is pregnant. So our kid will have a half-aunt (thorax or abdomen?) just a skosh older than he or she is. Pretty weird, especially if they get to meet one of these years. Hope you're all flourishing.* His scrawled signature followed.

She'd never met Rob. Squirt Frog and the Evolving Tadpoles hadn't come through L.A. after she started hanging out with Colin. She was happy for him and his wife anyway. Babies were good things.

She carried in the mail. Marshall said something foul when he saw the SASE. "I've got good news, too," Kelly said.

"Yeah? Like what?"

"You're gonna be an uncle. And Deborah will be an aunt—or a half-aunt, depending on how you look at things." She held out the postcard.

Marshall took it. "So this is what Guilford looks like. Or what it looked like whenever they snapped that photo." He read his brother's note, then nodded. "Okay, you're right. That *is* good news."

"Uh-huh. I'm going to call your dad if I can," Kelly said. Power was out, which meant the cell towers were out, which meant her cell phone was a chunk of plastic and semiconductors: useful as a paperweight, but not for talking with people. Sometimes, though—not always—landlines worked when cells didn't. They were on a different grid, or something.

She got a dial tone when she picked up the handset. "Colin Ferguson," said the voice on the other end of the line, and then, when he saw which number had called him, "What's up?"

"We just got a card from Rob. He and Lindsey are going to have a baby."

"So I'll be a grandfather, huh?"

"That's right. How does it make you feel?"

"Officially obsolete instead of just obsolescent," he said. Kelly laughed—not so hard as she had about Playboy or the sperm whale, but she did. Colin always sounded like Colin. It was . . . she supposed . . . one of the things she loved about him.

Louise Ferguson flipped through James Henry's first-grade reader and spelling book. Her mouth tightened down to a thin, hard line. You couldn't expect little kids to read Shakespeare or Thoreau. You couldn't expect them to spell words like *unconstitutional* or *dystrophy*, either. She understood that.

But . . .

Maybe her memory was playing tricks on her. People always thought they'd walked uphill both ways when they went to school, and that they'd had to shovel through snowdrifts taller than they were—this, even if they'd lived in Laguna Beach. Louise understood that, too. It was part of the recipe that cooked up old farts.

Again, but . . .

The little stories in the reader sure *seemed* dumber than the ones Rob and Vanessa and Marshall had had. And, back in the day, those had seemed dumber than the ones she recalled from her own childhood. The vocabulary was tiny. The writing was bad: clunky bad. It wasn't interesting; it didn't make you go on and see what happened next. They weren't stories you'd read because you wanted to, not even if you were only six years old. The only way you'd read them was if you had to. Even the illos were hackwork.

And every story preached. Louise wasn't racist. She wasn't likely to have had a kid by a Mexican-American if she were. She had nothing against gays, lesbians, bisexuals, or transgendered people. Celebrating diversity was one thing. Singing hosannas about it over and over and over one more time was something else again. It was boring, was what it was.

Yes, education was propaganda. You taught kids the values you wanted them to have, then hoped like hell those values would stick when they got bigger. But did you have to use such a big trowel and lay them on so thick? This stuff was as bad as what the schoolmasters who taught about the dictatorship of the proletariat or that the Führer was always right had used.

If she complained about it to James Henry's teacher, what would happen? The books wouldn't change. The Los Angeles Unified School District had its commandments, and one of them was *These materials shalt thou use, and no others.* And Ms. Calderon would decide she was a reactionary, maybe a dangerous one.

Ms. Calderon already had her suspicions. James Henry could read even when he started kindergarten, for one thing. All by itself, that made teachers and administrators suspect Louise of being an elitist parent. What else could she be, when she'd already done some of what they got paid to do?

She made a small, discontented noise. If they did a better job at what they got paid to do . . . She remembered what had happened in one Orange County school district—just south of L.A.—before the eruption. The staff there, in its infinite wisdom, had decided that the *whole* alphabet was too hard for kids in kindergarten to learn. So they'd left out four or five of the less common letters, figuring those would keep till the first grade.

When news of this educational innovation leaked out, everyone who heard about it screamed bloody murder. The district backtracked as fast as it could—it didn't believe there was no such thing as bad publicity. But, as far as Louise knew, none of the educators who'd had the brainstorm got fired. Thanks to tenure rules, even sexual predators could be hard to can.

She made that noise over again as she paged through the speller. Her dog could spell most of these words, and she didn't even have a dog.

She knew what the problem was. L.A. Unified wasn't geared for kids like James Henry. He came from a middle-class background, and his first language was English. That made him stand out from the rest of the herd like a zebra with polka dots. L.A. Unified was about turning immigrants and immigrants' children into citizens. It didn't do that any too well, either, but at least it tried.

Private school? Catholic school? Louise was about as Catholic as a petunia, but even so. . . . *Even so, what?* she wondered. No matter how much she wanted to send James Henry somewhere better than the local public school, she couldn't afford to. The public school was free. The others wanted—insisted on— cash on the barrelhead.

You get what you pay for. That was one of the oldest and saddest truths in the world. If you could cough up the money and escape from LAUSD, you got your kid a halfway decent education. If you couldn't, Junior was stuck with this brain-dead pap instead. Good luck forty years down the line, too. He or she would be washing dishes or standing behind a cash register, waiting on the successful people whose folks had had the jack to buy them a head start.

She knew she'd left homeschooling out of the mix. Homeschooling was cheap, as those things went. It was also aggressively practical for a single mother, wasn't it? "Yeah, right," Louise muttered. You could stay home and teach your kid every single thing you wanted him to know. Sure you could—as long as somebody else went out to slay the antelopes and put antelope-burgers on the table.

James Henry wandered into the bedroom. "How come you're looking at my books, Mommy?" he asked. "Don't you already know that stuff?"

"Yeah. I do," Louise answered. "The trouble is, so do you."

"It's okay. The work is easy." James Henry might still be pretty new to this whole school thing, but he'd already figured out that skating through it meant he had more time to do stuff he actually liked. He wasn't a dummy, not even slightly.

"It's not okay. You should be doing more," Louise said. "You know you can do work that's harder than this."

"I will." James Henry wasn't worried about anything, which was why being a first-grader was so nice. "When they give it to me, I will."

Louise sighed. "I know. But will that be soon enough?" She imagined him learning the multiplication table just in time to graduate from high school. That wasn't fair; she knew she exaggerated. Without a doubt, they'd teach it to him by the end of his junior year.

When she laughed—it was either laugh or cry—James Henry asked, "What's funny, Mommy?"

"Your school is funny, that's what," Louise answered.

"It sure is," James Henry said. "There's this one kid—his name is Adrian—and he eats boogers."

"Thank you so much for sharing," Louise said dryly. Her older offspring had brought back tales out of school like that, too. Remembering her own days as a first-grader, Louise was sure she'd also been surrounded by little monsters. The kid who'd jumped up and down in a puddle of puke, for instance . . . When you started remembering things like that, you understood why you forgot so much of your childhood. It was one of the few mercies life doled out.

Disgusting Adrian probably wasn't hurting anyone but himself. But the horror who'd jumped up and down . . . What was his name, anyhow? Now she'd go nuts trying to bring it back. But what must his mother's face have looked like when she saw—and got a whiff of—his shoes? And his pants, too. He would have splashed the stuff all over them. Of course he would.

"Jimmy!" Louise exclaimed.

Her youngest son sent her a quizzical stare. "You never call me that. You get yipes stripes when people call me that."

Yipes stripes were his name for the frown lines she got when he did things she didn't like. And he was right—she didn't like it when people called him that. But . . . "Jimmy isn't your name," she agreed. "James Henry is your name. Jimmy is the name of a boy I went to school with when I was in the first grade."

"Oh." James Harvey digested that. "He must be an old man by now, huh?"

"You say the sweetest things, dear," Louise replied. She wondered what *had* happened to Jimmy. Was he the one who'd joined the Marines as soon as he got out of high school? She thought so, but she wasn't sure. The only thing she was sure she remembered him for was that one morning at recess.

How come they hadn't called him Old Pukey Shoes or something else just as elegant all the way through the rest of school? If he'd joined the Marines, maybe he hadn't been anybody you'd want to mess with even when he was a lot smaller. She didn't remember that one way or the other. Girls mostly didn't have to worry about whether boys would knock their block off. Mostly.

"Do you guys ever have fights on the playground?" she asked.

"You get in trouble for that," James Henry said.

Louise needed a moment to notice it wasn't what the lawyers called a responsive answer. "Do you ever have any fights?" she asked again.

"I never got caught at one," James Henry said after a visible pause for thought. Louise decided that would do. What you did mattered to you. Everybody did things he—or she—wasn't necessarily proud of. What you got caught at mattered to the world. Any number of disgraced politicians and athletes and celebrities could testify to that.

James Henry seemed glad to go do something else then. He must have figured he'd get in trouble for admitting he might have had playground fights. If he'd bragged that he went around starting them, he would have. As things were . . . Colin had told Rob and then Marshall *Don't throw the first punch, but do your best to make sure you throw the last one.* Louise had no use for her ex, but that still seemed a good recipe for not ending up in very many brawls.

It was much too late to worry about what her life would have been like had she not walked out the door on Colin. That didn't keep her from doing it, of course; plain and obvious truth never kept anybody from doing such things. The answer seemed plain and obvious, too. She'd have more money and fewer nagging little worries than she did now. But she'd also be emotionally dead.

This was better. She kept telling herself so. It could have been really good, if only Teo had wanted the child he'd fathered. If only. *My granny could have been a bicycle, too, if only she'd had wheels,* Louise thought. She shook her head. Granny would have saved a fortune on gasoline, too. In Granny's day, though, they hadn't cared. Well, too bad for them.

XII

Back in California, Bryce Miller had never paid that much attention to the Weather Channel even after the supervolcano eruption. When he did pause there in his channelsurfing, it was to see what Mother Nature was doing to some other part of the country, not what she had in mind for him and his friends. SoCal led a charmed life.

But he wasn't in SoCal any more. He was smack dab in the middle of the flyover states. Back in California, he'd used the term with the light irony it deserved . . . if you came from one of the coasts, anyhow. They used it here, too—bitterly, angrily, hopelessly. This was the part of the country the parts of the country that made (and that spun) the news ignored. Roman citizens of the second century A.D. who lived in Spain or Pannonia or Cappadocia would have said *provincial* the same hangdog way American citizens who lived in Nebraska said *flyover states*.

And, in this part of the country, the Weather Channel had the urgency of a kick in the teeth. That had been true even before the eruption. It was truer now. Satchel Paige famously said *Don't look back. Something might be gaining on you.* Around here, you did need to look ahead, to see what was rolling down on you.

This particular Weather Channel talking head was a very pretty Asian woman. She was pretty enough to make Susan notice. "You don't mind the blizzards so much when she tells you about them?" she suggested.

"I could have the mute button on, and I wouldn't mind," Bryce answered. Susan gave him a dirty look. He winked at her. That helped, a little.

He discovered he didn't want the mute button on after all. The pretty weathercaster was saying, "The upper Midwest needs to brace itself for the arrival of the Siberian Express. This enormous cold front was born near the North Pole and has been rolling south like a freight train. It has already severely impacted Canada."

Bryce made a face at the bureaucratic language. He started to say something rude about it, but Susan shushed him.

Just as well, too. The talking head went on, "Edmonton's low night before last was minus sixty-eight. Saskatoon's high yesterday—the high, mind you—was minus thirty-one. The storm reached Winnipeg last night. The low there was minus fifty-six."

A screen behind her showed a handful of people bundled up like Eskimos trying to make their way through swirling white. It was labeled EDMONTON, but it could have been any place up to and including the last frozen circle of hell, the one where Dante stuck Satan. Americans were preoccupied with their own misery. The eruption itself had hurt the USA worse than Canada. The disrupted weather was doing a nastier number on the neighbor to the north.

Even back in pre-eruption days, ninety percent of the people in Canada had lived within a hundred miles of the American border. That was where the climate had been sortakinda decent: like northern Minnesota, say, only a little rougher. A little rougher than northern Minnesota now, though, was on the ragged edge of human habitability. Or, judging by that footage, maybe over it.

"This is a big storm—a big, rugged storm. Even by post-eruption standards, this storm is very bad news," the weather-caster said seriously. "Lots of snow, strong winds, and frigid temperatures mean you should not go out in it unless you absolutely have to. And if you think you have to, think again. Staying inside may save your life."

Susan eyed the progression of the front on the CG map. It was just roaring over the border now. That put it about a day from Wayne. Maybe a little more, but you couldn't count on that.

"Don't go in to class tomorrow," she said. "You'd probably get there okay, but I don't know about coming back to town. What I do know is, I'm afraid you'd be dumb enough to try."

"Hey!" Bryce sounded indignant, which he was. "I don't do anything the people around here don't do."

"Yeah, well, even the people from around here aren't used to a blizzard like this," Susan answered. "Stay here. Stay . . . as warm as you can, anyhow." She couldn't say *stay warm*, because the apartment wasn't warm. But it was warmer than the outside would be, anyhow. How cold could it get here with the Siberian Express howling down? Colder than Bryce wanted to find out about, that was for sure.

He went to the Wayne State Web site. On the home page, an announcement in big red letters said DUE TO THE WEATHER EMER-GENCY, CLASSES WILL NOT BE HELD FOR THE NEXT TWO DAYS. A DECISION ON REOPENING WILL BE MADE AT THAT POINT IN TIME. THANK YOU.

Susan read it over his shoulder. "There," she said, a certain I-told-you-so in her voice. "Now you can stay home without guilt." Since guilt was exactly what Bryce would have felt for ditching his class without official approval, he maintained a prudent silence.

Al Stewart sang a song called "Coldest Winter" about, among other things, the winter of 1709. Along with the guys in Squirt Frog and the Evolving Tadpoles, Al Stewart was one of the few pop musicians with a sense of history, or even a sense that there was such a thing as history. No surprise that a classicist and ancient historian like Bryce had a lot of him on his iPod.

When the Siberian Express blew into and blew through Wayne and did its goddamnedest to blow the town over, Bryce decided that 1709 no longer came within miles of being the coldest winter in memory. Topping it might have taken more than three centuries, but this winter of the world's discontent froze every earlier competitor in its tracks.

The wind howled. It screamed. It wailed. The apartment had double-paned windows with shades, venetian blinds, and thick curtains. Cold seeped through them anyhow. Susan had a stuffed cat with a long, fat tail filled with sand that she used to keep chilly outside air from sliding in under the bottom of the door. That was fine, but how did you keep the chilly air from sliding past all the other cracks between the door and its frame?

For that matter, how did you keep cold from sliding in through the door, and through the walls? Yes, the walls were insulated, too. When the Siberian Express came to town, the insulation was fighting as far out of its weight as a flyweight forced into the ring against Mike Tyson.

Bryce had always been glad the apartment was on the second floor, not the first. When you had neighbors above you, you often wondered if a herd of shoes was migrating right over your head. Stereo sound you didn't want was another delight when it came through the ceiling.

That much, he'd known as long as he'd been apartment-hunting. But what he hadn't worried about till he got to Wayne was that heat rose. When the people down below tried to heat their place to the fifty degrees allowed by law, some of what their sorry heater pumped out also did its feeble best to warm this apartment. That feeble best might not be very good, but anything was better than nothing.

Against the Siberian Express, anything wasn't nearly enough better than nothing. After a while, Bryce and Susan spread all the blankets they had on top of the bed. They got in, fully clothed, and wrapped their arms around each other.

"I'm still cold," Susan said.

"So am I." Bryce nodded. "Well, if they find us frozen, we'll be one lump of ice, not two." He squeezed her tighter.

"You say the sweetest things," she murmured. For some reason, Bryce suspected her of imperfect sincerity.

He couldn't stay wrapped up with her all the time, not unless his bladder froze solid. When he flushed the toilet, he hoped it would work. They insulated pipes here, but not against weather like this. Sooner or later, those would start freezing up.

On his way back to bed, he pulled back the curtains and the blinds and the shade so he could look out the window. He saw a tone poem Whistler would have been proud of. White snow fell from a gray sky onto white drifts. The drifts might not have been as high as an elephant's eye, but they were gaining on it.

"What do you see?" Susan asked. She was too sensible to come out from under the covers herself unless she had to.

"Outside of a couple of woolly mammoths, just snow." Bryce adapted a line from Groucho Marx: "Inside the woolly mammoths, it's too dark to tell."

"Ba-dum-bum! Rimshot!" Susan said, and then, "Invite the poor things in for coffee. I'll bet they're freezing out there."

"Wouldn't be surprised." Bryce got back into the bed. As he chastely snuggled with his wife, he said, "Remind me again why I wanted to move to Nebraska."

"It's called a *job*." Susan pronounced the last word *yob*, as if it were some strange foreign term, possibly borrowed from the German. "They give you *money* for it." That came out as *mohnee*, as if it also didn't belong in English.

"Oh, yeah." Bryce nodded as if he'd forgotten. He wished he had.

After a while, bored by doing nothing under the covers, he started to do something. Susan slapped his roving hands away. "If you think I'm going to take my clothes off for you, Buster, you're out of your ever-lovin' mind!"

"You don't have to take 'em off," Bryce said—reasonably, he thought. "Just slide some of 'em down a little. Hey, what else have you got to do right now?"

"Now there's a come-on line," Susan muttered. But she rolled over so her back was to him. With a minimum of disrobing, the deed was done. Fornication with next to no bare skin wasn't nearly so much fun as fornication with lots of bare skin. It was a hell of a lot better than no fornication at all, though.

Bryce thought so, anyhow. "See?" he said, setting a hand on her bare hip. "We're warmer now."

"Oh, boy." Susan quickly made sure that hip wasn't bare any more. Then she rolled over to face him again and gave him a kiss. "You're crazy. I love you. I must, or else I'd be crazy, too."

They got out of bed to use the john, to eat, to make hot coffee for themselves if not for the woolly mammoths, and to check the Weather Channel and CNN for views of what the Siberian Express was doing to the Midwest beyond their frozen apartment and frozen Wayne. By then, the storm had got down to St. Louis, which didn't even come close to being built for blizzards like that. It was heading for Memphis and New Orleans. They were even less ready. Ready or not, here it came.

For Marshall Ferguson, the Siberian Express was a noise in another room. When the house had power, he saw a lot of white on white on the TV. Newscasters gave forth with the number of people found frozen. It was up into the hundreds by now.

His own problems were more immediate. He remembered hearing about someone who set out to be a writer. Naturally, the fellow cast his eyes on the tip-top markets like *Playboy* and *The New Yorker*. He declared he wouldn't bother to submit to any market that paid less. Either he starved or he found some other line of work, because you sure couldn't make a living that way.

For one thing, you were competing against the entire literate world. All the top writers aimed their top stuff at places that paid best. For another, those magazines weren't likely to buy more than one story a year from you even if you were Salman Rushdie or Stephen King. No matter how well they paid, they didn't pay well enough to let you make a living on one story a year, or even on one story a year to each if you could do that.

And selling pieces for two hundred bucks here, or four hundred fifty there, didn't feel the same after the big check from *Playboy* came in. His friends wondered why he couldn't do that all the time. So did his father. Dad nodded when Marshall explained the facts of a writer's life to him. He might understand them once he heard them, but they sure didn't make him jump up and down.

They didn't make Marshall jump up and down, either. If he weren't living at the house where he'd grown up, if he didn't pick up money on the side sitting for James Henry and Deborah, he would have had to look harder for a real job. He didn't get as much from his mother as he had because James Henry was in school and had teachers to babysit him.

After he took a shower and dried his hair one evening, he came downstairs. "Do you know somebody named Sophie Lundgren?" Kelly asked.

"Mrs. Lundgren? Sure. She taught me Spanish at San Atanasio High," he answered. "*Hay un elefante en mi ropa interior.*" It meant *There's an elephant in my underwear.* Mrs. Lundgren hadn't taught him that, but he wouldn't have been able to work it out for himself without what she had taught him. After a second or two, he thought to ask, "How come?"

"Because she called a few minutes ago—wants you to call her back. I wrote her number down." Kelly paused, too. "Sophie Lundgren taught you Spanish? She sure doesn't sound like she's from Mexico City."

Marshall shrugged. "I just work here. But yeah, she did. Hey, this is L.A. People here do all kinds of shit you wouldn't guess from their names."

"Well, you've got that right," Kelly said.

"What did she want?" Marshall asked. "I don't think I've heard from her more than once or twice since I graduated, and that's, like, a while ago now."

"She said she was calling some of the students she liked best. She's moving—moving a long way, I think. She wants help weekend after this one hauling boxes out to a truck. She say's she'll buy dinner for everybody who shows up."

That was bound to be a cheaper way to move than paying professionals. Still, Marshall had liked Mrs. Lundgren. Seeing her one more time might be a kick. "Where's the number? I'll call her back."

"It's on a Post-it by the landline phone."

"Okay." Marshall ambled over. So it was, with the name in Kelly's neat, legible script. *Accurate* was the word for Kelly, all right. Marshall dialed the number. It had a 310 area code, so it wasn't too far away.

Ring . . . Ring . . . "Hello?" Yes, that was Sophie Lundgren's voice—a whiskey baritone, or near enough. Marshall didn't know that Mrs. Lundgren poured 'em down, but that sure had been the rumor. Her voice did nothing to disprove it, anyway. If he'd taught high school for umpty-ump years, he figured he would have drunk, too, in self-defense if for no better reason.

"Hi, Mrs. Lundgren. This is Marshall Ferguson. I hear you

need some moving help weekend after this one. What time, and where do you live?"

"Thank you so much, Marshall!" his old teacher exclaimed. "Yes, Saturday a week, starting right after lunch." She gave him the address. It was down in Torrance, but this side of the Del Amo mall—not too far to get to by bike. He wrote it down on the Post-it, too. Next to Kelly's, his handwriting looked even sloppier than it did on its own.

"Who else'll be there?" he asked. "Anybody I know?"

She named two or three names he didn't recognize—they were from either before or after his time. Then she added, "Oh, and Paul and Janine Werber said they'd come."

"How about that? I remember them, yeah," Marshall said. He'd had serious hots for Janine Werber when he was seventeen years old. She'd been Janine O'Sullivan then: a gray-eyed blonde who looked as Irish as her name. She'd liked him okay, but not like that. She'd had eyes only for Paul. In high school, he'd already had his eye on becoming a CPA. Marshall thought Paul was the dullest thing that walked on two legs, but even he knew he might not be completely objective.

"Paul is . . . very reliable," Mrs. Lundgren said.

"Right," Marshall answered. If that was the best she could come up with, she thought Paul was the dullest thing on two legs, too. "Look, I'll see you about one Saturday after next, okay?" He said his good-byes and hung up.

"Somebody you knew way back when?" Kelly asked.

"Uh-huh. A couple—they've been a couple a long time, I guess. She was kinda cute then." Marshall didn't want to admit too much, even to himself. "He was kinda nerdly." That was an understatement.

One of Kelly's eyebrows quirked. "Okay." She left it right there. So did Marshall. If Paul and Janine were still an item all this time after graduation, what else could he do?

On the appointed day, he pedaled down to Torrance. Clouds blew past the watery sun. He got a couple of spatters of drizzle, no more. It was chilly, but he didn't mind that. He'd work hard enough to warm up.

Mrs. Lundgren's apartment was on the ground floor, which was good. He wouldn't have to lug heavy stuff down stairs. Piles of boxes stood everywhere. His old teacher introduced him to a couple of guys he didn't know. One of them said, "Hey, haven't I seen some of your stories online?"

"Yeah." Marshall grinned from ear to ear. He'd had one or two people recognize his name before, but only one or two. It was still a treat when it happened.

Then he forgot about it, because Paul and Janine Werber showed up. Paul had put on fifteen or twenty pounds; his hair was thinning. Janine looked . . . just the way Marshall remembered. Damn good, in other words.

Paul started gabbing with Mrs. Lundgren and even trying out bits of the Spanish she'd taught him. He'd always been a suckup—looked as if he still was. That left Marshall with Janine. "Long time," he said brilliantly.

"It has been, yeah," she said, and held out her hand. Marshall shook it. Then—Paul was paying zero attention to anything but his old teacher (and himself)—he kissed her hand and quickly let it fall. If she didn't like that, she'd let him know about it. If she did like it . . . He didn't know what he'd do then. It was like putting a story together. If you didn't write the first sentence, you'd never see how it came out.

Her eyes widened. Whatever she'd expected, that wasn't it. She didn't look mad or anything, though. "What have you been up to?" she asked.

"Got out of UCSB a few years ago," he said. "I write some stories. I sell 'em, but I'm not getting rich at it or anything. How about you? Kids and all?"

"No kids." She shook her head. "I'm a paralegal. It's not exciting, but it pays some bills. Paul's practice is doing pretty well, too. We're so busy all the time, we hardly get to see each other."

Was that a hint? He didn't get the chance to find out, because Mrs. Lundgren said, "Come on, people. You didn't come over here for Old Home Week. You came to work for your dinner. So work!"

Work they did, hauling boxes and furniture out to a big U-Haul parked in front of the building. They went on talking while they worked, of course. Mrs. Lundgren, it turned out, was moving to Copala, a town on the west coast of Mexico not far from Acapulco. She spoke the language, her money would go further there, and the weather would be better. She liked it hot—to her, L.A. these days might as well have been Minneapolis.

Marshall listened to her with one ear. With the other, he listened to Janine as much as he could without—he hoped—being too blatant about it. She seemed glad to see him and glad to talk to him. She'd always liked to talk. He remembered as much. But she seemed interested in him, too. "A writer!" she said. "How cool is that?"

He shrugged, as well as he could with a box of books—why did even a little box of books always weigh a ton?—in his arms. "It'd be cooler if I could, y'know, make a living at it."

"But it's so creative! All I do all day is look for papers and fill out forms," she said. He was sure she got paid more than he did for staring up to the ceiling and making feckless lunges at the keyboard. But if she wanted to think he was cool and creative, he sure wouldn't try to tell her she was wrong.

By the time the apartment was empty and the truck was full, Marshall felt bent-kneed and long-armed, like an arthritic chimpanzee. The restaurant, a Chinese place called Helen Yue's, was only a couple of blocks away. Had it been any farther, he might not have made it.

He told himself he sat down next to Janine by coincidence.

Even he didn't believe it, but he couldn't prove he was lying. Paul kept talking with Mrs. Lundgren, now about tax tricks for people who lived outside the United States. He didn't even notice when Janine gave Marshall her cell and e-mail, or when Marshall gave her his. Tax tricks, now, tax tricks *mattered*.

After dinner, they all went back to the Spanish teacher's now-empty apartment. She hugged her ex-students one by one. "You get to go back home," she told them. "Me, I get to see if I remember how to drive. I have a motel room rented for tonight, and I need to have that U-Haul at the pier by seven tomorrow morning. Ain't life fun sometimes?"

Just then, Marshall was thinking life might be fun sometimes after all. Mrs. Lundgren stepped up into the truck, started it, and drove away. She'd be Queen of the Road wherever she went. Nobody on a bike would argue with that big, noisy, smelly thing. Marshall remembered taking internal combustion for granted. No more. No more.

The former Spanish students shook hands with one another, unchained their bikes, and climbed aboard. "Take care, Paul," Marshall said. "See ya, Janine."

Paul Werber kind of grunted. "See you, Marshall," Janine said. Marshall pedaled back to San Atanasio several inches above the potholed pavement.

Colin Ferguson was reading Deborah *The Wind in the Willows*. It was an unabridged version, so she didn't come close to getting all of it. But it had plenty of colored pictures. She liked those fine. And she liked sitting on the couch with her daddy while it poured outside.

Marshall came downstairs. He didn't sound as much like a stampeding buffalo as he had when he was a teenager. He was wearing his plastic rain slicker. When he raised his bike's kickstand and rolled it toward the front door, Colin called, "Where are you going in this lovely weather?"

"Out." Marshall threw the word over his shoulder.

"Out where? Somewhere in particular, or kind of everywhere at once?"

"Out to lunch."

"Who with?" Colin knew Marshall and Vanessa both could have gigged him for that. He wouldn't have written it that way himself. But writing and talking were different critters. Dammit, they were.

"Janine." Marshall was out the door and had it closed and locked behind him before Colin could have answered even if he'd wanted to. As a matter of fact, he did want to, but he wasn't nearly sure what to say.

Deborah tugged at the sleeve of his sweatshirt. "Read more, Daddy!" Colin started to. Deborah let out an indignant squawk: "You already read that!" He had, too. He noticed once she reminded him. He straightened up and tried to fly right.

Marshall didn't get home till a quarter to four. Deborah had long since had as much of Mole and Ratty and even Mr. Toad as she wanted at one dose. Marshall settled his bike on an old towel and started wiping the water he'd brought in off the foyer tiles. "Long lunch," Colin remarked.

"Uh-huh." Marshall didn't look up from what he was doing.

"Have a nice time?"

"Yeah."

Colin sighed. "Am I wrong or am I right—she *is* married to that Paul fellow, isn't she?"

"Yeah—for now." Marshall still didn't look up.

Colin sighed again. "Look, son, I'm not gonna tell you how to run your life. You're a grownup. You're entitled to make your own mistakes. Lord knows I did. But I am gonna tell you this: anybody who'll cheat with you will cheat on you, too. That's how those things work."

"Not always." Marshall kept doling out words as if they cost as much as gasoline.

"No, not always," Colin agreed, which did make his son look at him—in surprise, if he was any judge (and he was). He went on, "Not always, but that's the way to bet."

Marshall squeezed the old dish towel they used to dry the tiles. By his expression, he would sooner have had his hands around his father's neck. In a voice colder than the Siberian Express, he answered, "It's my life. You said it—I didn't. So let me deal with it, okay?"

"Okay." Colin sighed one more time. Then, stubborn cop that he was, he also tried one more time, choosing what he said with care: "Cheating was what shot my marriage with your mother behind the ear, you know."

"Nah." Marshall shook his head. "That just shoveled dirt over it, Dad. Mom wouldn't've done it if she didn't think you guys were already dead. Besides, Janine hasn't got any kids."

"She's got a husband." Colin had to struggle to force out the words. Marshall might well have been right—from Louise's point of view, anyhow. But Colin wasn't used to looking at things from that perspective.

Marshall let out a dismissive snort. "Not hardly. Paul won't care. He only notices she's around when he gets horny."

"That's how Janine tells it," Colin said. "It might sound different if you were to listen to Paul." People who wanted to do something always told stories that showed doing whatever it was was the best, the most natural, thing in the world. They told those stories to other people, and they told them to themselves. They believed them, too. As a cop, Colin had seen that more times than he could count. You didn't need to be a cop, though. You just had to keep your eyes open.

Which Marshall wasn't doing right this minute. Janine, no doubt, was keeping her legs open, so he had the oldest excuse in the world. The best excuse, plenty of folks would have said. And it was . . . for a while.

"Dad—" Marshall wasn't going to listen to Paul. He wasn't going to listen to his old man, either. He'd listen to Janine, and to his stiff dick.

And Colin couldn't do thing one about it. He'd said as much to Marshall. His younger son wasn't so very young any more. If all this ended up without a happy ending, Colin could be there to pat Marshall on the back. That was about as far as it went.

It might have a happy ending. They might discover They'd Been Meant For Each Other All Along. Colin heard the caps in his own mind, as if he were listening to a movie trailer's voice-over. He never believed movie-trailer voiceovers. He didn't believe this would have a happy ending, either.

"Good luck," he said, and he meant it. "You'll get plenty of new stuff to write about, any which way."

Marshall rolled his eyes, as if to say *What am I supposed to do with such Philistines?* He went upstairs without another word. He was in love, or at least getting laid more often than he had been any time lately. No, he wouldn't listen to anybody who didn't see the world through similar hot-pink-colored glasses.

"Shit," Colin muttered. "I sure wish he would."

"Nothing we can do about it," Kelly said later, when Colin grumbled to her. "As soon as his old teacher told him Janine was gonna be there, you could watch the brains dribbling out of his ears."

"You know what the worst of it is?" Colin said.

"Tell me," Kelly answered, since that was what he plainly wanted to do.

"It's embarrassing, that's what it is," he said. "Far as I know, we've never had anybody in the family who broke up someone else's marriage. There's a name for people like that, and it's not a nice name."

"If she wasn't already hot to trot, he wouldn't have got anywhere with her," Kelly said. "And if he hadn't come along, she would have found somebody else."

"He said pretty much the same thing," Colin answered. "It's fine as far as it goes, but it doesn't go far enough. So Janine dumps Paul and grabs hold of Marshall. So yippee. But what happens when she gets itchy again six months from now, or three years, or five years? You know what happens as well as I do. But Marshall? Marshall hasn't got a clue."

"Or maybe he just doesn't care. It isn't quite the same thing."

"He may not care now. Why should he? Things are great now. He'll care when he's wearing egg on his face, though."

"Yeah, probably." Kelly sighed. "When that happens, try not to go 'I told you so' too loud, okay?"

"Who, me?" Colin did his best to seem perfectly innocent. Since he was anything but, the effort fell flat. He poked his wife in the ribs. "Okay, I'll try. Won't be easy—I'll tell you that."

"Try," she said again. "Anyway, it may blow over. Once she's had her fling, Janine may decide she likes Paul better after all. CPAs make a lot more money than writers."

"Huh! If it wasn't for that *Playboy* sale, I'd say the stupid cat made more money than Marshall." Colin knew he wasn't being fair. He also knew he was being less unfair than he wished he were. Marshall wasn't the most practical person ever hatched, but maybe Janine was. A paralegal married—for the moment—to an accountant? She didn't sound like a love-struck waif.

No matter what she sounded like, a couple of weeks later Marshall reported, "Paul's moved out of their house."

"Oh, boy," Colin said—not quite the cheer his son might have been looking for. He went on, "And when do you move in?"

"Umm . . . Haven't worked that out yet," Marshall answered. "Probably won't be too long."

"Well, good luck and all that," Colin said. "We won't rent your room out to refugees—not right away, anyhow."

"That's nice," Marshall said. He wasn't usually as dry as his father, but every once in a while. . . .

Colin chuckled, acknowledging the zing. Then he said, "I hope this works out for you, son. Honest to God, I do."

"Why wouldn't it?" Marshall returned. So many reasons sprang into Colin's head, all of them clamoring to go first in line, that he couldn't get any of them out. Which was bound to be just as well; Marshall knew what a rhetorical question was. The younger Ferguson added, "Who knows? You may get grandchildren who aren't a whole country and a glacier or two away."

"Have you talked about children with Janine?" Colin hoped his voice didn't show his alarm. A breakup without children in the middle of it was bad. A breakup with college-age kids in it, like his, was worse. A breakup with little kids stuck in the middle was worst of all. Gabe Sanchez could sing more verses to that song than Marshall would ever want to hear.

"Not really," Marshall said, which eased Colin's mind . . . a bit. But Marshall went on, "She has said she wants kids one of these years. She's, like, my age, so she's starting to hear her clock ticking. Gals don't get second chances the way we do." He glanced at a photo of Deborah on the mantel.

"Tell it to your mother," Colin replied. "You've made a fair pile of cash babysitting her second chance."

"Hey, she didn't have him in mind," Marshall said, which wasn't the smallest understatement in captivity. If Louise had thought there was any chance she might catch, she would have been more careful. Then she and Teo would be lovey-dovey to this day.

Unless they weren't. Maybe Teo would have run into a girl he'd been sweet on in high school and found out she wasn't attached—or wasn't too tightly attached. Stuff like that happened all the time. And the rage that went with it was one of the many reasons police forces wouldn't go out of business day after tomorrow—or millennium after tomorrow, either.

XIII

It was May. In what Bryce Miller kept thinking of as normal times, the countryside around Wayne State would have been bursting with spring. The grass would have been green. New leaves would have decked the trees. The birds would have been singing their heads off. Half the sophomore girls would have been wearing as little as the law allowed. Nebraska or not, that would have made for some pretty fine eye candy.

Even after the supervolcano eruption, spring would at least have been thinking about showing up most years. Not in the wake of the Siberian Express and the two other, almost equally horrendous, blizzards that followed it. Good old Theocritus wouldn't have got very far with pastoral poetry about the landscape he could see in these parts.

Snow still lay on the ground—not here and there, as it had in some other post-eruption springs, but all over. The drifts were taller than a tall man. Bryce, a tall man, could testify to that. Daytime highs hadn't got out of the thirties yet. The weathermen kept hopefully saying they would real soon now. The weather kept making liars of the weathermen.

A crow hopped across the crusted snow. It cocked its head now this way, now that. Its beady black eyes were alert for anything that might be food. A mouse? A discarded parsnip fry? Crows weren't fussy. They ate anything people did, and more besides.

Compared to what the winter had brought, of course, highs in the thirties seemed wonderful. Bryce was just chilly as he walked over to the library to meet Susan—she'd come to campus to do some research for an article she was writing. She still hoped for an academic job of her own, but the hiring situation looked bleaker than ever.

The paths on campus were free of snow. Machines had done the hard work at first. There weren't enough machines to cope with the new winters, and fuel cost too much to keep them going. Like so much of what had been routine before the eruption, nowadays they were for emergency use only.

For non-emergency use, Wayne State had students with snow shovels. Throwing snow around wasn't a requirement like passing your English courses and U.S. history. But the college paid for the work, either in money or in meal tickets at the student union. From what Bryce had heard, more shovelers chose meal tickets. The food at the union wasn't great, but Bryce didn't think you could get great food at any restaurant in Wayne.

A student coming the other way on a bicycle raised one hand from the handlebars to wave to Bryce. "Hey, Professor!" he called as he went past.

"Hey!" Bryce waved back. Little by little, he was getting used to students calling him *Professor*. The student population stayed pretty much the same age, while he—dammit!—kept getting older.

He'd started noticing that back in L.A., when he taught at Junipero High. The boys there had all looked like kids. Some of the girls, though, were definitely edible, to his eyes if not necessarily to the eyes of the law. Just how edible some of them seemed was something he'd never discussed in detail with Susan. No, he'd never done anything about it. No, he'd never even intended to. But he'd never discussed it with her, either.

Students here were college-age, of course. He'd put on a few years, too, though. And he kept putting them on. These days, even some of the girls in his courses looked like escapees from middle school. They weren't, but they looked that way to him. It was almost reassuring that others still seemed pretty damn hot.

The girls, hot or not, also called him *Professor*. They called him *sir*, too, which made him feel all the more an antique. They were polite here, more polite than in SoCal. That part of the courtesy, he could have done without.

Susan waited for him outside the library. She never would have done that during the winter. They hugged and briefly kissed. "Find what you were looking for?" Bryce asked.

"Some of it." Susan sighed. "I've filled out an interlibrary-loan slip for the rest. Will you come in and sign it for me?"

"I'd better." Being on the faculty, Bryce had the power to call spirits from the vasty deep and obscure journals from libraries around the country. Susan, a mere spouse, didn't. That never failed to irk her.

They bicycled back to town after he put his John Hancock on the paperwork. In due course, the journals would arrive, scholarship would advance, and all would be well with the world— except the article still wouldn't win Susan a job.

Something was different when they got to Wayne. Several buses were letting people out at a stop not too far from their apartment. The buses were not the usual, ordinary but elderly, wheezers and groaners that hauled people around this part of northeastern Nebraska. These were elderly, but a long way from ordinary. One was olive drab. Two more were painted in faded desert camo. And a couple of others, while they sported ordinary paint jobs, had bars on the windows that suggested their intended passengers might not be thrilled about staying aboard.

"Hello!" Bryce said. "What have we got here?"

People were getting off the buses and milling around near them. By the expressions on their faces, a lot of them were getting their very first looks at Wayne, and were thinking pretty much what he'd just said. Either that or *What the fuck?*, which came close enough for government work.

And government work it was. The milling people sometimes hid and sometimes showed the paper banners taped to the sides of their buses. NEW HOMESTEAD ACT SETTLERS, Bryce eventually read. "Wow!" he exclaimed. If he sounded amazed, well, he was. "It really is gonna happen! How long since they passed that bill?"

"A year and a half? Two and a half years? Something like that," Susan answered. Bryce remembered seeing on the news that the bill had finally passed, but he couldn't recall how long ago it had been, either. Since it passed, there'd been more frantic wrangling in Congress about whether to appropriate any real, live money for it.

They must have finally coughed up the cash, because here were these buses of new homesteaders. Some of them looked as if they might possibly know something about living on a farm or in a small Midwestern town. Others seemed stunned. Bryce could read their faces with no trouble at all. *When I volunteered for this, I figured anything beat staying in that goddamn camp one more minute*, they were thinking. *That's what I figured, yeah, but maybe I was wrong.*

Locals were coming out of houses and shops to give the new-comers a once-over. They didn't act much happier about what they were seeing than the homesteaders did. And Wayne was a big small town, at least by the standards of this part of the prairie. People who lived here were used to the college students who came and went. Some of the smaller places in these parts, there were no strangers who came and went. Stephen King knew what he was doing when he set horror stories in tiny towns like that.

So how would those people react when buses dumped loads of new homesteaders on their doorsteps? You could recognize people just out of camps from a mile away. They were the ones with the worst clothes in the world. Polyester? In colors that would gag a K-Mart buyer? A little too big? A little too small? Somebody'd felt good about him- or herself by donating it to help the supervolcano refugees. And the poor, damned refugees had to wear it or go naked. Late-night talk-show hosts had been getting laughs from them for years.

One of these homesteaders, for instance, had on a sweater that looked as if it were made up of ragged vertical stripes of vomit in assorted colors. Once upon a time, someone had designed it. Factories had turned out the style by the thousands, in assorted sizes. Some tasteless fool had bought this one and given it to a friend—or possibly to an enemy. And the recipient had sent it to a camp, where this poor fellow got stuck with wearing it.

The truly scary thing was, he might have pulled something even worse out of a bin.

Two Hispanic kids, a boy maybe four and his sister half his age, stared at everything in Wayne with wide-eyed wonder. They clung to their mother the way a limpet clings to a rock. They'd been born in a refugee camp, Bryce realized. Till the bus ride that brought them here, they'd never known anything else. The outside world was an idea they'd have to get used to a little at a time.

Quietly, Susan said, "Watch what happens. The first time anybody who's lived here a while has anything stolen, he'll blame the homesteaders."

"Wouldn't be surprised," Bryce agreed, also quietly. But he also wouldn't be surprised if the homesteaders did some boosting to get things they didn't have. The camps were full of that kind of petty—sometimes not so petty—crime. No surprise that they should be; there just wasn't enough stuff in them to go around.

And he'd spent a lot more time listening to Colin Ferguson

tell stories than Susan had. Maybe that had rubbed off on him more than he'd thought while he was doing the listening. Or maybe his wife made a better liberal than he did. It wasn't against the law to be a conservative in a college town, as long as you did it discreetly and washed your hands afterwards.

But he wasn't really a conservative, either, at least not one of the Know-Nothing variety that trumpeted out of the elephant's trunk these days. He was just a cynic. Could you be a cynical liberal? It wasn't easy.

A man in a nice wool topcoat—plainly *not* someone newly escaped from a camp—called, "Attention, homesteaders! Attention, homesteaders! Please form a line and follow me to the Wayne city hall. You will receive your homesteading allotments there."

They queued up with a speed and smoothness that would have impressed Brits, let alone a watching American like Bryce. That, by God, they knew how to do—they had it down solid, in fact. How many times a day for how many years had they lined up for food, for clothes, for complaints, for the chance to charge their cell phones, for everything under the watery sun? Often enough to get really, really good at it: that was plain.

The homesteaders tramped off toward City Hall. Bryce and Susan rode back to their apartment building. The mail was junk—well, junk and a utility bill. The bill would be horrendous, or whatever was worse than horrendous. As soon as they got inside, Bryce locked the dead bolt. He didn't always bother, but he did it often enough so Susan didn't call him on it this time. *Have to get better about remembering*, he told himself. That was definitely cynical. He intended to do it anyhow.

Vanessa Ferguson remembered the days when the post office on Reynoso Drive wasn't fortified like something in Baghdad's Green Zone. The post office had been that way for a while now: since long before the supervolcano blew. That she could recall how it had been in less paranoid times only proved she wasn't getting any younger.

She made sure she did a proper job of chaining her bike to the steel rack outside the building. Then she took the manila envelope from the carrying basket and went into the post office.

Her heart pounded as hard as it had when she discovered Bronislav had ripped her off. It might even be pounding harder now. But this wasn't rage—it was fear. It wasn't far from panic.

If this worked, it was also her revenge on the tattooed Serb pig. She had no idea—none!—what she'd ever seen in him. She must have been crazy to let him into her heart, and into her bed. She always felt like that about her ex-boyfriends. She had an extra-strength dose of it this time around.

She had such a dose of it, in fact, that she'd finally finished the story he said he'd been reading when he was really plundering passwords from her laptop. Not only had she finished it, she was going to stick it in the mail. That was why she was here. She'd mail it off. She'd sell it—first try, of course, because it was great. And, when she cashed the check, she'd do a fuck-you dance on the miserable, rotten memory of Bronislav Nedic.

God, this was scary, though! She didn't think Bronislav could have been more frightened when he fought the Croats and the Bosnians. (She also didn't think the Croats were Nazis and the Bosnians were al-Qaida clones any more. If Bronislav had thought so, the truth had to be something different.) Yes, part of her was sure the story would sell first time out. But she was . . . submitting . . . to . . . an . . . editor? What if he was jackass enough not to like it? He'd send it back. She didn't think she could stand that.

She hoped the line would be short. Hell, she hoped there'd be no line. Then she could get in and get out without spending time worrying about what she was doing. Yes, other people's bikes were already in the rack, but maybe those belonged to post office employees.

Forlorn hope. It was Saturday morning, the only time she could get here while the post office was open. Saturday morning was the only time most folks could get here. Seven or eight people stood in front of her. Only two windows were open. She'd be here a while.

And she was. When she got to a window at last, she started to explain about the return envelope inside the envelope, and how it would need postage, too. She'd worried about that along with everything else, and hoped the clerk wouldn't be too big a moron. But the woman smiled and nodded. "Oh, you must be a writer, too," she said. "A young man who writes comes in here all the time. He sold a story to *Playboy* not too long ago. *Playboy!* Isn't that something?"

"Right." Vanessa fought the urge to grind her teeth. The damned woman was talking about her own brother. The unfairness of Marshall's selling stories while she had to nerve herself to finish one and nerve herself all over again to put it in the mail gnawed at her.

She paid for the postage and stuffed the receipt into her purse. When the story sold, she told herself, she could write that little bit off her taxes. Then she almost ran out of there. She didn't want anything more to do with the perky clerk.

The post office was her last stop for the morning. She could have dropped in at her dad's house—it was only a few blocks away. She went straight home instead. She didn't like Kelly, and Kelly didn't like her, and that was the way that worked. Dad always sided with his new wife, too, which also struck Vanessa as totally unfair. After all, *she* was his flesh and blood.

And she didn't see much in Dad's new flesh and blood, either. Why he wanted another kid when he was as old as he was . . . Vanessa didn't get it, not when he already had three. At least Mom's little boy was an oops. Not Deborah. They'd gone and had her on purpose.

That Kelly might have wanted a child with Dad never crossed Vanessa's mind. After discovering they mixed like water and sodium, Vanessa thought about Kelly as little as she could.

She flicked the light switch by the door as soon as she walked into her apartment. When nothing happened, she said, "Shit!" Then she said something filthier in Serbo-Croatian. Then she said something filthier yet in English. She needed some mental floss to clean Bronislav out from between her ears.

Her nose wrinkled. That had nothing to do with the thieving Serb. The dishes were piled high in the sink. She'd let them slide for a while. Now they were telling her she couldn't get away with it any more.

"Shit!" she said again. If the power was out, the hot water would go in a hurry, too—as soon as whatever was in the heaters now ran out, it would be cold all the time. Doing dishes—especially dishes that had spent some time sitting around—with cold water was a pain in the ass.

Well, so was living in a smelly apartment. She plunged in. Anything would come clean with enough soap and water and cleanser and steel wool and elbow grease. *For sufficiently large values of "enough,"* she thought as she scrubbed away at an extra-dirty frying pan.

She swore again a moment later. Bronislav wasn't the one who'd come out with foolishness like that. No, it could only have come from Bryce. People you'd known and loved (or thought you loved) once upon a time didn't want to get out of your head, no matter how much you wished they would. No. They stayed in there like unwelcome guests, and every so often one of them would pop up and yell *Boo!*

The place did smell fresher once the dishes were out of the sink and in the drainer next to it. But that was a fight you couldn't win, not permanently. They'd start piling up again all too soon.

And she'd start ignoring them again, till she couldn't ignore them any more.

Monday morning meant a return to the widget works, and all the joy that went with it. The atmosphere was tense. There'd been waves of strikes back East and in the Silicon Valley because wages weren't coming close to keeping up with skyrocketing prices. Nick Gorczany hadn't given anybody a raise in quite a while. Everyone knew it.

Everyone also knew that doing anything about it would put you out on the street. Plenty of unemployed programmers and engineers and bookkeepers would figure low wages whaled the snot out of no wages at all.

And so people at the widget works grumbled and muttered and met in small groups for lunch. But that was all they did. Vanessa had always grumbled and muttered. She hadn't always bothered to keep her voice down when she did it, either. That made her more popular with the other hired peons than she'd ever been when things looked better.

There had been times when she'd wanted to be popular but wasn't. Now that she was, she discovered she didn't care. All she cared about was the electric jolt she seemed to feel—regardless of whether the power was on—when she put her key in the lock to her apartment mailbox. Every day she didn't hear back from the magazine to which she'd submitted was another day with a letdown in it.

She understood the mails were slow. She understood editors had to find time to sift through their slush. Intellectually, she understood all that. As far as she was concerned, intellectual understanding was for dweebs like Bryce. She wanted that acceptance letter *now*, dammit! She wanted the check that would come with it, too.

Some of her coworkers tried to draft her to tell Nick Gorczany they all needed more money. As politely as she could—and as rudely as she needed to—she declined the honor. She felt more than she thought, but that didn't mean she couldn't think. The messenger who brought the king bad news was the one who got it in the neck, not the people who'd sent him (or even her).

Mr. Gorczany did give people a raise: about a quarter of what they thought they were entitled to. In a note, he said *I wish this could be more, but the economy is tough on everybody, I included.* Vanessa curled her lip. That sounded just like him, all right. And, tough economy or not, he still drove his BMW from Palos Verdes Estates almost every day.

She started getting righteously pissed at the numbnuts editor who was sitting on her story. What did he think he was gonna do, hatch it? Only a small sense of self-preservation kept her from firing off a snotty query. If you made an editor mad, he'd reject *you*, not your story. The bastard.

Then, when she was starting to do her best to pretend to herself she'd never submitted in the first place, the return envelope showed up in her mailbox. Seeing it was such a rush, she forgot something Marshall had said. His words of wisdom were *It's the opposite of applying to college. Big envelopes are bad. Small ones are good.*

Vanessa tore the envelope open, right there in the lobby. Inside sat her story, with a sheet from the magazine paper-clipped to it. She pulled it out. It was a *Screw you very much for submitting* form rejection. Under the printed crap, somebody'd scribbled *Way too emo for us. Try the women's mags.*

"Emo? *Emo?*" The word tasted even worse the second time she spat it out. She'd sweated blood to show emotions honestly, and this was what she got for it? "Fucking emo?"

She stomped up the stairs. She slammed the door to her apartment hard enough to rattle half the building. Then she tore the rejection into a million pieces and flung them in the wastebasket. After a moment, the SASE and the printout of her story went in, too.

If she'd had the laptop on the kitchen table, it might have followed the papers into the trash. "Emo!" she snarled one more time. "Women's mags!" She made that sound filthier than any porn on the Net. "Cocksucking sexist shithead!"

She didn't usually drink by herself. Today, she poured a stiff shot of slivovitz—another leftover from Bronislav—and chugged it. It went off in her belly like a bomb. In minutes, the alcohol built a wall against the slings and arrows of outrageous editors.

All the same, she doubted she'd submit again. Certainly not any time soon. She wasn't going to try to deal with the cretins in New York City. She had to deal with too goddamn many closer to home. At least they paid her regularly—none too well, but regularly. The jerks who got paid for bouncing stories that were perfectly good . . .

"To hell with 'em! To hell with all of 'em!" she said, and she unscrewed the cap on the slivovitz bottle again.

It was pouring rain when Louise Ferguson walked into the Van Slyke Pharmacy. No lights were on inside. Well, the power was out at her condo, too. She'd do what she could do by hand, and she'd have things organized so she could quickly get the data into the computer if and when electrons started chasing themselves through wires.

"Good morning, Louise," Jared Watt said from behind the counter.

"Good morning, Jared," Louise answered, shrugging off her rain slicker. "Good and wet."

"It is. It is." The pharmacist nodded. Even in the indoor gloom, the lenses of his glasses made his eyes look almost as big as eggs sunny side up. "Back before the eruption, either we would have said the rain killed a drought or we would have complained because half of L.A. was washing into the Pacific."

"Well, we don't need to worry about it so much any more,"

Louise said. "Everything that could wash into the Pacific has gone and done it by now."

"And isn't that the sad and sorry truth?" Jared said.

You could always complain about the weather. They spent another few minutes doing it. Then a customer came in with a prescription. Jared filled it for her. He rang it up on a massive brass cash register that was almost certainly older than he was. The receipt book with carbons was new, but it was an old way of doing things making a comeback because the newer, niftier ways had turned unreliable.

The woman paused at the case of secondhand paperbacks. She pulled out a copy of James Michener's *The Source*: literature by the pound, because even in mass-market it had to be three inches thick. "How much for this one?" she asked.

"Three dollars," Louise answered. "With tax, three thirty-three."

"I'll take it," the woman said. "Looks like it's got enough inside to keep me going for quite a while." She pulled a five from her purse. Louise made change for her. The woman sighed. "Eleven percent sales tax is obscene, but what can you do? The state's as broke as we are."

Almost all the California politicians who'd raised taxes—again—no longer held office. The voters screamed that you couldn't squeeze blood out of a turnip. But the voters screamed just as loudly for all the services they'd enjoyed before the supervolcano blew. Sometimes you couldn't win no matter what you did. *After a supervolcano eruption* seemed to be one of those times.

Carrying her prize, the woman walked out. A man came in. He bought not one but two of the hideous ceramic ornaments that gathered dust on their glass shelves. Louise took his money in silent amazement. Back when the kids were little, there'd been a *Mad Magazine* spoof of junk like that. One picture showed *Clowns!* Another showed *Birds!* The next hyped *Clowns with*

Birds! And the last one was *Clownbirds!* The ornaments the man bought were definitely ugly enough to fall into the clownbird range. P.T. Barnum might have had the poor, kitsch-loving fellow in mind when he declared that one was born every minute.

However much she wanted to, Louise couldn't joke about that with Jared. He was the one who'd ordered the damn things. As far as she could tell, he doted on them. He carefully brushed away the dust they gathered. And when they sold (every so often, they would), he beamed from ear to ear.

He was beaming now. "Louise," he said, not quite out of the blue.

"Er—yes?" She knew her answer sounded nervous. Was he going to do an I-told-you-so? She'd never made any big fuss about the horrible things—politeness was her middle name. But he wouldn't have to be a mentalist to know they didn't float her boat.

That wasn't what he wanted to talk about, though. He sounded a little nervous himself as he went on, "I have a couple of tickets to the Galaxy's match next Saturday. I usually go with a friend, but Dave slipped in a puddle and broke his ankle. So would you, um, like to come with me?"

She opened her mouth. Then she closed it again without saying anything. She cared about soccer more than she cared about, oh, hunting tigers from elephantback, but not a whole lot more. On the other hand, the last time she'd been out with a man was the last time she'd gone to dinner with Teo before she found out she was pregnant. She'd thought she was done with that scene, not least because she hadn't met a man since who seemed interested in her. Once you turned fifty, you turned invisible. Only maybe you didn't.

When she hesitated, Jared quickly said, "You don't have to say yes because you work here or anything. I'm not going to fire you for saying no. This is the twenty-first century. I just thought it might be fun."

Fun. Louise wasn't at all sure that was a twenty-first-century concept. But she said, "Let me see if I can land a babysitter for my son. His half-brother's got a girlfriend these days, so I don't know. But I'll try."

Jared nodded. "That sounds like a plan." He didn't make any fuss. He might be strange some ways, but he was a grownup. He knew life came with complications, and that other people needed to take care of them.

The electricity returned that evening. Louise called Marshall and told him what she needed. She waited for him to tell her no. She waited for him to enjoy telling her no. Instead, he said, "Well, you got lucky. Janine's taking the train to Palm Springs Friday after work. Her law firm's going to some kind of convention there. She won't be back till Sunday night. So, yeah, I can do that. At the usual rate, I mean."

"I didn't ask you to do it for nothing. I'm glad you can do it at all," Louise said. She was even gladder he hadn't laughed in her face, but she kept that to herself.

The Galaxy (Louise discovered after a little research) played in Carson, which wasn't far away. She began planning bus routes. But Jared said grandly, "Don't worry about it. I'll pick you up in the car."

Before the eruption—even for the first couple of years afterwards—she would have taken that for granted. So would he; he wouldn't have needed to say it. Now . . . Now her own car had sat in its parking space so long, she doubted it would even start. "Hey, big spender!" she exclaimed.

"That's from *Sweet Charity*," Jared said, and started singing it in his erratic baritone. Soccer and musicals. Musicals and soccer. They made his world go round—but if she said so, he'd break into the number from *Cabaret*.

To Louise's relief, Marshall got to her condo fifteen minutes before Jared did. To her bigger relief, he was polite to the man who was taking her out—and who was also her boss.

"You're the one who writes stories," Jared said after they shook hands.

"Afraid so," Marshall admitted.

"Well, good. Keep doing it. We all need things to read, Lord knows." Jared turned to Louise. "Shall we go?"

"We shall," she said, and they did. Fastening the seat belt in Jared's Buick felt funny. No, she hadn't done it much lately. It was so much easier and more comfortable than a bike or the bus. It was also so much more expensive. She leaned back in her seat. "I could get used to this."

"So could I—if I lived at Fort Knox," Jared said with a wry grin. "But this is An Occasion." He pronounced the capital letters.

"It sure is," Louise agreed.

Their seats in the StubHub Center were near the midfield stripe. Only it turned out to be called the halfway line—soccer's jargon was different from American football's, and mostly imported from England. The Galaxy's foe was Real Omaha—*Real* with two syllables. Jared said they'd been Real Salt Lake till the eruption. "It means 'royal' in Spanish," he explained. "Several teams in Spain have royal charters, like Real Madrid. But Real Salt Lake and Real Omaha just sound dumb." Louise couldn't very well argue with that.

The game was . . . men running around in shorts, kicking a ball, and bouncing it off their heads. If you cared, well, you were one up on Louise. The home team (Jared called them a side as often as not, as if they were onion rings) ended up winning, 1–0. One–nil, not one–nothing or one–zero. Jared was pleased. Louise was pleased that Jared was pleased. He drove her back to her condo. Louise saw only a couple of other distant cars. They got back about half past nine. Louise invited him in. Marshall reported, "James Henry crashed maybe fifteen minutes ago, so he may pop out again." Louise nodded. That sounded like what she'd expected.

Her son by Colin didn't hold out his hand, but he would have if Jared hadn't been there watching. Louise paid him. He bobbed his head and took off.

James Henry didn't make a farewell appearance. Louise asked Jared, "Feel like a drink?"

"One, sure. Bourbon if you've got it, whatever if you don't. Thanks."

"I've got it." As Louise made the drinks, she wondered if she felt like a wrestling match. A man who thought a first date was a license to screw wasn't what she was looking for. No man was better than a man like that.

But Jared didn't reach under her blouse or into her pants. He clinked glasses with her and asked, "What did you think of the match?"

"I don't think I'll ever make a big fan, but it was more interesting than I figured it would be." Louise could say that much without worrying her nose would stretch like Pinocchio's. She added, "I enjoyed the company." Rather to her own surprise, she meant it.

"Good," the pharmacist said. "So did I, very much. Just so you know, I count myself lucky you walked in looking for work."

"Well, thank you. So do I," Louise said. Yes, she meant it not least for the paycheck. But she'd had worse bosses. Jared might be strange, but he wasn't high-pressure strange, the way Mr. Nobashi had been at the ramen works.

After Jared finished the drink, he said his good-byes. At the door, he pecked her on the cheek like a kid from junior high—middle school, they'd say these days. Then he disappeared into the night. Louise smiled after him. If he asked her out again, she knew she'd say yes.

XIV

Before the supervolcano erupted, Kelly Ferguson had never been in Missoula, Montana. She'd been there several times since, though, first to crash on a geologist who'd escaped the eruption with her and who taught at Montana State, and then to use it as a base camp from which to study what the caldera had done and what it was doing.

Missoula was the closest functioning city to what had been Yellowstone National Park. It had got a layer of volcanic ash after the eruption, but not a thick layer. All the prevailing winds—even the jet stream—blew from the direction of Missoula toward Yellowstone. Missoula got a layer of ash anyhow. No mere winds could completely defy the supervolcano. But Missoula, unlike a lot of places farther away, didn't get an incapacitating layer of ash.

"Old home week," she remarked to Geoff Rheinburg as they met for dinner before setting out into the eruption zone.

"Well, yes and no," answered the man under whom she'd studied at Berkeley. "Back in the day, you didn't need to worry about how your husband and your little girl would like it when you disappeared into the wilderness."

"Colin's okay with it," Kelly said, which didn't stretch the truth . . . too far. "Deborah . . . I didn't have to worry about how much I'd miss her, either."

Rheinburg chuckled and scratched his mustache. It had more white in it than it had the last time Kelly saw him. "I remember those days," he said. "Enjoy 'em while you've got 'em, because they don't last. If I see my kids twice a year these days, I figure it's been a good year."

Kelly nodded. Colin's grown children went their own way and lived their own lives. Even Marshall was out of the house at last, though he was in someone else's and not his own. Kelly didn't dislike Janine, though she was damned if she understood what Marshall saw in his new squeeze.

The next morning, she stopped worrying about what was going on back home. Three helicopters thuttered out of the sky. They kicked up leftover dust as they landed in an empty parking lot at the edge of the Montana State campus. Parking lots, these days, were broad, flat spaces people used for almost anything but parking.

Geoff Rheinburg eyed the whirlybirds. "Before the eruption, people around here would have thought they were black helicopters from the UN, come to steal their liberty and lock it in a jail in Bulgaria. They would've started shooting first and asked questions later."

"They may yet—if they haven't got one or two other things to worry about in the meantime," Kelly answered.

She had one or two other things to worry about herself. The last time she'd jumped into a helicopter, it had snatched her out of Yellowstone half a jump ahead of the eruption. She hadn't told Colin she'd be flying in this one. *I can tell him after I get home,* she thought. *Then he won't have anything on his mind.* Man is, always has been, and always will be the rationalizing animal.

Daniel Olson waved to her as he climbed aboard another

chopper. He'd escaped from Yellowstone with her. He was the geologist with the slot at Montana State. She'd stayed with him till a cop buddy of Colin's found a way to get her back to California.

When she strapped herself into her seat, the pilot gave her a helmet with an intercom connection. She was glad to put it on. Helicopters were godawful noisy. Flying in one without protection was too much like taking up residence inside the world's biggest Mixmaster.

The pilot's voice came through her headphones: "Good morning, folks, and thank you for flying Off the Map Airlines today." Everybody thought he was a comedian. As if he'd read her mind, the man went on, "You may think I'm kidding, but it ain't funny. Where you're going, the supervolcano erased pretty much everything that was on the map, right? I mean, that's why you're going there. So for God's sake be careful, and try not to do anything too dumb while you're poking around in the middle of nowhere."

His opinion of geologists was about the same as Kelly's of three-year-olds. Kelly had her reasons. Well, maybe the pilot had his, too. This might not have been the first scientific expedition he'd flown into what was literally *terra incognita*.

Here be dragons, Kelly thought as the rotors began to spin. In spite of the helmet, the noise was bad. But the dragon under Yellowstone had always belched fire. Now it was asleep again. She hoped.

Up went the helicopter. Missoula dropped away and disappeared to the west. For a while, the pilot followed the line of I-90. The Interstate hadn't completely disappeared from the map, at least this far from the eruption site. In fact . . .

"Doesn't the road look a little clearer than it did when we came this way in Humvees?" Kelly's throat mike would carry her words to Geoff Rheinburg's headphones. Without the intercom, she would have to scream, and even then he wouldn't hear much.

"You know, I think maybe it does," the older geologist answered. "I didn't want to say anything, for fear I was seeing more with my heart than with my eyes."

"Makes sense that it should," Kelly said. "That was a few years ago now. Enough time for the wind and the rain to get rid of some more dust, anyhow." They'd made the trek to the edge of the caldera before Deborah was born. In anybody's life, few dividing lines are sharper than the one between childlessness and children.

Before they went too much farther, though, the dust began to obliterate the line of the Interstate and everything else. The supervolcano had belched forth too much of it around here for the weather to have cleaned it away. Most of the landscape went brownish gray. The part that wasn't brownish gray was grayish brown.

They weren't flying very high. Kelly snapped a few photos. She eyed the ground first with her Mark I eyeballs, then through 8x42 Bushnell binocs. She hoped to see a bush pushing up out of the ashfall or a jackrabbit hopping across the dun-colored ground. She saw . . . the dun-colored ground. Maybe she was still too high and going too fast. Maybe there was nothing like that to see this far east of Missoula.

Here and there, the crowns of dead lodgepole pines did stick up through the ash. When Kelly remarked on them, Professor Rheinburg said, "Five gets you ten they aren't altogether dead. They're probably full of wood-boring beetles chomping away and having the time of their lives."

Kelly nodded. "You've got to be right." Those beetles had been pests in Yellowstone before the eruption. The acres and acres of lodgepole pines they killed helped fuel the enormous fires of the 1980s.

Where I-90 dipped, or would have dipped, south toward Butte (or what would have been Butte), the pilot kept flying due east. "This is the line of US-12," he said, though only his GPS could have told him so. "We're about forty miles from Helena— say, half an hour."

Helena was not a big city. No cities in Montana had been big even before the supervolcano blew. The relative handful of people who'd lived in the state—under a million despite almost the area of California—had liked it that way. Now only the western fringe was even remotely habitable. The rest . . . Well, this exploration party was going in to see what had happened to the rest.

"I would have liked to try somewhere like Salt Lake City before we hit Helena. It was farther away, and it should be in better shape." Geoff Rheinburg shrugged. "The Mormons discouraged it, which is putting things mildly."

Utah hadn't been hit so hard as Wyoming, Montana, and Idaho, but it had taken a beating. "What do you want to bet that, if we did go into Salt Lake City, we'd meet some Mormons already there?" Kelly said.

"Wouldn't surprise me one bit," Rheinburg said. "Some people would rather worry about the wrath of God than HPO. Me, I'd sooner keep breathing."

"Me, too." Kelly nodded. The progressive, fatal lung disease, caused by inhaling too much volcanic ash, had already killed more than a million people—how many more, no one even seemed to want to guess. It had certainly killed more by now than the direct effects of the eruption. And it had killed most of the livestock from Calgary down to Chihuahua. North America would be years getting over that, if it ever did. Beef and lamb prices had shot up even higher and faster than gasoline.

The helicopter pilot pointed. "There's Helena, dead ahead. I'm going to look for a place where I can set us down without kicking up too big a dust storm when I do it."

You could tell human beings had built Helena. The shapes of buildings persisted in the dust. Some of them, the bigger ones, stuck out of it. The state capitol was only three stories high, but its dome—modeled, like so many, after the one back in Washington—had shed dust and ash better than many newer, taller structures with flat roofs.

Also thrusting up from the dust was what looked like a mosque's minaret. Kelly hadn't dreamt Helena had held enough Muslims to need such a grand house of worship. And, as things turned out, it hadn't. Professor Rheinburg pointed to the minaret. "That's got to be the Shriners' temple," he said.

"Oh." Kelly felt foolish.

"Can you put us down anywhere near there?" Rheinburg asked the pilot.

"I'll see." Cautiously, the man brought the chopper toward the ground. The rotors kicked up some dust, but less than Kelly would have expected. As if it were landing on snow, the helicopter had skis rather than wheels. They spread its weight over a larger area.

The copter crunched as the skis took up the weight. Kelly both felt that and heard it. The pilot cut the rotor. The blades windmilled to a stop. In the sudden quiet, Kelly took off her helmet and put on a surgical mask that covered her mouth and nose and a pair of tight-fitting goggles. She wanted to study the ash and dust. More intimate contact, she could do without.

Geoff Rheinburg also got ready to go outside. The pilot also donned mask and goggles as the other two copters landed not far away. When Rheinburg opened the door, the first thing Kelly heard was a raven's grukking call. Her old prof beamed—or she thought so, though the protective gear made it hard to be sure. "Something lives here!" he said.

"Or at least passes through," she replied.

His feet crunched in the fine grit when he got out. He took a few steps. His shoes printed waffle patterns and small Adidas logos at each one. Kelly's sneakers were old. Time had blurred their sole patterns: when she walked, she left no advertising for wind and rain to erase.

Geologists were getting down from the other helicopters, too. Professor Rheinburg threw his arms wide to draw all goggled eyes to him. Then verse burst forth from behind his mask:

> "'My name is Ozymandias, king of kings:
> Look on my works, ye Mighty, and despair!'
> Nothing remains besides. Round the decay
> Of that colossal wreck, boundless and bare
> The lone and level sands stretch far away."

"Wow!" Kelly said softly. "Oh, wow!" The poem deserved better; she knew as much. But that was what she had in her. Shelley, of course, was writing about ancient Egypt . . . and also about everyone who thought he was unforgettably splendid. Fate did its number on Ozymandias, and now fate was doing its number on the United States.

Daniel Olson took a picture of the dusty, grit-scarred minaret sticking up out of the ash and dust. "Well, we're here," he said, which also wasn't poetry but was true enough. "Let's see what we've got."

They didn't need long to find some small rodent tracks—like Kelly's shoeprints, without visible logos—in the dust. There were a few insects, and here and there a weed poked its way up toward the sun. It wasn't abundance. By any standards except those of the harshest desert, it was devastation. But it was life.

"We definitely have more going on here than we did when we went to the caldera," Rheinburg said. "We're farther from the eruption site, and more time has gone by. Bit by bit, the planet is healing up. A few thousand years from now, you'd hardly know anything had happened."

"Not on a planetary scale," Kelly said. "But that *you* you

were talking about, who he'd be, what language he'd speak, what he'd think and feel about what he was looking at—the supervolcano would influence all that."

After a moment, Rheinburg nodded. "You're right. It's a question of scale, isn't it?"

Kelly nodded back. When you looked at people and what they did, you saw one thing. When you looked deeper and wider, at plate tectonics and at magma climbing up through the crust till it burst out like pus from a popped pimple, you saw something else again. Which view was true? Was either? Did you need both—and others besides—to get some kind of feel for what was really there? Would you ever have any idea of what was really there? All you could do was try.

They walked along. They all had printouts of street maps from before the eruption. The minaret, the capitol, and the sun oriented them. Here and there, wind and rain had cleaned the ashfall away from bits and pieces of other buildings. Glassless windows stared back at them like dead eyes.

Rainwater had carved gullies through the ash and dust. *Erosion in action*, Kelly thought. *Geology 101*. Something glittered at the bottom of one of the larger new gulches, several feet down. "Is that a big flake of mica?" Professor Rheinburg asked.

Kelly peered down at it. "That," she said after a moment's study, "is a Coors Light can."

"Oh," Rheinburg said in deflated tones. "I suppose the water's gone through some buildings—and some gutters—uphill from here."

The geologists took specimens from the surface. They used probes to dig deeper into the volcanic ash and dust. Eventually, scientists would collect samples from all over the ashfall zone, at varying distances from the supervolcano caldera and at varying depths. As Kelly meticulously labeled another tube full of volcanic ash, she feared that *eventually* would be a long time coming. The resources and the drive to gather the data just weren't there.

After a while, Kelly said, "I wonder how long it'll be before people can start living here."

"Not in my lifetime," Geoff Rheinburg said. Like his mustache, the hair that stuck out from under his broad-brimmed hat was gray, almost white. But he went on, "Not in yours, either. In your little girl's? Maybe."

That sounded about right to Kelly. Krakatoa turned into a jungle again less than a lifetime after the roar of its eruption was a shot heard almost halfway round the world. Krakatoa had been a piddly little thing next to the Yellowstone supervolcano, but Helena was a lot farther from the eruption site than the edges of the Indonesian island had been.

They put up tents and stayed in the buried city overnight. MREs were uninspiring, but they did fill the belly. And camp stoves let the geologists and chopper pilots fix coffee and tea.

When morning came, they went into one of the buildings through a window. Volcanic ash and rain had done their worst inside. They found no skeletons during their brief exploration. It was a relief of sorts, but Kelly wondered if that just meant the people who'd been in there had died fleeing instead.

Years too late to worry about that now, she thought. All the same, she didn't like wondering about how many dead lay blanketed under the ashfall. Pompeii and Herculaneum, only spread out over the heart of a continent. She wasn't sorry to fly back to Missoula that afternoon, not even a little bit.

Deborah was excited to ride in a car, even if she did have to sit in her car seat to do it. It was a rare treat; Colin didn't take the old Taurus out very often. But, while Kelly was off in Montana, he made sure the beast ran. LAX wasn't far from San Atanasio.

Better for him to go over there and pick her up than for her to schlep luggage on the light rail line and the bus.

He drove carefully. He was out of practice. And the people on two wheels and three, who dominated the streets these days, didn't have enough practice at looking out for cars. Deborah's presence inhibited him from calling some of the pinheads what they deserved. He knew one cop who'd told his kids before the eruption that cussing in the car didn't count. He sympathized.

The twenty-first century was still in effect at the airport. LAX had generators to keep the power running 24/7/365. You wouldn't want the lights going out and the computers crashing when a 747 was fifty feet off the ground. The people on the plane *really* wouldn't want that happening. Cell phones and WiFi worked all the time around here, too.

And there were a lot more cars than Colin was used to seeing. If you weren't staying near the airport, cabs would take you where you needed to go. You would pay an arm and a couple of legs for the privilege, but you paid for everything these days. Oh, did you ever!

Still, traffic wasn't the insane nightmare it had been before the eruption—nowhere close. And Colin easily found a space when he pulled into a parking structure. That wouldn't have happened in pre-eruption days, either. He locked the car—one conditioned reflex that hadn't faded—and headed for baggage claim, making sure Deborah held his hand.

He hadn't been there long when his phone rang. Kelly was calling. "Yo, babe," Colin said.

"We're down," she told him. "We're taxiing to the terminal. Won't be long."

"Sounds good. Love you. 'Bye." He stuck the phone back in his pocket.

"That was Mommy!" The idea was so exciting, it made Deborah jump up and down.

"Nah. That was a salesman, trying to get me to buy spinach and beets." Colin named two of Deborah's least favorite vegetables.

"Silly!" Deborah tossed her head in scorn. She'd never heard *I didn't come to town on a turnip truck, Charlie*, but that was the vibe she gave off. "You said 'babe.' You said 'love you.' So that was so Mommy!"

She was her own little person. She could walk. She could talk. She could think. She was good at it, in fact. "Okay, Sherlock. You got me," Colin said.

"I'm not Sherlock. I'm Deborah! Talk sense, Daddy!"

Instead of talking sense, Colin tried bribery: he gave her a granola bar. She chomped away. The bar declared that it was gluten-free. It was, too: the grains in it were buckwheat and oats. Wheat wasn't so hard to come by as a good New York strip would have been, but you couldn't take it for granted any more.

People coming out of the boarding area started gathering at the carousel for Kelly's flight. Colin remembered the days when you could meet somebody right at a gate. Those had vanished long before the supervolcano blew.

"Mommy! Mommy! Mommy!" Deborah saw Kelly before Colin did. She streaked toward her, running a little faster than light. Colin followed more sedately, as befit his years and the small paunch he still had in spite of all the bike riding.

Kelly picked Deborah up and kissed her. Since she already had a backpack and an overnight bag, she was handling a lot of extra weight. Despite wiggles, Colin took Deborah off her hands. "My turn," he said. "I want to kiss your mommy, too."

"O-kay," she said grudgingly—that was in the rules, even if it wasn't too far in them.

As they walked out to the car, Colin asked, "What was it like, going into a town where nobody's been for years?"

"Eerie," Kelly said. "That's the only word that fits. Geoff Rheinburg quoted from 'Ozymandias.'"

"What's Ozymandias?" Deborah asked.

"Not what, hon—who. He was a king in ancient Egypt—a pharaoh, they called them—a long time ago. A man named Shelley wrote a poem about the ruins of his statue."

"Haven't thought of that one in a long time," Colin said. "Not since English lit in high school." But, once reminded, he did bring back the images of arrogance and desolation. Slowly, he nodded. "It fits, all right."

"I thought so, too. Maybe it fits too well," Kelly said. "Everything we worked so hard to build . . . all ruins now."

They'd got to the Taurus. Colin opened the trunk. With a groan of relief, Kelly shed her backpack. Colin threw her bag in it with it. "Most of us did the best we could most of the time," Colin said. "That's about as much as you can expect from people."

He had to pay to get out, even though he hadn't been there more than a few minutes. Like every public institution these days, LAX grabbed every nickel it possibly could. You got less, you paid more, and they expected you to thank them for it.

"See any scavengers in there?" Colin asked. "I know Vanessa ran into some—and even into some survivors—when she did cleanup work in Kansas."

"That was on the fringes of the ashfall, though. This was only a hundred and fifty miles or so from the eruption," Kelly said. "Nobody could survive there. You might be able to ski in from Missoula or something, but you'd have to take all your own supplies and you couldn't bring out anything much."

"Snowmobile?" he suggested.

"Mm, maybe," Kelly said. "But there's still an awful lot of dust to kick up. And if you broke down, you'd be an awful long way from a garage. I wouldn't want to try it, that's for sure."

"Yeah, Triple-A service might be on the slow side," Colin said.

"What's Triple-A?" Deborah asked. With magnetic letters on the fridge, she was starting to learn the alphabet.

"They're people who help fix your car if it breaks down," Kelly explained.

"Did they help Ozymandias?" Deborah remembered the name. She'd be dangerous when she got older. She was already dangerous, in fact.

"Ozymandias didn't have a car. They didn't know about cars when Ozymandias was king," Colin said.

"Why not?"

"Nobody'd thought of them yet," Colin said. How were you supposed to explain the idea of technological change to a preschooler? Hell, plenty of allegedly adult elected officials didn't get it.

Luckily, he didn't have to try. Deborah didn't start the endless *Why?* routine that drives so many parents straight up a wall. A few months earlier, chances were she would have. She was changing, sometimes, it seemed, every day. She was growing.

Colin, on the other hand, was getting to the point where he wanted things to stay the way they were for as long as they could. When you saw sixty looming ahead like a giant pothole in the road, all the changes ran in the wrong direction. You got older. You got creakier. You saw your father-in-law the dentist more often, and for more horrible things. He'd retire for real pretty soon, and you'd go see some kid instead.

He turned right off Braxton Bragg and on to the street where he lived. A few blocks later, he turned in to his driveway. He stopped the car and killed the motor. "We're home," he announced.

"Yay!" Deborah said. Colin couldn't have put it better himself.

Louise Ferguson walked into the Carrows on Reynoso Drive to have lunch with Vanessa. Marshall was babysitting for James Henry. That would cost more than the lunch did. If he'd known why Louise wanted him to keep an eye on his half-brother, he might not have come at all. He didn't go out of his way for anything that had to do with his older sister.

As the hostess led her to a table, Louise wondered why she kept coming to this Carrows. She'd had some seriously unpleasant lunches here with Vanessa and with Colin. Habit, she supposed. She'd been coming here since long before the eruption, since the days when she was still married to Colin. And the food was never too bad or too expensive. You could do worse.

She might have known the server would put her at the table where she'd sat with Colin when she had to tell him she was pregnant and Teo had bailed on her. She'd had days she remembered more fondly. Yes, just a few.

Here came Vanessa, on a bicycle. She chained it to the rack in front of the restaurant. That hadn't been there before the super-volcano went off. Weeds pushed through cracks in the asphalt of the parking lot now. From where Louise was sitting, she couldn't see any cars parked on it.

She waved when her daughter came inside. Vanessa hurried to the table. Louise stood up. They briefly hugged, then drew apart again. "How you doing, Mom?" Vanessa asked as they sat down across from each other.

"I'm here," Louise answered dryly. "You?"

"Here," Vanessa agreed. "Still trying to climb out of the hole that miserable Balkan bastard left me in. The goddamn cops in Alabama just *won't* go after him. He didn't steal from anybody there, so for them it's like it never happened. SoCal might as well be Mongolia as far as the rednecks are concerned."

"Are you ready to order?" Carrows seemed to specialize in bright-eyed, smiling waitresses. This one must have heard the end of Vanessa's snarl, but she didn't let on.

"Let me have the bacon and eggs and hash browns," Louise said. Vanessa chose the same thing, only with a slice of ham in-stead of the bacon. Eggs, pork, potatoes . . . You could still get those. The selection didn't come with toast, the way it would have before the eruption.

When the waitress took the orders back to the kitchen, Vanessa asked, "What have you been up to? Are you getting any?"

Louise wouldn't—couldn't—have been so blunt if you'd put her on the rack. "You always were charming, dear," she murmured, and sipped at her water. Water was still free. Los Angeles, these days, had more than it knew what to do with.

Vanessa just shrugged. "Hey, why waste time beating around the bush?"

"As a matter of fact, I am," Louise answered, and had the satisfaction of startling her daughter. She didn't say the man she was sleeping with was her boss. Vanessa would have had some remarks on that score, all of them no doubt pointed but none germane. She did add, "He's very nice. It's . . . comfortable." She looked for the right word, and found it after a moment.

"Comfortable!" It wasn't a word, or an idea, to suit Vanessa. "What good is that? I want a man who makes my heart pound, a man who's exciting!"

"Wasn't it exciting when Bronislav siphoned all the money out of your savings?" Louise couldn't resist the jab. Truth to tell, she didn't try very hard.

Vanessa glared at her. "That's a low blow, Mom."

"Well, if you can take shots at what I'm looking for, why shouldn't I be able to do the same thing back?"

Vanessa didn't answer. Louise didn't need to do a mind-reading act to know what she was thinking, though. She was thinking she didn't like to be on the receiving end. She never had. Unfortunately, life didn't let you dish it out all the time. It would have been a lot more fun if it had.

Before they could start slanging each other for real, the waitress came back with their food. "That was fast," Louise said—talking to someone besides her daughter might take the edge off things.

"We want to keep people happy," the girl said. No doubt they also wanted to move as many customers as they could through the tables they had, but that didn't sound so friendly. The waitress went on, "Remind me who had the ham and who had the bacon."

After they sorted it out, Vanessa said, "She's supposed to remember that, or else write it down." But she didn't grumble loud enough for the girl to overhear.

Nothing like bacon and eggs—except maybe ham and eggs—to improve your attitude. The silence in which mother and daughter ate was grim at first. It grew more companionable as their plates emptied. "That's pretty good," Louise said when she was almost finished.

"It is, isn't it?" Vanessa sounded surprised the lunch was good, and even more surprised to be agreeing with her mother.

"I think the hash browns are from fresh potatoes. That's what does it," Louise said. "They're more trouble than they're worth to do at home. But the frozen hash browns you can get aren't the same when you cook 'em."

"They sure aren't." Vanessa agreed with her again. "Potato bricks. They've got about as much taste as cement, too."

"They do." Now Louise was doing the agreeing, and laughing while she did it.

"You know," Vanessa said, "the way things are these days sucks. I mean, sucks bigtime."

"Now that you mention it, yes." Louise couldn't very well quarrel with that. No one in her—or even his—right mind could. "And we're lucky, as far as these things go. Power on and off, too much rain, a little snow in the wintertime . . . Your brother in Maine would trade in a minute, I bet."

"If Rob doesn't like it, why doesn't he move back here?" Vanessa said.

"Well, I don't exactly understand that, either," Louise admitted. When Rob's wife got pregnant, she'd thought that would make a perfect excuse for leaving the permafrost behind. But Rob and Lindsey and, by now, the baby were still there.

"Besides, I wasn't just talking about the weather," Vanessa said. "Prices are flying so high, you can't even see them any more. Nobody can afford to drive a car except my boss, the asshole. And men are worse than ever, if you ask me. More depends on muscle now, so they think they're hot shit in a crystal goblet. Makes me want to puke."

Vanessa was touchy. She always had been. She got affronted even when she had no good reason to. When she did have a reason . . . Well, anything worth doing was worth overdoing, as far as Vanessa was concerned.

She had plenty of good reasons here. All the same, Louise asked, "What can you do about any of that?"

"I'd like to knock some of their stupid heads together, smack some sense into them." Vanessa muttered darkly about cold diarrhea in a Dixie cup, which was the other half of what she'd said a minute before. Her mouth twisted. "Most of what I can really do is piss them off. Better than nothing, but not enough better."

The waitress brought the—handwritten—bill. Louise paid it. She and her daughter walked out together. As Vanessa unlocked her bike, she lit a cigarette. "When did you start doing that?" Louise exclaimed. "It's not healthy."

"You live. Then you die. So what? While I live, I want to *live*, dammit, not just exist." Vanessa blew out smoke. A little sheepishly, she went on, "I don't smoke much. I can't afford to. These friggin' things are *expensive*."

"You shouldn't do it at all," Louise said.

"Yes, Mommy," Vanessa said, which meant she wouldn't listen. When had she ever? She pedaled away. Sighing, Louise walked toward the bus stop.

XV

Rob Ferguson tried never to miss a Guilford town meeting. You had to make your own entertainment around here these days, and town meetings held more of it than anything else he could think of. They didn't charge admission, either.

Jim Farrell stood at the pulpit in the Episcopal church. That would have been worth the price of admission if there were one. The wind outside made the windows rattle. It was below freezing out there, but not really *cold*. Rob's ideas about what *cold* meant had gone through some changes since he came to Maine.

"I have word from On High," Farrell said, as if he were the minister who officiated when Sunday rolled around. "Well, actually I have word from up north and word from down in the wilds of Washington. For people *will* write to a harmless backwoods hick in the wilds of forgotten Maine. They *will* unburden themselves to him, knowing full well that nothing they say in their letters will ever reach the news channels they still enjoy to the fullest in their oh-so-civilized lands."

"Subtle, isn't he?" Lindsey whispered to Rob as chuckles ran through the church.

"Like an avalanche," he whispered back. Their son, Colin Marshall Ferguson, dozed in his arms. Lindsey hadn't wanted to name the baby after any male in her family. Her mother and father had gone through a divorce at least as unpleasant as the one that split Rob's folks. Her father's current girlfriend was drop-dead gorgeous . . . and about her age.

The more or less benevolent more or less dictator of Maine north and west of the Interstate rolled on: "One of the things they tell me is that a big part of northeastern North America's power grid depends on electricity from plants along the chief rivers in northern Quebec. Now, friends, with all due local pride I say that there are not any great number of places with more miserable, colder climates on God's half-frozen earth than this patch which we ourselves infest. But northern Quebec, I kid you not, is one of them."

More chuckles from the packed house. Farrell acknowledged them with a tip of his trademark fedora. He overacted and overwrote. He would have bombed on TV, but live he was terrific.

And he had things to say: "So far, they've managed to keep those hydroelectric plants going in spite of what the supervolcano has done to the weather. So far. But the winters keep getting worse. If those rivers freeze up and don't thaw out, the power plants up there can't make power. And if that dread day comes—no, when it comes—do you know what happens to the power grid in most of the Northeast?"

"What happens?" a voice called from the audience. Not just any old voice: Dick Barber's voice. When you needed a particular question asked at a particular time, you planted a shill to make sure it would be. You did if you were a cynical old fox like Farrell, anyhow.

The retired history professor beamed out at his erstwhile campaign manager, as if surprised and pleased he'd inquired. *Yeah, as if*, Rob thought.

"I'll tell you what happens. The grid goes down, that's what," Farrell answered. "So millions upon millions of people get to find out what we've enjoyed ever since the eruption."

He still sounded droll, but nobody was laughing any more. People up here, people in thinly populated, self-sufficient northern Maine, had more or less managed to muddle through without much in the way of electricity. How would New York City or Philadelphia or Buffalo do? Rob was no prophet, so he couldn't be sure ahead of time. But he could guess, and none of his guesses was optimistic.

"And on that cheerful note, I give you back to more local concerns," Farrell said. "You do need to know, though, that the rest of the land of the free and the home of inflation may forget about us altogether, not just mostly."

There was commerce with the rest of the country at high summer, when things thawed out enough to permit it. New clothes came in, and canned goods, and batteries. So did such essentials as whiskey and rum and wine and beer. Moonshine popped up all over the place in these parts. The turnips and potatoes that gave their lives in the service of distillation did not die in vain. What the amateurs turned out was longer in kick than in flavor, though. When summer lasted long enough for barley to ripen, there was homebrew beer, too. Some of that was pretty good, but supply never matched demand.

This past summer, a little weed had made it up here, too—unofficially, of course. Rob smoked some. It was as much about nostalgia as about getting loaded. And smoking anything hurt when you hadn't done it for a long time. But for alcohol, he was pretty much locked into the Aristotelian world. So was everyone else in these parts.

After news that a big chunk of the country's population might have to find a way to live without Twitter and streaming Netflix and porn (to say nothing about details like lights and water pumps), arguments about things like moose-meat rations and the proper punishment for public drunkenness seemed less important—and less amusing—than they would have otherwise. When little Colin started fussing, Rob was glad for the excuse to leave early.

"Brr!" he said as soon as he and Lindsey and the baby got outside and the wind hit them. But it was an ordinary complaint, not the kind that meant they'd all turn into icicles if they didn't get inside in the next thirty seconds.

The sky was clear. A million stars blazed down from it. Rob had never seen skies like this, skies where the Milky Way really was a glowing river through blackness, in SoCal or anywhere else. You didn't get skies like this unless you went somewhere far, far from electricity—or unless the electricity went somewhere far, far from you.

Northern lights danced. Some of the streamers were maroon, others golden. A shooting star scratched a brief, bright, silent trail through them. Somewhere out there were the probes the USA had launched in happier times. For all Rob knew, they were still sending back data. Once upon a time, he'd thought space exploration was the most important thing humanity could do. He couldn't imagine it would ever mean anything to him again.

"That's sad," Lindsey said when he spoke his thought aloud as they made their way back through the darkness.

"Yeah. It is. But my thoughts have pulled back—pulled in. It's like I told you when you wanted to head south after Colin was born: I'm a small-town guy now. My horizon barely has Newport in it these days, let alone Mars or Jupiter."

Newport was the small town—small, but bigger than Guilford—where the road up to here branched off from I-95. It wasn't even forty miles away. Without a car or a bus or a railroad, though, forty miles was two days' travel. Now he got why, before the Industrial Revolution, most people never went farther than twenty-five miles from home their whole lives. He'd known the factoid for a long time. Here in this postindustrial corner of the world, he got it.

He got why darkness was such a big deal in those days, too. Without electric lights to push it back, it was always there at night, always lurking, always waiting to reach out and drown you.

Matches were another thing that came in when the weather was good. Rob used one to light a candle that sat on a table just inside the door. The flame gave out a dim, warm, yellow light—enough so you wouldn't break your neck, not nearly enough to make you forget the darkness it pushed back a little. You could get candles or torches any time. He saved the battery-powered lamps for when he really needed them.

The candle also gave out a strong, hot smell. It was made from moose tallow. Someone in *The Jungle*—a book everyone got grossed out with in high school—said they used every bit of the pig except the squeal. Had moose squealed, some clever soul in Guilford would have found a way to get some mileage from the noise.

Lindsey fed the stove firewood. It was as much of a heater as the apartment had. Little Colin's crib sat close to it, to get the most benefit. The baby went to bed without much bother.

Rob and Lindsey walked into the bedroom. It was a good deal chillier, though Dick Barber would have had no trouble getting through a night in it with just a Russian greatcoat. The two of them had more than a greatcoat to keep them from freezing. The bed was piled high with quilts and coverlets. Rob couldn't imagine any bed in this part of the world that wasn't.

He yawned as he slid under the thick layers of insulation. "Getting ready to hibernate through another winter," he said.

"You think you're kidding," Lindsey said, settling in beside him.

"Who says? When it's dark, dark, dark as soon as the sun goes down, what do you do? What can you do? You fall asleep.

And you stay asleep till the sun decides to come up again, no matter how long that takes. I bet the Eskimos at the North Pole sleep six months straight."

"Well, you can do *something* in the dark besides sleep," Lindsey said. "If you couldn't, we wouldn't have Colin."

"A point," Rob admitted. "But not tonight, Josephine. I'm pooped. Shall we make a date for tomorrow?"

"Sure, if we aren't too pooped then," Lindsey said. When they made dates like that, they did try to keep them. If life got in the way, though, then it did, that was all. If not tomorrow, the day after. Grabbing his jollies right this minute mattered less to Rob now that he was well past thirty.

Lindsey got up before daybreak, because Colin still woke up hungry in the middle of the night. Messing about with formula in near darkness, getting it not too warm and not too cold, would have been a major pain in the ass. Breast milk was a hell of a lot more convenient.

Rob said so after Lindsey got the baby settled and came back to bed herself. "Oh, Lord, you'd better believe it!" she exclaimed.

"And it comes in much nicer packages," he added slyly.

"Hey! Don't handle the merchandise!" she said. "You were the one who was pooped. Well, I am, too, and I want to go back to sleep."

Some experiments worked. Some didn't. You never knew which were which till you tried them. Before long, not too miffed because his experiment failed, Rob was also asleep again.

In the old days, the first thing he would have done when he got up was to check the Net for news about Quebec's hydroelectric plants. If he'd had a smartphone with a satellite connection (and, not so incidentally, some way to pay for the charges it ran up), he still might have done it. Since he owned no such critter, he didn't spend much—or any—time worrying about it. If the lights went out from Boston down to Washington, he figured word would get here sooner or later. And if that turned out to be later rather than sooner, his life wouldn't change one whole hell of a lot.

Back in the days when he'd enjoyed such quick, effortless connectivity, he wouldn't have believed that for a second. You had to keep up. You had to stay informed. Right now, or you'd kick yourself for not knowing.

He shrugged, yawned, and went into the kitchen to take a look at his son.

Marshall Ferguson was still getting used to the view of a new back yard. He'd spent his freshman year in the dorms at UCSB, and the rest of his time there in the kind of ratty apartment that had had a swarm of college students in it before him and probably had yet another sophomore or junior making a mess of it right now. Other than that, he'd lived at his folks' house—well, his dad's house these past good many years—since he was a little kid.

So he knew what things were supposed to look like when he raised his head from the typewriter (or, when there was power, the computer) keyboard. And they didn't look that way any more. It took some getting used to.

For one thing, he wasn't on the second floor any more. The house Paul and Janine had had—the house he and Janine had now—was only one story. It was in Torrance, but at the north end of the town: closer to San Atanasio High than he had been in San Atanasio, in fact. It dated from some time in the 1960s, from just before the days when all the built-ins would have been harvest gold or avocado green. Paul and Janine had got it as a foreclosure, which meant the payments were as near nothing as made no difference.

The house was small. The yard was good-sized. Back then, they hadn't believed in filling the entire lot with architecture. A big old oleander grew in one corner of the yard. There was one at Dad's house, too. The pink flowers were pretty, but you had to be careful with kids around. Oleanders were poisonous.

Marshall typed a sentence. He frowned, used some correction fluid, and took a stab at fixing it. He nodded to himself. Yes, that was better. He frowned again, looking for an interesting way to get from where he was now to where he wanted to be.

It was, perhaps not surprisingly, a story about a man who meets a woman he used to like just at the time when her marriage is coming apart at the seams. He was having trouble doing a good job with the woman's soon-to-be-ex. The guy kept coming out like Paul, and Paul, dammit, just wasn't dramatically interesting.

When Janine told him to go, he'd gone. He hadn't made much of a fuss. Hell, he hadn't raised any fuss to speak of. Maybe getting his marching orders was as big a relief for him as giving them was for Janine. The thing was over, done, finished, *finito*, and they both knew it.

Which, in a way, relieved Marshall. If somebody knocked on the front door, it might be a salesman. It might be a neighbor who needed to borrow some sugar. It wouldn't be Paul with a Glock in his hand and revenge in his heart.

Paul had moved back in with his folks and his scummy brother. He was a CPA; his brother preferred armed robbery to the kind you pulled off with the tax code. Phil was out on parole after his latest misadventure. Janine didn't like him, but had been fond of his two little boys (though she didn't care for their mothers).

In real life, an accountant who moved back in with his parents was reassuring. He'd be dull in a story. Marshall pondered ways to perk him up without turning him into someone who toted a Glock.

He was deep in thought and far from the real world when somebody kissed him on the back of the neck. *Somebody*—that was what went through his head while he jerked and jumped. Even before his butt hit the chair again, he realized the somebody wasn't real likely to be anyone but Janine.

She giggled and ran a hand through his hair. "You looked so

cute sitting there with your face all blank. You didn't even know I'd come home."

"Cute. Right." Had anybody else done that to him, he would have been furious. He still was, but when the person who'd distracted you was your girlfriend-going-on-fiancée there were, or could be, compensations. He pulled her down onto his lap and kissed her. But when he started to take her back to the bedroom to finish what they'd started, she wiggled away.

"Not right now," she said. "I just wanted to, you know, wake you up."

"Well, you did. Now—"

"Now I've got to go shopping," Janine said.

"What? It won't keep for half an hour?"

She shook her head. "Not enough hours in the day as is, not when I've got the day job. We'll see what happens after dinner." She fluttered her fingers and hurried off.

Because she had the nine-to-five, Marshall did a lot of the shopping. He didn't know what she had to get that was more urgent than fooling around. Muttering to himself, he tried to pick up the story again. He wouldn't have been so irked if this were the first time she'd teased him while he was writing and then not come through. She'd done it twice before, though. That wasn't good. That was a trend, and not one he liked.

You had to get used to certain things when you started living with someone. Marshall grokked that. Janine hated peas and zucchini. Okay. Marshall knew his world wouldn't end without them. She folded towels and T-shirts in ways different from the ones he'd learned. He could deal with that, too. He could even handle her squeezing toothpaste from the middle of the tube, no matter if he heard his father growling inside his head whenever she did.

Cockteasing, though . . . That was harder to handle, especially when it was cockteasing that interrupted his work. He wondered if Janine knew she was doing it, or how badly timed it was.

He also wondered if he wanted to make an issue of it. She went on and on about how controlling Paul was, and how that drove her nuts. Wouldn't she think Marshall was acting the same way?

He scratched his head, mumbled, and eventually got back to writing. He was making up his story as he went along. He was making up living with Janine as we went along, too. He'd had girlfriends before, but the only people he'd lived with were his folks and, for that freshman year, the Korean guy he'd roomed with at the Santa Barbara dorm.

Janine, on the other hand, got what she knew about living with a man from her time with Paul. Marshall wasn't just like her ex. That was one of the reasons she'd dumped Paul for him, or it should have been. But she'd got Paul to pay attention to her by yelling. So she yelled at Marshall, too, often snarkily.

That wore thin even faster than getting teased while he was writing did, because it happened more often. Finally, Marshall said, "Hey, you don't have to go on like that, you know? I was already taking care of it."

His new squeeze looked astonished. "You were, weren't you?"

"Um, yeah," Marshall said. The dishes had been going from the drainer into the cabinet. As soon as that got done, the silverware would go into the drawer, and the glasses into the cupboard over the stove. If you noticed what was happening and what was likely to happen, it should have been obvious before you started yelling.

"Whenever Paul would do stuff—and he didn't do much—he'd crow like a rooster or like he wanted a medal for it," Janine said. "You just went ahead and did it, and it, like, went under my radar."

"I'm not Paul," Marshall said pointedly. Trying to soften that with a joke, he added, "I'm not even the walrus."

"The what?" Janine didn't get it.

"Never mind." Marshall didn't bother explaining. He was

fuzzy on the details himself, anyway. The Beatles were a band from long before his time, a band people older than his father listened to on oldies stations.

"You come out with the weirdest shit sometimes," Janine said.

"Yeah, well, that's what you get for messing with a writer," Marshall said.

"What else do I get?" She grabbed him below the belt. She didn't tease all the time. The silverware and the glasses went into the drawer and the cupboard later than Marshall'd thought they would. Since Janine didn't bitch about them any more, that didn't bother him.

She did keep coming on to him and not following through while he was writing, though. She thought it was a hoot. He was less amused. "I wish you wouldn't do that," he said at last. "It's like . . . I don't know . . . like grabbing somebody's arm when he's driving."

"Nobody drives any more. Not unless you're in a bus or a truck." Was Janine missing the point because she was dense? Or was she wiggling around so she wouldn't have to argue about what bugged Marshall? He wasn't sure himself. He wasn't sure she was sure, either.

He made a couple of sales not long after he moved in with her. That felt mighty good. He didn't want her saying he brought in no money. He wasn't going to make as much as she did, but he needed to make something. He didn't want to think of himself as her kept man, and he didn't want her thinking of him like that, either.

The day-to-day grind ate most of his life, the way it eats most people's lives most of the time. He was happy enough. Was he happier than he had been while he was still living with his dad and stepmom and little half-sister? He was getting laid a lot more often, which certainly didn't hurt.

He rarely had the time to ask himself *Do I want to be doing this for the rest of my life?* He did sometimes wonder. From the looks Janine sent his way every so often, he suspected she sometimes wondered, too. He was still trying to figure out what a relationship was and how you kept it going. She'd just had one blow up and sink.

"It wasn't your fault, Marshall." She said that a lot. "I was already in the water, and you were a life ring."

"Glad to be of service," he would answer. In a way, it was reassuring. He didn't want to blame himself for her leaving Paul—for her kicking Paul out of this house, if you wanted to be exact. Her ex still had boxes of junk in the garage. Marshall left them severely alone.

He didn't want to blame himself, no. But every once in a while he did wonder what would have happened if he couldn't have gone to help old Mrs. Lundgren move. Would Janine and Paul still be together? Would she have found herself some other life ring instead? Would that different life ring be living here now? Would he be asking himself these same unanswerable questions?

Or would he just count his blessings, figure Janine was more than cute enough and not impossible to get along with, and go from there? Most of the time, that was what Marshall did himself.

Rain came down as Kelly got out of Colin's Taurus at the airport. It could rain any old time of the year in L.A. these days, but winter was still the season with the most wet stuff. She leaned back in to kiss Deborah in the car seat. " 'Bye, Mommy," Deborah said tragically.

"So long, sweetie," Kelly said. "I'll be back Monday."

Colin got out to haul her carry-on out of the trunk and to hug her and kiss her before she went into the terminal. "I'll miss you, too, you know," he said.

"Well, I hope so. And I'll miss you," she answered. "But I'm not going to Helena or any other part of the end of the world this time. It's just Chicago, for the geologists' convention."

"It's winter," Colin said. "In Chicago, it's *really* winter."

"That's why they have it this time of year," Kelly reminded him. "Since the eruptions, everybody holds conventions in the summertime, when it's—"

"Warmer," Colin finished for her.

"Well, yeah." She nodded. "But hotel rates and everything are a lot cheaper this time of year, and the convention committee really got its rocks off on that."

Her husband winced. "You've stuck around with me too long." He turned back toward the open driver's-side door. Traffic wasn't a fraction of what it had been once upon a time. "See you Monday. Have fun with all your scientific buddies." One more hug and he was gone.

The flight to O'Hare was routine. The cost wasn't. If her department hadn't sprung for some of it, she would have stayed home. The convention had laid on a shuttle bus to the Hilton. A good thing, too. Some Internet work had shown that cab fares were as bad as in L.A. Without every seat filled and a couple of fare-savers riding in the trunk with the luggage, no human being who wasn't an All-Star second baseman or point guard could have afforded a taxi. Even a millionaire wouldn't stay a millionaire for long if he took taxis very often.

At the hotel, most of the people in the check-in line were also in her line of work. She said hello to friends and acquaintances even before she got her key card and took her stuff to her room. Like the front desk, the bar was on the second level. It was only Thursday afternoon. The convention hadn't officially opened. Kelly could see the bar was already doing a land-office business anyhow. She'd never gone to a professional gathering that worked any other way. From what Colin said, it was the same with cops. It was probably the same with birders and stamp collectors, too.

She met Geoff Rheinburg for dinner. "Better food than in Helena. Better beds, too," she said.

He was presenting a paper on what they'd learned on their excursion to the abandoned capital of Montana. "Lord, I hope so," he said. But he seemed distracted. He looked out through the glass curtain wall at the snow sifting down.

"You okay?" Kelly asked after several minutes when he said nothing else.

"Me?" He came back to himself with a wry chuckle. "Yes, I'm fine, Kelly. I'm wondering about Manic-Five and La Baie James, though."

"You're wondering about . . . what?" Manic-Five sounded like a band whose songs she'd almost heard. She didn't know what La Baie James sounded like. Nothing she was familiar with.

Patiently, her mentor answered, "They're Hydro Québec power plants. Manic-Five is on the Manicouagan River. The others are even bigger. They're at, well, La Baie James—James Bay, it'd be in English. It's the little bay at the southern tip of Hudson Bay. They've been putting power, more and more power, into the grid since the 1970s. And it's cold up there. I mean, it's really, really cold up there, and it gets colder every winter with all the supervolcano crud in the stratosphere."

"Cold enough to freeze the rivers?" Now that Kelly knew what he was talking about, she could connect the dots. "What happens if it is?"

"We all find out," he answered with what might have been gallows humor or the simple truth. "The grid's . . . complex. It's gone out for weird computer glitches, and it's stayed up for the hell of it. But I don't like the way I've had to learn about the situation through the back door. It tells me the people who know more about it than I do don't want word leaking out."

Kelly looked out at the snow, too. "Even these days, cold in L.A. or Berkeley's just a word. Turn off the lights and most of the heat in a town like this in the middle of winter, though . . ." She didn't go on, or need to.

"Uh-huh," Rheinburg said. "If we can get out of the airport and back to California before things hit the fan—or before the ice up there stops the turbines—I'll be a happy man."

"If you feel that way, and if you know that much, I'm surprised you came to the convention," Kelly remarked.

"If I were a totally rational man, I wouldn't have," he answered. "That's about the size of it. But things up there may last till we get home. They may find better workarounds than I expect. I want to see some people here I may never see again if the Northeastern grid does crap out. And what the hell, Kelly. Sooner or later, we'll get home again even if things do fall apart. It may mean standing in line for a train ticket and not making it back for three weeks, but we'll get there."

"Easy for you to say," Kelly told him. "You don't have a little kid who expects you back Monday no matter what."

"Well, no," Rheinburg said. "Although I might, if I were in the habit of hitting on my students. I've been tempted a few times, but never enough to do anything about it."

He'd been married to the same woman as long as Kelly had known him, and for a fair number of years before that. There'd never been any hint of scandal about him. He was, if anything, scandalously normal. At a campus like Berkeley, that stood out more than it might have somewhere else. Kelly wondered, not quite for the first time, if she'd ever tempted him. She didn't ask. This wasn't science. Just because you wondered something didn't mean you had to know the answer. Sometimes you were better off not knowing, in fact.

When the waiter came by again, Rheinburg ordered a second gin and tonic, which he seldom did. Then he said, "If I were you,

I wouldn't keep anything you really need in your room. You may have trouble getting back in there. The computer key may not work if there's no power. I don't know that. I haven't researched it. The door units may have batteries in them. Why set yourself up for hassles you can duck, though?"

That was such a good question, it prompted Kelly to say, "Anybody would think you were a grownup or something."

"I doubt it, even if I can play one on TV," Rheinburg answered. She laughed. They finished dinner. He grabbed the check. She squawked. He wouldn't listen. "I'm senior to you. Hell, these days I'm senior to damn near everybody. I can do things like this. I can afford to do 'em, too."

There were receptions and cocktail parties after dinner. Kelly got a little buzzed, but only a little. Some people did use them as an excuse to drink hard. Some people needed no excuse to drink hard. And some people used drinking as an excuse to come on to others, while, again, some people needed no excuse. Still, there was less of that than there had been in the days before cell-phone cameras and harassment lawsuits.

Buzzed or not, when Kelly got back to her room she made sure she stuffed everything she had to have into her purse. Normally, she would have thought leaving it here was safer. From what Geoff Rheinburg said, these weren't normal times. She wondered if there'd been any such thing since the supervolcano erupted.

The presentations got rolling on Friday. Kelly went to Professor Rheinburg's, and made a couple of comments from the audience. She bought a fat book on the supervolcano at the Oxford University Press booth. Oxford books weren't cheap, but weren't so bad as the ones from Cambridge. Since it was deductible, the price didn't seem too outrageous.

More geologists poured into the Hilton. There were more receptions and parties in the rooms Friday night. Kelly kept a drink in her hand in self-defense. As long as she had one, people didn't try to press others on her. She still did some drinking, but less than she would have otherwise.

Because she did some drinking, she needed to get up in the middle of the night. She'd left the light on in the bathroom when she went to bed. She always did that in hotel rooms. Enough light leaked around the door so she could get there if she needed to without breaking her neck.

Except she couldn't tonight. The room was pitch black. The digital clock on the nightstand was out. So was the red LED at the bottom of the flat-screen TV. The smoke detector's red LED still worked—it had to be hooked to a battery. But one firefly didn't spit out enough photons to do her any good.

She groped for her purse. Fumbling in it, she found her phone. It showed no bars. "Oh, shit," she said softly. But she could—and did—use it to show her the way to the john. The toilet still worked. She went to the window. The light-blocking curtains did a good job. Little more light came in when she pushed them aside. Chicago and Chicagoland had just fallen back into the nineteenth century.

No—there were some lights way off in the distance. Maybe that was O'Hare, running on generators. Whatever it was, it had precious little company.

She thanked the God in Whom she didn't particularly believe they'd given her a room on the sixth floor. When day gave light, she could use stairs to get up and down. If she were on the twenty-sixth, she might go down once but she wouldn't want to come back up again.

And if she were in an elevator on the way up to or down from the twenty-sixth floor when the lights went out . . . she'd probably still be in that elevator now. Did the cars have battery-powered emergency lights? She sure hoped so. How long would the lights last? What kind of arrangements were there for evacuating passengers in a power outage? She was glad she could wonder about such fascinating questions in a nice, comfy bed.

How long would the room stay comfy? It was eerily quiet—the fan and the heat were out. Pretty soon, the chill outside would start leaking in; lows for this weekend were expected to be right around zero. Kelly used the light in her phone to go to the closet and grab the spare blankets off the shelf. She piled them on the bed. They weren't spare any more.

This is the way the world ends, not with a bang but a whimper. She'd read the poem in some lit course. Well, the bang had already come. It didn't end the world, but the whimpering aftermath wasn't much fun. And either her imagination was working overtime or it had already started getting colder in here.

XVI

"Thanks, Marshall," Colin said to his younger son. He added a one-word editorial: "Adventures."

"Yeah, well . . ." Marshall gestured vaguely. "I'm glad for you and Deborah she's finally getting back. I'm kinda sorry for me, on account of I'll miss the paydays I've got from you."

"Nice to be loved for myself alone," Colin said. Marshall laughed. Colin stepped out into the night. Marshall had it easy tonight—Deborah was already asleep. With any luck at all, Marshall could do as he pleased and get paid for it.

Colin tried to remember if he'd driven at night since he'd taken Kelly to the hospital to give birth. A few times in the line of duty, yeah. He'd driven to the station in the wee small hours when Mike Pitcavage killed himself. They'd already had Deborah then. And some other times on police affairs. Not many, though.

He'd have to be extra careful tonight. Too many people forgot any cars remained on the roads. They didn't bother with lights for their bikes or trikes. If a car encountered one of them before it could stop, he or she would be sorry . . . but not for long.

He picked his way east along Braxton Bragg Boulevard, heading toward the Harbor Freeway (though more people called it the 110 these days). He hit no stupid cyclists, though he had one near miss. When he got to the onramp, he smiled to himself. He'd faced down the LAPD over a big petroleum shipment right there. But the smile quickly vanished. He'd led San Atanasio's finest in that caper at Chief Pitcavage's orders.

He wouldn't have had to think about any of that if Kelly were flying back to LAX. But the delays for flights were even longer than the ones for train travel. O'Hare had limited flights and limited hours. If it hadn't been the busiest airport in the country before the grid went down, it wouldn't be operating at all. Midway wasn't, along with plenty of other airports back East.

So . . . Union Station instead of LAX. San Atanasio was only fifteen or twenty minutes from downtown L.A. by car. Amazing how little downtown impinged on the suburb, though. Most of the time, Colin had neither need nor desire to go there. He and Kelly had spent their wedding night at the Bonaventure Hotel. That was the night snow came back to L.A. Since then, he'd been there only a handful of times.

Braxton Bragg ran above the freeway. He sped down the onramp and onto the 110. Before the eruption, you could have found a traffic jam here at any hour of the day or night. You probably wouldn't have after nine at night, but you could. Now the freeway was nearly empty. Most of the traffic on it was eighteen-wheelers. They hauled supplies from the port at San Pedro to the rest of the Los Angeles area.

Colin wondered whether Bronislav Nedic was making a go of his restaurant in Mobile. If he wasn't, he might be behind the wheel of one of those growling monsters. That would serve him right.

Once Colin got downtown, he pulled off the 110 and groped his way to the train station. This wasn't like LAX; he didn't come here often enough to do things on automatic pilot. That was how he thought of it, anyhow. Bryce would have said you had to be familiar with the rituals. The rituals Bryce was familiar with pre-dated Christianity, but he would claim the principle didn't change. He might be right, too.

No trouble finding a parking space. The attendant who gave Colin his ticket didn't seemed surprised to see him; it wasn't so bad as that. But, as with LAX, it wasn't what it had been in pre-eruption days, either. *In the old days*, he thought. One of the di-vides of the coming world would be the chasm between people who remembered life before the supervolcano blew and those who didn't. He was and always would be on the wrong side of that divide.

Finding his way around the station didn't turn out to be too bad. Signs guided him where he needed to go. And it was laid out in a familiar way, with track numbers taking the place of gate numbers at an airport. *No, the other way round*, he realized. Airports must have learned a lot of their licks from the way train stations worked.

He got to where he was supposed to be twenty minutes be-fore the train was due. He'd built in both travel time and fum-bling time. The Navy and the police had taught him not to be late no matter what. Early was acceptable.

Early, here, meant buying a cup of coffee and the skinny little sheet the *Los Angeles Times* had become and standing around waiting. So he did that. He hoped Marshall was using time back at the house better than he could himself.

He gave the cup back to the guy behind the counter and got his five-dollar deposit refunded. Washing china cost less energy than going through waxed cardboard or styrofoam, and saved the expense of hauling in all those disposable cups. You put out some money to make sure you wouldn't walk away with the one they gave you, then got it back once you returned the artifact.

There was no deposit for newspapers, but there was a recycling bin right next to the newsstand. The less pulp the *Times* had to bring in, the better off it was. Colin had just chucked his paper into the bin when the PA announced that Kelly's train was arriving.

She got off two cars back from where he was standing. When she saw him, she waved and ran and hugged him. "Take me home!" she said. "I am *so* grubby and *so* sick of wearing the same clothes! Oh, my God! I mean, I got some new stuff, but still. . . ."

"On our way," he said. "We'll wake Deborah up. *When's Mommy coming home?* It's worse than *Are we there yet?*—I swear it is."

"Let me take a shower first. Is there hot water?"

"Yup." If the power were out here, Colin would have produced hot water for her even if he'd had to chop down one of the trees in the back yard. But the electric lights showed he didn't need to do that.

"Everybody on the train cheered when we got to country that had more than emergency generators going," Kelly said. "They cheered like their team just won the Super Bowl. It was bad back there—I mean, *bad*. They aren't used to outages the way we are, and it was cold like you wouldn't believe."

"Well, you're finally back, and Deborah's not the only one who's glad to see you." Colin squeezed her hand.

They went outside. It was in the forties, and probably fixing to rain, though it hadn't started yet. Kelly did a couple of dance steps. "This is *won*derful!"

The ride home was quick and easy, though he almost creamed another fool riding a lightless bike after he got off the freeway. He leaned on the horn. The noise seemed all the louder for being so unusual now. He hoped it made the jerk on the bicycle piss his pants.

Kelly dropped her bags in the foyer and ran rejoicing to the bathroom. The water in the shower stall started to splash. Playboy recoiled from the bags. They were large and unfamiliar, which might mean they were going to kill him. But, when they didn't jump up and start ripping the cat limb from limb, he cautiously approached and sniffed them to find out where they'd been. By the way he sniffed and sniffed, they'd been some interesting places.

The water stopped. The blow-dryer buzzed. Kelly came out wearing different clothes and a blissful expression. "God, that was great!" she said. "*Now* I want to see Deborah."

"I'll get her." Colin went upstairs to his daughter's room. He scooped her out of bed.

"Daddy?" she muttered. "What's going on?" Even as he carried her down to the front room, she wasn't more than a quarter awake.

"Who's that?" he said. One of her eyes opened just enough to see who it was. When she did, both eyes opened—wide, wider, widest.

"Mommy!" she squealed, and started trying to run even though Colin was still holding her. He set her down so she'd quit kicking his ribs. She squealed again while she was charging Kelly. Playboy thought she might be charging him and flew up the stairs. Deborah did her best to tackle her mother. She might be outweighed four to one, but she had momentum and enthusiasm on her side.

"Hello, sweetie!" Kelly picked her up and hung on to her and kissed her. Right that minute, watching them, Colin was as happy as he'd been in his whole life. He gave Marshall an extra fifty when his son headed back to Janine's place.

"Hey, too much," Marshall said. He was a solid kid—not that he was such a kid any more.

"Don't worry about it," Colin told him. "It's all good tonight."

"Hey," Marshall said again, and then, "Thanks." He rolled his bike out the door and pedaled off into the night. *He* had front and rear lights—Colin checked to make sure.

"You didn't come back," Deborah was saying to Kelly. "You didn't come back and you didn't come back and you didn't come back and—"

"I couldn't come back," Kelly broke in when she saw that would go on for some time. "Things in Chicago stopped working, like they do here when the power goes out. Only they couldn't start it up again. There's a whole big part of the country where the power doesn't want to start back up. And it's cold back there, too."

"It gets cold here," Deborah said. "It's cold now."

"Not when I've got my arms around you," Kelly said, and Deborah giggled. "But I mean cold, cold, cold, way colder than it ever gets here."

"Yuck," Deborah said, which was just what Colin was also thinking.

Kelly nodded. "Yuck is right. You know what a pain it is when the power goes off. And when it's cold like that and the power goes off, it's even worse."

"People turn into ice cubes." Deborah thought it was funny, because she didn't know it was real.

Colin knew too well it was. Not a whole lot of video was coming out of the frozen Northeast and Upper Midwest. By the nature of things, you had to bring your own power supply with you to shoot video when you wanted to do that in places where it was out. Then you needed either a satellite hookup or time to get your tape to some place that did have power so you could broadcast. Hundreds, maybe thousands, of people had already frozen to death. More would, till things got straightened out. If things got straightened out.

Playboy came back downstairs. He stalked over to Kelly and

rubbed against her, as if to admit he remembered her. Then he flopped at her feet, rolled over onto his back, and started to purr, as if to admit he was glad he remembered her. And well he might have been. She fed him and gave him water and changed his cat-box more than anyone else. Cats were honest about remembering and appreciating things like that. From everything Colin had seen, they were a hell of a lot more honest about it than people were.

Squirt Frog and the Evolving Tadpoles had a gig in Greenville, up at the base of Moosehead Lake. That was more than twenty miles from Guilford: no laughing matter with the snow as high as LeBron James' eye. Part of the deal was that the promoter had to lay on a sleigh to take the band both ways.

It wasn't Jim Farrell's sleigh. There were others up here. No: this one belonged to Doug Kincaid, Rob's father-in-law. Rob didn't know what kind of arrangement Doug had made with the fellow who'd set up the concert. Whatever it was, he would have bet Doug hadn't come out on the short end of it. Whatever Doug Kincaid did, he did well. He made a point—often an annoying point—of doing well.

Before the band set out, Lindsey told Rob, "Keep your hand in your pocket whenever you have anything to do with my dad. That way, you'll make sure you come back with your wallet."

"If he wants my wallet, he can have it," Rob answered. "My license and the charge cards long since expired, and I hardly ever have cash in there—not that cash is worth a whole hell of a lot around here any which way."

She gave him a wifely look. "Don't be more difficult than you can help," she said, which proved she had a fair handle on the character of the man she'd married.

Before the sleigh arrived, Justin Nachman said, "I want another look at your father-in-law's lady friend. IIRC, that was one seriously hot babe."

"You haven't sent a text in years, but you still talk like one," Charlie Storer said.

Rob had more things on his mind than dialectical immaterialism. "Try not to say that where the guy doing the driving can hear you, okay?" he told Justin. "I don't know what kind of grief Doug can give you if he gets pissed off, and I don't want to find out. I don't think you do, either."

"Hey, I'm cool," Justin said. "If 'Don't get the locals mad at you' isn't the number one mantra for a band on the road, it oughta be."

"Okus-dokus. You got that one right," Rob said.

"'Okus-*dokus*'?" Biff Thorvald dug a finger into his ear, as if to say he couldn't have heard what he thought he'd heard.

Slightly shamefaced, Rob answered, "I got it out of one of the books in the tower at the Mansion Inn. I've been looking for a place where I could throw it in."

"Yeah, well, now you can fuckin'-A throw it out again," Biff said. After a little thought—it didn't take much—Rob decided that was a good idea.

He hadn't gone north and east of Guilford since the last time he hunted in this direction. Pretty soon, the sleigh took him farther than he'd walked. He stared at the unfamiliar scenery. It didn't look much different from what he saw around his home town, but he didn't know what came next before it came. That felt distinctly odd.

When he said as much, Justin nodded. "Yeah. I was thinking the same thing," he agreed. "Pretty weird."

"We used to throw shit in the vans and drive for three states without even thinking about it," Rob said wonderingly. "Half the time, we didn't even bother looking out the window. It was just, like, the road. What we had to go on till we got to where shit mattered again."

"That world is dead as shoe leather," Justin said. Rob nodded and smiled to himself at the same time. Justin had had the room under the tower at Dick Barber's domain. No doubt he'd read some of the books on the shelves up there, too. Rob was pretty sure he knew which one that figure of speech came from.

They went through the little down of Monson on the way to Greenville. Any town that looked little after Guilford had to be, well, little. Monson might or might not have had a hundred people before the eruption. If it held half that many now, Rob would have been amazed.

"Trees around here still grow pretty close to the road," Charlie said. That was another way of noticing the same thing. Where there were people in any numbers, the second-growth pines fell for the sake of firewood. Without warmth through the winter, you couldn't live. And, where winter stretched from September into April, a lot of trees went up in smoke.

The twin towns of Greenville and Greenville Junction, though, had had a pre-eruption population of over two thousand. Like Dover-Foxcroft, that made them a metropolis next to Guilford. Moosehead Lake was something to see, too. Manhanock Pond, on the way to Dover-Foxcroft, was a lake by the standards of someone from L.A., even if not to the locals. Moosehead Lake was a lake by anybody's standards. On the map, it actually looked like what it was named for. That made it as unusual in geography as the constellation Scorpio was in astronomy.

At the moment, Moosehead Lake looked like a frozen moose. The sleigh glided past what could have been a movie director's dream of an Old West Indian trading post: all logs and rococo type on the sign. It had been a you-can-get-anything-here kind of place even before the eruption: grocery store, hardware store, clothing store, and drugstore all in one. These days, all things secondhand passed through it. Just about every surviving store north and west of the Interstate dealt in secondhand things, because so damn few firsthand things were running around loose in these parts.

Doug Kincaid and the promoter, a fellow named Bill Gagne, greeted the band closer to the lake. The promoter pronounced his name *Gag-nee*. "Yeah, I've got cousins in Quebec," he said. "They go *Gahn-yay*. But my people've been in Greenville since Maine was part of Massachusetts. So we're *Gag-nees*."

"Looking forward to the show tomorrow," Rob's father-in-law said. "Never figured Lindsey would marry a guy in a band I'd heard of. I still think it's awesome."

"These days, we're just glad to get a chance to play," Rob said. Justin, Charlie, and Biff all nodded. "Reminds us of what we used to be once upon a time." They could have got out of Guilford the first summer after the eruption. Biff was the only one who'd had a local girlfriend then. But they'd stayed, and now it didn't look as if they'd be going anywhere.

"You could be in plenty of worse places right this minute," Doug Kincaid remarked. "Here, at least, we know what to do with really cold weather."

"We know how to hunker down, too," Gagne put in. "You live where things were tough before the supervolcano screwed the pooch, you learn that shit. So we know how to do without, 'cause we already were. The folks farther south, they're only starting to find out."

"Ayuh," Charlie said, so naturally that neither local even gave him a funny look. When Rob meant *yeah*, he said *yeah*. He didn't try to fit in by talking like the natives. If Charlie wanted to, though, Rob supposed he had the right.

However you said it, the agreement was deserved. Some power had come on in parts of the Northeast and upper Midwest. A lot of places still went without, though. Their winters weren't quite so horrendous as the ones here, but they weren't anything delightful, either. And places like New York and Pennsylvania and Ohio had a lot more people to try to feed and keep warm than upstate Maine did. Things were bad, and not getting better very fast, if at all. Battery-powered radios brought Jim Farrell's domain such news of the wider world as it got.

Doug said, "Sylvie's really looking forward to hearing you guys play, too. She had you on her iPod back when iPods worked all the time."

"How about that?" Rob said—one of the few phrases, his father had told him, that were safe most of the time. His bandmates didn't let their tongues hang out like hungry hounds, either. He was proud of them.

The bed-and-breakfast where they spent the night plainly didn't do much business any more. But their room had a wood-burning stove and enough fuel for it to keep them not too cold till morning. Rob had long since decided that being not too cold was as much as anyone could hope for in post-eruption Maine.

They played in a high-school auditorium. It had no windows. The doors stayed open, which let in some light but also let in the cold. Torches burned in sconces that had plainly been mounted on the walls after the supervolcano blew. Soot streaked the industrial-strength paint above them and darkened the ceiling. Such soot stains were part of life here. Rob suspected they would get to be part of life over much wider stretches of the country.

They didn't practice enough. Their harmonies were ragged. They fluffed chords. Measured against any of their recordings, they were crappy. The audience didn't seem to care. People weren't measuring them against their recordings. Unless you used up precious batteries, or unless you had vinyl and a windup phonograph, you couldn't listen to anybody's recordings any more. People compared them to a day without entertainment. By that standard, they were dynamite.

Rob felt almost embarrassed to take his bows. He didn't think they'd ever got such a fervent reception. They played four encores, and got out of doing more only by miming exhaustion.

"Wow," Justin said as they left the stage at last. "I mean, wow. That really happened. And we weren't even loaded." Maine north and west of I-95 remained something close to an anti-pot zealot's dream. Except that once the summer before when some weed showed up, Rob hadn't got loaded on anything but alcohol for a hell of a long time. And with alcohol, less was definitely more. A little buzz was great. When you got massively drunk, you acted like an asshole and then you felt like dogshit the next day. Not worth it—not for him, anyhow. Other people did look at it differently.

Bill Gagne said "Wow," too. "You guys filled the joint. We'll clean up on this one."

"That's cool," Rob said. A concert like this did operate on cash. He'd have to find something to do with his greenbacks. Well, there were worse problems to have.

His father-in-law brought Sylvie backstage. Not even multiple layers of warm clothes—the kind of things that turned most folks into the Michelin Man—hid her emphatic curves. "You guys were awesome," she said.

"She's right," Doug Kincaid agreed.

"Hey, at least," Charlie said. Everybody laughed. Rob knew they hadn't been that great, not by pre-eruption standards. They'd prided themselves on their tightness then. It was nowhere to be seen now. By all the signs, though, no one who wasn't in the band noticed or minded.

Wayne, Nebraska, still had electricity. With the Siberian Express' aunts and cousins howling in every winter now, Bryce Miller was damn glad of that. It meant the heat worked. It also meant the computers and TV and cell phones worked, keeping them connected to the outside world.

TV was a less vast wasteland these days. Much of the American product came out of New York City. With the Northeast having so many power outages, a lot of channels on the cable package were blank a lot of the time.

The Omaha PBS station picked up the BBC by satellite and rebroadcast it. Even before the Northeast's troubles, Bryce had liked BBC news better than American versions. Unlike those, it presumed its viewers had something better than a room-temperature IQ.

These days, room temperatures in Wayne rarely got above forty-five. American news did its best to live down to them. If it bled, it led. The other staple was assurance that the climate would go back to normal any day now. American news shows ran stories like that about twice a year. They didn't seem the least put out when each one proved untrue, any more than they ran retractions about medical "breakthroughs" that somehow didn't confer immortality after all.

On the BBC, you got the idea things were bad now and were getting worse. Maybe that was a British attitude. Maybe it was just an adult one. Either way, Bryce preferred it to the usual American bullshit optimism.

"It appears clear that the massive power failures in the American Northeast and upper Midwest show we have reached the other side of an historical watershed," a BBC commentator said. American news didn't talk about history; American news had forgotten there was such a thing. Had an American newsman by chance remembered, he would have said *a historical watershed*. Two countries separated by the same language, sure enough.

"As the new Russia emerged from the collapse of the old Soviet Union as a strong state, a state to be reckoned with, but no longer a global superpower, the United States now finds itself in a like position," the Brit went on. "Its problems were not caused by an inadequate political system, but by a natural catastrophe that beggars the word *Biblical*. Regardless of cause, however, the effect is similar. When the most populous sector of the nation is at risk of death by cold or hunger, no American government can possibly contemplate military adventure beyond its borders. Whether any other country will seek the role of global arbiter, or whether a balance of power amongst the stronger states will prevail as it did before the First World War, remains to be seen."

Bryce turned to Susan. "If you're going to have your obituary read, nice to have it read with such a classy accent."

"Hush!" she said. "He's not done yet."

And he wasn't. "One would have thought that the mere fact of the supervolcano eruption should have cast the United States down at once from its perch atop the hierarchy of nations. That this has in fact taken most of a decade to transpire is a tribute to the USA's resilience and former abundance. By now, though, the surplus of times past is largely exhausted. The United States must attempt to make do with what it can produce for itself at this moment. In spite of everything, that remains considerable. But the nation's wounds and problems are enormous. The USA can scarcely be expected to look anywhere but inward for some years to come."

"'The United States is washed up. Anybody got a cigarette?'" Bryce quoted.

"How about a beer instead? We have some of those," Susan said.

"Sounds like a plan." Bryce got off the couch and went to the refrigerator. The beer was homebrew, turned out by a History Department colleague from local barley. Bryce had got it by translating some Greek for him. As far as he was concerned, he'd won the exchange. Any microbrewery would have been proud of this IPA. Stuart didn't care about that. He made enough for himself and his friends. He enjoyed brewing and he enjoyed drinking. Bryce and Susan enjoyed drinking what he brewed, too.

By the time Bryce came back with the bottles, the BBC newsreader was talking about Chechen nationalists and their long, ugly guerrilla war against the Russian government. The TV showed lean, black-bearded men in anoraks and skis with Kalashnikovs slung across their backs. Whether they had right on their side or not, they were terribly in earnest.

One of them—a leader—gave forth with a stream of impassioned gutturals. It wasn't Russian; Bryce could speak a few words and knew the sound of the language. It had to be Chechen instead. Over his words, a few seconds later, came the suave voice of a British translator: "No matter how bad the weather becomes, no matter how hungry we grow in the mountains, we will fight on until we are free at last. Allah is great, and He is on our side. He punishes Russia with this evil weather more harshly than He lays His hand on us."

The screen cut back to the anchorman, snug in his warm London studio. The studio might be warm. London wasn't. Pundits worried about the failure of the Gulf Stream. If that happened, northwestern Europe would start looking like Labrador. They were on about the same latitude. As bad as things were, it was always interesting to contemplate how they could get worse.

"Mr. Kerashev may well have a point," the BBC man said gravely. "Russia has declined to release agricultural statistics of any sort the past two years. The ones that did come from the Ministry of Agriculture before that are widely regarded as suspect even by Russian standards. Suspect though they may be, they show a sharp decline in the harvest when measured against pre-eruption benchmarks. Russia is known to be an active buyer of grain on the international market, paying for its purchases with revenue from sales of natural gas and oil."

For the first time in its history, the United States was also a buyer of grain, not a seller. Bryce didn't know what America was selling to finance its purchases. Selling gas and oil might mean more people would freeze. Not selling gas and oil might mean they would starve. That was what you called a bad bargain.

Now the BBC showed people in long white robes milling around and waving their arms in despair. Behind them were houses that looked like sand castles slumping into the sea. And that turned out to be pretty much what they were.

"Climate change from the supervolcano is global in its impact," the newsreader declared. "What you see here is an Egyptian village about seventy-five kilometers south of Cairo. It could be any number of villages up and down the Nile. Since weather patterns altered in the wake of the great eruption, Egypt has got far more rain than at any time since measurements have been recorded, and very likely since the dawn of civilization five thousand years ago."

One of the robed men shouted in Arabic. This translator spoke elegant British English with a faint Middle Eastern accent: "My house fell down! All the houses are falling down! We have lived here for generations, my family, always in this house. What are we going to do now?"

"Most buildings in Egyptian villages are made from sun-dried mud brick," the BBC man in London noted. "This material is cheap, easily available, and adequately strong—as long as it stays dry. When rain hits it, though, it returns to the mud from which it was born."

He paused to adjust his glasses. They sat almost as far down his nose as Bryce liked to wear his specs. "As I say, rain has come to Egypt. By European or American standards, it is a modest rain. In a country used to none, however, even a modest rain seems a monsoon. And it does more damage than a monsoon. Like a plague loose amongst people without immunity to it, Egypt has no defense against the rain."

The screen went to more pictures of collapsed houses. Wailing women were dragging a child out of one of them. Another cut brought up a crowded urban scene. *Cairo*—the word appeared in glowing red letters. Some buildings there were made of stone or baked brick. But others—the ones poor people used, mostly—were falling apart.

An imam at a crumbling mosque and a priest with a bushy white beard and a large crucifix around his neck both implored their God. "In most places, people pray for rain," the BBC man said. "Here, Muslim and Christian alike pray for drought. Egypt gets its water from the Nile. Any additions seem excessive to the populace."

The next story was about Manchester United's shocking defeat in Bulgaria. Bryce didn't care enough about soccer to be shocked. He thought some more about rain in Egypt instead.

His Hellenistic poets had moved to Alexandria and worked there. The Ptolemies, in their day, were the richest patrons a poet could have. But Alexandria lay right on the Mediterranean. It had always got rain every once in a while—not very often, but enough so builders made sure what they ran up didn't fall to bits the first time it got wet.

That wasn't true farther south. Egypt preserved things from long-gone days because it was so dry. How many papyri would molder because rain fell on them, or on the ancient rubbish heaps that held them? The number wouldn't be small, whatever it was. And nobody could do anything about it.

Susan was thinking along the same lines. "Before the eruption, we would have sent all kinds of aid if something like that happened to Egypt," she said. "But it's hit us harder than it's hit the Egyptians."

"Hasn't it just?" Bryce finished his beer. He thought about another one, but decided not to. "It's like the fellow on the Beeb said. We've got so many troubles here at home, we can't worry about anything farther away."

"Speaking of which," Susan said, "when I went down to get the mail earlier this afternoon, the apartment manager told me the police finally caught that guy who was breaking into places."

"Good," Bryce said. The burglar had hit seven or eight houses and apartments, including one on the ground floor of this building.

"Good—I guess," Susan said. "It was a Hispanic fellow—one of the homesteaders. 'They should ship 'em all back to the camps,' the manager said. 'They're nothin' but a pack of thieves.' "

"Oh," Bryce said. "No, that's not so great." The towns of northeastern Nebraska got on warily at best with the newcomers. It was worse in the smaller places than in Wayne. The people in those places cut no one any slack, not even their own neighbors. And it wasn't good here. The apartment manager's attitude was widespread. A homesteader who lived down to a stereotype wouldn't help.

XVII

Through her father and on her own, Vanessa kept doing what she could to get some payback on Bronislav Nedic. Her family might hail from Scotland and Ireland, but she had a Balkans sense of revenge. Bronislav had wronged her. He'd stolen from her. He'd pretended to love her—and to like her story—so he could steal from her. Yes, he was long gone and most of the country away. She'd get even anyhow, one way or another.

When she had electricity, she created dummy e-mail addresses for fictional people who lived in and around Mobile. She used them to write savage reviews of his restaurant. *Unity should be broken up*, one of them began, and went downhill from there. The others were just as sweet. She slammed the food, the location, the service, the prices—anything she could think of. One of her fictitious alter egos agreed with another about how lousy things were. Yet another chimed in with new complaints.

She had no idea how much harm she was doing. The restaurant stayed open, so she wasn't doing enough to suit her. She wanted Bronislav to crash and burn. If he started up again somewhere else, she wanted him to crash and burn there, too.

And she kept trying to work through the police. The cops in California were sympathetic enough. The Mobile police, though, and the state police operating out of Montgomery, just didn't give a damn. Bronislav played nice in Alabama. That was all they cared about.

After she saw a court case on TV, she went to the FBI. That meant taking a day off and riding the bus downtown, but she did it. She explained what she wanted at the front desk. The woman there sent her to an agent named Gideon Sneed. His looks were against him—with his eyes set close together, he reminded her of Micah Husak, whom she'd seen and tasted too much of back at Camp Constitution.

Hoping against hope, she did some more explaining. "He stole my money and took it across state lines," she said. "That's what you people do, right? Go after bad guys in interstate commerce?"

Agent Sneed grudged a nod. "Theoretically, yes, that's what we do," he said. "But from what you've told me, there's nothing here important enough for us to put any enforcement effort into it. We're stretched too thin the way things are. The whole government's been stretched too thin since the eruption."

"Oh, fuck the eruption!" Vanessa said furiously. "Whenever people feel like sitting on their hands, they use it for an excuse."

"We're not sitting on our hands. That's the point." Agent Sneed worked hard to stay polite. If he hadn't had a good-looking woman sitting in front of him, he probably wouldn't have bothered. Vanessa wouldn't be able to play that card forever—maybe not even for too much longer—but she still could. The FBI man went on, "Do you have any idea how much smuggling there is along the I-10 corridor that keeps L.A. fed?"

As a matter of fact, Vanessa did. Bronislav had told her stories about it, and laughed while he told them. Cigarettes, liquor, steaks . . . Anything that was either taxed or packed a lot of value into not much bulk was at least as likely to move in mysterious ways as it was to go with official blessing. More likely, if you believed his story. Of course, you were asking for trouble if you believed anything that lying fuck said. Vanessa had believed him for a while, and look at the trouble she'd wound up with.

She said none of that. She hoped not too much of it showed on her face. It must not have, because Gideon Sneed went on, "And this is just nickel-and-dime stuff next to what's been going on in the Northeast since the lights went out there. They had the pipelines in that part of the country all set up already. They've been smuggling cigarettes for years and years, and they were hauling up moonshine even before that. Now?" He rolled his eyes. "Half the stuff that gets up there isn't legit. More than half, for all we can prove. We can't stop that traffic, but we do try to slow it down as much as we can. The Federal government and the states are in desperate need of all the tax revenue they can lay their hands on."

Half of what went into the Northeast was smuggled? Maybe Bronislav had been telling the truth about life on the road, then. He was still a lying fuck.

He was still a crook, too. Vanessa said as much, adding, "It's not like you'd have to call out the bloodhounds to catch him, for Christ's sake. Whenever that restaurant is open, he's there. For all I know, he sleeps there, too."

"I understand that, Ms., uh, Ferguson," Sneed said. "But he's not what we would classify as a target of urgency. We can't come close to going after all the people at the top of our prioritization scheme, let alone the ones who aren't. . . . Is something wrong?"

"Never mind," Vanessa said. Nick Gorczany would have been proud of coming out with a six-syllable piece of horseshit like *prioritization*. For Agent Sneed, plainly, it was all part of the day's work. But you couldn't tell people who talked like that, people who thought like that, how awful it was: they talked and thought that way because they had no idea how awful it was. The blatherers shall inherit the earth. By the available evidence, they already had.

"I am sorry. You did have a criminal offense perpetrated against you," Sneed said. "You might be able to gain restitution through the civil courts."

"I've thought about it," Vanessa said. It would take Lord only knew how long. It would cost money up front that she didn't have. She doubted a lawyer would take the case on a contingency basis—his share of what she stood to make even if she won wouldn't be big enough to interest one of those mercenary bastards.

"I'm sorry I can't be more helpful. I'm sorry the Bureau can't be more helpful," Sneed told her. "We are as severely impacted by the resource reductions since the eruption as any other agency. We have to pick and choose which cases to pursue with great care."

"My tax dollars. Inaction." Vanessa walked out. If Gideon Sneed wanted to think she'd said *in action*, she was stuck with it.

The Federal building wasn't far from City Hall. Once upon a time, City Hall had been the tallest building in downtown L.A. Earthquake codes had limited others to a max of twelve stories. Vanessa didn't remember those days; the codes had been reworked before she was born. Now City Hall lived in the shadow of newer, taller skyscrapers—when the sun came out to make shadows, anyhow. At the moment, it looked as if it was gearing up to rain. Vanessa had an umbrella in her purse. *Don't leave home without it*, she thought: borrowed wit and wisdom from some old commercial.

In the shadow of City Hall lived the denizens of skid row. Los Angeles' weather was less attractive to the homeless than it had been before the supervolcano blew. It was wetter. It was colder. In winter, you really could freeze to death here these days. Food and clothes were harder to come by; ordinary people could afford to spare less for the unlucky, the mentally damaged, and the addicted.

But if it was bad here, it was still better than it was in most places. Vanessa shivered, imagining trying to live on the streets in Boston or New York or Pittsburgh. Because of that shiver, she gave a badly shaved man in a newsboy cap and a dirty tan trenchcoat five dollars when he went into his spiel for her. She usually did the big-city pretend-they-aren't-there thing with panhandlers. Not today, though. Her milk of human kindness might have been low-fat, but it hadn't curdled.

She soon found herself wishing it had. When you gave to one homeless guy, you bought yourself a swarm of homeless people, all of them with a hand out for a handout. She didn't feel like emptying her wallet to keep them in drugs or Ripple or even cheeseburgers. As soon as they figured out that she didn't, they called her some names even her father might not have heard in his Navy days.

The San Atanasio city bus pulled out of the same station Greyhound used. Vanessa had enjoyed lots of walks more than the one over to the station. The homeless people followed her. Sometimes they followed her in front of her, like a cat. They must have realized they wouldn't get anything out of her. If they wouldn't, they'd make her sorry. They succeeded at that, anyhow.

A hulking security guard with a pistol on his hip discouraged her adoring fans from going inside with her. "Thanks," she told him sincerely.

He touched the brim of his black Stetson. "You're welcome, Miss," he said. "It's what I'm here for. I know them, and they know me, too. Oswald—the tall, skinny dude with the Dodgers cap—he's a pain in the neck even around here."

Vanessa hadn't thought that skid row might have its own standards. Wherever it got them, Emily Post would not have approved. "I brought it on myself," she said. "I gave some money to one of them, so they all tried their luck."

"That'll happen, yeah," the guard said. "It was a Christian thing to do, though."

She never knew how to answer when somebody said something like that. Her family had put up a Christmas tree and dyed Easter eggs, but that didn't make her a Christian. Her father mostly ignored religion. Her mother had grabbed at every New Age fad for years. Mom didn't seem to do that so much now. Maybe she'd decided enlightenment didn't come freeze-dried and prepackaged after all.

Signs that said things like No SOLICITING! and No LOITERING! hung all over the bus station. More guards made sure people paid attention to them . . . up to a point. As long as someone sat quietly and nursed a coffee cup or a little something to eat, they let him alone, even if it was dollars to donuts he wasn't waiting for a bus. That seemed fair to Vanessa.

The ride down to San Atanasio took her through South Central L.A.: a ghetto since before World War II and now ghetto mixed with barrio. Storefront churches; heavily fortified liquor stores; equally strong check-cashing and quick-loan places; fried-chicken joints and taquerias; old, faded stucco houses, many with Spanish tile roofs; newer, just as faded apartment buildings; gang graffiti on walls and fences; burglar bars on every other place's windows . . . Vanessa didn't like coming through this part of town, not even a little bit. Hers wasn't the only white face on the bus, but she didn't have much company.

Nobody hassled her, though. People got on. People got off. Some people stared out the window till their stop came. Others blocked the outside world with earbuds. Those were way better than boomboxes, which could annoy whole city blocks. Here and there, people who knew one another chatted in English, Spanish, and Korean.

Vanessa got off at Oceanic. Farther east, the same street was called Compton. It had been Compton here in San Atanasio, too, till the city council decided it wanted nothing to do with the working-class (a euphemism for poor and tough) town with the same handle. *What's in a name?* she thought as she walked to a bench around the corner to wait for the westbound bus that would get her close to home. But she and the city council knew what, even if Shakespeare didn't. Money was in that one.

As soon as she sat down, the rain started falling. "Shit," she said resignedly, and popped open her umbrella. She'd wasted a day. She'd feared she would, but she'd gone anyhow. And, the next time she thought of something that might do Bronislav a bad turn, she'd gladly waste another one.

A long time ago—Louise couldn't remember quite when—there'd been a sappy movie about an affair between two people over the hill. They'd called it *Love Among the Ruins*. Louise did remember that it had made something of a splash. Most of the time, especially if you were a woman, Hollywood forgot you had those feelings as soon as you turned thirty—thirty-five, tops.

She and Jared were younger than the people in that movie had been. Still, she didn't expect a director would come sniffing around for their story any time soon. Her boobs sagged. Her seat spread. She had stretch marks. Jared had a potbelly and that haircut that looked as if he'd done it himself with tin snips. No, they weren't the most photogenic couple anyone could have found.

He did remember the movie when she mentioned it, though. She didn't have to explain herself to him, the way she had so often with Teo. (She hadn't had to explain herself to Colin, but he hadn't cared. That mattered a lot.) "Oh, yes," he said. "Too sweet for its own good, but they've cranked out plenty worse. What about it?"

"I was thinking that, if they ever made a movie about us, they could name it *Love Between the Ruins*," Louise said.

Jared broke up. He had a loud, high, shrill laugh, one that filled the bedroom in his neat little house. "I like it!" he said. "I like it a lot. The movies do kind of forget that people our age get horny just like anybody else, don't they? Maybe not quite as often, but we do."

He scratched, not seeming to notice he was doing it. His belly had a scar on the right side, a souvenir of the day he and his gall bladder had parted company. Louise was a member of the Zipper Tummy Club, too. She had an appendectomy scar, just about the minimum qualifier. She hadn't needed a C-section with any of the kids.

She set her hand on his. He would never win any World's Greatest Stud competition. But then, Louise didn't suppose the Hollywood Madam would be ringing her cell phone and requesting her services any time soon, either. When they fooled around, Jared cared about her as another person there with him, not just as an instrument of his own pleasure. As far as she was concerned, that mattered a lot more than size and gymnastics.

"It's . . . nice with you, you know?" she said.

"With you, too," he answered seriously. "That's kind of the point of things. Or if it isn't, it should be."

"I'm not arguing," Louise said.

"Good." He nodded. "Don't. Arguing will get you a yellow card. If you do it too much, it will get you a red."

She'd soaked up enough soccerspeak to know that a yellow card meant you were in trouble, while a red card meant they threw you out of the match. She had no idea what she would do with her arcane knowledge, but she had it.

She poked him in the ribs. Colin had almost never reacted to that. Neither had Teo. Jared wiggled; he was gratifyingly ticklish. "Guess what?" she said.

"What?" Jared said. Not *Chicken butt*, the way Colin would have. He hadn't noticed even the kids stopped thinking it was funny after a while.

Louise poked him again. "You can't fire me now, you know. If you try, I'll hire an attack lawyer and our whole sordid story will come out in court. It would be in the newspapers, too, only the newspapers don't pay attention to anything any more."

She didn't faze him. Well, she hadn't meant to. You couldn't (or you'd better not, anyhow) say something like that unless both you and the person you said it to knew damn well you were kidding. "If I'd thought there was any chance I would ever have to fire you, I wouldn't have made my lewd advances to begin with," Jared said with as much dignity as a naked man could show. "And since you don't seem to understand that, I see I'm going to have to give you a severe tongue lashing."

Which he did. Louise wasn't sure how severe it was. She was sure that, after he got done giving it, all she wanted to do was roll over and go to sleep. That was supposed to be what men did, which had nothin' to do with nothin'.

The only problem was, she couldn't. Instead, she went into the bathroom. When she came out, she started getting dressed. "I've got to get home," she said regretfully. "Otherwise, Marshall will soak me even harder for making sure James Henry doesn't burn down the condo."

Jared sat up. He reached down, picked up his slacks, and pulled out his wallet from it. He extracted an engraved portrait of U.S. Grant. "Here," he said. "Throw this into the pot."

"You don't need to do that!" Louise had a touchy pride about making it on her own if she could. It sometimes bent—she'd touched Colin for money more than once when she was desperate. You did what you had to do, which wasn't always what you wanted to do. She didn't have to take money from Jared now.

He had pride of his own. Setting his thick glasses on his nose, he gave her a stern look. "Who said anything about needing to? I want to. You're here because you feel like being with me for a while—at least, I hope that's why you're here. So why shouldn't I chip in?"

After a moment's thought, Louise decided arguing was a losing proposition. "Thanks," she said, and stuck the fifty in her handbag.

Jared put on his clothes, too, so he could go to the door with her. He kissed her good-bye. "See you Monday," he said. "Of course you know I'll dock you if you're late."

"Of course," she said seriously. She made her hands tremble. "Look—you can see how worried about it I am." They both laughed. She swung onto her bike and pedaled away.

No stars in the sky: clouds covered them. With the power working, the streetlights were on. They did a much better job of warning her about bumps and potholes than her little headlight could. That was more to let other people know she was there than to show her the road ahead.

It was after eleven. Not many other people were on the road. An owl hooted from a tall tree. She never would have heard that if she were in a car. Off in the distance, a siren started to scream. Louise cocked her head, listening. Police car? No, an ambulance. Like any cop's wife or ex-wife, she knew the difference in the notes. She hoped whoever was in it or whoever it was going for would be all right. For ordinary people getting around town, bicycles were okay. In an emergency, you still wanted internal combustion.

"Hey," Marshall said when she walked into the condo.

"Hello," she answered. "How's James Henry?"

"Asleep."

"I sort of had in mind when he was awake."

"Oh, yeah." He nodded, as if that hadn't occurred to him.

Louise tried to sniff without showing it. No, he hadn't got baked. He was just being difficult. "He's cool," he said after another pause. "He, like, beat me a game of checkers."

"Did he? How much help did he have?"

"Not enough for him to notice. Not as much as you'd think, either. He's a sharp little guy."

Louise already knew that. She didn't mind other people noticing, though. Oh, no! She was smiling as she asked, "How's Janine doing?"

Marshall hesitated. "She's okay," he said after that little stop-and-think.

"All right." If Louise had felt nasty, she might have done some poking there. But she didn't feel nasty; she was about as happy as she'd been since the day before the day Teo left her. So she asked, "And how about your little half-sister?"

"Deborah's cool." No hesitation there.

"All right," Louise said again. She didn't want Colin's new child to be sick, or anything like that. Such vindictiveness wasn't in her. If Deborah were homely, though, or bad-tempered, or stupid . . . Plainly, she wasn't. Life would go on even so. Louise handed Marshall money. "Here's some more you don't have to tell Uncle Sam about."

"Uncle Who?" he said as he stuck it in his pocket without looking at it. They exchanged knowing smiles, grownup smiles. You gave the government what you couldn't help giving it. Anything more? You hung on to that. Louise was sometimes surprised her younger son by Colin—the kid who'd been her baby for so long but wasn't any more—had got old enough to own a smile like that. But there you were.

And here she was.

And here Marshall wasn't. "I'm gone," he said, and out the door he went. Louise locked it behind him and worked the dead bolt. Yes, she was old enough that her onetime baby was no baby any more. Someone still liked her—loved her—just the same. It made a hell of a lot of difference.

Kelly puttered around the house on a Saturday morning. She'd hoped to spend it with Colin, but he'd had to go in to the station this morning. She couldn't do a lot of the things she would have liked to do, because the power was down. When that happened once in a blue moon, it irked you every time it did. When you knew it could happen any old time, you worked around it—or you sat there cursing the darkness, which did you no good.

Okay. She couldn't get online. Her cell had no bars. Even the landline was out—she checked. No TV, either. But she did have a battery-powered radio. Some local stations went on generator power during outages. And, with a lot of local stations off the air, she could pick up signals from ones farther away. Sometimes she could, anyhow. When the atmospherics were right.

She'd got Seattle once, in the middle of the night. Las Vegas, Phoenix, Albuquerque . . . They were all possible, but none guaranteed. San Diego stations came in better, but usually went off the air at the same time as their L.A. neighbors.

She clicked the digital station-changer, moving up ten kilocycles with every click. Here was *bandera* music, maybe from the Central Valley, heard through a waterfall of static. And here, a few clicks on, was the local news station, loud and clear. "We'll stay with you till the generator runs dry," the broadcaster said genially. "Or maybe the power will come back before then. In that case, we'll stay with you till the lights go out again."

He sounded resigned and amused at the same time. It wasn't as if he'd never gone through this before. Everybody in SoCal had. There weren't many places in the country any more where people hadn't.

Sure enough, he went on, "Brownouts and power rationing continue as the Northeast tries to adjust to the loss of power from

Quebec. In Boston, electricity is available from five a.m. to eight a.m. and from six p.m. to nine p.m. In New York City, the hours are six to eight a.m., eleven a.m. to one p.m., and seven p.m. to nine p.m. Philadelphia is the same as Boston. In Cleveland, the power comes on only between six and nine p.m. Consumers are anything but happy with the restrictions authorities have imposed."

A new voice with a thick New York accent said, "This is a"—*bleep!*—"nightmare! It's a"—*bleep!*—"joke, too."

A woman's voice, more educated: "This is like that city—Bucharest, that was it—before Communism fell. Can't we do better than that?"

"If we can do better than that, it's not obvious," the newsman said. "We talked to Professor Emeric Brody of the economics department at Johns Hopkins University, to ask him why our difficulties seem so long-lasting."

"Until the shutdowns in Quebec, we were using as much power as the grid could produce," Professor Brody said. "When something close to twenty percent of it abruptly became unavailable, distribution systems were badly deranged. Outages and damage to equipment only made the situation worse."

"What is the solution?" the newsman asked.

"If we are going to consume power at our previous level, we have to produce more," the professor said.

"Wow! Ya think?" Kelly like to talk back to the radio.

But Emeric Brody hadn't finished. "Oil-fired powerplants seem impractical now. Petroleum is expensive and needed for other kinds of fuel. But plants using coal and nuclear plants can be built. The main obstacles are political, not economic. Congress and the President have not been able to agree on what kind of plants to construct or where to put them. And so the Northeast has gone through what it has gone through. Maybe close to a hundred million angry voters will force action. Maybe—but they haven't done it yet."

"That was Johns Hopkins Professor Emeric Brody," the local newsman said. "Thanks very much, Professor. My engineer on the other side of the glass has just shown me a sign to let me know we'll have to shut down in ten minutes. I'll come back with more news and the five-day forecast right after we give you these important messages."

The messages were important only to the station's bottom line. Kelly didn't waste battery power listening to them. She went to see what Deborah was doing. Her daughter was playing with hand-me-down toys: stuff her folks had put in boxes when she outgrew it. They figured a granddaughter might enjoy it one of these years, and sure enough. . . .

Deborah was feeding a Cabbage Patch doll a plastic drumstick and apple. "Now, Barry Woodrow," she said, "you've got to clean your plate." That Barry Woodrow wasn't equipped to do any such thing didn't bother her. She was a little kid. Like a novelist, she was allowed to make things up. She glanced over at Kelly. "Hi, Mommy! Want some lunch?"

"Sure," Kelly said. "It smells delicious."

"You're silly," Deborah told her.

"Thank you," Kelly said.

That made her daughter laugh. Then Deborah said, "Read to me? Barry Woodrow has to digest for a while."

"I'll read to you," Kelly said, which was how she almost always answered that request. She wondered where the devil Deborah had come up with *digest*. Wherever she'd found it, she knew what to do with it. "Do you want Oz or Commander Toad?"

"Oz," Deborah said.

They were working their way through *The Hungry Tiger of Oz*. That was one of the books written by Ruth Plumly Thompson after L. Frank Baum died. Most of the time, novels by someone who continued a series were worse than the ones by the person who created it. Kelly thought the Oz books an exception to the rule. Thompson was a smoother, more clever writer than Baum. She gave Baum full props for inventing the world; Thompson probably couldn't have done that. But Thompson did amusing things with what she'd inherited.

Deborah had enjoyed Baum's Oz books, and she liked Thompson's Oz books, too. She didn't worry about which were better or why. As long as the stories were good enough—and as long as Mommy or Daddy was reading them—she just rolled with it. There were definite advantages to being a kid.

She wasn't old enough for *The Hobbit* or *The Lord of the Rings* yet. Colin said his older kids had been seven or eight before he could get through those with them. The movies came out not long after that.

He also had an evil scheme for when it was Deborah's turn. Apparently, he'd pulled it on all of his children by Louise, and looked forward to doing it again. When the story got to Shelob's lair, he'd taken a fat rubber spider and stuck it in his pocket. As soon as Shelob came onstage at last after the big buildup, he'd yanked it out and waved it in the kids' faces.

"Should've heard 'em screech," he'd said with a reminiscent chuckle.

Kelly'd wagged a finger at him. "You're wicked!"

"Yeah, but I have fun," he'd answered. "What I don't have right this minute is a spider. Don't know where that other one got to between then and now. Well, I expect I can come up with another one." Kelly expected he could, too. And she expected he would.

Playboy ambled into the front room. He hopped up onto the couch and meowed for kitty treats. He did everything but put on sunglasses and wave a tin cup in Kelly's and Deborah's faces. Kelly finally fed him something to get rid of him.

"He's *our* Hungry Tiger," Deborah said.

"If he were a hungry tiger, he'd have *us* for lunch, not his crunchies," Kelly said. Deborah thought that was funny. Well, Kelly did, too . . . up to a point. Every once in a while, when Playboy got annoyed, she'd see that I'd-eat-you-if-I-were-big-enough gleam in his eye. Since he wasn't, he had to put up with being adored. Cats had a rugged life, all right.

He was an indoor kitty. Kelly didn't want him going out and meeting dogs and raccoons and other cats with balls. So he saw birds and squirrels and such delicacies through the windows. Deborah called them his TV channels, which wasn't a bad way to look at it.

He hunted, killed, and devoured crickets that got into the house. He hunted flies that got in, too. He also hunted the occasional buzzing bee or wasp. So far, he'd been lucky—he'd never caught one of those. He had proudly presented Kelly with the corpse of a small lizard he'd assassinated in the laundry room. She'd praised him and petted him and fed him kitty treats to distract him while she flushed the poor thing down the toilet. She didn't think she'd distracted him well enough. He spent the next hour giving her reproachful looks, as if to ask *Why didn't you eat the tasty goody I brought you?*

Deborah thought Playboy was the best kitty in the world. Every once in a while, he'd scratch her—or Kelly, or Colin—while he was pouncing on a piece of string or playing with a cat toy. He didn't mean those; they were accidents that came from living with an animal that had claws.

Because she was still little, sometimes Deborah would literally rub him the wrong way or treat him too much like a squeeze toy. Then he'd swing with intent to hit. Where he was acting in plain self-defense, Kelly would spray Bactine on the scratches and remind Deborah she had to play nice with the cat.

Playboy was a good-natured beast. He had the manners of a gentleman—of a gentleman cat, anyway. But even a gentleman could lose his cool. When Playboy scratched or nipped without a good excuse, he got exiled to the laundry room till he yowled pitifully for release.

Gentleman or not, he definitely wasn't the brightest cat that ever came down the pike. He knew—he *knew*—string and ribbon were a basic feline food group. He would swallow them whenever he got the chance. And, of course, then he would york them up again in short order, usually on the rug. Or sometimes he wouldn't. Cat poop decorated with ribbon showed up in his box every now and then.

Colin had brought home a helium balloon with a ribbon to hold on to for Deborah's third birthday. She'd liked it. Playboy thought it was the greatest cat toy in the history of cat toys. He launched himself through the air time after time at the ribbon while the balloon bounced against the ceiling. He sprang up onto the backs of chairs and the couch so he could bat at the ribbon and try to get it into his mouth. He even jumped onto the dining-room table, where he was totally not allowed. He knew going up there was a laundry-room offense. He knew, but he didn't care. In his small, fuzzy brain, the quarry was worth the punishment.

"You've turned our cat into a criminal," Kelly told Colin. She was only half kidding.

"Looks that way, doesn't it?" Colin had sounded bemused.

Two or three times since then, though, he'd come home with more helium balloons to give Playboy something to do. Kelly'd bought him one or two herself. Playboy never got bored with them. And sometimes the great hunting beast would triumph. He'd snag the ribbon and scarf down a few inches before his people could take it away from him. Then it would reappear in one less attractive setting or another.

"Hey, when you've had your balls chopped off, you've got to make your own fun however you can," Colin said.

"I guess," Kelly said. "I just don't see why he thinks it is so much fun."

"Maybe he thinks they look like mouse tails or something," Colin said, which seemed sensible even if Kelly didn't know whether it was true. Most of the things Colin said seemed sensible. That made his deadpan jabs at the way things were all the more dangerous.

Which was what Kelly was thinking this morning when she heard a car out in the street. That didn't happen every day any more. She looked up in surprise. It stopped somewhere close by. Two doors slammed. Footsteps came up the walk.

She went to the door. Looking out through the little panes of glass set into the wood, she saw two uniformed cops approaching and a San Atanasio PD black-and-white at the curb. "What's up?" she asked as she opened the door.

"Mrs. Ferguson?" one of them said somberly.

Her world swayed. "Colin," she got out. "Is he all right?"

"No, ma'am. I'm afraid not. I'm sorry, but you better come with us."

XVIII

Willie Sutton used to say he robbed banks because banks were where the money was. Colin doubted one modern robber in a thousand had heard of Willie Sutton. Whether the crooks had heard of him or not, the principle remained the same. This was the first time the check-cashing place on Sword Beach had been knocked over . . . this month.

It was a nice day for riding a bike, anyhow. It was in the mid-fifties, with a few clouds but nothing that looked like rain. When not behind one of the clouds, the sun shone as bright as it ever did since the eruption.

Gabe Sanchez used the trip over as a chance to get his nicotine fix. As he and Colin turned right from Hesperus onto Oceanic, he lit a fresh cigarette and said, "I met a gal."

"Cool," Colin said. Gabe had met a fair number of gals since his marriage exploded. He hadn't stayed with any of them long. He sounded a little different this time, though, so Colin asked, "Who is she? What's she like? What's she do?"

"Her name's Ruby, Ruby Crawford. She's black, but maybe half a shade darker'n I am. She's, like, I dunno, somewhere between forty and forty-five—got a teenage daughter. Sergeant in the Hawthorne PD. I *like* her, y'know? Haven't said that about a woman in I don't know how long."

"Cool," Colin said again, this time in a different tone of voice. Cops often hung out with other cops. Who else was likelier to understand the crap they went through? Another thought crossed his mind: "Does she smoke, too?"

Gabe laughed. "Bet your sweet ass, Charlie. Yeah, we're both junkies, all right. Her kid thinks it's gross—can't wait to go off to college and stay in a smoke-free dorm. Then she'll light up the other shit instead. You wait and see."

"Ha! Mine sure did." Colin mimed toking. A little old Asian man in a floppy hat was trimming roses in his front-yard flower-bed. He waved to the cops as they went by. Colin waved back. He came this way fairly often. The old man probably knew he and Gabe belonged to the police.

They swung left from Oceanic onto Sword Beach. Colin ped-aled harder. Smoker or not, Gabe stayed with him. The check-cashing place was about halfway from Oceanic to Braxton Bragg Boulevard. A black-and-white motorcycle and a bicycle with po-lice lights were out in front of it.

A swarthy man had come out from behind his fortifications to talk with the uniformed cops. He gave his name as Farid Hariri. When Colin asked him why he hadn't trusted to the metal and bulletproof glass, he answered, "Because the asshole had an AK-47. This stuff is supposed to be okay against pistol rounds, but not against military ammo."

"You recognize an AK, do you?" Gabe asked.

"I used to carry one in Lebanon," Hariri said. "I haven't touched one for twenty-five years, but I could field-strip it in my sleep."

"Okay. You know one when you see one," Colin said. He thought of Bronislav Nedic. How many men who'd fought in far-off wars were making honest or even not-too-honest livings in America these days? He'd have to wonder about that some other time. For now, he asked, "How about describing the crook?"

"Mexican. Maybe twenty or twenty-five. Medium size, medium build. Shaved head. Hoodie. Jeans. Nikes. I didn't see no tats."

"Doesn't narrow it down a whole lot," Colin said, suppressing a sigh. There were a hell of a lot of tough Hispanic kids in and around San Atanasio. "What did he get away on?"

"He ran," Farid Hariri said.

That was, or could be, a break. A guy running with an assault rifle and a sack of cash wasn't exactly inconspicuous. But, with the power down, even somebody who wanted to call the police might not be able to. How had cops nabbed perps back in the days before telephones?

Colin and Gabe had their two-way radios to cope with times like this. So did the uniformed officers. One of theirs squeaked for attention. "Markowitz," he said into it, then held it to his ear to listen. A moment later, he went, "Roger. Out," and turned to his superiors. "Maybe we got lucky. A citizen flagged down one of our guys on bike patrol. Sounds like the perp's holed up in a house on 146th, maybe a block east of Sword Beach."

That wasn't far away at all. Well, it wouldn't be, not if the robber was on foot. "Let's go get him," Colin said. Out the door they went. Markowitz jumped on the motorcycle and roared away. The other uniformed cop and Colin and Gabe followed more sedately on their bicycles.

Colin had time to remember that he wasn't wearing a bulletproof vest. Neither was Gabe. They hadn't figured they'd need to worry about it. The .38 in his shoulder holster didn't seem like much when set against one of Sergeant Kalashnikov's finest, either. Well, if they could establish a perimeter and make sure the bastard didn't get away, that would do till the SWAT team showed up.

Gabe was smoking like a furnace. Colin wouldn't have minded something to ease his nerves just now. From what he'd heard in the Navy, there was nothing like combat for turning abstainers into two-pack-a-day guys. He hadn't understood that back then. Right this second, he thought he did.

The houses on 146th were at least sixty years old. A lot of tracts in San Atanasio were of this vintage. They'd gone up after the Second World War to house the vets and their Baby Booming families. Jobs were easy to come by and paid good money, the houses were cheap, and San Atanasio boomed along with the babies.

Then the neighborhood changed. As blacks bought in—the houses were still pretty cheap—whites and Japanese-Americans moved to Torrance or the Valley. Some stayed, but they said the city wasn't what it had been any more. There'd always been Hispanics in San Atanasio. Some of them had been there longer than anybody else. Now more came. A big chunk of police work started to involve riding herd on gangs.

As he and Gabe rode up, a uniformed cop pointed to a yellow stucco house. "He's in there!" she called to them.

"He didn't run out the back door and hop the fence or anything?" Colin asked.

"Don't think so, Captain," the uniformed woman answered. "We've got a guy in the house behind it, the one that faces on 145th. He's probably in the back yard now, and he'll be able to see if the perp tries to bail."

"Sounds good." Colin nodded. "Anybody else in the yellow house? Does the bad guy live there? Does he have friends? Or are there hostages?"

"I don't know," the uniformed officer said. "Nobody's screaming or anything. No shots fired."

"Okay." Colin got off his bike and walked toward the house. He stopped across the street, behind a parked car whose tires had gone flat. Maybe this would be easy. Maybe the kid in there would realize he couldn't get away and come out with his hands up.

To help him realize that, Colin yelled, "You can't get away! Come out with your hands up!" Then he yelled it again, in his bad Spanish.

A yell came back from inside the house, out through a partly open window: *"¡Chinga tu madre!"* English followed a moment later: "Motherfucker!" Not quite an exact translation, but close enough. The robber went on, "Don't fuck with me, assholes, or I'll blast the shit out of all of you!"

"That won't do you any good," Colin said. He didn't say the kid couldn't do it. A guy with a pistol might well miss him from across the street. A guy with an AK might well hit him. The bullets could punch right on through the stupid car he was standing behind, too.

He'd carried a gun for the San Atanasio PD for more than twenty years. He'd drawn it a few times, but he'd never once pulled the trigger except on the practice range. He was proud of that; it was the kind of thing he wanted to keep intact till he retired. He especially didn't want to try shooting it out against an AK-47. Not quite coming to a gunfight with a knife, but the next worst thing.

"You cocksuckers better clear outa here or you're gonna be sorry!" the robber shouted. "I ain't bullshitting, dude!"

To show he wasn't bullshitting, he started shooting. Glass exploded out from behind that partly open window. Colin had thought the guy was there, but curtains had kept him from being sure. Well, he wasn't in much doubt now.

A bullet cracked past his head, maliciously close. Next thing he knew, he was on his belly behind the car. His suit would never be the same. *Better my suit than my carcass,* he thought as he yanked out the .38.

Pop pop pop pop pop pop! Those were all the San Atanasio

cops' pistols going off at once. The bastard with the assault rifle was still banging away, too. The AK's reports were louder than those from the pistols, and seemed to come about as fast as all the pistol shots put together. It wasn't even full auto, either, or Colin didn't think it was. Fully automatic assault weapons were illegal in the States, and hard to come by. Semiautomatic fire seemed quite horrible enough, thankyouverymuch.

"Holy fucking shit!" Gabe yelled from somewhere behind Colin. That summed things up as well as anything.

The cops' fire began to stutter as they paused to reload. There was also a brief pause from inside the yellow house. As soon as the robber swapped out his empty thirty-round banana clip and slapped on a full one, though, he was back in business. The barrage from out here must have left the front of that house looking like a colander. Why the hell hadn't it left the bad guy looking the same way?

A bullet blew out the windshield on the car. It was safety glass, but even so. . . . A sharp fragment bit Colin's left hand. He swore and slithered toward the front bumper. He could pop up behind the engine block, and it would shield him some while he fired.

He popped up. He fired three times, as fast as he could. There went all those years of being a peaceable cop. And then he felt as if somebody'd slammed his left shoulder with a Louisville Slugger. Next thing he knew, he was lying on his back. A Louisville Slugger wouldn't've hurt this bad. A Louisville Slugger wouldn't've made him bleed like a stuck pig, either.

"Colin's down!" somebody shouted. "We've got to take that fucker *now*!"

That sounded like a good idea. Colin groped for something he could stick in the wound to slow the bleeding. Soldiers carried first-aid kits. Mostly deskbound cops didn't, dammit. *I could use a morphine needle, too*, he thought vaguely. He'd never hurt so much. The world grayed out. He'd just started to worry about it when he couldn't any more.

Kelly'd last been at San Atanasio Memorial when she had Deborah. This time, she'd had to give Deborah to the neighbors across the street. She wanted to call Marshall and Vanessa. (No, she didn't much *want* to call Vanessa, but she knew she should.) She couldn't even do that, not with the power out. All she could do was ride in the cop car and numbly worry.

"He's in surgery, ma'am," one of the uniformed men said. "Ambulance took him. It got there as quick as it could, as soon as the bad guy couldn't shoot it up any more."

"Couldn't shoot it up because he's dead?" Kelly asked.

"Yes, ma'am."

"Good!" Kelly said. The fury of her response amazed her. Any punk who shot her husband had no business staying alive afterwards.

"He tried to beat it out the back door," the cop explained. "And our guy in the yard of the house behind the house where he was at, he stopped him."

"Shot him, you mean."

"That's right."

"Good," Kelly repeated. Most ways and most of the time, she was a liberal. But no, she couldn't find sympathy for someone who'd hurt her family. "Can you tell me more about how Colin is?"

"No, ma'am. I'm sorry, ma'am. All I know is, they took him into surgery. The doctors, they'll be able to tell you what's going on."

Only they didn't—they were too busy doing what they needed to do to patch Colin up and put him back together again. She sat in a waiting room whose couch and chairs wore the hide of a particularly hideous Nauga. Gabe Sanchez was already there. He gave her a hug and showed her about where Colin had been hit. "He'll pull through," he said. "He's a tough son of a gun."

"I know," Kelly said, wishing Gabe didn't sound so much like a man whistling in the dark.

After a bit, Gabe gave an apologetic bob of his head and ducked out of the waiting room. *Cigarette break*, Kelly realized. She glanced at the magazines on an end table. None of them went back to the days before the eruption, but a couple came close.

When Gabe walked in again, he had Malik Williams with him. The chief hugged Kelly, too. "They'll fix him up good as new," Williams said.

"Yeah." Kelly made herself nod. The hospital had lights, computers, all the fancy gear that repaired people in the twenty-first century. Everything worked. Faintly, she could hear a generator chugging to make sure it all kept working. Most of the world could learn to live without electricity a lot of the time. It was a pain, but it could be done. Not in a place like this.

A doctor in surgical scrubs walked into the waiting room. "Mrs. Ferguson?" he asked Kelly. He had very tired eyes.

"That's me. How is he?"

"He'll make it," the doctor answered, and a great stone of fear tumbled off Kelly's chest. The doctor went on, "He lost a lot of blood, but we've got that stabilized. I'm afraid he will lose some function in his left arm. I don't know how much yet. Part of it will depend on how he heals. He may need some additional procedures after he recovers from the initial trauma here."

More operations. Kelly translated that from doctorspeak into English. More pain. More recovery. She didn't know what she could do about that, except be there for Colin and take care of him when they happened. For now . . . "Can I see him?"

The doctor frowned. "He's still pretty dopey. He's in the recovery room." Then he took another look at her face. "Well, for a little while. Come on with me."

They gave her scrubs, too, and a mask. Colin lay on his back on an electronic bed. He was alarmingly pale—almost gray. He had an oxygen cannula under his nose and an IV running into the back of his right hand. His left shoulder was a mound of bandages.

Hesitantly, Kelly went up to him. Even more hesitantly, she said, "Colin? Honey?" When he didn't respond, she said his name again, louder this time.

If he'd stayed out, she would have drawn back and waited. But his eyelids fluttered. As if it took a lot of work—and odds were it did—his eyes opened. For a second, she didn't think anybody was home even so. His lips moved. Not much in the way of noise came out, but she lip-read "Hey, babe."

"How are you?" she asked: your basic foolish question.

He considered. This time, she could hear him when he answered, "I was born to hang." She yipped startled laughter. Behind her, the doctor snorted. Colin ignored them both. He forced out a question: "Did we catch the guy?"

"They told me he was dead," Kelly answered.

"Okay." Colin managed a small nod. Then he said, "I don't feel so real good."

"I bet you don't. But you'll get better," Kelly said.

"That's about enough." The doctor touched her arm. "We'll give him some rest now, and you can see him again when he's a little more with it."

"Thanks for letting me in." When the doctor guided her out of the recovery room, she shed the scrubs and the mask. Gabe and Chief Williams still stood in the waiting room. She gave her report: "He was sort of awake. He talked and made sense. He asked about the robber, and I told him the guy was dead."

"That all sounds good," Malik Williams said. "He was still doped to the eyebrows, I bet."

"Oh, yeah." Kelly nodded.

"All right. Do you want that car to take you home?" the chief asked. "I know you've got your little girl at the neighbors'."

"Yes, please," Kelly said. "If the power's back on outside, I have to call his son and his daughter—his ex, too, I guess. If I can't call, I'll drive over to Marshall's and get him to watch Deborah for a bit while I came back here."

"That sounds like it ought to work." Chief Williams spoke with the air of a man who was used to putting plans together on the fly.

"I'm glad he's gonna pull through." Gabe Sanchez hugged Kelly again. "I'm gladder'n I know how to tell you—he owes me fifty bucks." She poked him in the ribs. They both laughed, more in relief than at the quality of the joke.

Before Kelly could get back to the police car, she had to run the media gauntlet. The local TV outlets had got word of the shootout. News crews thrust mikes in her face and asked her how Colin was doing, what she was feeling, and about the gun battle (of which she knew as little as they did, maybe less). "I don't have anything to tell you. Please excuse me," she said, and she kept saying it till she pushed her way to the car, got inside, and slammed the door. Then—and only then—she added, "Stupid assholes."

"Yes, ma'am," said the cop behind the wheel. "Take you home now? How's Captain Ferguson doing?"

"He's out of surgery. They think he'll be okay," Kelly answered. "And yes, take me home, please."

"You got it, ma'am. That's good news."

She retrieved Deborah from Wes and Ida Jones, who made horrified noises when she told them Colin had been shot. Ida said she would pray for him. Kelly didn't know a lot of people who took their religion seriously. She knew even fewer who took it seriously and were still nice. Ida qualified on both counts.

"Daddy got hurt?" Deborah asked.

"Daddy . . . got hurt," Kelly agreed. "But he's going to get better. He'll be in the hospital for a while, and then he'll finish getting better at home. He'll be home all the time till he's well enough to go back to work."

They went across the street. The power was still out. Kelly was as sure as made no difference that her ancient Honda wouldn't start. Keeping two cars alive these days felt like insane ostentation. She had to look up Marshall's new address before she stuck Deborah in the Taurus' car seat and drove over there.

When she knocked on the door, Marshall looked amazed. "What are you doing here? You and the artichoke?"

"I'm not an artichoke!" Deborah said, laughing—it was a game they played.

"Your dad got shot," Kelly said baldly.

"Oh, shit." He sounded less surprised at that than he did at finding Kelly and Deborah on his doorstep. A cop's kid knew it was possible even if it wasn't likely. "What happened?"

She told him what she knew, finishing, "Will you come back with me and babysit while I go to the hospital again? That'd help a lot."

"Sure. Lemme write a note for Janine—she's over at her folks'. And I'll throw my bike in the car so you don't have to drive me back here. Do Vanessa and my mom know?"

"Not unless they're listening to a radio with batteries. Power's been out all day. I'll call 'em as soon as I can."

"Gotcha. Yeah, the power's down, all right—I've been pounding on the tripewriter all day. Be right back."

Kelly took him and Deborah to the house where he'd grown up. Then she drove to San Atanasio Memorial again. She was almost there when she realized her license had been expired for a couple of years—one more thing she hadn't worried about. Back in the day, the DMV had renewed it pretty much automatically as long as your record stayed good. It stopped bothering after the eruption. She wasn't likely to hit another car. She did have to be careful not to take out anyone on two or three wheels.

She had to get through the TV crews on her way in this time. She said "Please excuse me" over and over, in a tone that couldn't mean anything but *Get the fuck out of my way.*

They'd moved Colin to a regular room by then. He looked pinker than he had when he first came out of surgery. He looked more alert, too. "Some hero you married, huh?" he said.

"I married the guy I love," Kelly said. "How do you feel?"

"Like an angry alligator found me at the snack bar," he answered. "But you told me the other guy is talking with his mortician, didn't you?"

"Uh-huh. I wasn't sure you remembered."

"Oh, yeah." Now Colin could nod better. "What did they say about the arm?"

"That you may have some damage." Since he was able to remember, Kelly wouldn't lie to him. "They don't know how much yet. That'll depend on how it heals."

He nodded again. "All right. But I'm still here, and I guess I'm gonna stick around and annoy you a while longer."

Tears stung her eyes. "You'd better, Buster. Or else!"

When Vanessa's phone rang after dinner, the number the screen showed wasn't one she recognized. She said "Hello?" anyway. She was so glad to have bars again, she might even have talked to a political pollster. He wouldn't have liked what she had to say, but she would have talked.

But it wasn't a pollster. "Vanessa? This is Kelly. Have you seen the news or anything tonight?"

"No. Why?" Next to talking with her stepmother, a pollster's bull seemed downright cheery conversation.

Then Kelly said, "Okay—you don't know. Your father got shot this afternoon."

"Oh, Jesus! What happened? How bad is it?"

"An armed robber with an AK was holed up in a house and started shooting. Colin got hit in the shoulder. He's at San Atanasio Memorial—he had surgery. He'll make it. That's the main thing. They don't know how good his left arm will be afterwards, but he will make it."

"Thanks for letting me know," Vanessa said. "What happened to the robber?"

"Deceased." Kelly packed a lot of sour satisfaction into the word.

Vanessa understood that down to the ground. "Good!" she exclaimed.

"I said the same thing when they told me," Kelly said. "I guess I'm not as civilized as I'd like to be."

"Screw civilized," Vanessa answered. "Civilized people don't shoot cops with assault rifles." For once in their touchy relationship, they were on the same page.

"I would've called you sooner, but I've been waiting to get a working line," Kelly said.

"Yeah, it's been down all over," Vanessa said. "I had to go in today to edit some stuff. Double time on Saturday—yeah! But people at work were playing with manual typewriters. An old engineer brought out a slide rule, if you can believe it."

"I've used one a few times when the power just wouldn't come back on," Kelly said. "Feels medieval, but it works."

"If you say so." Vanessa wasn't on the same page as Kelly any more.

Her stepmom must have realized as much. "Listen, I'll let you go," she said. "I guess I need to call your mother next."

"Have you ever talked to her before?" Vanessa asked, honestly curious.

"No, but it needs doing, doesn't it?"

"Yeah, probably." Vanessa might not have been sorry to hear

some of her exes had stopped a bullet. If Bronislav stopped one, she'd give three cheers. But her mom didn't despise her dad the way she despised men she no longer loved. Maybe raising kids together had something to do with it. Or maybe her mom was just more sentimental than she was.

"Then I'd better do it," Kelly said.

Realizing she was about to hang up, Vanessa quickly asked, "Can Dad have visitors? I should get over there."

"They let me in to see him. You're family. They should let you in, too." Kelly paused. "I guess I'd better tell them to let your mother in, too, if she wants to come. They're liable to raise a stink unless I say it's okay."

"I wouldn't be surprised," Vanessa said. "Maybe I'll see you at the hospital."

"Yeah. 'Bye." This time, Kelly did hang up.

"Fuck!" Vanessa said as she set down her phone. You hoped you never got a call like that. Getting it from someone you disliked made it worse, but the Holy Ghost couldn't have given her that kind of news without rocking her. She went into the kitchen and pulled the bottle of slivovitz off a high cupboard shelf. It tasted like plum-flavored napalm and burned as if it were on the way down. Worse, it was left over from her time with the Serbian freedom fighter, chef, and thief.

At the moment, she didn't care. She filled a shotglass full and chugged it. It was just as venomous as she remembered. Bronislav could drink it like that without even coughing, but he must have had his gullet copper-plated or something. Vanessa coughed plenty after it went down. She didn't do this often enough to get used to it, assuming a human body could get used to it.

In a little while, though, the plum brandy put up an invisible shield between her and the bad news. Just as well she didn't do this very often; she might get to like it too much if she did. Her father had done a lot of drinking after her mother walked out of their marriage. He did seem to have eased off since. Maybe Kelly was good for something, hard to believe as that might be.

You were never further from real misery than one bad break or a few inches. If the dumb shithead with the AK had missed, Dad would have a story to tell for the rest of his life. A few inches the other way and he'd be dead. He got the story this way, but he earned it with his pain.

Vanessa filled the shotglass again. The slivovitz scorched less going down this time. Her nerve endings still had to be stunned, or something. And it definitely did numb her up. That suited her just fine. The less she had to think about the gruesome orgy they always made of the funeral for a cop killed in the line of duty, the happier she was.

"If you'd told me sooner you wanted to go over there," Jared Watt said to Louise on Monday afternoon, "I would have brought the car and driven you. It wouldn't have bothered me. I know you were married to him for a long time."

"It's all right. I'll take the bus," Louise said. Driving her to see her ex in the hospital might not have bothered Jared, but it would have bothered her. Life was crazy enough even when you didn't try to fit together pieces that weren't supposed to mix.

Instead of crossing Van Slyke to wait for the bus, she stayed on Reynoso Drive. The bus that stopped at this bench took her east, not south. She went past Hesperus, past the Carrows and the post office and the B of A, past Sword Beach. This part of town felt achingly familiar. She'd come to these places all the time while she lived with Colin. She'd shopped at the Vons past Sword Beach as long as she could afford to drive. Now she went to a smaller market much closer to the condo.

She hadn't been to San Atanasio Memorial since James Henry was born not long after the eruption. It only seemed a million years ago and in another country, one where almost everything still worked all the time. Inside the hospital, things still did. But you paid a stiff price for that, not only in money but also in health and pain.

She cross the street. An electric eye opened the sliding glass door for her. A young Hispanic woman at the reception desk raised a polite eyebrow when she came up. "I'm Louise Ferguson," she said. "Which room is Colin Ferguson in, please?"

"He's in 476," the receptionist answered. "Please use the stairs. We save the elevators for emergencies." She pointed. Maybe they were trying to save power. Or maybe not quite everything was sure to work all the time, even here.

Louise dutifully went up the stairs. *My exercise for the day*, she thought. She found her way to room 476. There was Colin, looking like somebody in a hospital bed. And there, in a chair by the bed, sat a rather wide-shouldered woman whose short, dark-blond hair had some gray streaks in it. That had to be Kelly. Absurdly, Louise was miffed. Her picture of her visit to her ex hadn't included his current wife.

Kelly's picture might not have included Louise, either. But no—she wouldn't have said to come if it hadn't. Louise stepped into the room. She introduced herself to Kelly, who wouldn't have been in much doubt about who she was. They cautiously shook hands: life's little, or not so little, awkwardnesses. Then Louise turned to Colin. "How are you doing?" she asked.

"I'm drugged," he answered matter-of-factly. "I'm still pretty sore. I'm due for another shot before too long."

"All those years without ever needing a gun . . ." Louise said.

"Yeah." He let out the dry chuckle she remembered so well. "Watch that first step. It's a doozy, I tell you."

"I guess!" Louise said. "You weren't the one who got him, then?"

"Oh, heck, no. I was out of it by then. I fired three rounds that didn't do any good, and then he nailed me."

"How long will they keep you here?"

"If everything goes okay, a few more days. They want to make sure I don't have an infection in there. Then I have to heal up and see how the arm is. I can wiggle my fingers some. They say that's good."

"Has, uh, Deborah seen you since you got hurt?" Louise asked.

"I brought her for a few minutes this morning," Kelly said. "She said this was a weird place and it smelled funny. But she was glad to see her daddy even so."

"That's good." Louise nodded. "And this *is* a weird place, and it *does* smell funny."

"Thanks for coming," Colin told her. "Nice to know I'm still irresistible."

"Oh, right. At least," Kelly said before Louise could decide whether to laugh or get mad. Only the pitch of her voice differed from Colin's; the inflection was his to a T. If that meant anything, odds were it meant they'd made a good match. While Louise had put up with what Colin called his sense of humor, she hadn't tried to imitate it much.

A nurse came in and shooed Louise and Kelly out into the hall. Sweeping the curtain around the bed closed, she said, "One minute, ladies. I have to give him an injection."

"I hope that's his pain shot. I think it is," Kelly said. "He's hurting more than he lets on."

"That sounds like him," Louise replied.

The current and former Mrs. Ferguson eyed each other, looking for something to say. Kelly spoke first: "I do appreciate that you came. And so does Colin. You still mean something to him— I know that."

"He means something to me, too," Louise said. "We were together a long time. And it wasn't a horrible divorce. I tried not to make it one, anyhow. I just . . . had to go in a different direction, that's all."

"I've got the car here," Kelly said. "For this, I've been using it. When you go, do you want me to drive you to your place?"

"Thanks, but that's okay," Louise answered. Kelly didn't try to insist. Now Louise had met her, but making friends or even owing her anything pushed it further than she wanted to go. She'd made her choices before the supervolcano erupted, and she'd stick with them.

XIX

Rob sometimes got mail from other people who lived in this cut-off chunk of Maine. There were occasional fan letters. Flounders, he and his bandmates called those, from the line in *Rocky and Bullwinkle*: "Fan mail . . . from a flounder." There were also occasional invitations to play, sometimes even offering money or other interesting inducements.

Mail from the rest of the United States came rarely enough to make him open his eyes wide when it did. The last time he'd heard from his father was the letter letting him know he had a new half-sister. Dad had never been one for Christmas or even birthday cards. Idle chatter wasn't his style, any more than it was Rob's.

But here was another letter in his small, neat script. Here at last: by the California postmark, it had been a month on the road. The Pony Express could have got it here faster—unless the ponies died of HPO trying to cross what had been the Great Plains and was now the Great Eruption Zone. The stamp said FOREVER + 2 and SUPERVOLCANO RELIEF. That didn't mean it was good forever and two days. It meant you paid first-class postage plus two bucks, and the two did what they could to help the cleanup.

Dear Rob, the letter said, *I have joined your club, and if it weren't for the honor of the thing I would rather walk. A punk with an AK put a round through my shoulder. Not the arm I eat and write and shake it off with, but even so not a whole bunch of fun. The punk is dead, and I don't miss him a bit.*

"I bet you don't!" Rob said. Dad had never been one for wasting sentiment on crooks—few cops were—and he really wouldn't waste any on somebody who'd come too close to punching his ticket for good.

So I am on the shelf right now, his father continued. *I stay home and I get in Kelly's way and I read Deborah stories. I make sure she sits on my right side so she doesn't jostle the other shoulder. It may not matter. I've got plenty of plaster and fiberglass armor. I mostly sleep on my back on the recliner in my work niche.*

"Ouch!" Rob exclaimed. He hadn't thought about how awkward a cast there would make lying down or rolling over.

When the cast comes off, I will start going to physical therapy, Dad wrote. *That is supposed to be even less fun than going to the dentist (Kelly's father would kill me if he read this). The dentist numbs you up first. With the physical therapist, it's supposed to hurt. But I need to do it if I'm going to get any use out of the arm. Some would be good.*

"No shit," Rob agreed aloud. The drummer in—was it Def Leppard?—had lost an arm in a car crash or something. He'd fixed up his kit so he could do amazing things with foot pedals, but it wasn't the same. You came equipped with a right and a left for good reason.

I may need more surgery, too. Whether I do, and how much I get back, will all figure in to when I go back to work—and if I go back, Dad finished. *I have more than enough time served to retire if I want to. That would be one thing. Retiring because I have to would be something else, something I don't like so much. But I may not have a choice. Hope you are doing well. If you get close to e-mail or if you find a camera and film for it, send me photos of Lindsey and little Colin. I already know what you look like. Love anyway, Dad.*

Rob read through it again, shaking his head. It sure as hell sounded like his old man, all right. And, knowing his father, he feared he knew how much Dad wasn't saying. How bad did the wound hurt? How worried was Dad that he wouldn't get back much function in the arm? Both ways, probably more than he was letting on.

Lindsey was at the high school. How much use for chemistry kids here would ever have was another interesting question. But this technically was still part of the USA. They might move to some place where knowing such things mattered. And going to school got them out of their parents' hair for a while.

Little Colin would have been in Rob's hair right this minute, since he was playing househusband. But the kid was down for a nap, so Rob could make like a grownup. Only there wasn't much to do. No TV. No radio, not when he was low on batteries. No Net. It was quiet quiet quiet. He was trying to get his hands on a spring-powered record player and some records to play on it. That would, or at least might, be better than nothing.

Meanwhile . . . Meanwhile, it was as nice a day as Guilford had seen since the eruption. The sun shone. Much of the snow had melted. Grass and even a few flowers were trying to grow. It was in the fifties—beach weather, the way things were these days. It probably wouldn't get down to forty tonight, either.

All over Guilford, people with vegetable plots and green-houses would be cheering for the good weather to go on. The longer it did, the better the chance their vegetables had of matur-ing. Rob cheered for the good weather even though he didn't have a plot. The more veggies there were, the better the odds of getting through the next grim winter would be.

When Maine north and west of the Interstate was just an amusing outlier, the rest of the country could afford to throw it a bone during the short stretch of time when the roads opened up. Now the whole Northeast was in trouble: the really densely populated part of the USA. Who would bother remembering the handful of people up here?

After a while, little Colin woke up. Rob changed his diaper. The fresh one, like the wet one it replaced, was cloth. Pampers didn't get up here, nor had they for quite a while. He'd got pretty good with safety pins. He'd stuck himself a fair number of times, but the baby only once.

When his son was dry, Rob carried him and the letter over to the Trebor Mansion Inn. His bandmates had met his dad back in the days before the eruption, but all they would do now was make *Oh, wow!* noises. He hoped for more from Dick Barber. No guarantees, but he hoped. Dick was ex-military himself, and was within shouting distance of Rob's father's age. He reminded Rob of his dad, too, maybe more than Rob realized with the top part of his head.

He was chopping wood when Rob got there: chopping wood without a shirt on, as a matter of fact. "Showoff!" Rob called. It wasn't all *that* warm. One of the Maine Coon cats the folks at the Inn bred also watched in disapproval—though more, Rob judged, from the scary noises than from the sight of a bare-chested Dick Barber. Dick was lean and fit these days. Most people around here were. Surplus calories didn't grow on trees any more.

"As long as I keep working, it's not bad," Dick said. "Since I'm not . . ." He pulled on a sweatshirt. "What's up?" Rob showed him the letter. Barber held it out at arm's length to read it. "Good God! At least they got the bastard with the Kalashnikov."

"Yeah. But that doesn't do Dad a whole lot of good," Rob said.

"True. At least it *was* an AK-47, not a more modern military piece with a small-caliber round and a really high muzzle velocity," Barber said. "Some of those, the shock of a hit can kill even when the wound itself might not."

"Happy day!" Rob exclaimed.

"I know." Dick skimmed through the letter again. "Your dad sounds like someone with his head on tight. If he does have to retire, my guess would be that he'd be able to find something interesting to do with his time, not just sit around and wait to die of boredom." He reached out and gently touched little Colin on the end of the nose with his right index finger. "Not easy to be bored when you've got a small child in the house, is it?"

"Now that you mention it," Rob said, "no."

"That should help," Barber said. "If he were a certain kind of man, he might make some money by writing a book about what led to unmasking the South Bay Strangler. But, from things you've said, he's not that kind of man, is he?"

"Now that you mention it," Rob repeated, "*no*." He got a chuckle from the proprietor of the Mansion Inn. His father was about as far from being that kind of man as anyone could get. If a person could be aggressively private, that was Dad. And Rob gave Dick Barber points for seeing as much.

"With the weather this good, you might want to think about going down to Newport or over to Bangor to see if you can find a working phone line and call California," Dick said.

"There's an idea." It was one that hadn't occurred to Rob. The twenty-first century, or some of it, was only a couple of days' travel away. He would have to find a pay phone, of course, or someone whose cell he could borrow. Even if he could charge his old one, he hadn't paid a bill for years. No cell-phone company would keep anybody on the books for that long. He wouldn't have himself. "I may do that before it starts snowing again."

"Bite your tongue," Dick said, so Rob did. The older man laughed. Little Colin didn't know what was funny, but he laughed, too. Rob sketched a salute and turned to go. Dick Barber returned it with, well, military precision.

When Lindsey got back from the high school, Rob showed her the letter, too. She made horrified noises, which was reasonable enough. "Do you want to fly back and see him?" she asked. "The airport at Bangor should be open."

"Umm . . ." he said.

"Oh," his wife replied.

"Yeah."

He could scrape together enough cash for a phone call. For airfare? Not likely, and the airlines didn't run on barter. His credit cards were at least as expired as his cell phone. So was his driver's license, come to that—and the clean-shaven guy on it bore little resemblance to the shaggy fellow he'd become. Even if he could have paid for a ticket, with that for an ID they might not have let him on the plane.

He shook his head, marveling. "I don't belong to that world any more. Nobody in Guilford does, or in Dover-Foxcroft, or Greenville, or . . . anywhere up here. It is what it is, and we are what we are, and what we are is on the outside. If we got connected up again, the first thing the Feds would do was charge everybody with tax evasion. Most people would lose their houses, too—who's sent mortgage money to Chase every month?"

"Nobody," Lindsey said.

"You got that right," Rob agreed. "Maybe over the weekend, though, I will hop on my bike and go to Newport and see if I can make like ET and phone home. Lord! I wonder if I still know the number!"

"If you think you can get back by six Monday morning, you

should go," Lindsey said. But it had started raining by the weekend, so he didn't. He wrote a letter instead.

When Bryce Miller walked into his apartment, Susan pointed to a fat envelope on the kitchen table and said, "Looks like your article's finally in print."

"Woohoo!" he said, and tore the envelope open. Sure enough, inside were two copies of *The Journal of Hellenic Studies* with his comparative analysis of the prosody of three of Theocritus' pastorals. One copy would go on the brag shelf that housed his and Susan's scholarly publications and the little magazines that had printed a handful of his poems.

The other copy, he would send to his mother in California. She had a brag shelf of her own, one she used to impress her relatives and the neighbors. The article would be Greek to her in more ways than one. She wouldn't care. It was a sign that Bryce was doing well for himself. She would care about that.

Bryce cared about that, too. Publishing articles was one of the hoops you had to jump through to win tenure. That this one made a Congressional budget report seem exciting by comparison, that perhaps three dozen scholars in the whole world would give a flying fuck about what he was saying . . . Next to jumping through the hoops, those were details.

"Anything else in the mail?" he asked.

"Utility bill."

"Do I want to know?"

"Unh-unh. And it'll get worse with fall coming on and winter right behind."

"Yeah, I know. Well, we're still here." He'd walked away from a secure job at the Department of Water and Power to teach Latin at a Catholic high school in the San Fernando Valley for a lot less money. He'd left that job to teach at a college in rural Nebraska. If he'd worried about getting rich, he never would have spent so much time memorizing irregular Greek verbs.

Susan had encouraged him to bail from the DWP. She'd married him while he was getting on people's cases—especially the ablative—teaching Latin. She'd come to Nebraska with him, and if that wasn't love, what the hell would be? She'd finished her own thesis while she was here. She'd looked for a job of her own, and looked, and looked.

She was still looking. People cared no more about the Holy Roman Empire than they did about Hellenistic poetry. By all the signs, they cared even less.

Or maybe that wasn't fair. Bryce had landed the Wayne State job by luck: good luck for him, bad luck for the previous holder. Professor Smetana, who had been teaching here, died of lung disease brought on by breathing crud from the supervolcano eruption. He'd been one of several hundred thousand—no, probably over a million by now. The list got longer every day, and would keep getting longer for years to come.

Do I want Susan to get a job enough that I want somebody to die so she can? Bryce wondered. Put that way, the answer had to be no. But if someone who held a job that Susan could land *did* die, he wanted her to land it. She wasn't one to put on a big show when things bothered her, but living here and living here and not getting a job and not getting a job was wearing on her. Had worn on her, in fact.

"Honey?" he said.

"What?"

"Do you want to move back to L.A. at the end of the academic year?" There. He'd said it.

She looked at him. "And do what?"

"I don't know. Whatever. I'd find something, and so would you. You'd be a lot happier than you are here."

"Don't be dumb. Don't be dumber than you can help, anyhow," Susan said. "I'll be okay. And you're only a couple of years away from tenure. You want to throw that away because I've got a case of the blahs?"

At least she admitted she had them, which probably meant she had them bad. Most of the time, she denied everything. "No, I don't want to do that," Bryce answered. "But I don't want to come back from campus one day and find a note on the kitchen table and you gone, either. That's more important, as far as I'm concerned. Colin had that happen to him about the time Vanessa didn't want me around any more."

"Well, I'm damn glad she didn't, because I like having you around," Susan said. "And I'm not going anywhere, thank you very much. Except to the bathroom." When she came back, she asked, "How's Colin doing, anyway?"

"Last time I talked to him was about a week ago." Bryce was willing to change the subject. If Susan said she wasn't going anywhere, she wasn't. It was when she didn't say anything that you had to worry. He went on, "He says they'll take the cast off pretty soon. He's righteously ready for them to do that. He says he hasn't been able to scratch where it itches since he got shot."

"I believe that," Susan said. "I broke my wrist when I was, I dunno, eight or nine. Fell off my bike—lucky I didn't break my neck. It was summer, and it was hot. The itching and the sweating drove me nuts." After a moment, she added, "I guess he doesn't need to worry about sweating so much, even in L.A."

"No kidding!" Bryce had learned about the shooting in a laconic note. *He won't shoot anybody else*, Colin wrote. *No thanks to me, but he won't.* That was very much his style. You knew police officers could find themselves in danger, but you didn't think it would ever happen to anyone you knew. In all the time Bryce knew him, Colin had never fired his gun in anger. From what he said about this, he had now, but it hadn't done him any good.

Then Susan said, "Tell you what—let's see where we are at the end of the year. Maybe we'll talk about it some more. Or maybe I'll find something. Or—what's that line you use?—maybe the horse will learn to sing. That's it, isn't it?"

"That's it," Bryce agreed. "Huzzah for old Herodotus!" So things weren't even slightly good, then. He liked teaching at a college. He liked being married, too. If he had to choose one or the other . . . He figured he could find another job a lot easier than he could find another woman crazy enough to put up with him.

"I wish I didn't think I was casting notes into the void when I sent out applications," Susan said. "It's like everybody and her granny is after every job there is. And with the Northeast all screwed up, half the profs there are looking for slots in places that still have power most of the time. That only makes things worse."

Bryce started to say there might be jobs in places like that. He swallowed it. For one thing, those universities were getting the hindest of hind tit. For another, the towns they were in were a lot worse off than Wayne, Nebraska. That BBC commentator had got it much too right. All the USA's bills, social and economic, were coming due, and no one had anything to pay them with.

Marshall heard the car pull into the driveway. He used to take that sound for granted. Now it was something out of the ordinary. He turned to Deborah, who was building something out of the ordinary—just what, only she knew—from Duplos. "Your mom and dad are home," he said.

She nodded. "Daddy gets his arm back today."

"Is that what he said?"

Deborah nodded again. "That's what he said." By the way she answered, if Daddy said it, that made it so. There had been a good many years when Marshall was convinced that, if his father said it, that made it BS. He didn't automatically believe that any more. He did believe his dad had a particular way of saying things. This sounded like him, all right.

The key turned in the lock. Kelly opened the door. She came in, followed by Colin Ferguson. He was out of the armor plating he'd worn since he got shot. "Do you have your arm back, Daddy?" Deborah yelled.

"Sort of," he answered. It was in a sling. He waggled his fingers and thumb, just to show he could.

"Way to go, Dad." Marshall meant it. Even with a long sleeve covering his father's left arm, it looked thinner than the right. Well, fair enough—it hadn't done anything for a while.

"Power's still working, right?" Dad asked. When Marshall nodded, his father went on, "Oh, good. First thing I need to do is scrub this poor hunk of dead meat with a wire brush. I've got all those weeks' worth of dirt and sweat and dead skin under the cast. It's grotty to the max. Past the max. So I'm heading for the shower." He started upstairs, toward the bathroom off the master bedroom.

"Hang on to the banister," Kelly said sternly.

Dad started to come back with something snarky. He started to, but he didn't finish. Instead, he took a firm grip on the metal banister with his good hand. "Yes, ma'am," he said, and up he went. He would have sassed Marshall's mother; Marshall was sure of it. How did Kelly get him to behave himself? However she managed, Marshall wondered whether they could bottle it. If they could, world peace would break out day after tomorrow.

The water in that upstairs bathroom started to run. When it stopped, Kelly said, "I'll go up there and give him some help. He didn't have an easy time putting on his shirt after they removed the cast. He can do things with his hand, but the arm isn't much more than a deadweight. They said it would get better once he starts putting some strength in again."

She hurried upstairs herself. By the way she talked, she was trying to convince herself along with Marshall. She wanted to believe everything would get back to the way it was before Dad got hurt.

People all over the country—hell, people all over the world—wanted to believe everything would get back to the way it was before the supervolcano erupted. And people in hell wanted mint juleps to drink. Satan wasn't running the julep concession. The country and the world wouldn't get back to normal for nobody knew how many years. Next to those two, the chances for Dad's arm seemed pretty decent.

He and Kelly came down again. "Better?" Marshall asked.

"Better, yeah. Not good yet, but better," Dad said. "It's—a process. I scraped off the outer layers of crud, so the arm's not *as* rank. Next time, I go after more of the onion."

"You've got an onion on your arm, Daddy? Yuck!" Deborah said.

"I sure do, sweetie. I've got potatoes in my head, too," Dad answered. That was what he called looking for a word but not being able to find it. He struck a pose, as well as he could with his bad arm back in the sling. "I'm a regular vegetable garden, I am."

"You're silly, you are," his daughter said.

"Well, that, too." He went over to her and ruffled her hair. When he looked up, he said, "Feels funny not having all that weight on my left side. I leaned away from it to keep my balance. Now I'm like this." He mimed someone leaning back and to the right and about to topple over.

"Like not having your land legs after you've been at sea for a long time," Marshall suggested.

"*Just* like that!" Dad sent him an admiring glance. He felt good—he didn't win them that often. Dad went on, "You ought to be a writer or something."

"Or something," Marshall echoed. "Would be nice if I could make a living at it, or even come close. Janine's making noises like I ought to get a real job."

Playboy wandered into the front room. Here were a bunch of people who knew him. Obviously, they'd gathered together for no other purpose than stuffing him full of kitty treats. What else were humans good for? God had given them thumbs so they could open the packages He magically provided. Playboy stropped the ankles of each of them in turn. He purred like far-off thunder. The better his routine, the more he got fed.

Marshall petted Playboy but didn't reach for the goodies. He wished they hadn't named the cat after his big sale. Every time he saw the fuzzy beast, he got reminded he hadn't made another big sale any time lately.

"Can I, Mommy?" Deborah asked.

"Okay, but only two," Kelly said. Deborah fed Playboy. He inhaled the treats and then beat it. Now that the humans had done what he wanted, he didn't need them any more. Till the next time.

"What kind of real job would you get?" Dad asked.

"She's talking about something in, like, advertising," Marshall said. "By now, I've sold enough stuff that I've got kind of a résumé."

"Yeah, you would, wouldn't you?" Dad said thoughtfully. When he looked at a problem, he eyeballed it carefully and from all sides. He looked at it like a cop working on a case, in other words. "Job market's not what you'd call great, but selling a bunch of stories could make you stick out—and that's what you want. Nothing wrong with a regular paycheck, either."

"I know." Marshall also knew he wouldn't have passed his thirtieth birthday without ever getting one if not for the kindness of family and lover. Even so . . . "I'd rather go on doing what I've been doing."

"If you're gonna do that, you've got to find a way to make it pay more," Dad said.

"We talked about novels a while ago," Kelly said. "Novels pay better than short stories, huh?"

They had indeed talked about them. Marshall had thought about tackling one more than once, in fact. Every time he did, the amount of work involved, and the effort to keep all his balls in the air and make everything come out the way he wanted it to, scared him too much to let him keep going. So he said, "Yeah, they do," and left it there.

"You've got some chops now," Dad observed. "When you try to sell a novel, you can say you've had stories here and there and in *Playboy*. You're not Joe Shmo who doesn't necessarily know the alphabet all the way through."

"I guess," Marshall said. He'd still be trying to crawl out of the primordial slush pile. But his father had a point. He wouldn't be bubbling up from the reeking ooze at the bottom of that pile.

"And," Kelly said shrewdly, "if you can sell a novel or two, it may keep you from trying to write chewing-gum ads or whatever."

Somebody had to write chewing-gum ads. Otherwise, there wouldn't be any. What would happen to chewing gum then? No one wanted to find out. But Marshall would have bet that whoever did write those ads didn't come home from the office feeling proud of himself for having done something cool every day. More likely, the guy gulped a slug of Old Overshoes and figured *Well, okay, two more weeks and we can afford to fix the roof.*

Next to that existential—not despair, but resignation, which might have been worse—wasn't the fear of jumping in over your head by starting a novel a small thing? Mm, not a small thing, but a *smaller* thing? "Mm, maybe," Marshall said, as much to himself as to his father and stepmom.

———

When Vanessa got to the bus to head for another delightful day at the widget works, the driver handed her a small sheet of paper. He had a little pile of them near the fare box; he was giving one to everybody who boarded.

Vanessa sat down in the first empty seat and read hers. *Due to budget constraints, the number of buses traveling each route on a daily basis must be reduced. Effective November 15, the following schedule for this route will be implemented. If this is impactful on your commute, the inconvenience is apologized for. Should more funding become available, we will attempt to facilitate a restoration of service.*

Calling the writing wretched gave it the benefit of the doubt. The bureaucrat who'd cranked it out must have grown up without a native language. If Vanessa thought that was bad, she let out a yelp of pure horror when she looked at the new schedule. Seeing the Mummy or the Wolfman couldn't have dismayed her nearly so much.

This bus got her to work about a quarter past eight, which was okay. After November 15, it would go the way of the dodo and of Yellowstone National Park, though less spectacularly than the latter. There would be one that got her to work a little before seven, and one that got her there going on ten. No happy medium.

"Man, this sucks!" That wasn't her; it was the African-American woman who'd got on right after her. But she couldn't have put it better herself.

Several people swore at the driver. "It ain't my fault," he said. "They gonna cut my pay, too, on account of I ain't drivin' as much."

"That's terrible! You ought to sue them," Vanessa exclaimed. She leaped as passionately into causes as she did into everything else.

"Not me. I ain't suin' nobody." The driver shook his head. "I got two little kids. Ain't gonna do nothin' to mess with my job, not when I got them rugrats to feed." Vanessa had no answer to that. She thought children were a ball and chain, but she didn't suppose the bus driver would want to hear her say so.

When she got to the widget works, she showed Mr. Gorczany the bus-schedule change sheet. "Can I change my hours so I can still ride in?" she asked. "Earlier or later—whichever you'd rather."

Her boss pooched out his lower lip like a spoiled little boy. "That would be inconvenient, because you wouldn't be interfacing with the rest of the staff as much," he said.

She hadn't thought anyone used that stupid piece of jargon any more. She'd underestimated him. "I don't think I'll be the only one the new schedule affects," she answered. Try as she might, she couldn't make herself say *impacts*, much less *impactful*.

"Well, let's examine some alternative choices," Nick Gorczany said redundantly. "Could you drive in?"

That was straightforward enough. It was also more than clueless enough. "Could you double my pay?" Vanessa blurted. He still tooled around in his BMW. Did he think everybody else was made of money, too?

"No," he said, which was also straightforward enough. "Could you ride a bicycle? Most people seem to have bicycles these days."

"I have a bike. I could ride it in, I guess, but it would be a pain," Vanessa said. "I don't live real close to here. That's why I take the bus."

"Well, let's see what we can work out. I don't want to inconvenience you too much, but I don't want to impair our efficiency, either," he said. The haggle that followed would have made a secondhand-parts dealer in Lagos jealous. They finally agreed she would ride her bike Monday, Wednesday, and Friday of one week and Tuesday and Thursday of the next, taking the bus and coming in early on the days when she didn't ride. It was a fifty-fifty split between what she wanted and what he wanted, in other words.

She supposed she ought to thank her lucky stars she'd got that much. She thought about asking him if she could adjust things when it rained, but decided not to. If she walked in dripping wet one morning, that might flick his conscience—assuming he owned such a critter.

Back at her desk, she worked out some of her anger at the transit district and at Nick Gorczany by eviscerating a proposal the company was getting ready to submit. She had a red pen run dry in the middle of her edit. She pulled out another one and kept on cutting. The engineers who'd drooled the first draft onto paper would turn fourteen different shades of puce. She didn't care. This was what Mr. Gorczany paid her—not enough—to do.

If they wanted to take it to the boss, she also didn't care. If he backed them and the widget works blew the contract as a result, she didn't care much about that, either.

Or maybe she did. Because if that happened, what would they do? Blame her for not editing well enough. Of course they would—otherwise they'd have to blame themselves, and what were the odds of that?

The power was on, which was good. She took the edited draft to the copier and made a set for herself. Only after she'd preserved (and stashed) a record of what she'd done did she return the draft to the engineers who'd produced it. Sure enough, they bleated like sheep being sheared.

"If you'd written it in English the first time, it wouldn't look like this now," she said.

"Did you have to do all that?" one of them asked unhappily.

"No. I could have left it alone," she answered. "The agency with the funding would have laughed its ass off if I had, but why worry about things like that?"

She hoped they would try to argue grammar with her. They'd grown leery of trying that; she won easily but not graciously. One of them plucked up his courage if not his common sense and asked, "What's wrong with this? The spellchecker didn't mind it."

"That's because the spellchecker is a moron." Vanessa didn't say *and so are you*, but the suggestion was there. "You wrote 'We are lead to propose the following goals and objectives.' Never mind the passive. Never mind the clunky structure. The present tense of the verb is l-e-a-d, pronounced *leed*. The past tense is l-e-d, pronounced *led*. L-e-a-d, pronounced *led*, is the metal that anyone who thinks it's the past tense of l-e-a-d, pronounced *leed*, has between his ears instead of brains."

"You're not a good team player." If the engineer couldn't come down on her for being wrong, he'd come down on her for being right.

"If I were playing on a good team, I would be," she answered, and walked away. If they fixed things, fine. If not, tough titty.

An hour or so later, Nick Gorczany stopped at her desk. "Try to work on your attitude," he said. "Try."

"When they defend the indefensible, it pisses me off," she answered.

"Try anyway," Mr. Gorczany said. "You know the old saying about catching more flies with honey than with vinegar."

"I was trying to get rid of the flies," Vanessa answered. Her boss rolled his eyes and went off to share old sayings with somebody else. That suited her fine.

XX

Colin Ferguson looked at himself in the bathroom mirror. He whistled a few bars of the *Mission: Impossible* theme. "Your job, should you choose to accept it," he said as dramatically as possible, "is to button your shirt with both hands."

Kelly was reading on the bed. "Go for it, honey," she called. "Tom Cruise ain't got nothin' on you."

Tom Cruise had nothing on him except umpteen gazillion dollars and two good arms. Colin's left elbow and wrist worked all right. Whenever he tried to move his left arm from the shoulder, it felt as if he'd whacked a hornets' nest in there with a stick. The physical therapist insisted that time and practice would make it easier, if not necessarily easy. The puckered scar from the 7.62mm AK round and the surgeons' knife marks (some smaller ones newer and pinker than the rest—they'd gone in again, arthroscopically, to clean out more bone fragments) insisted that the therapist didn't know what she was talking about.

Well, he had to try. He did. "Ffffudge!" he said—not quite a slip in front of Kelly, but mighty close.

"You want help?" she asked.

"No. What I *want* is to be able to do this by myself," Colin answered. "I want it not to hurt so darn much when I do it, too. I can almost manage the first part. The other half isn't there yet, though. Not even close."

"I'm sorry. You got torn up, from what the doctors say," Kelly told him.

"Yeah, I know." He was still trying to decide whether buttoning down from the top hurt more than buttoning up from the bottom. He hadn't made up his mind. Where he was right now, both seemed equally horrendous. He'd started getting good at doing buttons with just his right hand. Going back to normal felt like more trouble than it was worth. He kept at it anyhow. At last, he said, "There! I did it. And I didn't age a day over five years."

"Want a pain pill?" Kelly asked. "You've still got some left."

He did want one. He shook his head all the same. "Thanks, but no thanks. I'm trying to do without 'em as much as I can, so I don't get to like 'em too well."

"Okay, but they're there for when you really hurt. You're making noises like you really hurt," Kelly said. "You're also making noises like a cop who's scared to death of drugs."

"Well, if I am, I've earned the right," Colin retorted. "I don't know how many people I've seen who messed up their lives 'cause they found out how much they liked getting loaded."

"I can't see you knocking over a pharmacy next week," Kelly said.

"No, and I want to make sure you can't see me doing anything like that," Colin said. "Anyway, it's kind of eased off now that it's just hanging again."

"Okay." By the way she said it, it was anything but. She didn't push it any further than that, though. One of the things wives—and husbands—needed to learn was when to back off.

Putting on jeans wasn't such an ordeal—his left arm didn't

need to do as much. "I'm only glad I'm not a southpaw, and that the punk didn't get me in the other shoulder," he said. "Then I really would've been wrecked."

"I'm not glad about any of it, not even a little bit," Kelly declared.

"Well, neither am I," Colin said. The more he tried to make his wounded arm work, the more he wondered if he'd ever be able to go back to the cop shop. He could do the part of the job that involved sitting at a desk. In the field, though, he'd be a liability—hell, a danger—to himself and to whoever was with him.

For that matter, he'd be a danger going to and from the station. You could ride a bike with one good arm as long as nothing went wrong. The second anything did, you were screwed. The same held true in a car, even one with automatic. You couldn't even think about it if you had a stick.

He carefully went down the stairs. He could use the banister climbing them. It was on his bad side descending. If he slipped, he'd either fall or try to catch himself with his left arm and then fall. Stairs were dangerous. They got more dangerous when a cat fell asleep on them.

"Move your fuzzy butt," Colin told Playboy. Playboy ignored him. Colin stepped around the cat. One of these days, he wouldn't see the lazy beast. Then they'd both be sorry.

He ran water into a Pyrex measuring cup to nuke it to make coffee. As long as they had electricity, he'd enjoy it. When he finished his joe, Kelly fixed some. He went into the front room and turned on the TV. He'd developed a new tolerance for it since he got hurt. Watching cost no effort, and he could work the remote with one hand.

Which he did, as soon as the picture came on: it was Barney and Baby Bop. PBS was fine most of the time, but not all the time. He switched to CNN. A Viagra commercial was running. He muted it. It was at least as irksome as the sappy purple dinosaur. A commercial for backyard chicken coops followed it. He wouldn't have seen that before the eruption. But meat and eggs, these days, were more do-it-yourself than they had been for many years.

"Hey, hon!" he called.

"What?" Kelly answered from the kitchen. The microwave hadn't dinged again yet.

"If I do retire, what do you say I start raising chickens? We could use the poop to fertilize the garden."

"If that's what you want to do," she said. "Make sure it is before you start, that's all." He nodded, though she couldn't see him. It sounded like good advice. So did most of what she said.

At last, a newswoman came on. "A bill to construct seven new nuclear plants has passed the House," she said. "Fierce debate is expected in the Senate. Polls show that most Americans want more energy, no matter how it is produced. But less than one person in four wants a nuclear power plant built within a hundred miles of his or her home."

Colin sipped his coffee. "Everybody wants to go to heaven, but nobody wants to die," he said.

"Say what?" Kelly brought in her cup. She hadn't heard the story. He explained. She nodded. "Oh. Yeah. One of the things I haven't heard many people say is that the supervolcano coughed out a lot of radioactive crud. Not by percentage, of course, but when over six hundred cubic miles of junk come out, even a tiny percentage makes a fair-sized raw number."

"If the EPA finds out about that, I bet they declare the eruption illegal," Colin said. "Then all our troubles are over, right?"

"Right." She sent him a severe look. He grinned back.

On the TV, the newswoman said, "The Administration hopes the disastrous outages in the Northeast last winter will allow this bill to pass both houses at last. The nuclear plants will add to the grid a large part of the power lost as a result of the freezeup in Quebec. Environmental groups vow to fight construction through the courts if the bill does pass."

"So they'll start building them about the time the climate finally gets better on its own," Colin said.

"That may not be for hundreds of years," Kelly reminded him.

"And your point is . . . ?" he said. She stuck out her tongue at him.

CNN ran more commercials. When the news came back, it was with a report from London. The reporter stood outside in the snow, bundled up as if near the summit of Everest. It wasn't winter yet—it wasn't far into fall—but he looked cold anyway. "The continued fading of the Gulf Stream from stream to trickle has dealt Britain and all of northwestern Europe a catastrophic blow," he said somberly. "The United Kingdom has endured winters of discontent every year since the eruption. And they have grown progressively worse. As has often been remarked, we are on the latitude of Labrador. More and more, we have a climate to match."

They cut to clogged roads in London, to fields full of drifts, to Stonehenge all ghostly under a mantle of white. Then back to the fields, to cattle trying to dig their way through the thick snow to whatever greenery lay beneath.

"Our livestock is not so drastically afflicted as that in the United States," the reporter acknowledged. "Yet forage for our cattle and sheep has decreased as the climate worsens. Last year, the Home Counties—for our American friends, the ones surrounding London—had a winter that once would have been reckoned harsh even in the Scottish Highlands. Forecasts for the long cold season ahead are even grimmer."

Another cut, this time to a poorly shaved farmer in Wellingtons and a thick anorak with the hood over his head. "It's a balls-up, all right," he said, his accent much less suave than the

BBC man's. "I've got to buy more fodder from abroad, because my flocks can't get as much from the fields when they're mostly frozen. And sweet suffering Jaysus, the prices! I'll have to charge more for my animals when I sell 'em. Everyone will. It's a pity. It's a great pity, but no help for it I can see. My main hope is, I can get through the winter without losing half the beasts from a blizzard."

A 3-D graph showed three steeply rising lines. "These are the prices of petroleum, wheat, and beef since the eruption," the reported said, in case his audience couldn't read the dates at the bottom of the screen and the words PETROLEUM, WHEAT, and BEEF. "No end to this inflation seems to be in sight. Production has dropped sharply in all three commodities, whilst demand has remained constant or even increased. A more classic recipe for exploding prices can scarcely be imagined."

This time, the picture cut away to the bustling port of London. A correspondent standing on a wharf said, "There is concern the Thames may freeze for an extended period this winter. If it should, one of the busiest ports in the world will have to shut down. Two new icebreakers have entered service since the supervolcano erupted, and five more are on order. If the port does fail, the effect on the UK's economy will be staggering."

They shifted to a different reporter, this one on a beach under as bright a sun as the world got these days. People in Speedos and bikinis invited skin cancer. The beach was in . . . Greece, by the unreadable letters on a taverna. "More and more inhabitants of Britain and Ireland and Scandinavia are abandoning their homelands for the more congenial climes farther south," the reporter said. "Immigration within the European Union is easy—so easy that Greece and Italy and Spain have begun to worry that they may be swamped by newcomers. Some politicians in these Mediterranean countries have proposed stricter controls and higher taxes for aliens coming to their warmer shores. That the

EU constitution forbids such discrimination fazes them not in the least."

"I know the weather is bad farther north," a Greek official with a bushy mustache said in excellent English. "But this is our country, our homeland. We were here first. We have more than anyone else the right to live here now. We will not let foreigners buy our nation out from under us."

Colin turned to Kelly. "Change his clothes and his accent a little and he could be from Orange County."

"He has the same troubles we do, and for the same reason: his weather's got worse, but it isn't terrible," she answered. "And his supplies don't move along I-10 to get to his country, either. Compared to us, he's well off."

"And compared to England, he's in hog heaven," Colin said. "The Russian war in the Ukraine seems to have bogged down pretty well, too. Ain't everybody got fun?" He stood up to fix himself some more coffee. By now, he was good at doing that one-handed.

Rob had eaten a good many strange things before he wound up in Guilford. That was what he got for liking weird restaurants. He'd had sea cucumbers at a Chinese place in San Diego. The taste was briny and innocuous, but the texture put him in mind of something halfway between custard and Play-Doh. He'd eaten a stewed sheep's eyeball and other odd bits of the head at a Moroccan restaurant in . . . was it Tucson or Phoenix? He couldn't remember. He liked tongue, but for anyone who grew up with Jewish friends that hardly counted as strange.

But he was absolutely, positively sure he'd never eaten chitlins before he got here. Maybe if he'd grown up with friends from South Central L.A. . . . . Since he hadn't, pig guts had flown under his radar till now.

He and Lindsey ate them for the same reason slaves in the

antebellum South and their sharecropper descendants had: they couldn't afford to waste anything. When she made chicken soup, she threw in the feet these days along with the rest. They thickened the stock a little, and you could get bits of meat and skin off them if you worked at it.

But chicken feet were a difference of degree. Chitlins were a difference of kind. Somebody in Guilford had a cookbook that told you what to do with them, even if it called them chitterlings. That was necessary at first because, unlike in the deep South, they weren't a part of local pre-eruption cuisine. These days, you didn't throw out anything you could possibly use.

Since Rob spent more time at home than Lindsey did, he got to deal with them. You turned the guts inside out. You scraped them. You soaked them in cold, salted water for a day. You washed them half a dozen times. Considering what had been going through them, that struck Rob as an excellent plan. Then you cut them into two-inch lengths, stewed them with onions and whatever other herbs you could grab, and ate them. The first time Rob and Lindsey tried them, they were surprised at how tasty they were.

You could also deep-fry them. You could if you had cooking fat to spare, anyhow. Even though Rob and Lindsey had got some lard along with the chitlins, they didn't. Fat was hard to come by, and you used it with care. Lard, schmaltz, duck fat, goose grease . . . They were luxuries, delicacies. He couldn't recall the last time he'd eaten butter. Olive oil? Olive oil was right out.

Chitlins and parsnips. Pig's feet and potatoes. Duck and barley stew. Sauerkraut. Homebrew beer. Moonshine. Baked potatoes with salt and a little schmaltz for flavoring. Rye bread that was all rye, not the domesticated stuff groceries called rye bread. Moose meat. Wild turkey—a much skinnier, stringier bird than its domestic cousins. Berries. Mushrooms.

All of it added up to just about enough to live. Even Jim

Farrell had had to have his trademark suits taken in. "I resent being skinny," he said on a sleigh-borne swing through Guilford. "But I suppose I would resent being dead even more."

"Seems a pretty good bet," Rob said. They were sitting in the parlor of the Trebor Mansion Inn, enjoying the warmth of the fire blazing in the fireplace. With malice aforethought, he added, "You probably wouldn't be so noisy about it, though."

Farrell aimed a baleful glare not at Rob but at Dick Barber. "See the trouble you got us all into when you tossed a bone to these stray polliwogs or whatever they were?"

"Well, if I hadn't they would have caused trouble somewhere else," Barber answered. "It might as well be here in Guilford, where they can entertain us while they do it."

A Maine Coon kitten started to climb Rob's leg. He knew how kittens climbed legs: the same way they climbed trees, with their claws all the way out. Maybe trees didn't mind. His leg did. He gently removed the kitten before it made too many flesh wounds and set it on the couch beside him. It let out an indignant, squeaky mew.

"Take it easy, you dumb thing," Rob told it. "I was just trying to keep you from shredding me. And now you're up here."

"He talks to cats," Dick Barber said to Farrell. "I've seen it before."

"When he gets them to answer, that's when we have to worry," Farrell replied.

"Well, I'll talk to you, too," Rob said to the retired history prof. Farrell touched the brim of his fedora—as regal a gesture as Maine north and west of the Interstate was likely to put up with. Rob went on, "Are we going to make it through another winter? Not one whole heck of a lot got up here this summer."

"Which is an understatement. I was keeping track, so I have unfortunate reason to know." Farrell sighed, muttered to himself, and then went on, "Most of us should make it. Guilford should do all right. But the closer you get to Canada, the less came up from the south."

"Not so many people up there. More moose to shoot. More pines to cut down," Barber observed.

"I like to think there's more to life than cracking moose bones for marrow in front of the fire pit," Farrell said. "Neanderthal Man could have done that. Neanderthal Man did do that, as a matter of fact. How have we advanced over the past fifty thousand years?"

"If we've got a satellite phone with a charged battery, we can take a picture of ourselves cracking moose bones for marrow and post it on our Facebook page," Rob answered.

"Well, yes, certainly," Farrell said. "But how have we advanced?"

"We've lost some more people this year," Dick Barber said. "They decide they want their cell phones and their Facebook pages, and they leave for places that still have them. Or they just get sick of shoveling snow and chopping firewood."

"The really interesting question is whether it's that much better anywhere else in the United States." Farrell waved objections aside before they got raised, like a man swatting at gnats that hadn't landed on him yet. "Oh, I'm not talking about places like Florida and Southern California. Those were barely part of the country even before the eruption."

"Thanks a bunch," Rob muttered.

"Any time," Farrell said. "But from things I hear, you will endure shortages and outages and dreadful weather if you move to Ohio or Tennessee or any of those other heathen places. And the people already infesting California or Florida want no more company for their fortunate selves. Hawaii, now, Hawaii is doing everything but sowing mines in the Pacific to discourage new arrivals. If only it could come within light-years of feeding itself, it might try to regain its aboriginal independence."

Rob looked at him in admiration. "I don't think I ever heard anybody use 'aboriginal' in a sentence before."

"Your servant," Jim Farrell said modestly. "Ambrose Bierce defined aborigines as 'Persons of little worth found cumbering the soil of a newly discovered country. They—'"

"'—soon cease to cumber; they fertilize,'" Rob finished for him. "Sorry, Professor. But I found *The Devil's Dictionary* when I was, like, fifteen. My dad had it. It's warped me ever since."

"Your father is a man of parts," Farrell said. "Did I hear that not all his parts are working the way they ought to? A robber with an assault rifle?"

"That's right." Rob nodded. "Last letter I got, he still didn't know if he'd be able to go back to the force."

"Chances are he's made up his mind by now, then," Dick Barber said. "Our connections to the regular U.S. Post Awful aren't what you'd call great."

"I know. We're lucky to have any at all, when we're pretty much off the grid and off the map as far as they're concerned," Rob said.

"It's partly because the postmasters in Newport and Bangor remember we're here even if Heap Big Chief Postmaster in Washington doesn't want to. And it's partly because Jim"— Barber pointed at Professor Farrell—"threatened to talk to Canada Post if the USA stopped sending things up this way."

"I did not threaten. I merely stated an intention," Farrell said. "Hard to believe as it may seem, someone at the Postal Service is still possessed of a vestigial sense of shame—and we are still possessed of a vestigial link to the rest of the land of the corporate and the home of the resigned."

Rob grinned. "Even if that doesn't scan real well, I may steal it."

"You can't steal what's freely given," Jim Farrell replied.

He was fun to listen to, more fun than anyone else in Guilford—probably more fun than anyone else in his little not-quite-duchy. When power outages made entertainment at the flip of a switch only a nostalgic memory, that counted for a hell of a lot. Farrell's sentences had grammar. They had wit. They had just enough purple passages to make listeners smile . . . and to camouflage his underlying hard common sense.

"Thanks, Professor," Rob said, and then, not quite apropos of nothing, "I like it here!"

"You must. Otherwise, you would have bailed out as soon as the runways at Bangor or Portland thawed out enough to let planes land and take off," Dick Barber said. "You. Y'all. Youse guys. You and Biff and Justin and Charlie. All of you."

"I understood you," Rob said. "We'll always be outsiders—"

"Like me," Barber broke in.

"Yeah, like you." Rob nodded. "But it's okay. The people whose people have lived here since Maine was part of Massachusetts, like Bill Gagne in Greenville, they let you talk at meetings and everything."

"*Then* they call him an idiot," Jim Farrell put in.

"Hey, I didn't know Maine *was* part of Massachusetts once before I got here," Rob said.

"Well, I am an idiot sometimes. Sometimes I'm not, too, though, and they see that." Barber eyed Rob. "Sometimes even you're not."

"Maybe sometimes," Rob allowed. Another kitten wanted to climb him. He picked it up, put it on his lap, and started petting it. He'd never dreamt Guilford, Maine, would end up his favorite spot in the whole wide world, but there you were. And here he was.

Marshall took another sheet out of the typewriter and eyed it. The ribbon was starting to go. The next time he had power, he needed to order a new one online. Editors had eased up on typewritten submissions. That started to happen pretty soon after the eruption, but gathered steam after the big outages in the

Northeast. They did insist on black copy, though, for best results when they scanned to OCR.

I can get a few more pages out of this one, anyhow, Marshall thought. He fed a fresh sheet of paper into the old portable. By now, he'd got used to it. It wasn't user-friendly, not the way a computer was. He had to think things through before he set words to paper. Sometimes he fiddled around in longhand till he got his sentences the way he wanted, and then transcribed them. But he could use the typewriter to do what he needed.

Tap, tap, tappety-tap. He had the touch down now. And he was getting close to twenty thousand words into what might turn out to be a novel. If it did, when it did, he intended to dedicate it to Kelly. How many stepmoms got a novel dedicated to them? She was a character in the book, too, renamed and (he hoped) suitably disguised.

After he took out the next page, he looked at his watch. Like a lot of people his age, he'd started wearing one when his phone wouldn't reliably give him the time. "Shit!" he said. It was later than he'd thought.

He filled a pot with water. A match got a burner on the stove going. He cut up potatoes, carrots, and onions, and then a chunk of pork shoulder. They all went into the pot, along with salt, pepper, some other spices, and a bay leaf. The pot went onto the stove. He put the lid on it. In a couple of hours, it would be pork stew.

Pork. Chicken. Chicken. Pork. Fish (or sometimes squid). Pork. Chicken. Chicken. Pork. He couldn't remember the last time he'd eaten beef. McDonald's and Burger King sold so many pork patties these days, they'd had Muslims and Orthodox Jews picket them. Lamb? Marshall sighed. Lamb had been too goddamn expensive since long before the eruption.

Back to the typewriter. The real world receded in favor of the world inside his head. He looked up in surprise when Janine's key chunked in the lock. He also looked up in surprise because it was getting dark. He could still see the words he was putting on paper. Past that, he hadn't cared about anything. He was lucky he'd remembered to get the stew going.

He stood up and kissed Janine. "Hey, babe," he said, sounding more like his father than he knew. "How'd it go?"

"I looked stuff up," she answered. "I filled out some forms that don't need lawyers. I interviewed a little old lady who may have been allergic to an antibiotic her doctor prescribed for her. She's trying to decide whether to sue him. The firm is trying to decide whether to take the case if she does. Another exciting day in the life of a paralegal."

"Right," he said, and lit a kerosene lantern. All over L.A., people were doing the same thing. If the Big One chose this moment to hit, a million lanterns would fall over and a million fires would start. It would be like San Francisco in 1906, only more spread out.

"Stew smells good," she said, sniffing. She sounded as if she deserved part credit, and she did: it was her recipe. After the sniff, she asked, "What else did you do?"

"Couple thousand words," he said, not without pride. "It's starting to feel like it's going somewhere." He'd approached it with . . . fear was the right word. He wasn't some teenager, who might plunge into a novel and finish because he didn't know how hard it was. He knew, all right. Maybe he knew too well.

"Okay." Janine didn't read a lot for fun. She read more now than she had before the supervolcano blew. Everybody did, because less in the way of other kinds of entertainment was around. But she still didn't read all that much, not like Marshall. She went on, "When are you gonna see if you can sell it?"

"Two or three more chapters," he answered. "I should have enough then to see if I can get an agent interested."

She started to say something, then let it go. She looked

under the lid on the pot instead. She stirred with a serving spoon. "It's coming along," she said. "Do we have any wine in the icebox?"

Another old word reviving with the thing so many refrigerators had turned back into. Rob pulled out a bottle of Chablis. He poured for both of them. He'd done his duty on the work front. A little buzz would be nice. The wine would go with the stew, too.

He wouldn't crack *Iron Chef* any time soon, but dinner turned out fine. They killed the bottle of wine. Marshall wondered if Janine was drinking herself into the mood. Kerosene lanterns made lousy reading lamps. The most fun you could have with the power off, you made in pairs. It was also the most fun you could have with the power on, but it had less competition now.

But that turned out not to be why Janine was nerving herself. Instead of doing dishes, she said, "Marshall, this isn't working out. You're not bringing in enough money to make us go, and all you do is sit and pound that typewriter. You don't have enough ambition."

"What? Being a writer isn't an ambition?" he said, because he knew too well he had no comeback for the other.

"Not when it doesn't make you anything, and it doesn't," she answered. "And I was hoping for more, well, excitement when I told Paul to hit the road. Coming home to somebody who hardly even notices I was gone doesn't cut it."

"So what do you want me to do? Pack up and leave?" he asked, hoping against hope she'd tell him no.

But she nodded briskly. "Yes, that's about it. Oh, you don't have to clear out of here by tomorrow morning or anything. I know it's not simple without a working car. It isn't like you don't have anywhere to go, though."

Back to the old house—again, he thought unhappily. "And how long till somebody else moves in here?" he asked. He was just being snarky—if she was out looking for that somebody else, he had no clue about it.

Or he hadn't had a clue about it till her jaw dropped. Even by lantern light, he thought she turned red, but it might have been his imagination. The other damn well wasn't. "That's got nothing to do with anything," she said, her voice a little shrill.

It had a lot to do with everything, as he knew perfectly well. *Anybody who'll cheat with you will cheat on you, too.* Marshall heard his father's words in his memory. Not for the first time, Dad knew what he was talking about, dammit. "Okay," Marshall said, even if it wasn't. "I'll leave as soon as I can pack up my shit and get a car. It was fun while it lasted, wasn't it?"

"Some of it." Janine's mouth twisted. She was gonna be like his sister. She'd erase the good times, so all the bad stuff would be his fault. That sucked, but what could you do? Except move out, anyway?

Kelly grunted when she lifted a box out of the Taurus' trunk. "What did you put in here?" she asked. "Anvils?"

"That one's got manuscripts and shit like that in it," Marshall answered. "A sheet of paper doesn't weigh anything much, but a box of paper's heavier than a box of lead. If I did sci-fi, I'd figure out some bullshit reason why."

"I always thought the same thing. Nice to know I'm not the only one." Kelly lugged the box to the open front door. Playboy was shut in the laundry room to keep him from getting loose (not punishment—he'd been bribed inside with treats). Deborah, however, remained underfoot. "Get out of the way!" Kelly told her, not for the first time.

"C'mere, kiddo. I'll read you a story," Colin called from the front room. Deborah went, but she'd gone before, too. With his bad arm, Colin wasn't helping Marshall move back in. Not to put too fine a point on it, Kelly'd told him she would break his good arm if he tried carrying stuff.

I'm getting too old for this myself, she thought as she hauled the box up the stairs. She did give Colin a certain amount of credit. He hadn't gone even slightly I-told-you-so on Marshall. He'd just told him to come back and made sympathetic noises that sounded as if he meant them. Maybe he realized Marshall was beating himself up, and he didn't have to do it for his son.

Marshall came upstairs right behind Kelly. His mouth wore a sour smile. "Gee, I wonder which way to turn from here," he said. "I mean, I've never set eyes on this hallway before, right?"

"Don't worry about it," Kelly said. "You've got a roof over your head, and plenty of people don't."

"Yeah, yeah." His nod was sour, too. "I don't mind being my dad's son. I'm kinda proud of it, to tell you the truth. But being my dad's kid . . . That gets old, you know?"

She did know, or thought she did. If Professor Rheinburg hadn't pulled strings or twisted arms or whatever he did at Cal State Dominguez, she would be scuffling herself.

"Times are hard," she said. "What can you do? When your novel sells, things'll start straightening out."

"Glad you think so. Janine didn't feel like waiting."

"Well . . ." What was she supposed to say to that? She tried, "When you hooked up with her, you weren't exactly thinking with the top part of your head, were you?"

"I don't know what you're talking about," he answered, deadpan, as Colin might have. Then he did something Colin wouldn't have in a million years: he grabbed his crotch. Kelly laughed so hard, she almost fell over.

"What's funny?" Her husband's voice floated up from below.

"Tell you later," she said. And she did, after Marshall's stuff was all in, Playboy was released (his irate meow said that, bribe or no bribe, they had no business living without a cat for so long), and Deborah went off to color or look at a picture book or play with dolls and dinosaurs or whatever else she felt like doing.

Colin chuckled. "He's got it figured out, too, then. That's good. If he could've seen it sooner—"

"He wouldn't've got laid so much once he moved in with her," Kelly interrupted.

"Yeah, there is that," Colin said. "But that doesn't guarantee a happy ending, not unless you're from Hollywood and you get to roll the credits before they start arguing about who didn't clean up after the party and whose turn it is to take out the trash."

"So what does guarantee a happy ending, O Sage of the Age?" Kelly asked, perhaps less sarcastically than she'd intended.

Colin reached up with his good hand. "Sorry—have to adjust my turban so the reception's better," he explained. Kelly rolled her eyes. He went on, "Dumb luck has a lot to do with it: finding the right person. Putting up with the annoying stuff the other person does, even if she—he—whatever—is the right one. Knowing that she—he—is gonna put up with your crap the same way. Making up your mind you're gonna ride it out no matter where it goes. Oh, and being happy in the sack with the other person every once in a while sure doesn't hurt, either."

Kelly considered. "Sounds good to me. Doctor Phil can get off the TV now. Look out for Doctor Colin."

"Look out, is right," he said. "So how are we doing?"

She spread the fingers on her left hand. The diamonds in her wedding ring weren't humongous, but they were sparkly. "I like it fine so far. Why don't you ask me again in about thirty years?"

"Okay," he said, and then, in a low voice, "Think Marshall'll be out of the house yet?"

"As a matter of fact, yes," Kelly answered. She saw she'd surprised him, but she meant it.

XXI

When Louise fell for Colin, it was girl-meets-boy, the kind of thing that happens to almost everybody. As with an awful lot of people, it was also the kind of thing that got more and more boring as year crawled after year. When she fell for Teo all those years later, it was her Grand Passion, and she went head over heels. It never got boring, not even a little bit. It blew up in her face instead. That was worse. It hurt harder, anyhow—maybe not more, but harder.

When she fell for Jared Watt, she hardly noticed she was doing it. She couldn't very well help noticing the outward trappings. He took her to soccer matches and to musicals—and, to be fair, to movies and to restaurants, too. They went to bed together. She always made sure they took precautions. This long after James Henry came along, she didn't *think* she could still catch. But she hadn't thought she could when she got pregnant with him, either. So: precautions. Every single time.

The games and the shows and the dinners were only outward trappings, though. For quite a while, even the sex was only an outward trapping. An enjoyable trapping, certainly. Jared always worked hard to please her. That made her want to please him as well. But, for a long time, she thought of the two of them as what her grown kids would have called friends with benefits.

That he was still her boss also complicated things. He went out of his way to assure her she didn't have to do anything with him. She believed him. If she hadn't, she would have said no at some point early on to see what his word was worth and whether it was worth anything. All the same, dating somebody who could fire you was interesting in ways she could have done without.

Firing her didn't seem the first thing on his mind, though. "I sure am glad the power wasn't working the day you walked in," he told her one morning. "I've said that before, haven't I?"

"Yes, but I still like to hear it. So am I—for all kinds of reasons," she answered. Why not? They were the only ones in the drugstore. Business on a cold, rainy winter morning wasn't going to be brisk.

The power was working now. It let Louise see Jared blush. "Aside from that—" he began.

"Yes?"

"Aside from that," he repeated firmly, and she let him go on, so he did: "Aside from that, if I had posted my want ad, I would've needed to sort through four dozen losers to find three or four possibles, and none of them would have been a quarter as good as you."

"How do you mean that?" she asked. "And how would you have tested them? Or don't I want to know?"

"I was talking about their job performance," Jared said primly. "Other things just happen. Or, more often, they don't."

"I'm glad they did this time." Louise meant it. Having someone interested in you that way was a sign you were still alive. It was a sign you hadn't disappeared, the way so many women over fifty seemed to. America often acted as if it wanted to push the disappearing age down to somewhere between thirty and thirty-five. That was insane, which didn't keep it from happening.

"Now that you mention it, so am I." Jared suddenly stiffened. "A customer!" He said it just the way Mrs. Lovett did in *Sweeney Todd*. That Louise knew he was doing Mrs. Lovett only showed she'd been hanging out with him for a while. People you hung out with rubbed off on you. You rubbed off on them, too. Louise sometimes heard bits of her own speech come back at her out of Jared's mouth.

The bell over the door chimed when the customer came in. She was a woman near the age of disappearing Louise had been worrying about a moment before. Her face had seen some hard times. So had her raincoat, which must have been ancient long before the supervolcano eruption made her need it more. She closed her umbrella and stuck it in the bucket Jared had put by the door for days like this.

"Horrible out there!" she said. "Horrible!"

"It is, yes," Jared replied. "Can we help you with anything?"

"Well, I hope you won't get mad, but I just came in to get out of the rain for a little while," the woman replied. Louise nodded to herself. If the gal had done business here, even once five years ago, Jared would have had a name to go with her harsh face. Louise didn't know how he did it, but he did.

"Glad to be your oasis," he said now. "Look around. If you want to spend a little money here while you dry out, we won't mind."

"No, huh?" the woman said.

"No. But we won't mind—too much—if you don't, either."

"Okay." She went over to the shelves of used books. She picked up a mystery, which didn't surprise Louise, and a book about the Battle of Gettysburg, which did. And she picked up one of the gaudy ceramic whatsits that Jared kept selling and Louise couldn't stand. Finally, almost as an afterthought, she got a bottle of aspirin.

Louise rang her up, took her money, and made change. She put everything in a plastic bag. "Keep the books dry," she said.

"Uh-huh." The woman nodded. "Wouldn't be much left of 'em by the time I got home if you didn't." She managed a smile that didn't quite reach her colorless gray eyes. "Now that I've made you both rich, I guess I can go back out in it."

"Try to stay dry," Louise said. "The two of us, we'll head for Tahiti on what you just spent."

"Don't you wish! Don't we all wish!" The woman took her umbrella out of the bucket, opened the door, unfurled the umbrella, and walked away. She hadn't gone far before the swirling curtains of rain hid her.

"Tahiti? I do wish," Jared said.

"Me, too. Who doesn't?" Louise answered. "The really scary thing is, L.A. still has good weather, at least as far as the United States goes. In spite of that, it does." She waved at the downpour outside.

"The good news is, you're right. That's only rain. It isn't snow. We don't get snow very often. We never get snow in July or anything like that. If there weren't so many people living here, this would be wonderful farm country. It wouldn't even need irrigation, the way it did before it filled up." The pharmacist paused for effect. "And the bad news is, you're right."

"Yeah." Louise sighed. "For anybody who remembers the way we used to be, this is pretty miserable. I feel sorry for James Henry and all the people who won't grow up remembering what it was like before the eruption."

"It'll be water to a duck for them," Jared answered. "Before too long, they'll get old enough to call us a bunch of nostalgic fools. You always need to find some reason or other to think your parents are fools. That helps remind you how wonderful you are yourself."

"Tell me about it!" Louise exclaimed. "I went through that

with my kids by Colin. Now I get to look forward to a rerun when James Henry turns sixteen. Isn't *that* wonderful?"

"Sooner or later, they'll end up doing a musical about it," Jared said.

"Sooner or later, they end up doing a musical about everything." Louise could tease him about it, as long as she didn't get mean.

"You're right," he said cheerfully. "But so what? That's part of what makes them fun to begin with. I wonder if I'll live long enough to see it."

I wonder if I'll live long enough to was a notion Louise hadn't had till she passed fifty. Before then, time seemed to stretch like a rubber band. Of course she was going to last forever, to live happily ever after. Only she wasn't. She wouldn't. Nobody did, no matter how much everybody expected to or wanted to. She might have thirty or forty years left. She might not have thirty or forty minutes. If she fell over from a heart attack, if the next person who walked into the drugstore was a strung-out crackhead with a Glock . . .

You never knew, that was all. Colin had dodged his brush with the Grim Reaper this past summer, but why? Only by luck, as far as she could tell.

Jared started reciting poetry:

> " 'Had we but world enough, and time,
> This coyness, Lady, were no crime . . .
> But at my back I always hear
> Time's wingèd chariot hurrying near;
> And yonder all before us lie
> Deserts of vast eternity.' "

Was he following his own train of thought or guessing hers from her expression? She remembered the poem from high school. The poet wanted to get laid, but his girlfriend wouldn't give it up. More meaning behind it, though, than she'd imagined when she was seventeen. Tears stung her eyes.

You couldn't live with men. Vanessa had proved that to herself to her full satisfaction—or dissatisfaction, depending on how you looked at things. When she was in high school, she'd been sure she would have Peter's babies. As soon as she met Bryce, though, old Peter didn't seem like so much of a much.

Bryce seemed okay . . . for a while. He was clumsy in bed, though—not that Peter'd been any too wonderful along those lines himself. And Bryce was horny *all* the damn time. When he wasn't horny, he didn't want to do anything except read or get into arguments on the Greek-history message boards (there were such things, no matter how perverse the notion seemed to Vanessa). He didn't want to shop. He didn't want to dance. She decided she was better off without him.

Which led to Hagop. He wasn't horny all the time. One of the things that had interested her in him was that he was twice her age. Hagop certainly knew things about screwing that Bryce wouldn't find out in a month of Sundays. But he was a self-centered bastard. He wanted her on his arm to show his fellow rug merchants what a stud he was.

If she hadn't followed him to Denver like a fool, she wouldn't have nearly died when the supervolcano blew. That Hagop almost certainly did die was some consolation—some, but not enough. Because getting out of Denver meant getting stuck in Camp Constitution.

You couldn't live without men, but Vanessa could have lived forever without Micah Husak. In exchange for services rendered, he'd got her better quarters and less obnoxious tentmates. In exchange for services rendered, and for her self-respect. Millions of people remained stuck in resettlement camps all these years after the eruption, New Homestead Act or no New Homestead Act. Vanessa would have bet anything she had that Micah and other FEMA flunkies still had more than their share of women who did what they wanted.

She'd managed to get away from that. It hadn't even cost her a zipless fuck—only a zipless blowjob to a National Guardsman whose name she never found out. You couldn't get much more zipless than that, could you? Erica Jong would have been proud . . . or appalled, depending.

After that, Bronislav. She'd been sure Bronislav was the real thing. Well, she'd been sure with Hagop, too (or as sure as she could make herself with him), and with Bryce, and even with Peter way back when. Being sure was part of what made her tick. She'd dumped Bronislav's forerunners. Getting dumped herself— and getting ripped off in the process—was a new, and nasty, variation on the theme.

So, while you couldn't live without them, you also couldn't live with them. Every so often, one of the guys at Nick Gorczany's widget works would try his luck with her. With monotonous regularity, she turned them down and shot them down. She'd always got as much mileage as she could out of being pretty. Now she wondered if it wasn't more trouble than it was worth.

Some of the engineers and programmers must have decided that, because they kept striking out with Vanessa, she had to be a lesbian. They must have gossiped about it, too, because a short-haired female programmer came on to her. She wasn't as blatant as the guys were, but she also struck out. Vanessa was straight. Choosing the right guy was the problem. So was wondering whether she could find him, and wondering where to look. Aside from *not at the widget works*, she didn't know.

Oh, she had an electronic profile or two out there. Who didn't, as long as the power stayed on? But, after meeting a couple of men that way, she decided those profiles weren't worth the paper they weren't printed on. The fellow who said he was five-eleven turned out to be five-five. Since he hadn't lied about his weight, he was also a good deal wider than advertised. The one who gave his age as forty had to be fifty-five. The pale band on the first joint of his ring finger said he was probably married, too. She made an excuse about needing to road-test her hamster and left as soon as she could.

She discovered that her high-school achievement-test scores qualified her for membership in Mensa. She sent in her forms, paid a year's dues, and got a membership card. She went to one, count it, one, meeting. The people there were smart. Very few had anything else going for them. They talked about how they'd be on Easy Street if only this, that, or the other thing hadn't happened to them.

Vanessa had plenty of complaints of her own along those lines. She didn't feel like listening to anyone else's. She wanted a winner. Winners plainly didn't go to Mensa meetings. After that first one, neither did she.

She was eating a dinner that made her long for MREs (and they said it couldn't be done!) when her phone rang. The displayed number and name seemed vaguely familiar, so she said, "Hello?"

"Hello, Ms. Ferguson. This is Agent Gideon Sneed, from the FBI," the man said. That was why she knew the name. He'd told her he wasn't interested in going after Bronislav.

"Yes?" she said. Her opinion of the FBI hadn't been high even before they didn't want to throw her thief of an ex in the slammer. In that, she took after her father. He respected the Feds' courage and diligence, but didn't think they were long on brains. Because they had jurisdiction over a relatively small range of crimes, they didn't need to be—not if you listened to him, anyhow. Vanessa had, for years, at the dinner table and in the car and while she was watching TV. His attitude sank in, and became hers without her ever noticing.

"I wanted to tell you that we may possibly be opening an investigation of Mr., uh, Bronislav, uh, Nedic"—Sneed made a horrible hash of both names, the way most people would reading them cold off a sheet of paper—"over issues that are unrelated to yours. If we do, we may append your charges as well, to increase our chances of winning a conviction on one count or another."

"Well, all right!" Vanessa said. "That's the best news I've had in I don't know how long. What's the asshole gone and done now?"

"You understand, at the moment these are only unsubstantiated allegations," Sneed told her. And only somebody like an FBI man could say *unsubstantiated allegations* often enough to bring it out as if it belonged to the English language.

For once, Vanessa had no trouble stifling the urge to copyedit. "Yeah, yeah, fine," she said. "Cut to the chase. What's he unsubstantiatedly alleged to have done?" If you couldn't beat 'em, join 'em.

Sneed didn't think her repetition was funny—he sure didn't laugh, anyhow. For all she could tell over the phone, he didn't even notice. Cops got so used to cop jargon, they took it for granted. "There is a certain level of tension between the Serbian and Croatian communities in Mobile," the FBI man said carefully. "It is possible that Mr. Nedic has participated in activities which would escalate that level of tension."

From what Vanessa knew of Bronislav, he didn't participate in activities. He shot people or blew them up. If those people were Croats, he got drunk on slivovitz and sang songs and danced afterwards, too. "That sounds like him, all right," she said. "But how big *are* the Serbian and Croatian communities in Mobile goddamn Alabama? Seventeen Serbs and nineteen Croats?"

"Larger than that," Sneed said. "Large enough that an incident between them could be a significant incident. If Mr. Nedic is trying to create such an incident, we need to prevent him from being successful."

"And stop him, too," Vanessa murmured. She couldn't help herself, or stop herself.

"I beg your pardon?" Sneed said.

"Never mind," Vanessa said. "So if you bust him on the terrorism rap, you'll toss in stealing my bank account and taking it across state lines like a cherry on top of the sundae?" *God, when was the last time I had a sundae? Much too long ago—probably before the eruption. Have to do something about that.*

"Yes, that's about right," Sneed said. "You have an interesting way of talking, you know?"

"I've heard people say so," Vanessa replied, which was true. Sometimes they meant it for a compliment. The FBI man seemed to.

"You do," he said now. "I noticed it when we met in person. I was very sorry that our prioritization process prevented me from implementing proceedings against Mr. Nedic at that point in time."

"So was I," Vanessa said: growled, really.

"That makes me especially glad to be able to bring you this information now," Sneed said.

"Okay," Vanessa said.

"In fact," the FBI man went on, "I wondered if it might be possible for the two of us to meet some time in a social setting."

"You mean, like, a date?"

"Yes."

She almost hung up on him right there. She wondered if the whole call was a setup. FBI guy finds a bulge in his pants, comes out with some bullshit about dropping on Bronislav so he'll look cool to the woman who can't stand the dude, then tries to get into her knickers. He hadn't said they were actually doing anything about the damn Serb, just that they were looking at it. If they didn't, he had all kinds of built-in excuses: Bronislav got cold feet, or there wasn't enough evidence, or some judge wouldn't issue a warrant, or yaddayaddayadda.

On the other hand . . . That he'd gone to the trouble of cooking up the scheme (if he was) said he was interested. And he was a cop of sorts. Vanessa knew how cops worked. She knew it the way a fish knew water: she'd grown up with it. That might turn out to be a plus, and maybe not such a small one.

"Ms. Ferguson? You there?"

"Yes, I'm here. Maybe we can try it," she answered.

"Good!" He sounded happy and surprised, which was about the way he should have sounded. *Amazingly lifelike*, she thought.

They settled on dinner and a movie Saturday after next: the opening of the great American mating dance for as long as there'd been movies. Vanessa went back to her current, interrupted supper. Getting cold hadn't made it much worse, because it hadn't been that good to begin with. When she finished, she added her dishes to the pile in the sink.

You couldn't win if you didn't bet. You also couldn't lose, but she chose not to dwell on that side of things. She hadn't told him to fuck off. Not this time. Not yet. *Maybe I'll get lucky this time. Maybe I really will.* If you told yourself something often enough, you could make yourself believe it. Maybe—just maybe—you could even make it true.

Across the street from the buildings and parking lots at Wayne State lay tennis courts, a soccer field (a pitch, if you were feeling like a Brit), a baseball field, a softball field, and a golf course: lots and lots of wide-open spaces punctuated by chain-link fences, a few rows of trees, and some bleachers. Snow held sway over them all, like the Red Death in the Poe story.

It drifted against the trees and the fencing. It turned the bleachers into mounds of white. The ground was white. Everything for miles around was white—*white as snow*, Bryce thought, and sneered at himself for perpetrating a cliché, even if he did it only inside his own head. Here and there, roads shoveled clear scribed asphalt-dark lines through the whiteness. He stood by one of them, waiting for the bus to town. It wasn't snowing right this minute—no more than a few scattered flakes, anyhow—so he could see the campus buildings, which were also unwhite, or at most dappled. When he pulled back his mental horizon, they didn't seem like much.

They didn't seem like much because they damn well weren't. Snow covered the whole damn continent north of the Rio Grande, with minor polychrome enclaves in SoCal, Arizona, and Florida. It lay thicker in some places, thinner in others, but it was everywhere. Europe was no better off. Most of Europe was worse off, because the settled parts there sat farther north than they did in North America.

Asia . . . Northern China had always had hard winters. Now it had worse ones. Southern China had been subtropical. It wasn't any more. People in Afghanistan were saying the winters they'd been getting (and the summers they hadn't been) were God's judgment upon them. God's judgment for what? For their sins, of course. And, in arguments over what those sins might be and just who'd committed them, several different ethnic groups were shooting at one another. As far as Bryce could tell, several different ethnic groups there had been shooting at one another since at least the days of the Persian Empire. Only the weapons and the excuses changed through the centuries.

"Hi, Professor Miller!" a coed called. She waved a mittened hand his way.

"Hi, Peggy!" Bryce waved back. She was cute. She wasn't dumb. The combo made her a pleasure to have in his class. Were he single, he might have tried to get her phone number once she wasn't in his class any more.

Not being single didn't stop everybody. The anthropology department had recently had a small scandal about a married prof carrying on with an ex-student. That the prof was female and the student a forward on the men's basketball team added variety to the spice but didn't change its essential nature.

A crow perched on the BUS STOP sign. People gathering close by didn't bother it. People who gathered at the bus stop often ate things while they waited. They didn't always throw what they couldn't finish into the trash. Knowing such things was one of the ways college crows made their living.

"C'mon, you stupid bus! I'm cold," said a guy who'd been standing at the stop longer than Bryce had. Several heads, Bryce's among them, bobbed in agreement. He'd spent more time than he wanted the past few years standing on one corner or another with his mittens jammed into the pockets of whatever overcoat or anorak he happened to be wearing. He'd been cold just about all that time. His nose, not the smallest peak in the range, felt as if it wanted to fall off.

He'd read somewhere that Asians might have evolved their flattish features during the last Ice Age, as a response to extreme cold. He didn't know if that was true. The anthro prof who'd frolicked with the basketball player might have had a better idea. It did strike him as reasonable, though.

Here came the bus at last. People climbed aboard with sighs of relief. It wasn't much warmer inside than out-. They'd escaped the wind blowing down from the North Pole, though. And they weren't just standing there. They were on their way into Wayne. *We're going somewhere, man*, Bryce thought.

A few hardy souls on bikes were also pedaling between college and town, and a few more coming the other way. Bryce wouldn't have wanted—hadn't wanted—to do that in weather like this, but no accounting for taste. College kids were a hardy bunch. They were also often a crazy bunch.

The bus shuddered and wheezed when it stopped in the center of town. The small local bus fleet had been old and rickety when Bryce came to Wayne. It was older and more rickety now, and smaller, too. A couple of the buses that had finally crapped out were being harvested for spare parts to keep the others going. There was no money to buy new ones. Bryce wasn't sure anyone in the United States was making new buses these days. Demand had fallen into the Yellowstone caldera.

He got off. The bus chugged away, leaving a trail of diesel exhaust in its wake. Global warming wasn't the big worry any more. Al Gore probably burned trash in his back yard nowadays.

A team of six or eight glum-looking men and a couple of glum-looking young women were shoveling snow off the sidewalk. Bryce remembered a *New Yorker* cartoon about synchronized snow shovelers. Then he noticed the bored cop keeping an eye on the team. His perspective shifted. Suddenly, the scene looked more like a frozen outtake from *I Am a Fugitive from a Chain Gang*.

In Wayne, people didn't get jail time for misdemeanors any more. As the town couldn't afford new buses, so it also couldn't afford to house petty criminals and feed them while they sat on their unproductive asses. It put them to work instead. About half the shovelers looked like college kids. Bryce recognized one unshaven older town guy who fought the cold by constantly keeping a high level of antifreeze in his blood. And he would have bet that the others were New Homesteaders. He wondered what they'd done, or whether they'd done anything. No, the town and the people who'd come here to get out of the refugee camps didn't always get on so smoothly as they might have.

The cleared sidewalks helped him get back to his apartment building more easily than he would have otherwise. Susan seemed happy when he walked in. That made him happy. He still wondered whether he would have to move back to SoCal when the spring semester ended. If the choice was between job and marriage, job would have to bend.

"How's it going?" he asked after he kissed her.

"Not bad. I got an idea for an article. Now I have to see if I can make it work," she answered. No wonder she was in a good mood.

"Cool," Bryce said. "What is it?"

"I want to see if I can connect Frederick's ideas about falconry with his foreign policy," Susan said. The renegade Holy Roman Emperor had written an enormous tome about hunting with hawks. Where he'd found the time, Bryce had no idea, but Frederick II was the kind of guy who made time when he felt like doing something. As for his foreign policy . . . The way it looked to Bryce, Frederick had flown himself against the whole damn world. He'd made it work for most of his reign, too.

"That *is* cool," Bryce said now. "Or it will be, if you can do it."

"Always if," Susan agreed. "But it'll keep me busy for a while, anyway. And when I publish it, maybe it'll make somebody notice me and go, like, *We need her in this department*. I can hope, right?"

"Sure, babe." Bryce nodded. You could always hope. A lot of the time, you had to hope. You could even live on hope for a while. Why not? What else was the whole country doing?

"Darn!" Colin said as he combed his hair.

Kelly knew that would have been something a lot stronger if she weren't around. "How's it doing?" she asked.

He looked down at his left shoulder as if it had betrayed him. Well, it had, but you couldn't blame it after a bullet smashed up its workings. "Y'know," he said, "I think the rehab's gone about as far as it's gonna go."

She'd been thinking the same thing for the past couple of weeks. She hadn't wanted to say so, because she kept hoping she might be wrong. All she said now was, "Are you sure? They say time—"

"—wounds all heels," he finished for her. She winced. While

she was wincing, he went on, "It may get a little better. I may be able to move it a little more without feeling like somebody's driving nails in there. But I won't go back to being a real, no-kidding, two-armed human being again. I wish I would, but I won't."

"Which means what?" Kelly feared she knew the answer, but she didn't want the words of ill omen coming out of her mouth. If they were going to get said, he needed to say them himself.

He came over and sat down on the bed next to her. "Which means the San Atanasio PD will just have to do without a certain captain of police. I know that'll be rough on them, but there you are."

"Are you sure?" she said.

He nodded. "Yeah, I'm sure. You think you and Deborah will be able to stand having me rattling around the house 24/7?"

"Oh, I'm sure Deborah will hate it," Kelly said. Their daughter loved having Daddy home all the time. She was even learning she had to be careful around his bad side.

"Yeah, well, she's still too little to know which end is up," Colin said. "How about you?"

"I like having you around," Kelly answered truthfully. "The real question is, will you be able to walk away from the office and into retirement? Or will you go batshit?" Just because he wouldn't swear around her didn't mean she couldn't swear around him.

"You never know ahead of time, but I don't think I will," Colin answered. "I've got enough here to keep me interested all kinds of ways." He set a hand on her leg, above her knee. "Only you'll have to get on top more often."

"I don't mind," she said, which was also true. "But you can't do that all the time."

"Ain't it a shame?" he said.

"If you say so," she answered. "What will you do when you're not lying on your back?"

"Riding herd on the kid will do for a start."

"For a while, sure. But she won't be a toddler forever, you know. Day after tomorrow—not really, but close enough—she starts school. She'll be gone for big chunks of time. What will you do then, here by yourself?" She hoped the anxiety in her voice didn't show. Cops' spouses too often had reason to worry about the people they loved.

How many interrogations had Colin done? However many it was, he heard the words behind the words she said. "Don't worry about that kind of stuff. I'm not gonna do anything stupid," he said. "I intend to get shot by an outraged husband at the age of a hundred and three."

"Oh, you do, do you?" Kelly said. "Well, I'll tell you what. If you're still around at a hundred and three and I'm still around to know, I give you permission to wander off the reservation—once. Just once. Till then, fuhgeddaboutit, Mister. After that, you can forget about it, too."

"If I'm still around at a hundred and three, I probably will forget about it right after that," Colin said. "My folks were pretty good about keeping their marbles, but none of 'em lived that long."

"Neither did mine," Kelly answered. "I had a great-grandmother, I think it was, who almost got to a hundred, but she didn't quite."

"Hon, what do you think about me hanging it up?" Colin asked.

"I won't be sorry," she said. "I'd get nervous every time you went out on a case from now on. I mean, I always knew bad things could happen to you, but nothing ever had, so I didn't worry about it much. Now . . . They say, anything that can happen can happen to you. Now I know in my gut that's true, not just in my head. I don't want to get the jitters whenever you stick your nose outside the station."

He nodded. "About what I thought you'd say. Well, I'd be

lying if I told you I wouldn't be hinky myself. After you get shot once, I don't see how you can help having the next time in the back of your mind."

"We're on the same page there, especially when your arm reminds you you got hit every time you move it," Kelly said.

"There is that," Colin agreed. "If I'd just got grazed, the way Rob did a few years ago, I might be able to not think about it. But from what he wrote, that really was a dumb accident. The guy who shot me, he did what he was trying to do. The next jerk who pulled a gun, he'd mean it, too."

"Uh-huh. He sure would," Kelly said. "So I'm happy you're going to retire, as long as you think you won't literally get bored to death once you stop going to the cop shop."

"Nope. Not me," Colin said. "The only thing that gripes me about it is that I've got to hang 'em up. I'm not doing it because I want to. It's kind of like the so-and-so with the AK won."

"Like hell it is!" Kelly exclaimed. "He's dead. He's pushing up the daisies. He's pining for the fjords, for Christ's sake. This is an ex–armed robber." She did a lousy British accent, but she gave it her best shot.

And she pried a laugh out of her husband. "Thank you, Monty," he said.

"Any time," she told him.

He put his good arm around her. "The company will be better here than it would be at the station—I'll tell you that. Prettier, too."

"Flattery will get you—somewhere, probably."

"I was hoping it would."

"Maybe not right now, though," she said when he got grabby.

"You're no fun," he grumbled. If he'd kept grabbing, Kelly might have gone along with it. Now that Marshall was back in the house, he was keeping an eye on Deborah right this minute. But Colin didn't push it. He was pretty good about not making a nuisance of himself too often. From what Kelly knew of men, that was as much as a woman married to one of the creatures could reasonably hope for. He did say, "If I'm home all the time, I'll drag you down in the bushes whenever I get the chance."

"Promises, promises," she said. They both laughed. That they could both laugh about it, she figured, spoke well for the state of their marriage.

XXII

Spring came to Guilford on little cat feet, like the fog in the poem. On the calendar, it arrived at the end of the third week in March. Except on the calendar, that meant diddly-squat. From what longtime locals told Rob, the vernal equinox hadn't meant much in Guilford even before the supervolcano erupted. You could get snow into April, once in a while even into May.

These days, you could get snow into July, even into August. *Snow—it's not just for winter any more!* Rob thought it made a terrific advertising slogan. For some reason or other—he couldn't fathom why—it never caught on the way he wanted.

But, around half past May, the weather slowly began to gain on the calendar's claims. It could still snow any old time. But it mostly didn't snow all the goddamn time, as it did in the no-shit winter months. Daytime temps crawled above freezing. Sometimes, instead of snowing, it rained. The drifts that had covered the ground for so long started to melt. That happened first on south-facing slopes that got whatever sunshine sneaked past the clouds. Shadowed stretches stayed snowy longer.

Before the supervolcano blew, Maine had been a birders' paradise. All kinds of feathered critters came here to raise families and gorge on the bazillions of bugs that hatched out as ponds and swamps unfroze. The unfreezing took longer and was less certain now. There were fewer bugs. Anyone who'd ever had Maine mosquitoes turn his face to steak tartare didn't miss them a bit. The birds did, though. Only the hardier kinds came here for the abbreviated summer now. They found the times cold and hungry.

Well, Rob found the times cold and hungry, too. He was down to about 165 pounds. On a six-one frame, that wasn't much. Jeans that had fit him fine once upon a time hung loose these days. He was about twenty pounds under what he'd weighed when he came to Guilford. He used holes in his belt he'd never thought about in the old days.

By pre-eruption standards, almost everybody north and west of the Interstate was skinny. People worked harder. If you had to go somewhere, you walked or skied or snowshoed. If you needed firewood, you chopped it. You didn't—you couldn't—hop in the car to go three blocks to the drugstore and another block to the Subway for a meatball sub with marinara.

Rob wondered when he'd last seen a tomato. Some canned ones had come in since the eruption—he was sure of that. Fresh tomatoes? Not even all of Jim Farrell's magic with greenhouses would persuade them to grow in what passed for a climate around here these days.

Plenty of things wouldn't grow. But some would. Some had: turnips and other roots, some of the extra-cold-weather potatoes for which they also had Jim to thank, onions, and, in the green-houses, things like lettuce and garlic. Along with game and pigs and chickens, they meant the people in these parts might be skinny, but few were in any real danger of starving.

Rob ambled east past the Shell station. That wasn't one of the many businesses that had gone belly-up since the eruption.

Mort Willard, the fellow who'd run it as a gas station, was a skilled repairman, mechanic, and handyman. He could fix damn near anything, and did, often using the tools that had once performed surgery on automobiles.

Ralph O'Brian no longer worked for Mort. He made what living he made by chopping wood and shoveling snow and doing other things that needed a strong back but not a whole lot of brains. Rob felt a certain amount of *Schadenfreude* about that. He knew Ralph hadn't shot him on purpose. Ralph had been aiming for the moose. He'd got a musician only by accident. Then again, Rob would carry that scar on his calf for the rest of his life. A couple of inches to one side and he might have lost that leg below the knee. So he hadn't lost any love for good old Ralph.

Of course, if you sported no worse than a scar and no more than a mild dislike for one of your fellow human beings after he shot you, you were doing fine. It didn't sound as if Dad had been so lucky. You always knew something like that could happen to a cop. But when it didn't and it didn't and it didn't, when you moved the width of a continent away, you stopped worrying about it. And when you stopped worrying about it, naturally, that was when it happened.

Guilford petered out fast when you walked along Highway 6. Freezes and thaws had pitted the asphalt. Some of it still lay under snow; some peeked out. If any cars or trucks did come this way, they would have a tooth-rattling time of it. Rob wasn't holding his breath. In the distance, somebody hammered nails into a board. That was the loudest noise he heard. No motor vehicles within earshot.

Off to the south lay the Piscataquis. The ice on the river was starting to break up, but not nearly done. Some pines and broadleafed trees still grew along the riverbank, though others had been cut down for fuel. The pines looked like, well, pines. The maples and whatever else kept them company thrust bare branches into the sky. They would get leaves for a little while, but they hadn't done it yet.

Rob stopped and looked around. Somewhere right about here, that Hummer had smashed head-on into the eighteen-wheeler. The resulting mess blocked the narrow road and made damn sure that Squirt Frog and the Evolving Tadpoles wouldn't make it up to their scheduled gig in Greenville. They'd ended up in Guilford instead.

If their two Ford Explorers had come by half an hour earlier . . . *My whole life would be different*, Rob thought. *All our lives would be different if we'd driven through Guilford without stopping.* Several local women would have different husbands, or no husbands at all. Several children wouldn't have been born. Others who might have come along had the band reached Greenville now never would.

And what was the difference? Just a little timing. There wasn't a person in the world who didn't have a story like that. If you'd been a little late or a little early, if you hadn't had that fender-bender back in the days when you could bend fenders, if that woman in the store with you had bought the secondhand book that changed your life when you read it, if this, if that, if the other thing, your whole life would be totally changed.

It made you wonder. It really did. Ordinary lives were so easy to jerk around that way. What about the lives of nations? Could all that *If the South Had Won the Civil War, The Man in the High Castle* stuff be true? If your destiny could twist like a contortionist slipping on a banana peel, what about your country's?

"Yeah—what about it?" Rob said aloud. His breath smoked. Suppose the supervolcano hadn't decided to go off for another hundred years? Or another ten thousand years? *What would I be doing now in that case?* Whatever it was, Rob was sure he wouldn't be doing it in Guilford, Maine, right this minute.

Little Colin Ferguson wouldn't have been born. Millions of

people in the middle of the country wouldn't have been buried in volcanic mud and ash or died of HPO and other horrible lung diseases or got stuck in the refugee camps that, from the reports trickling up into this forgotten backwater, lay somewhere between Indian reservations and the Gulag Archipelago on the sorry scale of man's indifference to man.

But the world had what it had, not what it wished it had or what it might have had. Rob crouched in the middle of a snowless patch of ground off to the side of the road. It wasn't all bare, black, lifeless mud: primordial ooze. Here and there lay a green fur of moss. A small, corpse-pale mushroom stuck up phallically. That looked pretty primordial, all right, but lifeless it wasn't.

And, here and there, blades of grass were sprouting. Their green was different from the moss'. It was paler and brighter at the same time. It made you think summer barbecues were right around the corner. It did till you looked at the lingering snow a couple of feet away, anyhow.

If the winters stayed harsh, one of these years the grass might not be able to come up at all. Even if that happened, though, by then whatever *did* come up in Labrador in the springtime might have found a new home here outside Guilford. One way or another, life went on.

"Ob-la-di, ob-la-da," Rob muttered. The Beatles had turned into golden oldies long before he was born. So what? Hemingway was a golden oldie, too. So was Mark Twain. Dickens. Shakespeare. Euripides, for God's sake. People were still reading them all. People were still riffing off what they'd done.

That was immortality, or as much of it as human beings were likely to get. So it seemed to the wise, perceptive philosopher and sage known as Rob Ferguson, anyhow. The philosopher and sage's knees clicked when he stood up straight. He needed to take a leak. That wasn't immortality. It was mortality, reminding him it was around. He strode over to the closest pine and took care of business.

His stomach grumbled. Last he'd heard, the Chinese place in Dover-Foxcroft was still a going concern. As he'd seen when transportation was easier, it had always been as much about what you could get in small-town Maine as it was about what you could do with that stuff if you were a Chinese cook. Had soy sauce come north in trucks? Did the gal who ran the restaurant raise her own soybeans under glass and ferment them?

It was probably an academic question, unless a bunch of locals decided to go to Dover-Foxcroft in a wagon or something. He supposed he could ride over on a bike if he wanted to badly enough, and if Lindsey did. They could plop little Colin into a seat behind one of them and make an outing of it. Dover-Foxcroft was only seven miles or so from Guilford.

"Only," Rob said. "Yeah, right." Seven miles wasn't impossible on a bicycle—nowhere near. But seven miles each way wasn't something you did with a casual case of the munchies, either. As far as time went, it was like a forty-mile commute each way through downtown L.A. back in the long-lost days of cheap gas and clogged freeways. You needed a serious jones for Maine-inflected Cantonese before you'd start pedaling. Otherwise, you'd walk over to Caleb's Kitchen and eat pork sausage and turnips or chicken stew or something like that.

He turned around and headed back to Guilford. He wasn't going to walk to Dover-Foxcroft today: that was for damn sure. There was such a thing as working up an appetite before you ate, but that took it too far. He didn't think he'd end up at Caleb's Kitchen now, but you never knew. If his stomach growled again while he was anywhere close, he might stick his head in and see if whatever Caleb was cooking smelled good.

Yes, grass and maybe even some things with flowers were coming up. Yes, the snow was melting faster than it was falling. Yes, that really was an optimistic rose-breasted grosbeak chirping as it flew by. Yes, the temp was edging up toward fifty, and might not drop far below forty tonight. Back in those long-lost times, this had been about as cold and miserable a day as Los Angeles ever got. For a post-eruption spring morning in Guilford, it was a corker.

Somebody coming Rob's way waved. He waved back—it was Justin. His bandmate wore a denim jacket over a ratty flannel shirt, and probably a T-shirt under that. He was dressed much like Rob, in other words. Justin's hair was still curly, but not permed any more. Like Rob's, Justin's beard showed the first traces of gray. Beards were warmer than bare chins. You didn't have to worry about blades, either, or learn to shave with a straight razor.

"What's going on?" Justin called.

"Not much," Rob answered. "It's just another perfect day—"

"I love L.A.!" Justin finished for him. They grinned at each other. After a beat, Justin went on, "I don't love it enough to want to live there any more, though. How weird is that?"

"Oh, pretty much," Rob said. "But I'm so the same way. When Lindsey wanted to head south after Colin was born, I was the one who talked her out of it. And she, like, grew up here. How weird is *that*?"

"*Plus royal que le roi*," Justin said in what would pass for French if no Quebecer happened to hear him. "I like it here, though, more than I ever did anywhere else. We're out from under, know what I mean?"

"I just might," Rob replied. "Yeah, I just might. Before the eruption, our taxes were making the accountant's eyes cross."

"Duh! How many states did we have income from the last year before the supervolcano blew?" Justin said.

"Lemme see. There was despair, lethargy, doped-outedness, rage, lust. . . ."

"Not quite what I meant, but close enough," Justin agreed. "He said our mileage was liable to get us audited all by itself."

"How come none of the IRS weenies ever went out on the road with a working band?" Rob asked.

"Because they're IRS weenies?" Justin suggested. "Because they wouldn't know picking a guitar from picking their noses? But any which way, we don't have to worry about any of that shit for a long time. We've fallen over the edge of the world. *Here Be Dragons*, the atlas says when it talks about places like this. We're off the map, off the chart, off the goddamn Internet. I don't miss it a bit. I don't miss my belly a bit, either." He slapped his stomach. He still carried more weight than Rob did, but he sure wasn't pudgy any more.

"I don't, either—now," Rob said slowly. "One of these years, though, I'm gonna have trouble with a heart valve or my prostate'll start trying to kill me or something else will go wrong. Then I'll wish I was part of the big club, not the little one."

"Hey, life is full of tradeoffs. If you have more fun while you're living but maybe you don't live as long—guys make that deal every time they light a cigarette or eat a pound and a half of prime rib. Do you really live longer or does it just seem longer 'cause it's all a bore?"

"Right now, I'm with you. I told you that," Rob answered. "Have to admit, though, I'm not sure I'll say the same thing in my sixties."

"Farrell does," Justin said, which was true, even if Jim was bound to be past his sixties and into his seventies now. Justin went on, "Besides, if you do get sick I bet you can game the system. Show up in Bangor with a Social Security card and what will the hospital there do? Throw you out so you freeze in the snow? I don't think so!"

Rob wasn't sure his friend had it straight. The eruption had made everybody a lot more hardnosed. When there wasn't enough to go around, people had to be. All the same . . . "And from what we hear, who knows whether things will be better anywhere else thirty years from now?" Rob said.

Justin nodded. "There's that, too. So lay back and enjoy it. Maybe this summer some dope'll make it this far north again, or some seeds so we can try our luck with homegrown. Even if it doesn't, hey, there's still rhubarb vodka."

"*Now* I've got a reason to move south!" Rob exclaimed.

They both laughed. The local moonshine wasn't as dreadful as it had been when amateur distillers first tried their luck after the eruption. It still wasn't anything you'd drink if you had a lot of choices, though. Some of the homebrew beer, by contrast, tasted pretty damn good.

"We're in another country. We're in another time," Rob said.

"The natives are friendly," Justin observed. "Which is bound to be another reason we're still here."

"Still here . . ." Rob tasted the words. They rang a faint bell in the back of his mind. "Broadway song about that, isn't there?"

"Yeah, I think so." Justin screwed up his face, trying to dredge it up and plainly not having much luck. "By . . . by . . . Cole Porter or one of those old-time guys. Whoever wrote it, he's right. We *are* still here."

"Yup. Here in Guilford, by God, Maine. Who woulda figured *that*?" Rub stuck out his hand. "Here's to us, here's to being here, and here's to being here in Guilford, by God, Maine." Solemnly, Justin shook with him.

There was a last time for everything. With a little technical assistance from Kelly, Colin put on his uniform for the last time. Because he'd lost weight after the supervolcano like so many other people, the navy wool tunic and trousers were on the loose side. The uniform smelled of mothballs. Colin didn't much care.

Kelly wore a pale blue suit herself. You didn't get a retirement bash at City Hall every day. Colin kissed her. "You look great, babe," he said. "But hey, you always look great to me." Except in the line of duty, he made a lousy liar. Fortunately, he meant that.

Kelly's smile showed she knew it. "Well, if you're gonna rattle around the house from now on, you may as well rattle around in a pleasant tone of voice. You all ready?"

He set the cap with the patent-leather bill on his head. "Now I am. I oughta wear this darn thing backwards like a gangbanger, y'know? What could they do about it? Fire me?"

"Come on. Be nice. You want your report card to say 'Plays well with others,' don't you?" Kelly kept smiling, but now she let her patience show.

Colin didn't give a damn what his report card said. But the idea felt funnier to talk about than to do. He went down the stairs with his wife.

Marshall was reading Deborah a Commander Toad book. He'd been bummed when Janine didn't feel like letting him darken her towels any more, but he wasn't crying into his sausage and sauerkraut every night or anything. He'd had a fling, it hadn't been Happily Ever After, so here he was again, not a lot sadder and probably not a lot wiser, either.

"You look like a policeman, Daddy!" Deborah said.

"Funny how that works," Colin answered. He hadn't put on the uniform more than a couple of times since she was born; she might not even remember it. He blew her a kiss and nodded to Marshall. "We'll be back when the gruesome orgy's over with."

"Right, Dad." Marshall was resigned to his lines. "You came down just when we were getting to the exciting part. They're about to go into hopperspace." He went back to reading to his half-sister.

Once Colin walked outside, he was glad for the wool. It was cool out there, somewhere in the low fifties. It had drizzled before, but it wasn't raining now. The sun ducked in and out of the clouds. Not the kind of day you would have looked for in L.A. in early June before the eruption. In fact . . . "Kind of reminds me of the weather in Yellowstone the day we met," he remarked.

"Maybe some. If we were by a lake here, though, it wouldn't still be frozen over," Kelly said.

"Well, no," he allowed.

They got into the Taurus. Colin sat on the passenger side. He had to do up the seat belt with his right hand, which was awkward. But his left arm still snarled at him outside of a narrow range of motion.

Kelly started the engine. "They'd better not pull me over," she said. "I've got a current ID, but my license has been dead for I don't know how long."

"Yeah, like you're the only one," Colin said, and then, "I never fixed a ticket in my life, but I think I just might be able to get you off the hook for that."

"Do you, now?" she said as she backed out of the driveway. "So you're getting corrupt on your last day?"

"If you're gonna do it, that's the best time," he answered, more seriously than he'd thought he would.

"Yeah, I guess it would be," Kelly said. "I've driven to the station before, but I don't think I've ever gone to the city hall. Do I park in the same lot?"

"You can if you want to," Colin told her. "Not a long walk or anything. But City Hall has a separate parking lot you get into off of San Atanasio Boulevard instead of Hesperus."

"Okay, I'll try that, then," she said. "If they haven't reserved a space for you, I'll damn well turn around and go home, too, and they can throw the party by themselves."

She didn't need to worry about that. Colin hadn't thought she would. No doubt she hadn't, either. The parking space nearest the entrance usually belonged to the mayor. Today, a paper sign was taped over the metal one: FOR CAPTAIN COLIN FERGUSON. Balloons and crepe streamer adorned the sign. "I ought to retire more often," Colin said.

"You don't think it would lose some effect after a while?" Kelly asked.

"Nah. Why should it?" Colin said. "They'd always be glad to get rid of me." There'd been too many times in his career when he wouldn't have been kidding about that. He pointed to the balloons. "When we go, we should snag one of those for Playboy."

A uniformed cop stood outside the glass doors that let you into City Hall. He waved as Colin got out of the car, then ducked through them. "What's he doing?" Kelly wondered out loud.

"Warning people. What else?" Colin answered, not without pride.

He and Kelly went through the doors a moment later. He held one open for her—he could do that with his good arm. The mayor's administrative assistant bustled up to them. She was a gray-haired, highly competent woman named Lois Tsuye. "If you'll just come with me, Captain Ferguson, Mrs. Ferguson . . ." she said.

Come with her they did. She led them through the city council chamber—which would have been superdupermodern fifty years earlier, right down to the city seal with the crossed freeways on the wall—and into a reception room off to one side. Blue tape that wouldn't hurt the paint held a big banner with Colin's name on it to the wall.

The crowd was split between cops and city dignitaries. There were also a reporter and a photographer from the *Daily Breeze*. The *Times* didn't think the retirement was a big enough deal to cover. That bothered Colin not in the least. If not for the honor of the farewell, he wouldn't have minded skipping it.

Malik Williams came over and shook his hand. The chief's head gleamed under the ceiling lights. "I'll miss you, Colin," he said. "When your phone rings, every so often it'll be me, calling to pick your brain. I've enjoyed working with you. You did this force a lot of good."

"Thanks," Colin said. "I appreciate that, believe me."

"Hey, I mean it," Williams said. "You could've undercut me eight ways from Sunday. I was new, and you'd been here a long time. You knew everybody. And—" Williams flicked a couple of fingers across the back of his other hand. Colin had seen that gesture from African-Americans before. It meant *I'm this color, after all.* The chief continued, "But you didn't. You didn't even try. You backed my play, and I'm grateful."

"I told you I didn't want the job, and I meant it," Colin said stolidly.

Malik Williams smiled a cop's knowing smile. "People tell me all kinds of things every day. And some of it's true, and some of it . . . ain't." The pause before the bad grammar reminded you he really knew better. He set a hand on Colin's good shoulder— he also knew better than to touch him on the wounded one. Then he nodded and walked over to the coffee urn.

"That was nice," Kelly said. "That's what you came for."

"Yeah, I guess," Colin said. "But Malik's okay. I thought so as soon as I met him, and it looks like I was right."

He started toward the coffee urn himself. Rodney Ellis intercepted him. "Dude, you dance like you've got two left feet and a broken leg, but you're the best cop I ever worked with, and it's not even close," the black detective said.

"You need to keep better company, is what you need," Colin answered, trying to hide how pleased he was.

"No way, man." Ellis shook his head. "You always went where the evidence took you. You didn't care if the perp was black or white or green. You didn't care if he was a big wheel's kid, either. You just went after him. That's how it's supposed to work, and too damn often it doesn't even come close."

"Yeah, well, you're not too shabby yourself," Colin said. "I couldn't've done it without you, you know, not when it mattered most." Ellis had led the team that arrested Darren Pitcavage for dealing drugs, setting up (though they didn't know it) Mike Pitcavage's suicide—and unmasking.

"You were the one who got the lead," Rodney said. He squeezed Colin's hand and let him go.

This time, Colin actually managed to get to the coffee, and to drink one sip from his cup. Then Gabe Sanchez waylaid him. "Had to wait till the brothers got through with you," Gabe said in mock-indignant tones.

"I just figured a wetback like you was too lazy to come over first," Colin said. Cops woofed on cops as automatically, and often as thoughtlessly, as they breathed.

"Didn't see any paddies ahead of me in line," Gabe shot back. "Man, it won't be the same without you, and that's a fact."

"You'll have to do the grumpy-old-man number for me from now on," Colin said.

"Who's old?" Sanchez pulled a hair from his mustache. It was white. He let it fall to the industrial carpeting. "Oh. Guess I am."

Colin patted his own gray top cover where it stuck out from under the cap. "Happens to most people. All you've got to do is live long enough."

"Uh-huh. I—" Gabe broke off. If he could have done double takes that good on cue, he would have wasted his time at police work. "Holy crap! Is that Caroline Pitcavage who just walked in?"

"Yup." Colin's voice went thoroughly grim. "Haven't seen her since . . . since we busted Darren." She had apologized to him after it came out that she'd spent her whole adult life married to the South Bay Strangler. Hardly anyone had seen her since then. Colin couldn't very well blame her for that.

Since she'd come here now, though, he had to go over and say something to her. *How've you been since your husband snuffed himself instead of a little old lady?* popped into his head. That might not do, no matter what the capering devil inside him thought.

He managed a nod as he walked over to her. "Thanks for coming, Caroline," he said. "I'm glad to see you."

"I heard about this, and I thought I ought to," she replied. She was closer to his age than to Kelly's, but still had the trim look of someone who'd been a high-school cheerleader. Her eyes, though, her eyes told of the hard times she'd seen lately. After a moment, she went on, "I'm sorry you got hurt. I'm sorry . . . I'm sorry about all kinds of things. These lemons make crappy lemonade, if you know what I mean."

"I guess." Colin figured that for the giant economy-size understatement. "Do you ever, uh, hear from Darren?"

"Once in a while a phone call. Once in a while a card." She sighed. Her son had got eight years. If he kept his nose clean, he'd likely serve about half of it. "I hope he gets his shit together when he comes out. I hope he doesn't go institutional and decide life in there is easier than it is on the outside."

"Me, too. I think he's got a decent chance." Colin meant that. As a police chief's son, Darren would be kept away from the general run of inmates for his own safety. He'd stay isolated most of the time. No prison camaraderie for him. You'd have to be a nutcase to want to go back to that. Colin had long thought Darren Pitcavage was a nasty prick. A nutcase? No, or not that kind, anyhow.

"Like I said, I hope. That's about what I can do these days." Caroline sounded bleak. Well, she had her reasons. "Enjoy your retirement, Colin. Enjoy your life. It's nice somebody gets to."

People stared as she went over to pick up a Danish and get some coffee. She seemed to move in a bubble of wide eyes and quiet. Then Malik Williams walked up and made small talk with her. Colin admired the chief for that. It took moral courage. He wasn't sure he could have done it if he were in Williams' shoes and not his own.

A city councilman came up and pumped his hand. Charlie

Yamada had run the Honda dealership at the corner of Hesperus and Reynoso Drive till the supervolcano killed that business. He still sold Hondas these days: Honda motor scooters. He also sold Segways and bikes and trikes. IF IT'S GOT WHEELS, WE'LL DEAL! was his current slogan.

"You did the city a great service, Captain," he said. "You deserve to be proud of yourself for it."

"Thanks." Colin left it right there. Yamada was a friendly blowhard, but he was a blowhard all the same. A service? Colin hadn't known Mike Pitcavage was the South Bay Strangler when he set up Darren's arrest. If he'd had even a small suspicion, he would have gone after the chief years earlier. Anyone would have.

Kelly was talking with Lucy Chen. Not for the first time, Colin thought the two of them might have been sisters, even if one was fair and Jewish, the other almond-eyed and black-haired. Regardless of looks, they shared the same straight-ahead style and drive to get to the bottom of things. If Kelly had told him to take a flying leap that morning in Yellowstone all these years ago now, he wondered if he would have been smart enough to ask Lucy out. He could have done worse—he was sure of that. Whether she would have been dumb enough to say yes was a different question altogether. Luckily for him, it wasn't one he had to worry about any more.

"Excuse me," he told Councilman Yamada—any excuse to get away seemed a good one. He refilled his own coffee cup, then went over to his wife and the DNA technician. Raising the cup in salute, he said, "Here's to the two women who saved my bacon."

"Phooey," Kelly said.

"You did what you were supposed to do, and the truth came out because of that." Lucy might think she didn't know him well enough to throw *Phooey* in his face, but what she did say amounted to the same thing.

"Thanks to you," he said—he wasn't going to let her get away with that.

He might have gone on, but Eugene Cervus chose that moment to stride confidently to the lectern. The mayor of San Atanasio wore a suit elegant enough that even Mike Pitcavage might not have disdained it. He tapped at the mike to see if it was live. When he found it was, he leaned forward and said, "Ladies and gentlemen . . ." That got people's attention. After a moment, Mayor Cervus went on, "Ladies and gentlemen, we're here today to celebrate the career of Captain Colin Ferguson, who's done his best for the city of San Atanasio since well before the turn of the millennium."

The assembled cops and dignitaries clapped. Colin thought the mayor should have stuck with *turn of the century*. The other made you think when you should have been just listening. Cervus continued, "Captain Ferguson saved his finest work for last. His investigations led to the end of the South Bay Strangler's reign of terror over this whole region. And, after that, he labored valiantly to restore the unity and the pride of the San Atanasio Police Department." More applause, this time mostly from the cops. That made Colin feel good. The mayor finished, "Here to speak more on that is Malik Williams, chief of the San Atanasio PD. Chief Williams!"

Colin joined in the hand the chief got as he replaced the mayor behind the lectern. Williams deserved it, as far as he was concerned. "When I got here, they told me Colin Ferguson was a cop's cop. They were right," Malik Williams said. People clapped some more. He continued, "They didn't tell me he was a smart cop, but I found that out pretty darn quick. I've been finding out *how* smart he is ever since. We'll be using his ideas about how to go low-tech when we have to, and how to mix low tech and high, for years to come. So will police departments up and down California. I'm sorrier than I know how to tell you that his injury is making him retire earlier than he would have, because he's a good man—a terrific man—at your back. And here he is. Give it up for Captain . . . Colin . . . Ferguson!"

Beside Colin, Kelly blistered her palms applauding. Lucy Chen clapped hard, too. He lumbered to the lectern as the crowd gave him an ovation. He would rather have run in the other direction. But you did what you had to do, not always what you wanted to do. His left shoulder barked while he took his place there. Yes, you did what you had to do, all right.

"Thanks very much, folks," he said after the noise died down. "I'm glad you think I did a decent job while I was here. We've had some hard times, what with the real-estate collapse and the Strangler and everything that's come after the supervolcano. But we're still in there pitching, doing the best we can for our families and our friends and our town. We keep going. We have to. The town will get along fine without me, and so will the department. I'm going to watch my little girl grow up, maybe raise a few chickens while I'm doing it. And I'm going to smell the roses— the weather may be rotten these days, but it's not too rotten for them to grow. I'm sorry to be leaving a little sooner than I expected, but every other way I can think of I'm a heck of a lucky man. Thanks again."

They gave him another hand when he stepped away from the lectern, probably not least because he'd kept it short. Kelly kissed him. Everybody else in the room shook his hand again—it sure seemed that way to him, anyhow. He drank more coffee. He ate a sweet roll or two. He stood around listening to people who mattered to him—and to quite a few who didn't—tell him what a wonderful fellow he was. If you believed a quarter of that stuff, your hat size would swell more and quicker than Barry Bonds'.

At last, he asked a question of Kelly with one eyebrow. She nodded. Colin broke out in a broad grin. He'd spent long enough here. Now he could retire from his retirement party. A last few handshakes, and he made his getaway.

It had started raining again. "Never *used* to do that this time of year," Colin grumbled, glowering at Kelly as if the supervolcano erupted because she'd studied it.

"Well, it's doing it now," she said, and pulled an umbrella from her purse.

They walked out to the Taurus close together, so the umbrella could keep them both dry. Colin remembered to grab a balloon off the sign in front of the car so he could make the cat's day.

After he got in, Kelly helped him fasten his belt. She backed out of the parking space and started home. They might not see another car on the road all the way there. Colin had no idea when he'd get into this one again, either. That was as much the supervolcano's fault as the revised weather was. But what could you do? See what Deborah'd been up to while you were gone, was what. It made a good starter, anyhow.